MW01229155

A COUNTRY GIRL

CONTENTS

DOWN ON THE FARM

MY FIRST MEMORIES of William are in a country church. I am fourteen and he is sixteen. The flies are buzzing against the plate-glass windows of the church and the hot sun is shining in through the glass. William is reading the weekly record of activities before the small congregation of about a dozen farmers, their wives, and many children. William is tall, blond, tanned from the summer harvest, well-muscled. William smiles. A quick, genial boyish grin, flashing white teeth, blue eyes. A refined soft mouth, sensuous lips with a small cleft in his lower lip. William is speaking. His voice is sure and deep. I am dreaming, listening to the flies buzzing at the panes, knocking themselves against the glass with little hitting sounds.

I am dreaming. William my first date, first love. My blond handsome hero.

But it is not so. At the time I fancied another boy. A wide-mouthed, black-haired, dark-tanned youth who rode a motorcycle. Smart-alecky, coarse and crude. Loose flabby lips that slobbered when we kissed. I was chaste at fourteen and continuously fighting off his large grabbing paws at my breasts.

I treated William badly at first. I stood him up to a ball game. He had promised to pick me up in his black 1948 Mercury. William was the pitcher, a star. I acquiesced. But my black-haired friend arrived a few minutes before William, putt putt along the gravel country road. I could hear him coming for a mile and I couldn't resist. I jumped on the bike behind him, my arms wound tightly around his broad back, smelling the suntanned odor about him, he grinning his white, wide smile in his tanned face, brown eyes smiling and I laughing. Putt putt down the lane waving goodbye to my anxious aunt and uncle. Turning at the end of the lane by the acacia tree and down the country road. William arrived a few minutes later to an apologetic aunt and uncle standing on the back porch.

William at the ball game. Chewing gum, pitching. A large safety pin holding the fly of his pants closed.

My girlfriend nudging me. Did you see that? Giggling. Look at that.

I was ashamed for him.

An old car suddenly coming on the baseball diamond driving round and round kicking up a funnel of dust.

It's Alice's old dad. He's drunk again.

William patiently waiting, chewing gum, smiling. Oh a darling.

I sat with my black-haired boyfriend and we rode off again in the dark after the game. Cars pulling away. William asking me if I wanted a ride home.

No, thank you, I said.

Sitting on the back of the bike, the crickets chirping in the ditches along the gravel road home, the mist hanging over the sweet smelling fields of clover and hay. The loud rat-a-tat-tat of the motorbike and the cool moist air whipping in our faces and sucking at our clothes. My friend reached back with his large hand and grabbed at my breast and grinned.

My first real date was with William. My first date into town. We drove nineteen miles across country roads to the nearest town to see a show. Waiting on the street corner, William took my arm. I can still see his large well-muscled arms and a tangle of blond hairs on his tanned forearm. In the show he puts his arm around my shoulder, but doesn't take my hand. He smells of the country.

Another time a show with his handsome brother. Meeting his brother in a dark house dim lights. Introduced to his stepfather, shaking hands all around. His brother was gorgeous, withdrawn, handsome beyond words. He was nineteen. I was instantly fascinated by him.

Sitting between them. Not watching the show, my eye on his dark-haired handsome brother.

And then three years later. I am seventeen visiting my aunt and uncle again for the summer on their farm and I am with William at a ball game. This time his girl. He is still pitching as good as ever and he is smiling. He has given me his red baseball jacket to keep me warm. I have been sitting for three hours in the heavy dew of a country summer night becoming chilled watching the game. I am not much interested in baseball or any sport, but William is playing, he is the pitcher, and this makes all the difference. I am very uncomfortable and I have to go to the bathroom so badly it hurts, but embarrassment keeps me from mentioning it and I suffer.

William drives me home along the same country gravel road to my uncle's farm that I traveled on the motorbike, and just short of the corner on which the church is located and a few hundred yards before their lane he pulls over in the heavy gravel under the elm trees and stops the car. There is a full moon and the shadow of the elms stretches across the road and our car.

I still have his red jacket on. He moves over beside me. I have been watching his lips in profile while he was driving, seeing his lips move as he speaks and his teeth, which are fine white in the moonlight. William doesn't talk much. He is quite shy and withdrawn. I wonder who is more afraid. But he seems confident. His strong well-muscled body exudes strength, a manly strength that seems electric in the car.

He moves over beside me and takes me in his arms. He puts his lips to mine and kisses me gently. We have never kissed and it is a beautiful sensation, his mouth unbelievably soft and well formed. He presses his lips against mine and I feel a fantastic thrill for the first time in my belly, a light tingling electric feeling darting from my lips down to my belly and throbbing between my legs. He draws back from me and I can see his face in the moonlight. He is very handsome and I feel strangely moved to be sitting so close to him and kissing him. He hugs me and says, Oh Angela. I know nothing about love at this stage, and I don't really know what to do, but I kiss his ear lobe and touch his hair and draw my cheek against him feeling the rough scraping of his beard on my tender skin. We entwine our fingers. He has strong hands and hair on the back of them. I want to caress the thick blond hair on his forearms, but I don't dare. His arms are bare and I wonder if he is cold.

Are you cold, William?

No, not with you. He smiles and presses me against his large chest. William is so well-built that I can feel the strength in him as he holds me. I feel safe and cozy in such strong arms. His lips touch mine again and his mouth is wet and soft and the taste is so sweet and refined. He places his hand on his jacket against my breast and presses my breast. I feel the swelling of my breast under his hand through his jacket and I like it, but I draw his hand away.

The car is silent. The moonlight and tree shadows silently fall against the car.

William starts up the motor and smiles.

I guess I better get you home, he says.

There is something thick about his voice.

Now, today, I would invite him, welcome him into my bed and love him the whole night long in the dark room with the moonlight across the misty fields. Then I knew nothing. I was shy. Afraid of what to say, dreading silences. Always so shy and frightened, my palms dripping wet, my heart beating so fast. Oh and how I loved him.

The car moved down the road. We could both see it all ending. William turned in to my uncle's farm by the two acacia trees and drove down the long lane past the wind row of pine as far as the barn and turned around under the yard light. He drove back to the farmhouse and stopped in the shadow of the cedars. The house was completely dark. The crickets throbbed all around.

I turned to him.

Goodnight, William.

We looked at each other and there was such a longing, such tenderness in our eyes.

11

William said, Angela, and reached for me.

His lips touched me. He kissed me hard and gently and furiously and our tongues crept into our open mouths and touched and curled around our wet lips and inside the soft flesh of our eager panting mouths. His lips. I will never forget the touch of him. It seems incredible. All these years gone and he is the one I would kiss again, kiss and kiss again. His lower lip was exquisitely soft and well-formed with a small dip, a slight indentation in the middle that I ran my tongue over. Oh if I could only touch him now.

We sat together hugging and kissing against the window on my side of the car under the shade of the cedar trees for three hours. How we could kiss for so long I'll never know, and I in my innocence not knowing much of anything kept on with the kissing never knowing we could do more but kissing and kissing until I was so hot and excited and love-filled that I could barely leave him. The soft touch. Strength and softness. Firm, hard muscles. To know the feel of those strong arms to be held so firmly and yet gently, and to have that ever-loving, adoring mouth on mine.

We said goodnight. I went to my room and stared at the ceiling in the dark and saw stars and then hopped out of bed in my bare sticky feet onto the linoleum and leaned my elbows on the window sill and stared out of the open window at the moon-flooded fields and thought of him. I tingled all over. My toes tingled.

The next day my lips were sore. I ran my tongue over my chapped lips and felt a tingling, such a joy. I blushed at the table whenever William's name was mentioned.

It is the harvest season. Late June and time for haying. I am at my cousin's farm. They are raking the hay and William is there. He is stripped to the waist because of the hot sun and exertion of hoisting the sheaves onto the wagon and I watch him. His incredible muscles, his wet suntanned body dripping with sweat, and his blond hair.

There is a pail of water brought out to the field for the men to drink and a tin metal dipper to take the water. I am there because I am driving the tractor. I love to drive the tractor. I hate women's work in the farmhouse kitchen baking pies, peeling apples, preparing meals for the men, woman talk. I like to be out in the fields in the open air in the hot sun, getting a tan. Listening to the men. I like to be with men. They need me anyway to drive the tractor. There are no small boys around to drive and all the men are pitching sheaves. William takes the dipper from the pail and tips the bowl into the water. He raises the bowl and takes a long drink. The sweat runs off his nose in drops and falls to the ground. I watch the water drip off his chin. His blue eyes shine in the summer sun. He offers the bowl to me. I take it and drink after him, thrilled to touch the metal rim that his soft lips have just touched.

William is threshing. Laying the bales of hay in the barn. The sweat is pouring all over his face and running in his eyes. The pieces of straw stick to his wet skin and

12

prick him. He has an animal smell about him. I want to take him and caress him and wash the sweat out of his eyes and take him home with me.

Oh William. Do you know that I love you?

We are riding home together. We are taking the tractor home to my uncle's farm. William is driving, and I am standing behind him on the metal floor. I am holding onto his broad bare shoulders. There is a smell of metal, sweat and sun on our hands and clothes. We have nine miles of country road to cross. Up and down shaded hills and along open fields in the suppertime sunlight. Evening coming on.

Let's run off together, I say.

Oh William you know I love you.

He writes me letters. He says: You are beautiful you are a doll. There is no girl like you. No girl so beautiful what a figure and so nice too. I love you I am crazy about you.

When we are together he can't say this so he writes me letters. But his eyes tell me everything. I know he loves me.

I dream of marrying William. We'll have a farm and about ten children and we'll always be screwing in that farm bed with the brass rails.

I have a date with William tonight. I am in the bedroom at my uncle's farm. A sweet strong breeze is blowing in the window and fluffing the curtains. I look at myself approvingly in the mirror. I am pretty I think. My eyes are green and my mouth is a nice shape. Curved like William's and inviting kisses. I open my mouth and look at my tongue. I brush my brown short hair and tip the perfume bottle behind my ears. Then I lie back on the satin spread on the bed and stretch my arms above my head. As I fall back I think of William crushing me on the bed and lying on top of me.

Now we are together again. We are skimming across the country roads in a friend's car. William and I are in the back. I look at the mist settling over the fields and the red sun going down. I hold William's hand.

Christ! What a bore to have another couple along. We are all going to a baseball game. William is pitching and I suppose it's nice to have the others along, but I want him I want him all to myself.

As we watch the last of the sun's yellow light on the fields I think I'll never forget this, here I am with William and we're racing across the fields and I can feel his wet palm in mine and I know what it is like to hold him.

Can you believe it? The game has been canceled. William, the star pitcher, won't be pitching. And now we are sitting alone in his Mercury overlooking a stubble field and the sky is still light. The other couple has miraculously left and we are alone. William is playing the radio and the Everly Brothers are on.

I never knew what I missed till I kissed ya.

Do you like them? he asks me.

Yes, I do.

William is chewing gum. He is always chewing gum. He offers me a peppermint stick and I take it. I never used to chew gum before, but now I chew it all the time.

William and I love each other. And when two people love each other, innocent or not, they get down to things fast. Fast, but we took our time.

After a while I permitted William to touch my breasts. At first it was only through my blouse. He would press them and circle his fingers around my nipples. I never wore a brassiere because I hated them. They were too tight and confining. Gradually he learned to slip his fingers under my blouse and touch my bare skin. Creeping with needlelike marks up my flesh to the curve of my breast and stroking the swelling, his fingertips lightly stroking the fat. Inching his way up to my nipple, touching my nipple lightly, then again and again, until it stood out hard like the pit of a cherry. Finally bringing his lips to my breast through my blouse, then his bare lips on my nipple and taking it in his mouth and sucking on it ever so gently.

We were lying in a field pressed against each other and William was stroking my breasts. He had my blouse up and was sucking my nipples. Then he moved his fingers along the waist of my jeans to my belly button and down in hot electric touches to my mound of hair.

I felt a shock as though I were suddenly naked to have him touch me there, that most sacred place, which I am both proud of and a little embarrassed about, seeing that big bush of dark hair puffed out in profile in the mirror like a powder puff or a rabbit's cottontail. Proud, and yet secret, and he was touching it. I wanted to do the same to him, so I reached my fingers into his pants but they were too tight and I undid the zipper and looked at him in the eyes. He was beautiful. He was. So beautiful. I had never seen a big one before. Oh my god. I could feel his swelling blond prick in my hand. Then it wasn't a prick, just his adorable dear thing because I had never heard such a word as prick when I was seventeen, but Oh my, it was still his beautiful big prick and I held it in my hot wet hand.

I was fascinated by it. So large and hard and standing up out of his pants with a life of its own. I stroked it incessantly.

Oh you mustn't do that, he said.

Why not?

You'll see.

I kept fingering him.

Suddenly he groaned and kissed me. A white fluid came out all over my hand.

What's that?

That's what happens when you do that to me.

Oh William. I didn't know. My hand was wet and slimy as I held him in my hands.

You're sweet. Now you know.

Yes, now I know.

He had his fingers on my crotch and fingered me there. I felt all tingly and excited. I was very wet.

William, William. I love you. He wrapped his arms around me and lay on top of me. William, you're beautiful. I took his arms and kissed his blond arm. I ran my tongue over the tangle of hair and sucked his arm. I licked his muscles down to his wrist and ran my tongue along the crease in the palm of his hand and in between each finger sucking up the drops of sweat. I took each of his fingers in my mouth and kissed them, nibbled his nails and rubbed his hand across my lips.

Christ! Have you ever felt like that? Such a sexy healthy beautiful fucking boy before you and not even knowing what it was all about?

Once I had made him come like that I wanted to do it to him all the time. Every time we were together I stroked his penis and he played with my wet cunt, carefully separating my lips and moving his fingers all over my slippery hot flesh and fingering me, inserting his finger, first one and then after a while two into my cunt and frigging me off. I used to get so hot and writhe on his hard active fingers that I felt a deep ache, a hot burn in my belly and my legs would tremble until finally I came on him and my cunt tightened over his fingers and throbbed. He would wait until I came, and then he would spurt his beautiful white gobs all over my belly.

I loved the smell. Salty and of the sea. Infinitely slimy and gooey. Slipping over my belly down to my curly hair. We had it all over our fingers. I loved up his fingers so much. I liked the *taste* of his sperm.

Oh lover lover I want to kiss your belly, he would write. Your white, beautiful skin let me touch it, let me kiss it.

The first time he went down on me we were parked in his Mercury on a lonely country road. I was scared as we were stripped from the waist down and a car had just passed. William had his pants down to his ankles and mine were off and lying on the seat.

Then a car stopped and William quickly pulled up his pants and I pulled down my skirt and shoved my panties into the glove compartment. We were sitting close together when a beam of light shone in our window. William rolled down his window, which was all steamed up from our activity, and a policeman said, Let's see your driver's license.

William opened his wallet and showed the cop his license. The cop flashed the light all around the car and saw that everything was OK and said, Thanks. Don't stay too long, and left.

William rolled up his window and I giggled.

Jesus that was close.

15

William put his wallet in the glove compartment and we sat together until the police car drove away.

They make it difficult, don't they, honey? he said.

I kissed him. I forgot about the cop immediately. William's hot mouth on mine. Honest to God, baby, you must have the hottest mouth around, I said. William smiled, and oh how I love him when he smiles, and pulled up my skirt and kissed my big bush of hair.

Let me see it, he says.

Oh, don't be silly.

Now I *am* embarrassed. He switches on the dashboard light and we have a look at it.

Each individual brown hair curled in the dashboard light. You're beautiful, he said. He put his lips down to my stomach and ran his tongue around in my belly button. Then he licked my belly and kissed my curly hair. He parted the hair and exposed the pink flesh.

I was curious. Not embarrassed. I watched him. I saw his tongue touch the pink bud and I felt a fantastic sharp, burning excitement.

What are you doing?

He kept on. Licking and tonguing me. His beard was rough and scraped the soft flesh of my inner thighs. He ran his tongue between my lips down to my vagina and darted his tongue in and out.

Oh my God, William! What are you doing?

Incredible! Not a finger, but wet and soft and exquisite like velvet, tingling.

Oh please don't go!

I grabbed his blond hair with my hands. I felt warm all over and a fire burning between my legs. His tongue flicked back and forth over the hard bud. I didn't know what he was doing to me, kissing me. It felt so nice that I arched my legs and tensed my muscles. My flesh throbbed under his tongue. He kept on and on I couldn't stop I grabbed his hair and held his head between my legs and there was such a throbbing, a delicate, exquisite, sharp throbbing such as I have never felt before and I came in his face. But he wouldn't stop. He kept on and on with his tongue tonguing me with quick, gentle soft strokes over and over on my pulsating clitoris until Oh my God I came again. Then he kissed me. On my mouth, smelling all musky and wet and cunty and I sucked his lips so hard that my lips tingled.

My mouth was all hot, and I wanted to suck him. I wanted to kiss him there. Kiss his sweet huge penis. Take it in my mouth. I put my face down on his erect stiff organ and put my fingers around the thick hard shaft and held him tight. I kissed the tip. I wet my lips and placed them over the bulging tip.

William leaned over me and sighed.

I touched the soft, swelling tip with my tongue, ran my tongue around the fleshy, spongy bulb until I came to a small join in the flesh, a tiny ridge, a delicate soft cord. I licked him.

He stroked my face gently with his hand. I looked up and saw his eyes. His mouth was open, his nostrils dilated, sharp beautiful nose, eyes dreamy watery, intense with excitement.

Let me do it to you.

No, no, he groaned and rocked my head in his hands.

Do it, William. Do it in my mouth. I'm going to make you do it in my mouth.

Oh yes! Oh yes! All the time I was running my tongue so delicately, so gently over his bulging cock, over the fat pregnant tip oozing a slippery clear liquid, licking it up, tonguing the soft cord, holding his penis so hard so firm in my hands as it swelled and grew bigger and harder and William started bumping in my mouth and groaning and grabbing me by the hair and pressing my face hard into his cock and I sucked and sucked and flicked my tongue so fast back and forth over the fine cord as he pushed and suddenly arched and spurted in my mouth again and again, bumping, arching, plunging deeply to the back of my throat until my mouth throbbed and ached with the stress and gobs of sperm filled my mouth. William panted and gasped and let out such a cry when he came that I thrilled so hard in my belly and I throbbed all wet and hot and warm between my legs.

William had arched in my mouth, his hard thighs thrust against my breasts, and now he lowered himself back on the seat and sighed.

Oh Angela. He petted my hair as I slowly worked around his wet slimy cock, slippery and silky, smelling wet and salty. I swallowed the thick gobs of sperm and it went down like the white of an egg slippery, salty, tasting like Camembert cheese, smelling like Camembert cheese. I was thirsty. My lips were sticky and my hand was wet from sweat.

William took out a Kleenex and handed it to me. I wiped my hand and stroked his hard muscular belly and watched his curling blond hairs in the light.

I was excited all over again.

William pulled me up to him and kissed my mouth.

You're beautiful. His voice was all husky and he had a dreamy look in his eyes.

William drove me home. The windows were open and a sweet dewy hay air blew in through the car. There was a large white moon high in the sky moving between clouds. Oh look at that, William! Look at that! We sat close together on his side, warm and peaceful, our bodies touching my head on his shoulder smelling him, smelling him getting all excited again loving him so much wanting to do it all over again.

William turned on the radio and the crickets stopped. He took out a stick of peppermint gum and ripped it in two. He gave me half. I put the fresh powdered

17

piece in my mouth and the cheesy sperm taste went and I tasted peppermint and the saliva began to flow and my jaw ached and lips were swollen, and he looked at me smiling, chewing, his teeth glinting that sweet boyish grin and innocence in his eyes and said, I love you.

I couldn't sleep that night. Always on the edge of sleep with William's face before me, his big prick in my mouth, tasting it again, overcome by the sensations of doing it. The suddenness of it all, the newness, feeling I wasn't a little girl anymore that strange things were happening to me.

I could hear the old farmhouse at night. Creaking floors, unknown footsteps, scurrying sounds across my ceiling which were the attic mice, bats, ghosts, the black dog on the back stoop barking, distant howling from another farmhouse, the crickets. I could almost hear the dew falling on the grass and bushes, and the vegetable garden out front which extended to the road. I was tired, so tired, so excited. Finally I slept.

William came by the next day at noon. An excuse to see my uncle. He came just as the bread truck drove in. A little frightened to see him, wondering if I'd be embarrassed. But no. His boyish smile, his blue eyes those arms again no, no, not embarrassed.

The breadman carrying in the loaves of bread. My aunt in her apron wiping her hands on her apron and saying, How are you today, William?

And William: Fine, ma'am.

The screen door slamming shut and dozens of flies swirling into the house.

We're over at Johnnie's tomorrow, my uncle was saying to William out on the uneven back porch. Take in the hay there, and that should do it.

My uncle closing his blue eyes as he talked and swaying slightly on his feet. Expect good weather tomorrow.

My uncle walking down the porch steps in his big rubber boots that he always wore, and heading off to the barn. My aunt going inside, the screen door snapping shut. The breadman banging closed the doors to his truck, hopping in and driving down the lane.

William sitting on the porch swinging his legs over the edge. The dog, a black mongrel, coming up and rubbing against William's back. A yellow cat walking in and out of the black dog's legs.

He looks at me and I could melt. I'm all feet and hands and awkward and don't know what to do standing still beside him. I sit on the porch steps and smile at him.

He reaches for my tight hand with his big tanned hand, knuckled, and curly blond hairs on his wrist.

Just the touch of him again. I can't stand it. I get a strange current in my crotch, and my eyes falter. I look down.

Oh William. I am breathless.

I can see him start to breathe heavy, and it's as if I'm paralyzed with desire. I ache. It hurts. But I can say nothing except: Oh William.

I think my eyes are filling with tears.

Angela, will you see me tonight?

Yes.

Where will we go?

It doesn't matter.

We could stay here.

I look surprised. William waves his hand out toward the hay field behind the house on the other side of the windbreak of Lombardy poplars. Out there.

Yes. We could.

Does it matter to you where we go? he says. We could go to a show if you like.

I place my hand on his hairy, muscular arm and giggle. What do you think, sweetheart?

William is wearing a blue and white striped shirt and I run my hand over his bulging pectoral muscles through the cloth. What time do you want me to come?

Now, come now, now now. But I say: Anytime after eleven. They're always in bed by eleven.

I'll wait until the lights are out, and then I'll whistle.

No, don't, they'll hear. Where will you be?

Anywhere you like. Over there in the orchard? He points to the old orchard overgrown with weeds filling the corner lot. The concession road runs by out front, and on the side, a narrow dirt road going back in steep hills to the river.

No. It's too creepy. All those weeds. It's better around the back. Closer to the house. There's a mock orange bush by the house. Meet me there.

At suppertime I couldn't eat.

Lovesick, are ya? Cat got your tongue? my uncle kidded me. Wonder what's wrong with her, Mother? asking my aunt. Do you think we know the boy? he said and winked.

My aunt looked serious as she poured out the tea.

Do you think it's that kid on a motorbike? he said.

Oh, now, Dad, leave the poor girl alone.

I picked at my food. I usually have a good appetite for my aunt's cooking: fruit pies, cakes, salads, meat and gravy, fresh vegetables from the garden. I picked off a few slices of cucumber doused in vinegar, salt and pepper with my fork, and slowly chewed them.

I'll just have some tea tonight, I said.

Are you feeling all right, dear? my aunt asked.

I'm fine, thank you. I'm just not hungry, I guess.

Cat's got her tongue, my uncle said.

Dad! Stop teasing her now.

You know, Mother, what I always say. Still water runs deep.

I blushed and tipped my cup of steaming tea to my lips.

My uncle winked at my aunt. You never know what they're thinking, eh?

My face was burning. I was mortified behind my cup of tea.

Now, Dad, eat your dinner.

Oh, what a life when you've got a wife! my uncle said.

I liked my uncle. My cheeks were still hot. I put my cup down and dared to smile at him.

He winked his cornflower-blue eye at me. Pass the pie please, Mother.

The farmhouse was completely silent. I brushed my teeth and hair and said goodnight to my aunt and uncle while they were watching television. I climbed up the steep stairs to my room on the second floor at the head of the hall and closed my door.

I could hear them moving around downstairs in the kitchen below my room. The sound traveled up in the heating pipe to the floor in the corner of my room where it was covered with a tin plate. When I lifted the tin plate I could hear them distinctly below and see them if they passed under the pipe.

My uncle was getting out the big bag of puffed wheat cereal for his bedtime snack. My aunt brought out the toaster and jam and butter and put the kettle on for tea.

Every night they went through the same routine. In thirty minutes they'd be in bed.

I looked at myself in the mirror and made a face in the dark. I splashed some perfume on behind my ears on my wrists and ankles, and kneeled in front of the low window with my elbows resting on the sill. The air was moist and sweet. I could smell the mock orange bush. I looked over at the orchard on the corner. Oh William. I'd run to you now. Where are you, lover? I could take off this screen and climb out of the window onto the front stone porch and jump down into the wet grass. I'd run down the lane into your strong arms Oh you're so strong and lovely I can feel you hug you kiss you.

My aunt and uncle were coming up the stairs talking, stairs creaking, door next to mine opening closing the crack of light under my door going out. Floor creaking as they walked back and forth scrape of hangers in the closet ringing sound of pee in the porcelain jerry, window opened wide and then the squeak of springs in their bed. Talk.

Now would be the time while they're talking. I can't wait until they're asleep. I slowly turned the knob on my door, my heart pounding. Waiting for talk. Closing the door behind me. A squeak as the stiff wood fits into place. On tiptoes one step at a time in front of their door. Stop. Quiet. Hear the crickets creaking, the curtain blowing on the sill of the window on the stair landing. My uncle's voice. And now I moved quickly past their door and stepped down the steep stairs. Stop. Again. One more, more another squeak the bottom no more, the door opening turning the knob at last, behind me, closing tight the door to the kitchen.

Made it. I hurried across the linoleum and pushed back the bolt on the door between the kitchen and the storage room past the baskets of fresh fruit on the counter, the pail of swill for the pigs, smell of cucumber peelings, sour milk, berries, damp wood, unlocked the back door, screen door, then outside on the porch.

Brushed by a cat. Meow, purring against my leg. The black dog gets up from his braided mat and wags his tail.

Poor Blackie. Poor dog. You're glad to see me. I give him a pat.

Free! Free! I'm out! I take a deep breath of warm moist night air. I love it! I love it! Oh running around the house in the wet grass running through the dewy grass. Oh I sing praises to you, my love. I sing your praises. Moonlight and stars. Body and sweet air. Your warm skin your loving arms your hot body pressing on top of me. Hear the crickets. Silence. The crickets. A black bat winging in the moonlight. Wait. Shadows. Stopping suddenly at the corner of the house to look at the mock orange bush. There he is! *William! William!* I want to shout Oh my love Oh my love, I am here! There he is. Standing there by the mock orange bush looking out over the front vegetable garden. The asparagus bushes are fine wisps in the moonlight. The moonlight slanting through the poplars across him.

He hears me and turns suddenly and smiles. Angela! We embrace, and he hugs me tight and lifts me off my feet and I laugh and then remember myself and say: Shh! We must be quiet.

Mmmm you smell nice, he says.

The mock orange smells glorious. Sweet orange blossom. I sniff the blossoms. I love these. William breaks off a sprig of blossom and tucks the stem behind my ear. He kisses me on the tip of my nose and chin and forehead, and then my mouth. I have hold of his strong arms, but I can't resist letting my hand drop down to his sweet groin and the tight swelling in his pants. Oh, William. He slips his arm around my waist my heart is beating fast. His voice is already edged with emotion, and he says, Where can we go?

Over there. I point to the Lombardy poplars. In the hay field.

Ducking under the branches of poplar which form a thick tangle of limbs sealing off the sweep of northwest wind that blows in the winter across the fields.

The hay smells fresh and damp, soft and perfumed.

William takes me in his arms again and holds me completely against him. We embrace and kiss and I feel his prick against me, his hard chest and thighs and strong arms around me. We kiss.

It was unbearable, I say. I thought the time would never come. I was dying without you, darling. I take his big hand in mine. My cheeks are flaming hot.

21

William holds my face in his hands and looks into my eyes. So long. Deeply looking at me. I feel such a thrill.

I love you, he says. His voice trembles. Come on.

I follow him, holding his big hand, walking after him watching the line and stride of his long muscular legs and strong muscular back. We walk along the edge of the hay field, which is as tall as our waist and Oh so sweet and fragrant, throbbing with crickets and field sounds, to a large elm on a knoll at the end of the field.

We can't lie down in the hay, William says. Your uncle would be upset. William should know as he works in the fields all the time.

Lie down, I think. Are we going to lie down? I am thrilled beyond words.

William takes off his shirt and lays it out flat on the ground. We can sit here. He is gleaming and all smooth knotty muscles in the platinum moonlight. The way I've seen him so often in the sun.

William.

He unzips his pants and steps out of them. He is standing in his underwear gleaming white in this half-light. There is a mild breeze.

You'll get cold, I say, not knowing what to say.

He slips out of his shorts and he's standing there naked in the moonlight, his beautiful cock raised full to its height and pointing at me. He isn't the least bit embarrassed, and there's such a look of gentle tenderness in his eyes.

He takes me by the hands and then he unbuttons my blouse. My breasts are bare underneath. He pulls my blouse off and looks at my breasts. I am very proud of my breasts. They're round and full with big nipples that stand out like two cherry stones when I am excited, and I know he likes them. He sucks my right breast.

That one's smaller than the other is, I say. And it's true, my left one is bigger.

Then it's my favorite, he says. He encircles my nipple with his tongue and sucks on my breast. When he flicks his tongue over my nipple I feel the same tight tingling in my clitoris. I sway slightly against him and sigh.

He unzips my jeans and I step out of them, balancing against him with my hands on his shoulders. I am eager now as he pulls down my panties and I step out of those too. I stand before him feeling as though I am swimming in the clear moonlight, facing him, facing his grand lovely prick standing up so high, facing him with my bush of hair and pointed breasts, holding back by a few precious inches of soft summer night air watching him waiting for him. He doesn't take me in his arms but caresses me as if delirious, a madman murmuring Angela, my love, drawing his tongue over my belly kneeling in front of me parting my lips sucking my cunt.

Oh William. I part my legs and lean on him.

Go on, go on, he says. Do it! Do it! I want you to do it, and I come off in his face, the third time since I've known him, and he feels me throb and gush against his mouth all wet on his lips. His tongue flicks incessantly on my clitoris, so much it hurts, and I twitch and say, Oh no! Stop stop, my darling, but he doesn't and soon the excruciatingly painful sensitivity turns to pleasure and the exquisite feeling comes again and I am building up to another fuck and I'm fucking him all over again in his mouth. My cunt throbs and contracts as I wrap my legs tightly around his head.

Oh, lover. I slide down on him I can hardly stand now. I collapse in the grass. Sleep. I'm tired, I murmur, but William is all over me and kissing me and Christ I can't resist that mouth of his. He opens his mouth on mine and I'm gone again. Oh you fucking beauty. I feel his prick hard against me, nudging me in the crotch, rubbing against my hair.

Oh baby, what are you doing?

I want in, he says. Let me in you. Let me put it in you.

Oh, William, you can't! What if I get pregnant? He pushes against me and I feel such a burning ache in my cunt for him.

No, sweetheart, you can't!

What day are you?

I don't know. I'm taken aback, and I have to think. Seven, I think. I'm seven.

It's all right then. You won't get pregnant.

My cunt turns to fire when he says that. Are you sure?

Yes. You can trust me, Angela.

He takes his prick in his hands and I ache. He guides his prick to my opening. Tight. He thrusts gently, and it's like a hot burning, a flooding of molten fire as he breaks through and slips in.

Oh, Angela, he moans. Oh Angela, I love you. I am burning inside on fire the walls of my cunt tingling with hot fire. He pushes to the back and I feel a dull sweet ache.

Love me! Love me! I say.

I am completely his. I will do anything for him I will give myself to him. My virginity, my maidenhood, my love, my flesh, my cunt. He slides back slowly to my opening and plunges in again with a new thrill, a hot burning ache. Slowly, rhythmically he draws his swollen hard prick in and out in and out of my cunt so tight against the walls feeling every movement every part of my flesh tingling slipping sliding together so tight kissing a feeling building in my cunt like a hot snowball coming larger and larger, Oh stop! Stop! You'll have to stop!

It's all right, he says, it's all right, come on! Come on! Let it come!

It's coming! I'm coming! He plunges fiercely in me, a few rapid hard strokes piercing me as he groans and throbs and convulses inside me and I too come all over his prick so tight and throbbing clamping down on his penis, the muscles of my cunt contracting hard on him sucking his penis dry with my cunt.

23

Oh! Oh! I say, I am now! Now I am!

Yes do it! Do it! I am fucking you I'm fucking you I love you, I love you!

We sigh. We collapse together tight in each other's arms. Oh my. My love, love. This fucking in me so warm and rich, I cry.

My tears. You're crying you're crying. No no. He's kissing my lips, my mouth eyes drinking my tears. You're crying, he's crying too. Oh William. Angela, Angela. Our noses rub together in our tears.

Do you love me? I beg. Do you love me?

I love you like the sun and moon and earth. I adore you, Angela. I adore you. You're mine. I'll hold you and protect you forever. He cries as he says this and holds me so tightly in his arms that I think I will break.

All the time the elm tree above us was sighing in the wind, but I heard it only now and again, lying together in my darling's arms under the tree in the moonlight.

It was three o'clock when we said goodnight. William waited while I closed the screen and kissed him again through the screen for what seemed like the hundredth time. As he stood there his face was a vision etched on my mind. We couldn't part, and yet he had to go. I hung on the inside of the screen watching him walk away, and then turn and wave and throw me kisses Oh how I longed to take him to bed with me Oh how deprived I felt not to lie in my lover's arms and wake to his glorious face and see his beautiful naked body in the morning.

Oh so sad lovers are always parted and parting never together.

Goodbye! Goodbye! I waved.

My cunt was sopping wet from William's sperm. He had handed me his handkerchief, which I tucked in there to soak up the gobs, but it was soaking wet now.

Where can I put it? I thought. I'm not going out to the outhouse now.

When I had tiptoed back to my room I rolled a fresh Kleenex around it and tucked it under my pillow so he would be near me and I could finger it and smell him, smell William.

I squatted on the jerry before going to bed, naked, knowing I was dripping into the pot. I felt a keen thrill knowing his sperm was running out of me.

It's happened, I said. It's happened. I'm different now. I'm no longer a virgin. Now I'm a mature woman. A woman. I know now. Now I know what it's like to be fucked.

I wonder if they can tell. Will it show in my face tomorrow? Anne told me your neck is thicker after you've done it. Will my neck thicken? I'll have to check in the mirror tomorrow. And circles under your eyes too, she said. It would be terrible if it showed.

I lie naked in bed fingering my cunt, smelling my fingers seeing William's face in front of my eyes his prick in me I think his prick I can't believe his prick in me thrill of excitement in my belly cunt I can feel him again in me doing it loving me Oh how I love him what will happen I want him I want to live with him I want to live in a house with him in the country and fuck him every night.

My parents ended it. They came to fetch me. I kept writing letters to them that I didn't want to come home that I wanted to stay at my uncle's forever that I hated the city and hated them and they got worried and came to collect me.

I cried in my room. My aunt came to talk to me and said, You know your mother is very unhappy. She can't understand why you won't come home. She said it's not like you at all you were always so considerate and she can't understand it. She was crying, you know. I've never seen your mother cry.

I'm sorry, Mummie, but I love him. Can't you understand?

And I'm not pregnant. I want to be pregnant with William's baby. William's blond, blue-eyed baby I can already see he'd look like his father.

William came by that same day, and he was his most charming, sweet, lovable best. Boyish, gentle, friendly, shy. My mother liked him. He's very nice, they said. But you have to come home with us.

No no.

I ran away from them crying.

Angela! my mother called after me.

Let her go, my father said. Let her cry it out.

I ran along the side of the house, along the path to the outhouse by the Lombardy poplars. I took the hook off the door and plopped down on the seat crying. The door was swinging in the wind.

I hear footsteps on the path see a hand grasp the door, and it is William. Can I come in, Angela?

He steps into the small outhouse with me, draws the door behind him, and hooks it from the inside.

They'll see, I say.

To hell with them.

Oh relief, my darling, together my sweet my lover.

He approaches me and I can't help but get excited. There's a strong smell of lye in the hole and the flies are whining on the walls.

He takes me in his arms and I weep. I cry so hard against him and he says, There there, don't cry, please my love don't cry.

Oh William, I can't help it! I love you so much.

I love you too, kissing my face and tears and breathing hard in my ear and hair. I love you too. We can't get married yet. You're too young. You aren't eighteen. We have to wait.

I can't wait, William. I can't wait. I want you now. I can't leave you.

25

You have to.

Suddenly I'm angry. How can you stand it? How can you tell me to go? How can you?

Oh Angela! His eyes are hurting. What can I do? I have no money, you're underage. I'm still in school, what can I do? His blue eyes are filling with tears. He is beautiful. So strong, his muscles his chest his arms.

Let's run away, I say.

We can't.

He's right. I don't want to admit it. William lives with his grandparents. His father was killed in the war, and his mother has remarried. It would break his grandparents' heart if he dropped out of school. William is smart. He needs to stay in school. He can do better than his brother who is working for the railroad because he got married and needed a job. William knows it, and I know it too. Oh and how I worship him.

Angela? His voice is suddenly soft and he lets his hand run over my crotch. Angela, let's do it.

The flies are buzzing and the wind rattles the outhouse door. The door doesn't fit tight and there is a crack of daylight the length of the door through which I can see the Lombardy poplars.

William is unzipping his pants.

I am panting. I reach under my skirt and slip off my panties. William pulls up my blouse and cups my breast.

How? I say.

This way. It doesn't matter how, anyway anyhow. Put it in, I say. William sits back on the smooth seat above the pile of stinking shit beneath us and I quickly climb on top of him and lower my cunt onto his rigid big cock which slides in me as I ease myself down and he groans and leans back on the seat stretching out his legs. I place my hands on his chest and watch his eyes and blow him kisses as I raise and lower myself on his tool pulling up and down easy on and off his prick in and out nudging my hole piercing through coming closer close, close easing out and him gasping and arching and me coming down hard on him for the final time thrusting pushing drawing up tight on him a ball my knees flat on the seat clutching him with my arms and legs and kissing his mouth and sucking his tongue when the electric tickle comes over me in a wave in a flood and he comes inside of me now now, he says, fuck me now, and I fuck him Oh I fuck him really well, and the smell in that shithouse is so pungent and thick it overwhelms me as the flies buzz around us with a wild drone and the wind outside sighs in the Lombardy poplars and the slight wooden door rattles on the hook and knocks against the wood siding of the outhouse.

UP ON A MOTORBIKE

THERE IS ANOTHER story to that. I didn't lose my cunt to William. Not by a long shot. Here's how it happened.

He rode a motorbike. A great big violent fucking machine. His name was Rex.

It all began with my hero. My hero was James Dean. I was fourteen at the time and had just carved his name into my bedroom floor and covered it up with a scatter rug. My mother discovered it right away the first time she cleaned my room. All she did was slide the pink mat away and there it was: *James Dean*, carved with a penknife in the floor.

He was dead. My first poem was about death. It was entitled: "Death". A seventeen-year-old boy was killed riding his bike home by a driver blinded by the setting sun. I knew the boy. He lived in England.

My next poem was about a graveyard. I would cry over my hero's grave, and he would emerge and we would make love. The birds were singing.

Or else we'd meet after death.

That was the answer. I began a death cult. I would die at twenty-eight in a motor accident. *He* died at twenty-four. I'd never live to be thirty. Of course I'd never marry. I was romantic, beautiful and sexually unfulfilled. I'd never make it.

My hero rode a bike. I fancied myself on a bike. I took to wearing black and leather. Tight jeans and windbreakers. I cultivated smoking a cigarette cupped in my hand and held backward, the way he did it.

I was disturbed. No doubt about it. My mood flew high and sank within minutes. I was very proud of my temperament.

I was shy and had few friends. I couldn't communicate.

Nervous, fearful, adoring to be loved. I would look at myself in the mirror for hours, chin too small, nose not straight enough, mouth downturned. Green eyes, long lashes. When I was a small girl my uncle said, you have bedroom eyes. Excited, flushed cheeks, staring at my image.

I was being interviewed. I was often being interviewed in front of the mirror. Rich, famous, sex queen, girl-child, an intellectual.

Who was your first love?

My first love . . . my mouth opens slightly, sensuously. He was Rex.

Where is he now?

I don't know.

Tell me about it.

Rex rode a motorbike. Rex looked just like James Dean. Now that was something in those days. I'll tell you.

Now it's the Rolling Stones and Mick Jagger but in those days it was the pretty boys, the beautiful guys with the sexy balls, you know in the tight blue jeans and the red windbreakers.

I was seventeen. Truly seventeen. Kissed a few times. Chaste.

Rex went to the same high school. He was a year ahead of me, a senior. He was always alone. Blue windbreaker. Tight blue jeans. Wild brown hair and eyes and a face—so help me—just like James Dean. I was fascinated by him. I had met my hero. He smoked his cigarette cupped backward in his hand. I first noticed him sitting on the back of a park bench. Leaning forward, elbows on his knees, black Wellingtons on the seat, smoking a cigarette. That gave me a thrill.

As I walked by him he stared and smoked his cigarette with his cupped palm to his mouth. It was late fall. The maples were down. There seemed to be nothing left of the season but cold and the sudden brief sunshine at noon against a blue sky.

Walking. I turned at the end of the driveway and walked back again. I was timid, coming into flower. Red lips, flushed cheeks, frightened eyes. I was beautiful. Boys chased me. One said to me in the hall: You know what?

What?

You're sexy.

I was so shy.

Boys called me up. Followed me. Sent me chocolates.

I paid no attention.

Rex. I watched him in his blue windbreaker. I was just beginning to cultivate my romantic bent.

Rex called me on the phone. He had the softest, most gentle voice. I could tell in an instant that he was shy.

My soul mate.

I met my dream on a November afternoon, the snow suddenly floating down out of the sky on me, covering his blue windbreaker with white flakes.

His eyes were brown. The same straight nose, shock of wild long hair. Those high cheekbones and pouting mouth.

I wanted to meet you for so long, he said.

He was short. Only a few inches taller than I am which is five foot four. But then James Dean was short, so it was all right. And then it was very nice with our two bodies pressed together being so close in height.

We went to a football game. I didn't like it; I had never been to one before. My feet were cold, and Rex took me under the arcade and held them in his warm hands. One by one he blew on my feet and warmed them, and then he kissed them.

You have green eyes, he said. He said my name over and over.

Rex. My sexy little bombshell. He drove a VW convertible, an old rangy automobile that he called the bomb, and grinned with his boyish grin that only heroes can have.

The rest of the time he rode his bike. A big Harley-Davidson, sucking down the cold streets, balling out noise and sex.

I loved him.

He had a girlfriend, three years together since the tender age of sixteen. But I cut nicely into that.

Of course I wore my hair long. It couldn't be anything but long. It had to be long. My hero's girl had long hair; I had long hair. I would never have it short.

I didn't wear a bra. That was a bore. Harnessed like a horse wasn't for me. I wore a sleek black leather jacket over my unfettered breasts.

Angela, Rex said. Angela, you're a living doll.

Fuck.

We had to meet outside. My parents wouldn't let me go out with Rex. A little too rough for them, just right for me.

I dreamed of bikes. Big, gleaming bikes. The speed. Mounting the shining black saddle. Astride, the feel of the bike between my legs. Pressing down with my foot. Kicking the starter, cupping the handlebars with my red cold hands, still smelling of nicotine.

Christ! What a charge! Wa-room! Wa-room! The big wheels rolling. Me on top of this wild machine, and flying down the cold streets like steel.

Shit.

Spring came. Cold. Leaky sunshine. Dry streets. Even the dry streets gave me a thrill. The dirt you could see again on the pavement. The dust rising in the dry, cold air and the cold bursts of sunshine.

I lived in the suburbs with my parents. A yellow house with blue shutters and a backyard enclosed by a cedar hedge. A few houses down there was a cross street with a lilac hedge the length of the street. It was along this street that they came.

Rex and his friends. Riding their bikes to drown the sky. Breaking up the small suburb with their crackling noise, calling to me like a bird on its migration.

I ran to my bedroom window to look out. Push up the sill and breathe in that April air. See their bikes parked down in front of my yellow house.

Rex looked up and smiled at me. If only I could get out of this room. Shut up in my room, fleeing my parents like a monk. Geometry problems and notebook open on my desk.

Fuck. I smoked a cigarette out the screen window and watched Rex sitting on his bike.

Four o'clock afternoon fading, longing. Oh let me out. Take me with you. I want to be free. I want to ride with you.

I jump on the back of the bike and wrap my arms as tight as I can around Rex. The April sun is brilliant and warm on us. Glinting on the rear-view mirror. Blue sky, bare hard streets.

The motor kicks, fucks the street, we're off moving rolling down the street on the big wheels around the corner and out of sight.

I've put my hands across his belly. Rex's belly is hard and flat. His muscular thighs rise in his tight blue jeans like sleek, hard bone. I want to grab his thighs. He turns his head and his small gentle mouth touches my cheek.

Like it? he says.

The sun is shining on my cheeks and I am radiantly happy. The cold wind flies through my long hair, sucks around my ears and eyes and blows cold and intimately over my body. I smell of cold air. I smell of sun and dust. I can taste already Rex's warm pink tongue and his sweet saliva.

Rex's father drives a bread truck. I sense that Rex is a little embarrassed by his parents since my father is a lawyer. This is foolish because it doesn't matter to me what Rex's father does, and I don't care at all that my father is a lawyer.

Rex had a sense of humor. A sweet delicious way of talking that makes me laugh.

He is copying biology notes down from the blackboard. He is wearing black horn-rimmed glasses. Looks just like James Dean with a twinkle in his eye, but I've said that before.

I like boys that are well-built. Rex is well-built. Hard thighs, muscular arms, narrow hips in his tight blue jeans. Masculine hands, the hands of a boy smelling of cigarette smoke.

Oh how I'd like them up my cunt now.

But it is his face that I find irresistible and that unruly shock of brown hair.

Rex. I say his name softly, afraid. I am sitting beside him in the biology lab. We are alone. Everyone has gone home. The four o'clock sun is shining in through the windows.

Angela, he says. We cut up a cat today in our biology class. You'd like that, you'd find that interesting. He is always teaching me, pointing out to me what I might like and he's right. I like everything he says.

He knows me well. He guides me like a brother. He turns from his notebook and looks up at me over his horn-rimmed glasses and smiles. I watch his soft lower lip spread and close.

I know he loves me.

It is snowing and I want to meet Rex desperately. I am skating at the rink a few houses away from his with my Jewish girlfriend Rosalie. It is terribly cold, Saturday morning. There is frost in the air and thick snow on the ground. We huddle in front of the oil stove in the small wooden hut beside the skating rink. The room smells of wet wool, puddles of snow on the floor. Two boys in the corner are lacing up their skates.

We are driving up the hill covered in snow balmed in snow in Rosalie's car. She is driving and chatting incessantly. Oh if only Rex would appear. Rosalie living so close to Rex. Here I am stretched like a coil, a piece of thin thread, waiting. The snow falling in the frosty air and the window wipers are going like mad.

There's a feeling going up that hill. A dreamy feeling like a Grandma Moses painting. Dreaming, grinding up that hill.

Rex lives in an old rundown wood house in a row of similar houses. Short walk, small front yard. They couldn't have much money, three kids, father driving a bread truck. His mother works. She goes as a cleaning woman for the government. Rex told me this only after a long time.

Rex is fabulous. He carries my books. His voice is soft. He smiles and he walks—Oh how he walks! With a sexy roll, a sweet swagger. Rex is cock of the walk, that's for sure.

My girlfriend, not Rosalie, another one, thinks Rex is a doll. I had a crush on him, she confides.

You're kidding. I'm terribly jealous. Did he ask you out?

Once. Offhand. I went, but that was all.

Liane, my girlfriend, is very sexy. I am attracted to her. Many years later I have a dream about her, and I can't understand what it means.

Liane is passionate and she guides me in my relationship with Rex. We pass notes in class and she says, He loves you. Be patient.

Rex is still trying to get rid of his girlfriend, who is to me a baby. Although I feel sorry for her.

Rex comes by again. On his motorbike. I hear the bike for miles. I am tuned in to the roar of a motorbike like my own name.

It is Sunday. Spring again. My parents have gone to a movie. I am alone for several hours. I do what I always do as soon as they leave the house I go to my father's liquor cabinet and pour myself some white rum from the bottle. I prefer white rum.

Then I masturbate. Various ways. Techniques. It seems I've tried them all. First I draw the curtains in the living room. The sun shines against the pink and yellow drapes and the small room is very pretty. Three o'clock. Quiet. I lie down on the chesterfield and pull off my jeans and panties. Then I start to finger myself. I play around with the lips of my cunt and rub my clitoris. I finger touch my hole and slip my finger in and out. I can feel myself getting wet, and knowing I'm going to do it gets me very excited. I think of nothing, not even Rex. Only the sensation in my cunt, and aware of the sun against the curtains and the room sweetly warm. I lick my fingers, make them dripping wet with saliva, since I've found this works well, then I stroke my clitoris, lightly at first, feeling a needle-sharp thrill, making it burn and pulsate, then harder, taking the swollen shaft between my fingers stroking the skin up and down like a baby cock rubbing my fingers over the sensitive tip, grinding my clitoris hard and fast against my pubic bone, arching up on the chesterfield in a bow my legs high and wide apart until my belly and thigh muscles are taut and hard and I am frigging rubbing myself into a delirium, and grabbing my nipple under my sweater I come in a burning aching spasm of pleasure waves and darts of exquisite delight and I convulsively draw my legs together and clamp down tight on my cunt. Jesus! It's beautiful fucking yourself on the living room couch in the afternoon, a Sunday afternoon with the record player up full blast going the limit and just expiring on a sweaty hand in my cunt, panting and then doing it again. Trembling from the exertion.

Suddenly a knock on the front door. Jesus! Who can that be? Fuck my hands wet and I'm shaking. Off the couch in a flash pulling up my panties and jeans, taking a deep breath, another, opening the front door.

It is Rex.

Hi! he says. I saw your parents' car was gone.

I smile, delighted. Come in! Come in!

Rex steps into the small carpeted hall which is full of sunlight on the stairs and I close the door behind me.

My hand is wet.

I take his hand and Rex puts his sweet gentle lips to mine. I take my sweaty hand and run it through his hair.

Rex. We smile. It is beautiful knowing that my parents are gone and we are alone. The air is charged.

Do you want a drink? I am playful like a child.

OK.

I pour Rex some white rum. The level has gone down considerably, so smiling I take the bottle over to the sink and run some cold water in. My father finds out later. About the rum, that is. And my parents think it's a big joke that I watered the rum and that my father first noticed it when his drinks started getting weaker.

Rex and I are standing in the kitchen embracing. Rex has the sexiest thighs in the whole world. The sexiest mouth. As for a tongue there never was a tongue like that. Sweet Rex.

He strokes my breasts and I feel a warm tingling. I fix him with my eyes. There is such a thrill holding him with my eyes.

Rex looks at me deeply. Brown eyes. Mine are green.

The clock is ticking on the stove, so loud. Taking his finger Rex outlines my eyebrow and nose and lip and chin my throat, my breast over my sweater. We are both looking at my breasts through my sweater. He raises my sweater and there are my white breasts and pink hard nipples. Rex takes my nipple in his mouth, all the time looking at me and drawing his finger down to my belly button.

I am sitting on Rex's lap in the kitchen chair. Rex slowly slips his hands between my jeans and my belly and runs his hand down to my hair. I know when he's touched the hair. He stops. It's like an electric shock. Suddenly each hair becomes special, charged with electric current. We are both amazed that he is touching my cunt hair.

Rex groans and stretches out lengthwise on the kitchen chair. His cock is hard in his pants because I can feel it under me.

Suddenly I am wild. I don't care about anything. I unbutton his jeans and zip down the blue denim so fast I think Rex is afraid he'll get caught in the zipper.

Abruptly freed, his beautiful prick bulges under his white pants. With great reverence I gently slide his underpants down on his silky, springing prick and kiss him. I can't resist. It is so beautiful and warm and soft. I have never done this before and yet I feel as though my mouth should grow on him, suck him forever. I don't suck him. I only kiss him like a butterfly. A soft, butterfly kiss and then I'm gone because I'm shy. I stare at him in his eyes and I feel in me a breaking. It's as though I'm cracking up inside. A wild cry. A spring ache. Everything delicate I've ever known. Oh Rex you are a daffodil. You are a summer street a spring air the first tender blade of green grass. Your prick is beautiful like the pistil inside a yellow daffodil, your prick is gentle like the perfume of a hyacinth in spring, your prick is hot like the yellow sun.

Rex's prick is enormous. He stretches back in the chair and I stroke him as though my hands were born to this, so light I hardly caress him, then stronger, gripping him hard like a firm steel pipe standing in my hand.

Christ! what a joy. It's like a big tree or a thrusting green shoot. Tender bud. I kiss his prick again and lost in my senses I begin to caress him with my tongue.

There is a natural way. My tongue seeks the small slit of his penis and sucks around his cord. It's never-ending. Eternal like the fields in summer, deep I can't resist it. I am sucking kissing grasping his prick so hard his groans seem faint and sweet, and then excite me terribly, and I go on and on.

Rex draws back and small round blobs of white sperm spurt out onto the kitchen floor.

Oh baby, I say.

I rush for some Kleenex on the counter and mop the white drops off the kitchen floor. Smiling. That's a new one for this floor, I say.

Rex is a doll. He laughs and pulls back his foreskin and inspects his prick.

Come here, he says.

I come over, obedient like a slave.

Angela. Rex unzips my jeans and pulls down my jeans and panties to my knees. I pull them off my feet and leave them in a heap on the floor.

Oh Angela. His eyes are black, dark brown. Angela, Angela. His prick rises. He parts the lips of my cunt with his fingers and strokes my pussy.

I am all hot. I pant, and this excites Rex further. He moans against my bare flat belly. Angela. He takes his prick and puts it to my hole. Feeling round and hard and aching like a sweet burn, a throb. Oh I want it in me. He pushes against my tight lips, my body strains and uneasily he nudges through my wet cunt. Only a fraction of an inch and Rex groans. Our bodies are straining with the tension of holding ourselves apart like this. It is like fire Rex's prick in me. We stay perfectly still not moving. I can feel the throbbing of Rex's prick. Easily, slowly, he pushes his big lead pipe into me. Never before have I had a hot prick inside me. Everything else: candles, bananas, wieners, rolled-up washcloths, toothbrushes, hairbrushes never before a real one a big one a hot smooth silky one, burning prick. I clasp my legs around his thighs on the kitchen chair and push him deep inside me. There is a rush of tingling, a ball of hot sensation running in me that I don't know what it is, it is not like fucking myself that's for sure and it's coming so fast. Oh Rex! Oh Rex! It comes and I go over the top and now my cunt is throbbing like his prick, but still he lies still, the beautiful boy, still he holds back.

I don't know much about anything and so when he says, Are you safe? I don't know what he means. But someone in grade ten had said to me, you know you can do it if you aren't up to fourteen then you'll get pregnant, so now I know what he means.

I've just finished my period.

You won't get pregnant.

I'm terrified. Pregnant. A new world of mothers that wasn't for me. Free like a swallow.

Do you believe me?

I look at him intensely, passionately. I see him again riding his bike his strong thighs fucking the wind.

Oh yes! I believe you.

I believe him. He is my dream. I am dying for him. I am dying, I think, at twenty-eight, for him.

It's all right, Angela. It's OK.

I know. I know. I know then that he's going to fuck me and I don't mind. I don't mind at all when he starts to pull back slowly and push forward deep into my cunt, and drawing back, plunging in, he strings his bow reams my cunt fucks my guts as he comes harder and harder in me and shouts: Angela! Angela! Oh Angela! and I come again on him, clamping down my hot wet cunt on his prick convulsing on him fucking sucking his prick with my cunt, and we die together, we come together, and are reborn.

Love. Spring days. The daffodils first come out around the side of the yellow house and then the tulips come. In the corner of our backyard under the deep cedar hedge a profusion of lily of the valley grows into bloom. There is nothing more delicate and pure than the fresh white bellflowers of lily of the valley.

I pluck a bunch and take them to my room and stand them in a small crystal drinking glass.

You can never go back. You can never begin again. Once begun never to stop. Never to stop wanting always wanting it going on and on after that thrill charge in the cunt. Talking all around it about everything else. Philosophy, for example.

I'm an existentialist.

What's that?

I believe there's nothing.

Really?

Yes, don't you?

Then fucking like mad dogs. But that was after. First there was Rex. Rex, my spring blossom. My wild thing.

The resemblance of Rex to James Dean is uncanny. The same shock of wild hair combed high off his forehead, the wide brow deep eyes sharp nose. Even the mouth is the same, small pouting lips heavy jaw and sunken cheeks.

Catching Rex's eyes on the stairs in school between classes he holds me like an electric shock. I am confused in the noise of the crowd of students pressing up the stairs. My heart throbs. Rex is wearing a bright red shirt, black Wellingtons and tight blue jeans. He is not smoking, but I know he has grabbed a drag behind his locker door, changing books for the next class.

I am wearing a bright red sweater, blue skirt down to the calf and red knee socks. My breasts are fine and well-formed, and they point out high in my sweater. I can feel the boys looking at me. Some girls look too. My cheeks are flushed as they always are in school. My long brown hair shines over my back. I have the hair on top above my forehead cut short like Rex's.

It is Thursday. Rex and I always wear red on Thursday.

It is our sign.

I haven't seen Rex for weeks. At night I cry and listen to my transistor radio in the dark in my room. Sometimes I smoke a cigarette out the window.

Rex is having trouble with his girlfriend. He doesn't want to hurt her. My parents hate Rex. They fear him. His strength, his sexuality, his motorcycle. They forbid me to go out with him.

I am very disturbed. Lonely. I write poems to Rex and watch the snow falling outside my window.

I take long walks by myself in the snow in the noon hour at school along the path by the canal. The canal is drained for winter and is empty. Drifting snow and ice cover the stones.

I meet no one. I smoke a cigarette. Cupped reverse in the palm of my hand. I smoke it down to the butt nearly burning my fingers, which are sweating from excitement and fear and throw the butt into the snow where it drops like a hot stone.

There is a railroad yard directly across from the canal. Big lone boxcars stand on the sidings. The snow sifts down over everything.

I am passionate. Hot ice. I lie in the snow and think of Rex.

Angela, he would say softly, gently and hold my hand and kiss my fingers.

I hate school. I hate the bells. I hate the classes. I want to be free. I read poetry. I write poetry. I dream someday of being a famous playwright.

I'm late for school, running through the snow, the last bell ringing in the distance. Coughing as the cold air hits my lungs. Sitting at my desk in geometry class watching the pulse beat in the neck of the girl beside me.

I hate school. I'm going away. I ask my girlfriend if she wants to hitch a ride on a train. She likes the idea, but we give it up. For days I watch the trains across the canal. I get out a road map to see where the railroad lines go.

I take a book out of the downtown public library on suicide. Just the title thrills me: *Suicide*. I don't read the book; it is boring. It is four o'clock. I am standing on the sidewalk bridge over the canal near Union Station. Crowds of people pass. The sky is peach, winter light. I look down into the empty canal.

I'll die young, I know it. The idea excites me.

Rex wears red every Thursday. The winter passes. I don't see much of him because of the snow. It's like a country field outside the school in winter. No one is out but me. My tracks are the only ones in the snow.

Unexpectedly Rex calls me on the phone. He's very shy and stumbles over his words. His voice is so soft I can hardly hear him.

Yes, I say. I can hear him breathing deeply at the other end.

I can't forget you, he says.

Silence. I can't forget your green eyes. He's very quiet. 1 think he's crying.

Angela, he says and hangs up.

He calls all the time. Sometimes he doesn't speak. Other times he's outgoing and asks me what I'm reading.

You have to read *The Little Prince*, he says.

I do everything he tells me.

You have a future, Angela. You're smart.

No.

I buy myself a blue windbreaker. I wear my jeans to bed. I am him. He is me. I see myself married to him. I see him working in a department store. It doesn't matter to me what he does.

As it is he joins the Air Force.

Spring. Sand on the streets from the winter snow. Gutters running water. Warm sun. Daffodils, crocuses pushing up through the hard soil.

The streets are sexual. I find the bare spring streets, dusty and dry after a winter's snow, erotic.

Rex is coming for me. The sound of Rex's motorcycle coming to get me. A tunnel of roaring sound echoing down the streets.

I tell my parents I am going to a show. I get on the bus across the street from our house, and when the bus goes around the block I get off.

Rex is sitting on his motorbike at the corner waiting.

I am clinging to Rex on his bike. We are riding hard. The icy wind, fresh sun on our faces. The cold smell of jacket leather and oil.

We ride the streets for hours. There is nowhere we can go. There's nowhere to go.

We find a park. It starts to rain. Rex curbs his bike and we get off numb from the wind, the riding.

What are we going to do? I say.

Rex takes off his jacket and wraps it around me. The rain is streaming down our faces. It's not as cold as on the bike; in fact it is quite warm. It is a warm summer rain splashing on the grass.

Fuck. Let's take off our clothes in the rain.

The rain is running down Rex's face. His hair is flattened out in the rain. He takes out two cigarettes, which immediately become wet and tries to light them. They won't light.

Rex giggles and we huddle together under his jacket beside his bike.

What's worse here, he says, the rain or snow? The cigarette paper is soaked and the tobacco is falling apart. Rex tries to light them, but they don't. The cigarettes break and the tobacco crumbles in his hand. Shit. I'm dying for a smoke.

I kiss his mouth. The taste of nicotine. I kiss his hands. Nicotine. I suck his fingers.

Rex wraps his arm around me and we walk away unevenly together. He finds a nice spot in the grass under a tree. The rain has stopped. The white sky is turning blue. Smell that grass, I say. So sweet and moist I love it. I laugh and Rex looks at my mouth adoringly.

Rex, Rex. We press fingertips together and look at each other.

Rex is muscular and gentle, shy and passionate, soft and tough. He rides a bike. He walks alone. He hurts inside the way I do. He loves me.

Rex is looking at me so hard and gently so beautifully that it makes me feel sick inside. My stomach hurts. I am sharp and sick inside. He touches my face and wipes the rain off my cheek. My hair is soaking wet and curls on my shoulders.

Rex spreads his blue windbreaker on the grass and we sit down. There is no one else around. Bird sounds, wet grass. Waiting for dark.

What are you going to do next year, Rex?

I have to get a job.

You can't go to college?

No.

I know his parents are poor and there is a younger sister and brother at home.

I don't mind, he says. I don't like school anyway.

What about Carol? Carol is his girlfriend.

We've broken off. I feel a thrill. Three years they've been going together. Carol's parents are poor too. I've seen her. Long ponytail. Drab, cute in an ordinary way.

I would like to have an affair with you, I say. Rex is stroking his hand on the leg of my jeans. I would like to live with you.

We can't. Rex looks at his hands.

Why not?

He looks at me seriously, his eyes sad. Will you marry me?

I am shocked. Silent. Frightened, thrilled. He keeps looking at me.

Angela, will you marry me? His eyes so intense.

I don't speak. I love him, I do I swear.

You see. He hangs his head.

Oh no, it's not what you think! I hold his head in my hands and draw his face down on my breast. It's not what you think. I hold him hard. He's gentle against me.

I love you, I do. Oh Rex! How can I marry you?

He rubs his head against my breasts. I know, I know. His voice soft and hurt. I know, but you didn't.

I feel cheated and false. I mean what I say. You know I do.

Rex on his bike. Rex walking against the wind along the canal smoking a cigarette. The leaves sweeping in front of him. Rex telling me what to read. Rex kissing my hands and neck. Rex tonguing my mouth, caressing my nipple under my sweater, lying down with me in the snow.

Rex throwing stones at my window. Rex parked around the corner on his bike, night after night watching the light in my room. Sitting astride his bike under the oak trees, digging the heel of his Wellington into the soft dry soil.

I am seventeen. Do you know what that means? I am seventeen. Frightened. Passionately in love. I am afraid to marry. I will never marry. I will die at twenty-eight.

We'll wait and see, Rex says. He runs his fingers along the waistband of my jeans and my stomach quivers. He lets his fingers drop to my crotch and gently rubs my groin. My cunt throbs. I want him to touch me, suck my breasts. I kiss his lips. Our mouths suck together. Rex moans and turns the weight of his body against me. We lie together kissing furiously. Rex slides over on top of me and I feel his chest and thighs pressing into me. I feel the length of his body from his wild long hair to the tip of his boots. Warm. Oh you're so warm, Rex.

We wrap our arms so tight around each other it's as if we're suffocating. Tingling and suffocating all together.

The night is dark. Rex unzips his jeans and I feel a hot dart going through me. Rex slips out of his jeans and pulls down his underpants. I am lying under him fully clothed. Rex's bare white ass rises in the air. I can see the firm hard cheeks of his buttocks and his thighs covered with curly brown hair.

Christ! Rex is sexy. Even with those silly white jockey briefs around his knees.

Take them off, I say.

He has a look of agony in his eyes. His prick is fierce. High and hard and crowned at the bottom in a wreath of hair. The tip bulges fat and naked and slightly droops like a peony head.

Come here, I say. I have a thing for fat juicy pricks like this and I want to take it in my mouth.

I do. I take Rex's juicy prick in my mouth and suck him tenderly.

Rex is kneeling in front of me as I suck his prick. I can see his hairy thighs. I finger his sweating balls and cup them in my hands. Rex spreads his legs so that his thighs are outside mine. All the while I am sucking him he reverently strokes my long hair.

I keep sucking him until he throbs. Rex thrusts gently in my mouth and when I think he is just about ready to come he stops and says, I want to eat you.

I don't know what he means.

I want to suck your cunt.

When he says that I can feel my clitoris tingle.

I am embarrassed. His face in my cunt. I've never heard of that I say.

Yes. It's quite natural. You'll like it.

Oh, Rex. Do you want to? I am shy. I can feel myself blushing in the dark.

More than anything in this world I want to suck your cunt.

So I let him do it. He takes off my clothes and we fold them together in a little pile, and then we play sixty-nine. He turns around and lies between my legs with his face in my pussy and wrapping his legs around my head I take his prick in my mouth again. It is so big I nearly choke. He is all slimy from excitement and I am sopping wet too.

Rex parts the lips of my cunt and feels for the tip of my clitoris with his tongue. I can feel when he touches it as it feels like an electric shock. My clitoris is hard like a small bone. He knows he is on because my legs twitch and I can't stop trembling.

My excitement makes Rex terribly excited. I can feel it. His penis is swollen and throbbing in my mouth and I know he is just waiting until I come. I love the two fat halves of his head like two huge cotyledons, smooth and soft and swelling. I encircle his head with my soft tongue and Rex flicks his tongue back and forth on the fat pea end of my clitoris where the two flaps of skin join together. We are on the same place in each other, I licking his cord so fast and wet and he tonguing me like a dream.

I'm sucking your cock, he says. I'm sucking your little cock. He fastens his mouth onto my clitoris and sucks with gentle suction until I tingle. I arch and bump in his mouth and I imagine I'm fucking his mouth with my big prick that I'm choking him with my huge cock as he fucks my mouth and rams his bulging cock deep to my throat I'm coming I'm coming, I say, he arches and comes off in my mouth in a convulsion of spurts and the hot salty sperm floods into my mouth and I tingle and come at the same time.

Rex's prick throbs and gradually grows smaller in my mouth. I keep sucking him as he keeps on at me, and I like his prick so much, it's such a fat, soft sausage I can take his whole prick in my mouth at once now and it's like sponge rubber, springy and floppy and tastes so good.

Rex won't stop. He keeps licking my cunt.

Oh stop! It's too sensitive! I can hardly bear it! I twitch and yet he keeps on and soon the unbearable sensitivity becomes acute desire and I'm building up again and if he keeps on with his tongue on my clit like this I'll come again I do I draw my legs together and strain and my cunt clamps down and I blow off again.

Rex is the most tender lover. He has turned around and is sucking my lips. The lips of my mouth and stroking my long hair.

I feel like a dove. A soft cooing dove. At peace. I am warm. Rex's arms are around me. His hairy legs are crossed over mine.

The night air is warm. The smell of spring. A bursting joy. Fucking outdoors.

I'm not cold. Rex covers my hard nipples with his shirt. I'm not cold at all.

Rex is getting hard again. It is inevitable as we lie here together like this. He lies on my naked belly. I feel his prick growing on my stomach. He slips his hand between my legs and groans. We stay like that. Poised like a sculpture. Rex's hand on my cunt, his fingers slipping into my pussy, and his cock rigid on my belly. We are kissing like we're drinking water. Sucking, sucking.

I put my hand on his cock and he shudders, I can feel a tremor through his whole body. I stroke him diligently and cup his head and make a cunt of my fingers by encircling them around his prick and drawing his foreskin up and down. He is breathing hard in my mouth and panting.

My cunt aches for him. When he nudges his penis down between my legs so that it is still outside but pressing against me, I am melting into a big hot ache and I want more than anything to feel his hard flesh ease inside me. He rubs against my cunt hair and as he gets closer to the wet, bare soft flesh I tell him, It's O.K. I can hardly say it I'm so excited. It's all right now.

Rex doesn't waste any time getting in. He plunges his burning prick deep inside me in one long thrust up to the hilt and I feel as though I have been pinioned on a sword. I am nothing but palpitating, exquisite, erotic, cunty flesh as he comes and comes inside me, pulling back and plunging deep, sticking me over and over again.

We are lying entwined. I feel his soft sausage inside me and so help me Christ if I move just the slightest, just a little grabbing his prick with my cunt, I am coming again.

Fucked out. Wet and fucked out. Floating in a dream.

Why do we bother with anything else, Rex says, when this is so good?

Rex joined the Air Force. He had a thing about planes. Just like his bike.

Fuck! That big beautiful boy in the sky. And me down here on the ground.

He called me up two years after and we met by the sundial on top of the hill by the Parliament Buildings.

It was noon. It gave me a thrill just to see him.

I didn't remember him being so short, but maybe it was because I was standing on a slight incline. Rex was slumped against the sundial. He was going bald on top. Just a little. He'll probably be bald by forty, I thought. His face was the same.

How's it going, Angela? The same voice. The same curve to his mouth, the pink tip of his tongue.

Oh you fucking sexy bastard.

All right, I said.

He placed his hand on mine on the sundial. I felt an agony of separation, distant lives. We'd never meet.

What are you reading now? he says.

Not much.

You should read Klee. You'd like him.

Same old Rex.

We don't speak. He just looks into my eyes. The people pass by in their noon hour. What could we say?

It's a long time, Rex says.

Long time long long time my beautiful boy, my doll in the blue windbreaker, my beauty riding his machine.

Yes. Sundials are crazy, stupid things, I think.

Yes. Rex.

What are you thinking about?

Yes. And then I knew we'd never make it.

ANY WAY YOU LIKE IT

I KNEW ELIZABETH for five years. Six, in fact, if I include my last year of high school when she shared a locker next to mine. But I didn't know her well until my first year at university. We shared biology classes. We were lab partners.

Elizabeth was intelligent, ambitious, social, and yet inclined to be alone around campus. Elizabeth's idea of fun was public debating and shaking hands with the mayor in the evening papers.

Picture: Elizabeth smiling, long blond hair, wide blue eyes, turned-up nose, pointed chin.

Caption: Full support all the way. She is wearing a button and two blue ribbons on her breast. *Vote Liberal* is printed on the button.

The thing about Elizabeth was her breasts. She had the largest breasts of any girl on the campus. I don't know what she was, but she must have been a forty-two for sure. She always wore black sweaters and stuck out in front like two cannons.

The girls were quite nasty about Elizabeth's breasts. Imagine looking like *that*. It was always a big joke, Elizabeth and her big cans. The most famous boobs around. They were jealous. They would have traded their flat tits any day for a set like that. I never joked like that. I didn't think it funny.

Elizabeth was tall. Long slim legs. Fantastic legs. She used to be a ballet dancer. Long blond hair, slim hips, and as I've said these delicious cans. But I'm getting ahead of myself.

We shared labs. We were biology partners. It was great fun. Dicing up nematodes, squids, starfish. Hanging over the same porcelain dish of formaldehyde, drawing the dissection, one eye on each other's work. We were very competitive. Not so much me as Elizabeth.

Elizabeth would tell me her problems. Sitting on our stools in biology lab looking out over the snowy trees and the frozen river, lying like a flat ribbon between the fields.

My periods are bad, she says. I get a lot of pain. Rushing out to the john to fix herself up and coming back and saying: I've just changed my diaper.

Elizabeth was a baby. She missed her mother. She didn't live at home.

What I need is a baby, she said. A baby's supposed to fix you up. Carefully dissecting *Ascaris lumbricoides*, her long blond hair falling in her face.

Elizabeth seldom dated anyone on campus. Occasionally there'd be a flurry and some unexpected boy would ask her out. She'd go and make hedging remarks to me. Nothing ever came of it. They were all after her tits.

A writer dedicated a book to her. *To my love, Elizabeth*, on the frontispiece.

Well, that was keen, I thought.

A painter worshipped her. He begged her to live with him. A rich lawyer wanted to marry her. A friend lent her his Cadillac for two weeks while on vacation. Elizabeth was seen tooling around campus in a yellow Caddy, fur coat and blond hair flying. Another friend gave her a topaz pendant. Elizabeth had it priced to see if it was genuine.

How come somebody lends Elizabeth his Caddy? a friend of mine asks me.

What's with Liz? another girl says.

We all wonder.

A boy in engineering has recently asked Elizabeth out. He has a car and drives her places.

She's just using him, we say.

When he calls her at home over the weekend, she's never home. Late at night, she's out.

What's going on anyway? he says.

Elizabeth tells me she has allowed Ted, the boy in engineering, to feel her breasts. We are standing outside the biology lab in front of the glass cabinets, which display mice and butterflies and shells.

Really? I say.

Yes. Do you think I should let him?

Well, I don't really know. My boyfriend and I are fucking the ass off each other several times a week and laying hands on each other in the library halls streets buses, and she wonders.

Christ! I don't know. Did you like it?

I'm not sure. Then she says: You know Ted says I'm a Lesbian I'm so cold.

Oh baby really?

Now I'm no Les, but at the time this interests me. I say nothing.

Later I notice Elizabeth smoothing my hair. It is hanging in my face as I look down the microscope. Elizabeth pulls back my hair and smiles.

Another time she says: You have such a lovely nose.

Me? A nice nose? I hate my nose.

Oh yes, it's lovely. Grecian. It's smooth and straight, not like mine that turns up like a ski slide. She turns sideways and I see the curve to her nose. I laugh with her.

Now we are at biology field school together. Elizabeth is meticulous. Here we are, out in the bush, and every morning she puts on eye shadow, mascara, lipstick and powder.

My God.

I personally will have nothing to do with this crap. No make-up for me. Sometimes a little lipstick. Jesus! I won't put myself out for anyone. But here she is preening like a cock in front of the mirror and it's christly six a.m. and we have to go down to the main cabin and make the camp breakfast. There's one boy in particular she mentions. He said, kidding around: I could take you with my big toe.

The first day that we arrive at the camp Elizabeth and I go off to the can together. A wooden outhouse. Elizabeth pulls down her panties and plops down on the wood seat and Christ, she's bare! A bald shaved cunt! I stare at it. She's hunched over the seat, but I can see the bare crack in her white curved pubis and all the tiny dark hairs sweet as a child, a little girl. I am shocked. I have never seen a bare cunt before except on little girls. It's childlike, I think. She catches my eye and says, I hate the hair. I always shave it off.

Peculiar, I think. Some people are strange. I am proud of my luxurious bush of dark brown hair, which is bleached blond on the inside strands of hair by urine.

I'm ashamed of it, she says. Elizabeth not only shaves her cunt, she shaves her legs and her arms too. I noticed her arms in class. Prickly blond hairs, sharp in the light on the back of her forearms. I couldn't believe it at first, then I did and was a little enchanted. I would never do such a thing, even though I am self-conscious of the hair on my arms.

Well, such things are not for me. I am rough and ready and fucking my boyfriend every other night, and day too when we can, and I am what you would call *au naturel*. I have long hair too, brown, naturally curly, and I am pleased no doubt when I am nicknamed 'Brigitte' by friends and develop an underground name as the same.

I had renounced sex when Elizabeth knew me and she went around saying, She's like a nun. She never goes out. She studies all the time.

I had just met my new boyfriend and he smiled when Elizabeth said I was a nun. We were standing in the foyer outside one of the classrooms. The sun was shining in through the large plate-glass windows. And that was so. For a while I was off it. But now we were fucking all the time.

Elizabeth said to me: You're so lucky, you and Tony, you'll get married. You love each other. Look at me. I'll probably end up marrying an older man whom I don't love. At another time she confided: If you hadn't met Tony first, I could go for him.

Sure. Maybe his balls. Tony wasn't her type. No money or car. Only fantastic good looks, wide straight shoulders in a cuddly soft sweater, tight cords. Flashing white smile.

Elizabeth and I stick together. She needs mothering, and I don't mind.

I see Elizabeth at the camp again. It's early evening and she's washing up. She is completely nude bending over the sink washing her breasts with a washcloth, her glorious breasts with the round pink tits, in a basin of water gathered from the well. I am fascinated. No doubt about it. I have never seen such large breasts in my life. They are grand.

And then Elizabeth says, Here, handing me the washcloth, will you wash my back?

So I take the washcloth and rub her back sneaking a look at her tits. She has large, flat pink nipples. If I had known what I do today I would have reached around and grabbed one of her titties, but in those days I was innocent and also in love with my boyfriend.

After I had washed her back carefully but chastely, I handed her the washcloth and she said thanks and looked at me in the mirror.

She brushed her teeth in front of the mirror still naked to the waist, completely unconcerned about her free-floating boobs. I was impressed. Then she walked over to her canvas cot and sat in the middle like a Buddha, boobs hanging flat down to her waist, and put on her bra, which amounted to a harness.

I was disgusted. Not by the boobs, which were truly beautiful, but by the fucking harness.

Jesus, I'm glad I'm not built like that and have to wear that thing, I thought.

Another time. It is night and I am asleep inside my army sleeping bag in my camp cot as it is cold in early May in the unheated cabin, and Elizabeth comes in alone after drinking down in the main cabin with the boys and the young professor and tips up the end of my cot and lets it drop with a bang, giggling.

Fuck I'm mad. There is a crunch and a creak and it seems as if the whole bed is falling apart, and suddenly Elizabeth is contrite when she sees how mad I am. A little girl's joke gone sour.

Then there is the time when we go outside the cabin. It is about six o'clock at night. The sky is still light blue, no sun, air warm, and Elizabeth squats down on the far side of the cabin so they can't see us from the main cabin and pees. I squat down and pee too. I can still see her gleaming white ass, the two fat cheeks clearing the ground.

Another time I am downtown. I go into the National Art Gallery, and there is a friend from high school. She is blond, a cute turned-up nose and bow lips. Round blue eyes like a baby and extremely pretty. Her figure is nice. The sweetest slim legs and fine ankles. Always a tan. No big boobs like Elizabeth. We get to talking and we discover that we both know Elizabeth.

In no time we get down to the nitty-gritty. I have in fact heard Elizabeth mention this girl before.

There's something strange about her, the girl says. I don't know.

I have my doubts too. I find the topic exciting. This girl is very pretty.

She wrote me a letter and told me she worshipped the ground I walked on. The girl seems incredulous. Her blue eyes are round and large and her voice soft. I find that strange for a girl, don't you?

Yes, I do.

There's something more to it than that, she says.

This girl is quiet. She used to be in my art class and only spoke when directly questioned. There is something naive and angelic about her.

I find that odd, don't you? she says.

Yes, I do.

We both are quiet and think about that.

Then I am having coffee in the tunnel that connects the Arts Building to the Science Building. I see my old chemistry partner, a country boy, but not stupid and now in math, sitting at a table.

We sit together. And soon we are talking about Elizabeth. This boy and I always said whatever we liked to each other. No pretense, no shit.

I am drinking my coffee and he says, Hey. Did you hear about Elizabeth?

No. I am greedy for any information.

Yeah. Well, she was seen, if you can feature this, running around on the driveway at four a.m. in a bikini with a boy.

Wonderful. Her life deepens by the minute.

I laugh out loud, and encouraged, he continues.

They were wrestling together on the grass.

Jesus. At four in the morning?

You know she's working at the TV studio? She's got connections. There's a rumor . . . I lean closer to him across the table . . . Yes, there's a rumor that they've got a ring going, a prostitution ring.

You are kidding—

And that she's in charge, you know, like the madam.

He swirls his coffee and takes a slug. He has a thick growth of black beard on his white skin and always looks as if he needs a shave.

No kidding!

No.

Do you think it's true?

I don't know. He looks disappointed. We are both eager for any tidbits from this sensational life.

He's interested in her because of her tits. I know that. There's no sane boy around who wouldn't give her a tumble.

I am interested . . . well, I'm her friend.

I am meeting Elizabeth. It is snowing hard outside. By a coincidence I ran into her today at the university. I haven't seen her for ages, months. It seems like years.

She looked different. I didn't even recognize her, sporting a new fur coat, high heels, a gray poodle at one end of a chain. It was the hair that was different. Platinum this time, she had it dyed. And it was shorter.

How are you? she said. The poodle was pulling on the chain.

Fine. You're looking good. I smile at the tanned blond face and platinum hair. I don't much like the hair.

What brings you here? I say.

Oh, I'm taking a course in economics. I thought it would help in my job.

What are you doing?

I'm working at the TV studio. I want to get out of it. I'm interested in law.

Law. Christ.

What are you doing?

Oh you know, the same old thing. I'm getting a Master's degree.

You're married now, aren't you? she says.

Yes, I'm married.

It isn't long before I find out that Elizabeth lives just across the street from us in the expensive apartment building on the corner.

What a surprise! she says. You'll have to come over. I have some fabulous pictures of my last trip to Mexico. You and Tony will have to come over.

He's very busy right now. Exams.

Well, you'll have to come then.

The dog is dancing on his chain and pawing the tiled floor.

That's a cute dog you've got there, I say.

He's nice, isn't he? and she scoops him up into her arms. He's a miniature poodle. What are you doing this afternoon?

Well. I shuffle my books. I don't know.

Why don't you come over?

I look blank.

We could have some tea.

Tea! I don't drink tea.

Well, we could have a drink then. For old times' sake.

So I'm going over to Elizabeth's. I am crossing the street in front of the house where I live with my husband of a few months and walking up the walk to her apartment. It is snowing thick.

I hate this snow, I think. It's running down my neck and I don't know why I am going here anyway.

What could I possibly have to say to Elizabeth? But then I am curious.

I ring the doorbell, and she answers through the intercom.

Come on up.

The door buzzes and I'm riding the elevator. She's doing well for herself, I think. Christ I couldn't afford a place like this. My husband and I are living with his parents for fifteen dollars a month.

I'm envious because Elizabeth is not nearly as smart as I am. I know that. And I'm even better looking. I haven't the boobs, of course, but mine do nicely.

So there she is at the door. Wearing a white sweater, brown skirt, her platinum hair sweeping over her shoulders and the poodle bounding behind her.

Come in, she says, delighted to see me.

The apartment is very nice. Tastefully done up. A thick Oriental rug on the floor. Plates on the wall, heavy drapes.

Well, I say, it's nice to see you again.

Yes, it is. What will you have to drink?

We are seated in opposite chairs drinking rum and Coke. Elizabeth puts a record on the stereo. She likes opera. I don't dig opera at all.

How's Tony?

He's fine. Studying hard.

Good.

The living room is silent, snow muffled silence like a tomb, except for the high sad voice of the soprano.

I sigh and take a sip of my drink.

Elizabeth is looking at me intently.

I am nervous.

When my drink is gone Elizabeth offers me another one which I take eagerly.

The snow is falling gently. There is an electric shock atmosphere in the room as though each flake is charged. I want to ask Elizabeth something instead I say, I saw your friend.

Oh, who?

I describe the blond girl.

Elizabeth is noncommittal.

She offers to show me her pictures. That is why I came. The slides from Mexico.

Oh, yes, I say.

53

We are sitting close together on the couch under the lamp and Elizabeth is showing me the slides.

Very nice.

Another one. Her leg is pressed against mine. I feel excited. The alcohol is affecting me. I watch her mouth open and close as she holds the viewer up to the light, describing the pictures to me.

I am attentive.

Yes. She turns and hands me the viewer. Her hand brushes mine.

Looking at the picture. I turn and hand the viewer back to her. Her lips and open mouth are inches from mine.

I betray myself. In my eyes. I can't help it. I desire her. It's going through me like a knife. I don't know what I am doing. I am swimming with desire.

Suddenly our mouths are touching. It is the most fantastic feeling in the world. Kissing a girl for the first time and finding out it's like kissing a boy, and yet knowing it's a girl. This is a surprise to me. I wouldn't have known this. Her lips are soft and perfumed. Her hair floats down in my face. The tips of our tongues touch, encircle, and rub together, wet and soft and hard, and a charge goes through me. We caress each other's mouths with our tongues.

Elizabeth takes my hair in her hands and kisses the long strands and murmurs, I've always wanted to do this.

I believe her I believe her.

She touches my breast lightly and I feel an ache where her fingers lie.

Elizabeth, I say. I am breathing hard, panting. I can see her boobs heaving under her white sweater and I want to eat her up.

I touch the wool of her sweater lightly, slipping my fingers down over the swelling deep flesh. My hands are trembling.

Elizabeth's hand with her long silver polished nails drops into my lap and lies there like a hot bird.

In spite of the drinks I am shaking.

My hands are on her fat cans, holding them in my hot sweating hands. Cupping them, squeezing them, caressing them, feeling for her hard nipples under her sweater.

I am hot to touch her bare flesh, kiss her darling tits. I fumble with her sweater, slide it up to touch her tits. She stops kissing me and draws back and reaches to her back with one hand and unhooks her bra and out fall her breasts down into my face as I bring my lips up to her hard pink tit bouncing in the air.

I am doing what I have always wanted to do. Kissing a darling tittie. Sucking a beautiful boob, fat round white heavy feeling the flesh between my fingers squeezing cupping holding never enough nuzzling bouncing sucking her stand-up pink tit,

54

sucking the slit, each bump around the areola, giving her goose bumps, touching all parts of her breast with my tongue.

And she loves it. She does. As much as I do. Look at her watching me. Her blue eyes are glazed, watering. I have never seen her like this and panting, her heavy boobs swelling, rising in my face.

Then all of a sudden her hand is up my skirt fingers burning my flesh in their ascent finding the rim of my silk panties she yanks them down and places her hot hand on my hairy cunt and eagerly fingers my blooming clitoris running her finger, two fingers inside my cunt and frigging me until my thighs tremble and encircle hers and just like that she's lying back on the couch, her skirt drawn back over her thighs and her panties off on the floor, and I'm on top of her, kissing her luscious mouth and pumping her fat dripping cans, rolling her nipples and rubbing my bare cunt against hers, her scratchy, prickly little girl cunt, and she's lying back and moaning and moaning and we rub and rub until we both come holding each other in our arms and rubbing ourselves to ecstasy.

I am not embarrassed. I go down on her immediately. And before she's had time to recover I am eating her. The first time in my life! I have never eaten a girl before, much as I've wanted to tongue some wet slit, but never, and here I am crouched down between Elizabeth's legs lapping her slimy cunt, wet and musky from excitement, the clear juice running out of her sweet hole. I part the lips and find the fat bulb and suck like I've never sucked before because I know exactly how it should be done, where the tongue should touch and caress, how fast, how slow, how heavy, the rhythm. It's easy. Elizabeth is rising to new ecstasy arching her legs taking my head of long hair in her hands saying over and over, Suck me suck me eat my cunt.

Elizabeth comes in my face pushing her fat bare pussy over my tongue. I can feel the little bulb throbbing and twitching as I draw my tongue back and forth, contracting with each slow flick of my tongue Elizabeth trembling each time I touch the sensitive tip. Her thighs are tight around my head and she is saying, Oh! Oh! Don't stop! Please don't stop!

I don't. I slowly tongue Elizabeth to a new peak and she throbs in my face and lies still like a doll on the couch.

I am done in myself and lie down beside her and we fall asleep in each other's arms, our long hair spread out together.

Elizabeth is so beautiful. I want to eat her pussy all the time. Her blue eyes, turned-up nose and such a pretty mouth. To think that mouth, those lips on me . . . it's beyond my dreams.

Elizabeth and I are in the bedroom, both naked. Elizabeth is lying back on the flowered sheet and I am sitting on the side of the bed bending over her and playing with her breasts. I hold them in my hands and jiggle them. They are a handful. I caress every inch of white fat flesh coming closer and closer to her nipple. Tiny bumps stand up on the wide pink areola, and her nipple in the center is hard and firm like a bud. Only a pin-prick hole at the tip—Elizabeth has never suckled a baby. I knead her fat breast with one hand, and in the other I fondle her other breast and finger her nipple. My hair is flowing all over Elizabeth. I pull up and look at her in her wide blue eyes and find that she is staring at me intently.

She caresses my cheek with the tip of her finger and says: You're so beautiful. I wish I looked like you.

Not as much as you, I say. I am very proud that such a gorgeous girl is telling me that I'm beautiful.

I like to smell her hair, feel the silky strands across my cheek trailing over my nipples and belly as she moves down on me.

Her tongue rides over the high mound of brown hair and disappears into my slit. Sliding down over the shaft of my clitoris and finding my sensitive tip.

Her tongue is warm circling the bulbous tip, outlining the two folds of skin that come together drawing it into her mouth and pulling gently with her lips. A burning. I feel a burning as her tongue flows over my clitoris. Her cheeks are smooth and soft against my thighs. Her perfumed hair flows over my belly and her two big boobs, her delicious darling cans, are flattened against the inside of my thighs. While she sucks I reach down and grab her hanging tittie, the one floating over the side of my leg. As soon as I grab the fat hot ball, my hand burns and my cunt tingles. A deep burning ache flows through my belly and down to my swollen slimy cunt, for I am all slime and cunty juice from her sucking and my hair is soaking wet. While she sucks her fingers play with my asshole. Caressing my tight pink skin, my round hole, stroking her silky fingers up from my asshole to my cunt my dripping wide-open hole, which she fingers and rubs and rubs, her two fingers deep inside. Her fingers are warm and I can feel them slipping inside while her tongue is on me and her soft wet lips suck my cunt. Sometimes she nibbles gently with her teeth and when I arch up and cry, more more, she tongues me again and I say: I'm coming, I'm going to come, I'm going to fuck your face Elizabeth, I'm going to shoot off in your face, and she pants and pants and winds her arms tight around me as I thrust and bump in her sweet beautiful mouth. And I come.

All the time I'm thinking: This is a girl sucking me a girl miss fuckface miss big boobs giant cans cunt fucking me, and I come.

Her cheeks are wet on my belly as she rests and licks my cunt.

Oh Elizabeth. I stroke her hair and cheek and play with her ear lobe. Let me kiss you.

She slides up to my lips and lies against me, dragging her big boobs all the way up. They're pressed against me, the sweet fat things.

Come on, I say, I have to suck your tits first. I take one of her breasts in my mouth and suck in as much as I can at once until I am choking on breast. I am sucking like a newborn baby with her mama. While I suck I fondle her bubbie with both hands. I need two hands because it is so big. The other one, the free one, swings in my face. I let the first one pop out and grab with a big sucking noise the second and tongue her nipple and then really suck hard. She is rubbing her cunt against me, her hairless little girl cunt, and I can just see the pink crack as she undulates up and down, moaning and begging me to eat her.

First your lips, lover. Your mouth.

We kiss like old lovers. Friendly mouths, mouths that are known, mouths that have gone down on each other, and it is so thrilling I'm still aching more more my cunt is worked up to a fever and I want more more.

Oh my pet, she says, my beautiful doll my gorgeous pussy my sweet cunt I love you I love you. I've wanted to eat you ever since I saw you I could hardly keep my hands off you. Remember when we went to the show together I was aching to feel you up, I wanted to touch your pussy. And when I saw you at the camp outside the cabin I wanted to go down on you right there. You don't know how many times I've rubbed myself off thinking of you. And your lovely breasts they're so sweet.

They're nothing.

Oh they are. She fondles my breasts. They're lovely, look at them not like mine, they're just right. She holds them in her hands and strokes my nipples. They're round and soft and you've got the darlingest nipples. They're so big, look at that.

They aren't at all.

They are. I love them. She holds on to my breasts by my tits and fingers them. They are the size of two large peas, and I suppose not bad.

But Elizabeth, I haven't the cans like you. You're magnificent. You're really beautiful.

She smiles and I know she is pleased. I love her breasts.

We are sitting facing each other, holding each other's breasts and I watch her small belly rise and fall and the black mole below her belly button move away from the smooth curve of her bare cunt.

I feel so hairy. My cunt is buried in a mound of brown hair. A puff rises between my legs, and you can't see anything unless you part the lips.

I want you to come again, she says. She looks me straight in the eye and holds my gaze and makes flicking motions with her tongue. I want you to come. I want to run my tongue over your clitoris and make you hot.

I am burning with excitement as she talks I can't take my eyes away from her. We are breathing hard, our bosoms rising.

I want to suck your hard little clit, Angela.

I can feel my pussy swell and my clit contract. I watch her soft lips and glistening tongue.

We play 69.

It's a new feeling with a girl. I've played 69 with boys until I could walk on my head, but never with a girl, and again it's the same incredible soft dreamy smooth cheek and long hair, and a soft hot fleshy body of breast and stomach and buttocks against you and knowing it's a girl a girl with a cunt, a wet sopping slit like yours that's sucking on your baby prick.

Elizabeth has a surprise for me, she says, after we've sucked and rested and she's gotten up and poured a beer each because we're more in the mood for beer as we're dry from lapping each other's cunts.

The surprise is a dildo. Something I've never seen, but the thought of a fake penis has had great charm as I plunge candles, bananas, wieners, bottles, toothbrushes, hairbrushes, anything that sticks and won't cut into my hungry cunt, and now I see one as she takes the large pink plastic organ and straps it around her narrow hips and I feel strangely perverse as I watch her.

Sucking, well that's friendship among girls as natural as kissing a baby, but this is something else. A phony prick, an imitation cock, I'm not sure about that, but I am strangely excited by the perverseness, the plastic prick that this girl, my cunt lapper, is strapping on and she says, I'll fuck you like a man.

And I think: Oh baby, you'll never replace a cock. Jesus there is nothing I love more than a friendly cock, but I can't say that, and I'm game for everything. So we kiss and fondle and play with each other's cunts and bums and she puts her finger up my ass and I do the same to her and then she mounts me and eases her prick in and says, now I'm fucking you, lover, the way you like it and we're rubbing the hell out of each other with our fingers up each other's ass and she is plunging her fantastic big organ into me and I am riding her like a frenzied dog until I am coming in two places at once, against her bald little girl cunt rubbing her clit against mine, and inside in waves deep and convulsing riding over the top like an explosion. I come again and again in a continuous orgasm of ecstasy. Elizabeth is moaning in my ear and riding with me. She comes at the same time and embraces me like a vise thrusting as if she's dying inside me and we come down together lying in each other's arms our heads thrown to the side, our hair dripping around us, soaking wet, our bodies wet with sweat, our cunts sopping with excitement.

Enough is enough. We're done in. We've fucked ourselves out and it's a wonder we can rise again.

Elizabeth is tender and caresses me as I put on my clothes.

You aren't mad, you didn't mind? She is worried that she seduced me.

Elizabeth. I fondle her big boobs and look at her blue eyes so tenderly that she knows she didn't seduce me didn't corrupt me that I came here wanting to be laid, wanting her to go down on me.

Are you going to tell Tony?

She is worried about my husband. That is natural. I'm not worried. My husband has fantasized this so many times he's going to shoot off in his pants when I tell him.

I don't know if I'll tell him, I say. I'll have to think about it.

Well I do tell him and he is just as hot to trot as a young billy-goat. The first thing that he suggests is that we do it again and he'll watch.

I don't know. We've only been married a few months and I'm not too sure I can trust him. I can see him popping into Elizabeth the first chance he gets. But what the hell? What the fuck, I say.

I arrange a meeting with Elizabeth and say that Tony would like to come along. Is that all right?

No doubt. Elizabeth is very happy.

The three of us are all on Elizabeth's bed. Naked as lambs. We've had a few gins to loosen up, and I'm all ready as before to go down on Elizabeth. We start kissing, the two of us, slowly, taking our time and working down to the boobs and then the belly. My husband is sitting there beside us on the bed with a huge hard-on and the biggest grin on his face. As I go down on one of Elizabeth's boobs, his fingers touch her other one and I know he wants to suck her and I say, Come on, honey, suck her giant tittie, and he's in there so fast, sucking her tits and squeezing her breasts that I'm sure he'll come off right then. I can see his pulsating prick, but he can't stop and I know he's going to come and he reaches with his prick for Elizabeth's mouth and she knows what he wants and goes down on him in a flash and he moans and thrusts his prick in her mouth and comes like a flood shuddering and convulsing and clasping her head, and then he sinks down in a heap and collapses.

He lies there like a baby with an angelic look on his beautiful face, his eyes closed, and a tiny grin just beginning on his lips.

I kiss his mouth. Honey, honey.

He gives a big sigh and I know he wants to sleep. I know my husband. He will sleep like a baby.

Sweetheart. I play with his limp cock and squeeze the spongy flesh. We're going to suck each other off. Don't you want to watch?

He opens his eyes and his prick gives a small flick.

You want to see us eat cunt, don't you? We're really good at it.

His prick is rising again wavering in the air.

Elizabeth and I start to kiss and fondle, but we're both so worked up by Tony coming off that we go down on each other immediately and start sucking like fiends.

Tony knows how I would like to get fucked the same time I'm being sucked so I'm not surprised when he starts hugging me, placing his stomach against my bum, and holding himself up on one arm so he can watch Elizabeth eating my cunt. His prick balloons against my bum as he nudges it between my cheeks and feels for my hole and Oh my god he slips it in and rams the cunt off me while Elizabeth is tonguing me to a come in my cock. I am sucking Elizabeth for all I'm worth and I can feel her pulsating, her hard little pea throbbing in my face when Tony comes in my cunt and I come under Elizabeth's tongue and she climaxes shortly after while I am still throbbing from the double attack of tongue and prick in my pussy.

My truelove sweetheart has had it. He's lying flat out on the bed on his back and doesn't want to be moved. He's not even looking.

But Elizabeth and I are excited again, lying back with each other's pussy in our faces. At first it's just a languid lick, and then a friendly caress, but our little cocks rise again and Elizabeth fingers my wet cunt and I finger hers and place another finger in her asshole while we suck off again.

My darling sweet husband is still asleep. He looks so adorable on the pillow, gleaming sweat on his lips and brow, curly black hair around his ears, black lashes closed on his cheek. I kiss his lips and nuzzle his throat. He doesn't move.

While he sleeps Elizabeth and I quietly, indolently eat pussy.

LAYIN' AND STAYIN' TOGETHER

IT TAKES TWO to tango but four to swing, doesn't it? Laying in pairs. Hanging out together. When did we begin?

Our first swinging couple took time to develop. They usually do. We were young, all of us, and newly married, and jumping into bed with someone else was out of the question. All our passion and lusts were spent on our married partner without question. You see, we were in love, and even the thought of fucking someone else was taboo.

We would be faithful to death and die *in coitus*. But the idea was there. It began long before we were married.

I knew Victor before I met my husband. Victor was tall, about six feet, blond, blue-eyed lovely face, you know, that sexy type of man with a dimple in his chin, hollow cheeks, square jaw. Rugged and boyish, which is a combination I can't resist. And connected to that lovely face there was an equally admirable body, broad straight shoulders, which seem to be quite rare, a wide muscled chest, strong thighs and arms, narrow hips, and a flat stomach. A girl's fantasy, no doubt. In fact, he reminds me very much of my husband who is quite the same only dark and not so tall.

There is no question that I was attracted to Victor. It was obvious from the beginning. I think he felt it too because there was always this deep look in his eyes, the kind of look when someone holds your eye and is really saying: I want to fuck you.

It was that kind of thing. Whenever Victor walked into the school cafeteria or library, everything changed and became important. Special. However, Victor had a girlfriend and I had a boyfriend and somehow neither of us thought much in those terms until much later.

Which isn't to say that we weren't good friends. We were. That's just the point. We were the best of friends. In fact I can think of no one other than my boyfriend at the time, who later became my husband, with whom I had so much in common.

Our personalities were the same, romantic, moody. Long walks, poems, rain. Digging through Walt Whitman in the library and saying: This is it! This is life! He was so sweet when he said that. So intense. I found him terribly attractive.

In spite of his girlfriend he would tell me about his conquests. We were quite intimate. Some cry out, some shout, some burst into tears. They're all different. Walking around the block as we talked in the slushy snow. Feeling this connection. Hanging on to intimacies.

I want to take you in the woods and make love to you under a tree, he said to me one day. What about your girlfriend?

It was this come here and don't come here thing. I want you but no. There's no doubt about it, when I think back now. I was a cockteaser, and at the time I didn't even know the word. My old school friend, that's what he was. Good old Victor.

There were times when he was fucked off with his girl. Sometimes she was a prick. Political meetings, recitals, dancing lessons. She left Victor one summer to take lessons in modern dance on the Coast. Imagine leaving a boy like that? She danced like an elephant. And to make things worse, she wouldn't come across. No sex until they were married. That would have finished her as far as I'm concerned.

She was pretty. Long silky golden hair down to her waist, a fine small nose, pale blue eyes. A charming angel face, a sexy face. But she didn't have a good figure. No tits at all, short legs. She was small and angular. But in spite of her figure she came across as a sex doll. Her face made her. You'd meet her and think: What a fantastic good-looking girl. This was her face. Doll blue eyes, soft wide mouth.

Daphne was very independent. It was my way or no way. Victor was weak and took a lot of shit. When Daphne had been gone for several months he came over to my room to have a talk with me.

He looked downhearted. His handsome face drooped on his broad shoulders. He wanted my advice.

Victor is so depressed with Daphne gone that he drinks all the time. Every night after his summer job he goes to a bar and drinks five quarts of beer. He says he thinks of killing himself, but he won't do it. One night he came home to his room and two girls downstairs invited him in for a drink. They were nothing to look at in their early twenties with old maid written all over their faces. After a few drinks when Victor is nearly out of his mind they ask him to get into bed with them. He does, lying between them, and knowing they want him to fuck them pretty bad, but he can't get a hard-on. His prick is limp like rubber. So he lies there all night between these two hot bitches soft as a cooked pea thinking of his girl on the Coast in her modern dance class and why not screw the asses off these bitches? soft as a baby boy and not coming across.

He felt guilty. Guilty for not screwing. Guilty for not being able to screw. Guilty for wanting to screw.

Suddenly he suggests to me: Why don't we have a bottle of wine and go to bed? The two of us.

I laugh and act like a virgin. He smiles too as if it really was a stupid idea, but we both know we want to.

We don't get together. Of course not. His girlfriend returns. They get married the next summer, and Victor works for a year in the government. My boyfriend and I are very much in love.

That fall when I haven't seen Victor for over a year, three months after he's married I run into him at the university.

It's old times again. He's smiling in the tunnel with the afternoon sun shining in his eyes. He's holding an arm of books like a schoolboy and I find out it's back to school again. I'm getting my Master's in math, he says. Jes I hate working, you wouldn't believe how bad a job is, and immediately we're back to our old intimacy.

What are you doing? he says.

I'm married.

You too?

Just this summer. So you finally did it? I say. He smiles at me. Good old Victor, he knows we were knocking it off all the time.

You'll have to come over, Victor says. It's Tony, isn't it? referring to my husband.

Yes.

Victor all excited running off a mile a minute. We're living in a little apartment, not much, sixty-five a month no toilet, we share it but it's home.

He seems happy. I'm glad for him. So he finally got it in.

I ask about his wife. She's home most afternoons. It seems she's taking extra courses too.

What a life. I'm telling you. He looks at me confidentially and suddenly blushes. I'm writing a novel.

A novel!

I'm jealous. It is my desire to write a novel and here Victor, my old school buddy whom I wouldn't trade places with for anything, is doing just that.

What about?

And now he suddenly becomes vague and I know it's not about much. Shit Victor never had any talent in that line, oh but I'm jealous. Imagine secret afternoons writing that book.

What are you writing anyway? I try again.

Porno. It's straight porno.

Oh Victor, you're off!

The silly ass. He's probably drinking himself out while he writes his filth, and I know he'll never amount to anything.

His wife? The usual. She's not doing anything special. Of course she's as cute as ever, but that's not much in the world, is it?

Victor drives Tony and me over to his place the next day. He gets down to things pretty fast.

I am shocked. My God, my darling Tony and I are like two peas in a pod, the Bobbsey twins. We're inseparable, and Victor says, I'm seeing this girl Celeste. She's a dancer. We all know Celeste. You can't miss her around campus. She has a gorgeous figure, classic boobs, fantastic legs. She's tall and blond.

I am sitting on my husband's lap in the front seat of Victor's sports car jammed against the gearbox.

Victor lights a cigarette. I have coffee with her and talk things over. He's up to it again, I think. Intimate with someone else.

You can't just stick to your wife, he says. You have to talk to other people.

What does Daphne think about it?

She doesn't mind.

The sap, I think. I'd thrash him if he were mine.

Celeste, the dancer, is very beautiful. Victor is seeing her constantly. Drives her home, picks her up. Stays overnight.

One time his wife calls up and says to Celeste: Is Victor there?

Yes.

Send him home please.

Victor goes home like a dog with his tail between his legs.

The two of them were lying together in bed naked and Victor was stroking Celeste's beautiful breasts. That's as far as it went. His prick was as limp as a tomato.

His wife became friends with Celeste. And I swear if Celeste hadn't quit school and gone on a world tour there would have been something brewing between the two of them. She was that kind of girl.

My husband and I lounged on the couch that afternoon in Victor's small apartment, and we talked about nothing really.

Daphne said she would go shopping in the afternoon, a few classes in the morning. Funny how shopping in a supermarket when you're newly married is fun. The two of you playing house, pushing a cart down an aisle picking up a few cans. How long does that last?

You can't be new at everything.

The next time we saw the two of them it was at our place. We were so inexperienced at having company that we were in a flap. My hair was still wet from the shower. The

66

dishes were in the sink and my husband was scrubbing out the toilet bowl. It was very important that everything look right so we were always showering or cleaning when our guests rapped on the door. For the first ten minutes they had to sit by themselves. Damp, beaded with perspiration we emerged, and then began.

My husband had a surprise. Since grade eight when he saw his first porno pack in the back of a grocery store, porno pictures have fascinated him. Eating, fucking, sucking, he wants to see it all.

So the doll got himself a set from a guy in the government who was really set up. He had a collection at home of stills and movies and rented them out to anyone interested. There was talk that the photography branch had a group going where they photographed couples and girls and made their own pictures.

We had the usual drinks.

What's for you?

Gin and tonic. Same all around.

We're all drinking gin and tonic and it's—well sexy, sitting around the four of us tender married ducks knocking back the booze and looking at each other's crotches.

It doesn't come off that way. You're talking, sure. And it gets deeper and more intimate, school, philosophy, morality; but it's all crotch work, that's all it is.

So we drink and laugh and get louder and Tony brings out the pack.

Jes, Victor says. What a pal. For Christ's sake it turns out that my old buddy has never laid eyes on a set before. He is the guy with the stacks of *Playboy, Sir*, nudie magazines, crotch shots garters and all, but no real deck.

He thumbs through the pack. And there he is the big blond beautiful bastard saying, Jes Tony, you're a pal.

My husband grins like a kid.

We all look at the cards. His wife smiles. We've seen them before. And frankly they don't do much for me. But then I'm a girl.

My husband is the one with all the bright ideas. Let's play strip poker, he says. He doesn't mess around and work up to things like: let's play spin the bottle, he gets down to what's on his mind.

This is exciting. Spinning the old Coke bottle and taking off the clothes. This beats ordinary conversation.

We deal the porno pack and low man gets to take off a piece.

It's fairly even at first. Daphne has taken off her blouse, and that is a revelation. She has the smallest breasts. But it's hard to tell in her pink brassiere, and furthermore it appears to be padded.

I shed my shoes and stockings.

Victor takes off his pants.

When it comes to me again I take off my dress.

Daphne is almost naked. In fact now she is naked. Her titties are the tiniest things ever, only the smallest swelling of a breast, no more than a well-muscled man would show, and there's her blond hairy crotch. Now that is more interesting. Her legs are heavy and not exceptionally well-formed.

My husband for some reason still has his tie on, white shirt and pants, only his shoes are off. He's a sexy bastard with his broad shoulders and curly black hair.

And then it's the big surprise. Victor has a choice between his T-shirt and underpants and he decides on the underpants, I guess to get it over with and I am surprised, we are all surprised, except his wife, because he has the biggest dong I've ever seen. Long like a reel of soft lead pipe, for it is soft lying there against the blond curly hairs of his crotch.

My husband, the sweetheart, has a hard-on. He still has his pants on, but he has a hard-on. I don't think his prick went down the whole evening.

Now we are all naked.

We are sitting in candlelight on the rug. A single candle burns at the center of our circle. The porno cards are strewn all around and dark shadows flicker on the wall from the jungle of plants we have in our apartment.

There we are. Naked. Watching the candle wax drip on the rug and the black shadows leap against the wall.

My husband has another bright idea. We'll act out the cards—except, and there is a rule to this game, only with our married partners and no groups. Well that eliminates most of the deck but we do our best.

We draw a fucking couple, so Tony lies down on the floor and I climb on top of him and get it in. Then he turns over and lies on me and we are in familiar easy territory, we're fucking again and getting carried away and forget all about the card and our rapt audience.

They draw a sucking couple and Victor goes down on his wife but doesn't hang around long and we get the feeling that this is not his specialty.

We draw a sucking couple. The woman sucking the man, and this *is* my specialty and I do my best, holding my husband's stiff prick and licking the tip, flicking the cord, sucking it, encircling his penis with my hand running my tongue from the tip to the base along the cord, rolling his balls and sucking his fat bulging head again. Clear juice leaks from his slit and I'm sure he's going to come as his prick throbs in the air—we are experts and it seems we're drawing all the good cards, but we stop just in time and leave our audience agog.

Then Victor is sucking Daphne's toes on the couch. What's wrong with him? Has he forgotten that when Daphne threw up her spaghetti a while ago some orange-colored juice dribbled on her toes? Too many fast glasses of wine because she was nervous. Now he has one hand on her pussy and is fingering her clitoris. She is holding his balls and stroking his penis.

Daphne has collapsed on the bed in the bedroom.

We ran out of cards to do because if you can't fuck anyone but your partner there's not much to do. I am sitting out in the living room with Victor and Tony. I am still naked and have my legs wide apart in the leather chair. I might as well have a pair of jeans on for all I care. I am comfortable with my legs wide apart and hanging over the chair. I have the bushiest cunt.

We're all naked. Daphne is in the bedroom on the bed. I am in the chair and my husband and Victor are on the sofa opposite me. We're talking about other things but I can't take my eyes off the two pricks, my husband's and Victor's. Looking from one to the other, they are both stiff as a board.

We two girls share the double bed. I am beat and have drunk too much. Daphne seems to have recovered. We lie together on the bed talking a little before we fall asleep. I am thinking how strange it is to be lying beside a girl.

The next morning Daphne is feeling fit and sitting up in bed with the pillow plumped behind her reading *Lucky Jim*. The sun is shining in the room and it's a bright sunny Saturday morning, nine o'clock. I don't appreciate the sun as I have a headache.

The two boys have slept out in the living room. Victor on the couch and my husband in the lazy-boy chair.

Daphne walks around in the kitchen. Her blond bare pussy standing out in the daylight. My husband goes out to see what she's doing. I am jealous.

Before they leave Daphne says we'll have to try some other poses. I have some really good ideas. We'll have to experiment.

I don't know about that, I say. Sun, dry mouth and I'm sure she's talking about fucking my husband.

Well I have some ideas too. Like that luscious husband of hers I'd like to lay my two hands on that prick. But these ideas are too much for me at the moment and I try to suppress them.

My husband and I sit around more or less stunned for the rest of the weekend. Images keep recurring. Tony is mounting me in front of the Mathews. Daphne is sucking Victor's penis. Victor is putting it in his wife's hole. We can see her hole as we get up right close and watch. Her asshole is pink and has a small flap of skin around the rim.

The two of us go at each other all weekend long. I don't know how many times we've fucked now but we're exhausted.

The next day in school I am sitting in my Physical Chemistry class watching the friendly, large professor write Heisenberg's uncertainty principle on the board. All I can think of is what will we do next?

69

I think that I would like to pee on my husband. We could take shots of that for Victor promised to buy a Polaroid as soon as he can. We could get the stream arching over his belly. Or Tony spurting—that would be good. Big white gobs shooting off. I could have my mouth up close, in fact suck him just until he comes and we could take that. I think of Victor's big prick. I feel the stirrings of marital infidelity. I didn't know he had one like that, I think. I am wet in the crotch. The chemistry class is over before I know it.

The next time the four of us get together it is over at their place. That small apartment with no bathroom. And good as his word Victor has bought a Polaroid for eighty dollars, a used one. It is one of the original makes and as big as a box. He has spent his preceding days mastering its operation so we're all set to be photographed. We haven't the cards this time, so we use our own imagination.

We're drinking, my husband and I, sitting on the piano stool. They have a piano and Daphne plays.

It is Christmas time. Presents are on top of the piano. One is for us. We open it. It is a nice green fruit bowl.

Thank you very much. A little embarrassed. We have nothing for them.

Victor takes a picture. The two of us. My husband closes his eyes when the picture is taken. My hair is hanging down over my boobs. I am wearing a black T-shirt, blue jeans and blue wool slippers. My mouth is open. We are both holding drinks in our hands. My husband is laughing. I look sexy.

Victor's wife moves over beside us. She sits beside my husband. We are all photographed together.

The picture changes quite fast. Our clothes are all off. We are naked for the second time. It wasn't the same as the first time. We know what each one looks like now. We feel comfortable in the nude, as though now we can get down to business.

Well the show starts. It's you do this and we'll do that and Victor is snapping the shutter like mad. Since he's the only one who knows how to operate the camera, he misses out on most of the action.

First, it's the two girls on the piano stool. Squatting naked, and taking two quart bottles of Canada Dry ginger ale and shoving them up our cunts as far as they will go. They go as far as the neck and that's it. We get a picture of that. My husband says he's heard of prostitutes shoving the whole quart bottle up their cunts. Some big cunt. Well we don't believe it.

We'll do anything. What's next?

Tony and I are on the piano stool and I am licking his delicious prick. I hold it tightly in my hand, encircling it with my fingers. A cigarette burns in my other hand. My hair hangs down over my shoulder in front of my cheek. My boobs droop. Nice curve.

We look at the picture. Very nice, Victor says. You have lovely breasts. I like that. My nipples stand out like two cherries. You can't miss my dark bush, it's in every picture.

We take one of Victor holding Daphne by her legs upside down her golden hair streaming to the floor, sucking her cunt. Her legs are wrapped around the back of his neck. Now that is a good one. It's one of my favorites.

Then we feature assholes. It's assholes up in the air and it's Daphne again and Victor is tonguing her asshole. Of course it's clean. That goes without saying.

I want to know what that feels like so my husband does the same to me. It tickles. Like running your tongue inside your mouth.

We've run out of film. We divide up the pictures. Each couple gets their pictures, but there are a few favorites, like me sucking Tony's prick. We have to toss for that one.

There's not much to do once the pictures are taken. We've run out of ideas. We aren't very adventuresome at this point. Such as mixing partners. Well we don't even think of that. Or do we? Who does?

We get together a few nights later. This is like a drug. We are exposed to something more powerful and intense than our everyday life. We can't stay away from it. All these naked bodies and cunts and assholes and tits. We can't think of anything else.

We take off our clothes again for the third time. This time speedily without any fuss and make a little pile of our own.

My husband starts the evening off by coming over to me immediately and caressing my inner thigh fingering my cunt, and without hesitating goes down on me and starts sucking. I lean back in my chair and spread my legs wide. My cheeks are flushed my hair trails over my shoulders and arms and I close my eyes while he tongues my clitoris until I'm close to coming and he says, Come on, lover, come on. Fuck my face, and I fuck his face. Arching and bumping and throbbing on his sweet lovely mouth and tongue and nose.

He keeps on tonguing me but I push him away as my clitoris is so sensitive that it hurts. He smiles and stands up. His prick is stiff as whalebone. I smile at the Mathews who look hot to trot. Victor's prick is standing full length which is phenomenal and Daphne looks like she's ready to rape him. Before we know it she's lying on the floor and Victor is in her and banging away, and Victor comes off in about two seconds flat. Daphne moans and cries out and I figure she's come too, but you never know, and this gets Tony and me terribly excited. So we're down on the floor beside them while they get up and sit down and we think oh maybe we should stop, but they say, no, no go ahead, so we do and Tony fucks my ass off really good this time and I come again and he shoots his load inside me.

We get dressed and Victor says he has a bit of a stomach ache so Daphne makes him an Alka-Seltzer. He can't swallow pills, she says, so I always give him this.

71

We're done in again, and it's late, so we leave.

My husband has forgotten his scarf and goes back. He and Daphne are at the door for a long time. What the fuck are they doing anyway? I am upset. Finally he comes and we go across the street to a diner and have a cup of coffee.

The next time we're together, it's our place again.

It's the usual scene, camera. Victor brought his camera along but we don't take any pictures and the four of us are lying in the bedroom on the bed, on the white bedspread, all of us naked.

Wait! We decide we *will* take some pictures. This time it's a threesome. The two girls and Tony. My hand is on Tony's prick, and I'm kissing his mouth. His hand is on Daphne's crotch. Shoot: it's a picture. While Victor is developing the picture with a hard-on, Tony fingers Daphne. I see his finger working into her cunt and I am just about fit to be tied. I don't know what to do pull his hand away, say nothing, give him shit I am burning inside.

It comes to me that it is all really a sneaky game, and I know now what is up.

I have a good look at Victor. He's like a sun god. Beautiful. The muscles look at those muscles and those sweet pink tits on him and that golden hair. Christ! What a beautiful prick and his mouth, I'm partial to mouths, they are right or wrong, and his is just right, the perfect fleshed-out lower lip and slightly protruding upper lip. The dimple in his chin and square jaw.

I would like to be crushed by those arms I think, I would like to have *his* prick inside me. I don't give a damn now about Tony fingering up Victor's wife. Go ahead. The sooner you two are under way . . . I dream of Victor's prick. Slowly going in, easing in and hitting bottom and instantly coming off—we're all fireworks, Victor and I.

Victor says, Let's turn out the lights and play scramble. Let's mix it up.

Tony says, No. What a prick.

Victor's wife smiles. She'd like to mix it up. I bet you Tony's finger felt good in her cunt.

What's Tony holding back for?

I look at Victor and he blushes. He's beautiful when he blushes. My husband is self-assured. Victor is not. He blushes all the time. Just like me. Oh how I would like to suck his mouth every time he blushes.

Instead my husband fucks me and Victor fucks his wife. What a bore. We are lying side by side on the bed, the two girls on the bottom, touching the length of our bodies and both boys pumping away on top of us. The lights are on. It is glary in the room, what with the white bedspread and white walls. I keep an eye open and watch Victor and Daphne. I see his hairy blond thighs pumping up and down and then when he is just about to come I catch sight of his face and he pumps deeply and groans. Daphne is quiet. Victor did it too fast, and she didn't come.

Daphne is lying inert on the bed. Victor is collapsed on top of her. Then we go to it. We were both watching and now Tony resumes his thrusting and plunges like a mad bull inside of me and I have no trouble coming and neither does he, and it's ecstasy, excruciating. Tony is crying Oh! Oh! Oh! and groaning as he spurts his big delicious cocksucking prick inside of me. We are satiated. I am ashamed of my earlier lust for Victor and lie content in Tony's arms.

It seems that we are beginning all over again. We are at their place and Victor has put on some records, the Beatles and Elvis Presley and we're sitting around chatting. My husband and Victor's wife are sitting on the sofa about three feet apart. I am sitting back in a soft orange easy chair, and Victor is sitting in a black leather chair in the far corner. We make a triangle if you draw a line from me to Victor and then to Tony and Daphne, who form the apex of the triangle, as they are sitting quite close together.

Daphne and Victor have moved. They are in a house now, out of that cramped apartment. Daphne is working and earning good money. She's a nurse. Victor is working too. He's teaching school. The school work didn't last.

Someone decides to dance. It's Victor. Of course we dance with each other's mates.

Victor is squeezing the death out of me. He is pressing his prick against me and I can feel that he has a hard-on. He smells good. A cologne I'm not used to. I like the smell of his freshly laundered shirt. Daphne takes good care of him. Victor is much taller than my husband and I can rest my head against his chest. I can feel his heart pounding in my ear. He is sweating profusely under each arm there is a deep stain of sweat on his blue shirt, which I touch with my hands. The palms of his hands are soaking wet. He breathes into my hair warm breath. I can smell the shampoo I used on my hair before coming over. I soaked in the bath for a long time and lathered my cunt with soap. I am clean. My cunt aches as Victor holds me. My tits ache. He has his hand on one of my breasts. The lights are out. He slips his hand into my dress and I feel his fingers on my bare breast groping for my nipple. He fumbles and I ache inside. Finally he finds my tit and fingers it. I moan against him. He reaches for my mouth with his and sucks me hard on my lips. Our tongues grope in each other's wet mouths aching to touch, touching with fire, outlining our lips, mouths, edge of our teeth, corner of our mouths sucking our big thick tongues knowing we mean a prick until Victor picks me up and holds me high against him, his bulging cock and balls hard as rock against my thighs. There is only one thing I want to do and that is to lie down and put it in me.

The lights go on.

My husband's hair is mussed. Daphne's clothes are disarranged. Her see-through blouse is open and her flat tits are exposed. Her skirt is up over her thighs and we can see her bikini black panties with pink bows. I suspect my husband was down on her. He has a hard-on like a banana in his pants. I am surprised that his pants are closed.

The music has stopped. When it starts again we dance with our own partners. Somehow things have come to an end for tonight.

That cooled it for a while. It seems things got a little out of hand. Tony questioned me extensively about what we did and I in turn asked him what he was doing. It turns out he only kissed Daphne's crotch through her panties. But the intention was there, you can't deny that.

Two months later and it's April. I feel like a bird out of a cage. I feel excited and expectant. Yellow daffodils, robins, green grass, warm wind wrapping around me, which excites me further. I am blown away and ready for anything.

They come over again. It is our turn. Well we don't waste any time this time and we are going to play a new game.

It's spin the bottle. Any bottle will do. We take one of our mixer bottles, an empty Schweppes tonic water. Out come the old porno cards again. It's easy to do things within the framework of a game. Structure everything and it's O.K. The new morality, my husband says.

The cards are there on the rug. My husband is giving instructions. You draw a card and spin the bottle. Whomever it stops at you have to do whatever is on the card. But wait a minute. There's a catch. We can't, he decides, fuck each other's partner. Yes we're all agreed on that—that is too much, too dangerous. We're in trouble as far as the cards go, so we decide to do it this way.

First, we'll start out with kissing.

Victor spins the bottle and it points at his wife. We are sitting nude in candlelight in a circle on the rug on our living room floor.

He quickly pecks her.

She spins the bottle. It hits my husband. She kisses him on the mouth. Slowly, generously. His hand slips up to her bare titties.

Hey, none of that! Victor says.

They stop satisfied.

My husband spins the bottle.

It hits Victor.

Let's skip that, he says. Is that O.K. with you, Victor?

Victor says yes.

He spins again. It hits Daphne. They kiss again, slow French kissing while we watch.

This is getting to be a bore, I say.

All right. All right, my husband says. O.K. Let's suck breasts now. He hands me the bottle and smiles. Here, you start. You haven't had a turn.

Goddamn right I haven't had a turn. I take the bottle silently and spin, praying for it to hit Victor.

Of course, it does.

Just a minute, I'm going to kiss him instead, I say.

No one says anything and Victor waits.

It is our second kiss. It is as good as the first. My body tingles. We suck lips and caress tongues. Victor puts his arms around me. So sweet. He feels so big. I nuzzle my nose in his neck and kiss his warm soft skin.

Victor loves that, his wife says. He's a great necker. So is my wife, Tony says.

They should get along just fine.

Victor has a dreamy look on his face and I go back to his lips.

Come on, you're taking too long, my husband says.

Just a minute. I slip my fingers over his muscled chest and stroke his hard tanned belly, which trembles at my touch.

His nipples, isn't that right?

I go down on his tiny nipple with a small areola of blond hair around the pink pigmented skin and lick. His nipple rises under my tongue and then I suck him lightly, gently, and stroke his chest.

Victor sighs.

His breasts are hardly smaller than his wife's what with the well-developed pectorals, his nipple is smaller, and of course he has a ring of blond hair around his tittie which his wife hasn't.

He seems to like that too, his wife says.

It's Victor's turn to spin the bottle.

Victor spins and it points to me.

I feel a thrill go through me.

It's sucking breasts, isn't it? I say as I wait for his mouth.

Yes. My husband sounds jealous.

Victor is having a treat. He takes my left breast in both his hands and fondles it. Strokes the fat, jiggles it. My breasts are nicely curved and fleshed round and protruding. Victor fingers and squeezes my flesh and then my nipples.

You're supposed to kiss them, his wife says.

I'm getting around to that. Victor grins at his wife. Blue eyes, boyish grin, flushed cheeks. His prick is standing up its full magnificent length. I put my hand on his prick.

I can feel the silence in the room as Victor sucks my breasts and I hold his prick. He tries to put my whole boob in his mouth, but can't. He doesn't let up sucking. Like a baby he seems content. I am holding his prick and lean back slightly. It wouldn't take much, I think, for Victor to lean forward and fall on me and put his prick between my legs. I'd help him get it in. That boy would have no trouble. We finally stop. A little bit guilty. We needn't have felt so. Daphne is licking my husband's prick and he is grinning like an idiot.

Aren't you getting ahead of yourself? I say. My husband keeps grinning at me and for an answer arches forward toward Daphne's mouth.

What's next? Victor says.

Let's suck cocks, my husband says. It's our turn. I'll spin the bottle. So he spins and it hits me.

He does a good suck on my cunt. Just to show he's friendly, I suppose. Maybe he's showing off, because that's not their specialty.

My turn.

I spin. It hits Daphne.

What do I do?

You suck her, Tony says.

Do you mind? I ask Daphne.

Oh no. She laughs.

I don't mind either.

First I finger her cunt. It's like my own, wet and gucky. I slip my fingers along her lips until I find her hole and then I poke my finger into it. Feels like springy, mushy rubber. Daphne has her legs apart and is watching me. Her lips are parted and she's smiling a little. When I rub my fingers up and down inside her she sucks in her breath and shifts on her fat bum toward me. She was leaning back on her hands, but now leans forward, and grabs one of my breasts which are drooping in front of her. She puts her mouth to my nipple and sucks.

These girls are great, Victor says. Simply great. I finger her soft puff of a breast and stroke her nipple. It's hard. While my fingers are in her cunt I kiss her breasts, one, then the other and I can feel her shudder. I take one of her tits in my mouth and it feels strange nice I am getting very excited as I gently suck her breast. I am breathing hard and so is Daphne. The boys can't help but notice.

Jesus girls. You're getting us horny.

I look up at Daphne's face. Her sweet angelic face with her long golden hair and say to her, Now I'll suck you.

Daphne is in ecstasy. Victor never goes down on her it seems, and she adores it.

She's moaning as my tongue toys with her clit, which is huge, simply huge, and hard like a marble. I'm terribly excited when I see how hot she is as I eat her cunt. I have a good hold of the lips of her cunt by her hair and I can see her throbbing clitoris.

I'm going to suck her off. My stomach is aching with the thrill and I can feel my cunt dripping as I kneel between her legs.

The boys don't say anything; they are fascinated by this spectacle.

Victor jokes, a little ill at ease, because he's never frenched his wife and says, You girls sure are breaking the ice, aren't you?

By Jesus we are doing that. Daphne is panting and crying out of her head. She's having the first French of her life. She is lying flat on her back and while I'm tonguing her clit I am also fondling her breasts and she's moaning and saying, Oh, don't stop! Do it to me!

That's what I do. I bring her to a peak and she arches in my face and thrusts on my tongue and shouts: Oh! oh! and then sinks back on the rug.

I come up for air and Daphne is lying back like the dead. Her eyes closed, a beatific look on her face. Her golden hair fanned out around her, she still heaving with excitement.

Christ! I'm pretty hot myself.

Her husband says: Well, now she'll be wanting it all the time.

Then you'll have to give it to her, I say, and think you fucking bastard, and make flicking motions with my tongue.

My husband has his arms around me and is squeezing my tits.

You're a real cocksucker, aren't you? he says and sticks his prick in my mouth. I suck the way I always do and his eyes are sparkling and dreamy. He caresses my long hair. Suddenly he pulls out and gets on top of me and plunges into my gaping, dripping cunt. We're bucking like wild horses, fucking like minks and we come together, a glorious high riding throbbing thrusting peak, exploding into tiny shards of ecstasy. Coming and coming, it never stops. After our wild rocking Tony lies inert on me and I feel a new passion, a new thrill and I arch on his stiff prick and rub my cunt with a few quick jabs until I'm poised again, ready to fly. I come off again as good as before. Oh! The exquisite touch, the wave of bliss, pulsating deep in my throbbing, contracting cunt.

Victor and Daphne had the same idea. Victor fucked his wife and we heard groans and gasps, but we were too absorbed in our own passion to watch. They're lying together, Victor is on top of Daphne. Now he rolls off his wife and sits up. He doesn't look as satisfied as my husband and I. Daphne is still out cold. Lying on the rug in an abandonment of satiation.

We've poured another drink, roused ourselves and are going to take pictures.

We mix it up a little this time. The two girls. Me and Victor. My husband and Daphne.

While my husband and Daphne are in the living room developing the picture, and from what I can see through the open door necking and feeling each other up while Tony counts off sixty seconds on his wrist watch, Victor and I are lying on our bed going through imitation fucking.

He's on top of me, his big tremendous prick between my legs. God, how my cunt aches! as he thrusts against my pubic bone.

Oh baby, why don't you put it in? Come on, they'll never know the difference. I'm still dripping from my husband's gobs of sperm.

Slip it in.

He breaks through and I moan. Like cutting ice, breaking through the magic circle. Jesus! it's great every time and in in like I've never had it in and oh my God! his prick is long long feel it so deep I am filled with prick. Christ! I'm going to come, and suddenly he whips it out and spurts all over my belly.

They're still developing out there. I quickly wipe the goo off our bellies with the bedspread and squeeze him tight.

Oh, honey, you're beautiful.

My husband and Daphne come through the bedroom door arm in arm to show us the picture.

It is of the two girls. Down on each other. It's imitation. Just for the picture.

We both smile and Victor says, It's tremendous. Look at the tit on there and points to my tit in the picture. Daphne's fat ass is high in the air.

We are relieved, chatty. They don't suspect a thing.

After that taste I'm ready for anything, but would you believe that's more or less it for the night, and we say goodbye? When will we see you next? I say at the door, and Victor says, more or less to me, for it must be obvious by now that we have the hots for each other, As soon as we can. I am left standing at the door with a throbbing cunt.

My husband seems to have had enough for now and is not sorry to see them go.

What a boring weekend after they leave. I can hardly drag myself around the apartment. Everything is an effort. Finally we order Bar-B-Q chicken and go to bed early.

I walk through the streets to my job, for I am working now too, like a somnambulist. Everything kills me. I am bored to extinction. I talk to people like a zombie. All I can think of is Victor's big prick in me. I am talking to my boss who says, We'll run these samples through on the X-ray spectrometer first and then we'll try fusing them to see if we get better results.

Scream! Scream! I want to scream I am going nuts I am truly going nuts. I watch the snow fall outside his office window and long for Victor. Just to hear his voice, his voice, imagine. Not even his prick. Just to lie beside him in bed and caress him. I fear I'm getting a crush on Victor. I am going too far I know it, but I can't help myself. I become obsessed with Victor.

We meet again. It is Christmas time again.

How many years is this now, my husband is saying, three? four? Yes, we've known each other a long time. We are old friends.

We are together again. I've dreamed of this moment for months; I don't know how I have existed until now.

The four of us are sitting in their living room. Log fire in the corner, flickering warm on the copper wall. It's wonderful. Cozy. Intimate. Exciting.

We talk for a while. We always have a lot to say. It seems we have quite a bit in common. And as I say, Victor and I are quite similar in personality. His wife and my husband make up the other two ends of our relationship and are not like Victor and I, but we all relate to each other in various ways. For instance, I am attracted to Daphne, there is no denying that. I went down on her and I loved it. She is attracted to me. It shows. Her gestures, the tone of her voice when she speaks to me. She likes my boobs.

She says: I asked Victor what would make him more jealous—if I had an affair with a man, or a woman?

Victor looks reflective and says: I don't know. I don't think I would really care if she had an affair with a man. And with a woman? Well. That's just another interesting possibility. Perhaps, then, the woman, as it's unexpected. Different.

We talk about the attraction we two girls have for each other.

It's perfectly normal, my husband says. Girls have this closeness, they understand each other. They're much closer than men. It's quite natural. It doesn't mean a thing.

He's got a hard-on, I notice, in his pants.

We are fully dressed. We don't automatically strip anymore when we get together because its like seeing your own body now, there's nothing to it, and besides it's a lot warmer with our clothes on.

Daphne says: Remember when we were in bed together? She's referring to our first night when we two girls slept together.

Yes.

You know I was thinking of touching you.

You were! I laugh. Isn't that funny, I was thinking of it too but I didn't dare.

You're kidding!

No. I wanted to touch you kiss you, you know. I had the idea you were thinking of it too.

She looks abject. If only I had known; can you imagine? Why didn't I? We could have had so much fun.

Baby that's true.

I love these girls, Victor says. There's no one like them. Look at Daphne. There's no one like her. Or Angela. They are unique, these girls. He stretches back on his black leather chair and takes on the warmth of the fire.

Come on. We aren't unique, I say, and take him on with my eyes. We're like any two hot girls anywhere.

Daphne has gone to the kitchen to make a sandwich. My husband quickly follows her.

Victor and I are left alone. He moves over on to the couch beside me and takes my hand in his.

Angela.

We look at each other and I think oh my God I'm falling in love with this guy.

I lean against him and moan. Oh my God. My passion for Victor makes me weak. I am ready to cry.

Victor. Oh Victor. I think of him constantly, dream of him, long for him, love everything about him, can't live without him. Dead.

I touch his lips his hair his tongue cheek, Victor. It is Victor I think of when Tony makes love to me. Victor.

He is kissing me, loving me, holding me so tight. Angela, I want you so much. Angela, Angela. He looks at me. I love you.

Oh, those beautiful blue eyes, that pouting mouth, I'm going to cry.

No, don't cry. Don't cry. He croons in my hair, caresses my face. We're the same, Angela. I know we're the same. You feel lonely, don't you? You're always alone. I know. I understand you.

All the time he's stroking my hair and kissing me. Why didn't I meet you first? he says. We could have children together. I want to have babies with you.

Babies. Blond, blue-eyed babies. I think of his blond baby.

Ah, this is silly, lover. You know I can't have your baby. But I can have you. I will have you. I caress his delicious beautiful face. Oh, you beauty. I must have you. You're everything to me now. I am obsessed by you. Driven by you. I don't know what it is your big beautiful prick or your gorgeous face or your body or knowing you know what I'm thinking and feeling the same way, I don't know what it is.

My hands lie quiet in his lap like a dead bird. Passion, emotion has drained me. I want to cuddle and sleep.

I notice that Tony and Daphne are gone. Where have they gone?

Shhh, he says. It's all right.

Yes. I know. It's all right. So they're off together. Do I feel jealous? No. Well, a little weary.

Victor sings me a song. He plays his guitar. He's very good on the guitar.

Here are a few verses, I say, showing him a poem I take from my purse, which I have recently written. Sing them for me.

He sings. A sweet, low soothing voice as he plucks the notes on his guitar.

And I think: How things have changed from that eager passion to tranquil desire. We are in love.

We go upstairs to bed, up the hardwood steps that Tony and Daphne have taken earlier. We are in the master bedroom. Victor undresses me gently, lovingly, and then takes his own clothes off. We lie together under the cool sheets in the large room hugging each other and warming up.

Victor's body feels delicious, familiar the length of me. We go through the ritual of love-making. Breast fondling, nipple sucking, kissing mouth belly cunt—Victor has no trouble going down on my cunt, he bites into my bush and licks my clit comes up on me again and raises his magnificent prick and guides it into my hole.

You know, it's all right, I tell him. He hasn't put on a rubber.

It is?

Yes. It's all right. You can fuck me, baby, and fill me up. Fill me up! Come on! Come on! I am rocking under him seeking his rhythm following him as we move, one tightly locked wet unit plunging on the white sheets, his long hard throbbing prick deep within my gaping pulsating cunt, and we are coming coming together for the first time and it is delicious ecstatic a thousand joys reeling fucking coming shouting falling together on the bed, tumbling over the climax of passion, intense joy, bliss exquisite pain, oh my lover. Victor bites the pillowcase in his heat and growls. He spits out a piece of linen and shudders in me on me, he spurts. Victor spurts. His giant, long hard swollen prick fucks off inside me, white spurts fucking into my cunt. My cunt fills up and runs over with Victor's hot sperm, juicy, running, burning suck flowing out of me.

Oh baby, Oh baby, he moans.

We hold each other in our arms. Wet, panting, exuberant.

Victor's prick is still within me. The big long snake, the gorgeous doll of a coil. You beautiful limp cock you fucking sweet worm. He rises. My baby rises again and I am pierced. He feels out my cunt with his prick and I am like a sensitive instrument playing to his chord coming, oh, I can't help coming again and he is too and we both come together with a moan and a sigh. And he holds me so tight.

It isn't long before Victor is plunging again and I say, If you do that to me I'll come off again. I'm still excited.

Come on, love pie, come again. I want you to. So I do.

Victor!

It's easy with that goddamn stovepipe in me fucking the tail out of me. But do you think he'd let up—Jesus! I need a rest. No, no, come on, and he thrusts and rams my cunt and I tingle all inside and it builds up to my peak again and rolls over, flicks over, and I say, Aaah!

I am running sweat. My hair is in limp strands. My cunt is sopping wet with Victor's sperm and aching. Wide open. Like a huge cavern. I don't think I'll ever close again, I tell him.

Victor falls asleep on top of me. I hold him tenderly, his big chest and fucking thighs, his gorgeous blond head. After a while he rolls off me and I too fall asleep.

Sometime in the night he tried to mount me but collapsed and said: Angela, I'm too tired. I wish I could.

The next morning when I awake the first thing I do is to go to the bathroom and wash my pussy. Victor is still asleep.

My husband comes into the bathroom while I'm flushing out my cunt in the bathtub with a douche and he says, What's going on?

What does it look like? I'm cleaning myself up.

He is very suspicious.

How are you? I say.

OK.

What did you do? I am dying of curiosity.

She sucked me off.

Is that all?

Yes.

How come?

I don't know. I didn't feel like it.

You must be sick.

I guess so.

But I know the reason, he's never good for more than one go and he shot it off sucking, which he likes best, so why complain? He got what he wanted.

After that we did everything together. We moved out of separate rooms and went at each other in one big pile on the floor. You and me, the two girls, two girls and a boy, two boys and a girl. My dream of one prick in my cunt, one in my asshole, and since there wasn't another prick for my mouth, Daphne's cunt hanging over my face while she squatted on me and I ate her pussy.

Two girls working on one boy, less interesting because there's only one prick and it's either in or being sucked.

A foursome of suckers. Victor sucking me, me sucking Tony and Tony sucking Daphne, who in turn is sucking Victor. Or the reverse, where we suck each other's partner and our own mate sucks us.

There is one thing we don't try. The two boys together. I am sorry about this, I would have loved to watch them play 69. It would have been tremendous, but my husband wasn't for it.

I have all I can handle with girls, he says. I'll let you know when I'm tired of it.

But that wasn't the point.

Once Victor grabbed his stiff prick and said: How about it? Why don't we try?

Tony said, Thanks Victor, but some other time and smiled. Friendly, but no deal.

It might be fun, Victor says.

Could be, my husband says, but I'll forgo that pleasure.

No hard feelings?

Come on, my husband says and grins. He's sweet when he's grinning. A lovely boy. Lovely white teeth and a toothpaste ad smile. Black hair. I'm fond of black hair.

Tony and Victor are jealous of the relationship Daphne and I have. Easygoing, eating each other every chance we get. Our tender kisses and caresses. Daphne is fond of my breasts and is always stroking and fondling my tits. I love her hair. Long golden sheen to her waist, and her ass is sweet, plump and good to hold firmly with both hands and give a light slap.

Well. Girls are different, it seems. They fuck anything—man, dog or beast, and fellow girlfriend.

But we have good fun together. It's the healthy indoor life. And there is no jealousy anymore. It's a four-way zap society. Loving each other up, as though we are all each other's pets.

It is fun. The snow falls. There are white storms. It rains. Summer, hot sun and blue sky with light balls of white clouds.

We fuck through it all. Rain or shine. Through the seasons. Coming together, coming off together with lovely warm naked skin and blond hair and sweet-smelling cunts and rampant pricks.

Will they never go down?

Remember when you couldn't get it up at first? I say to Victor.

That's a laugh.

We all laugh.

Looking at it standing up there a mile high waiting for a hole, waiting for a cunt, a mouth or an asshole.

We had fun with the asses. Slicked up with Vaseline, prick greased up and in it goes. Slowly, gently.

Pretend you're crapping.

All right: nervous.

And ease it in.

So tight.

So goddamn exciting. A thousand fiery needles of excitement along your prick in my asshole and I move rhythmically as my husband draws back and in, back and in carefully, regularly, easily until I am all hot, all burning from where I don't know, is it my cunt or my asshole? I don't know but I have such a fantastic urge to crap can't contain it building up and excitement tingling rising condensing growing until I come throbbing beating contracting and Tony groans and lets out a loud love cry for it is truly beautiful spilling in your wife's asshole with your hot white sperm spurting prick.

Tight. My God so tight, I thought you were going to strangle me, he says after.

The next stage in our relationship comes to us as the shock of our life.

It is mid-June and raining hard. Rain sluicing down the gutters, dripping from the trees, all leafy green and blossom.

My husband knocks on the door of their house. The rain soaks his hair and back.

We are paying a surprise visit.

Daphne answers the door.

Hi! Aghast. How are you?

Fine, fine. He stands in the rain. May I come in? I am sitting out in the car.

Daphne's pale blank face suddenly warms to a smile. Yes, come in. I'm sorry, it's raining.

We are all seated inside, Daphne, Tony and I. Daphne is talking.

You see, you never realized that all the time we were getting together Victor was having an affair. One after the other. A continuous succession of girls.

We are silent. The rain drips outside in the garden.

He never stopped. She gestures with her hands. I don't know what was driving him.

Her face is sad and sweet. Aching. I see the tears in her eyes. Her golden hair droops over her cheek. She looks thinner.

Have you lost some weight?

Yes.

How? It's wonderful to lose weight. A feat. Did you go on a diet?

No.

You didn't? You just lost weight?

Yes. Sad quiet eyes looking down.

I see. Yes, I see. Daphne not eating, unable to eat, each spoon held in her mouth unable to swallow tears welling in her eyes her throat a lump.

I nod my head. That's too bad, I say.

Where's Victor? Where is he? Where is my beautiful blond boy? Where is my gorgeous lover with the long prick?

Victor is living with Linda.

Who?

Linda.

Who is she?

A friend. Friends of ours. Her husband worked with Victor.

How did this happen?

84

I don't know. Daphne gestures sadly, wanly, angel face open, sick.

This is incredulous, I say. I can't believe it. The two of you were so compatible, you got along so well.

Not really.

But what about us? We had such a good time together, didn't we?

Yes. A long pause. Maybe that was the trouble.

What do you mean? my husband says.

Well, the girl, Daphne says, looks like Angela.

Like me? I am pleased, annoyed.

Yes. Like you.

Rain falling. Rain.

EATING OUT

HOW DO YOU recall a particular time of your life? A certain flavor, a taste that seems gone forever?

I must have been mad at the time. If not mad, I was certainly obsessed with a passion for Eugene. My waking life, and even my dreams, were distorted by my love, or perhaps I should say lust, for Eugene.

On the other hand, I'm not surprised. Eugene was a beautiful creature, a boy whom no sane girl could resist. Six foot three, black hair, brown eyes, broad shoulders, an athlete's build, and a handsome face. His nose was inclined to be large and slightly bent across the bridge, which didn't in any way detract from his appearance. He had very white skin against his black hair and heavy shaven beard. Eugene was a warrior. A black prince. Handsome, taciturn, rugged. How I longed to know him.

But it wasn't meant to be. Eugene was married to a beautiful intelligent girl. They seemed perfectly suited, although they were seldom in each other's company. His wife was a scientist. She was small, petite, also dark. Exquisite. But they were lacking this *frisson*, this particular passion where each would consume the other. From an outsider's viewpoint, there was no drive to bring their lives together. Eugene worked late in his office leaving his wife at home. On weekends when she wasn't working, she would take their only child, a girl, to a nearby park and never once stop by to see him. How foolish. She would see him only at mealtimes and late at night. But then Eugene never liked to be disturbed. He worked obsessively in his office on his project. I know they loved each other, but there was a maturity, a coldness, a distance that I never understood.

And yet there was something about Eugene that intrigued me. A passion, a hotness, a certain mystery. Did I read too much into his good looks and distant manner? Was he really just empty and boring like all the rest?

It took a long time to find out.

There are always two sides to a story. And my side was that I was dissatisfied with my husband. What had seemed for several years to be the perfect marriage was no longer perfect. Tony was trying to push me into a relationship with a couple that I didn't want. At least, I thought, if I'm going to screw around, pick someone I like and not just another prick.

And so Eugene came into the picture. The black-haired, gorgeous bastard.

Always cool, distant. Walking down the hall at work he skimmed the surface of the wall, never moved out in the open. I did the same thing. It was something automatic. Rounding a corner against the wall as a guide and protection. While he walked, tall long-legged stride and broad shoulders, he'd snap his fingers. I always knew when he was coming by the sharp snap snap of his fingers as he passed my office door.

Eugene was, as I've said, compulsive. He worked continuously on his project. Always studying in his small crowded office, looking over maps and diagrams and reading books.

He was confident, outgoing, speaking at meetings, introducing speakers, giving papers. In control.

And yet strange. Strange is the only word for it. There is something in his blood, mystic, barbaric, mysterious that I understand. For I have that in me too.

Eugene was unmapped territory. The unawakened dream. He was rigid, passionate. I sensed something deep and strong, something frightful beneath his taciturn surface.

It was up to me to awaken him, I thought.

This was difficult. I tried dropping hints. Something direct. Talk to him. We talked about writers. Hemingway. He had read Hemingway. Yes, he liked him, understood him. Not much there.

Art. He was interested in art. Movies? Yes, he liked movies. Sometimes he and his wife would go to a movie where there'd be explicit sex and they'd get all worked up and when they went home his wife would be very hot in bed after.

Well, I was getting nowhere there.

Affairs?

No, not that he knew of. No, in fact, none of his friends were having affairs. Well, yes, there were two, a woman who was a nymphomaniac, and another woman in her forties married to a man with a bad heart condition.

By Jesus! What have I stumbled upon here? Is life really like this? Are people faithful? True? Then what about my life, the friends I know? My life's not like this, I thought.

And then I told him about our nude parties. Walking around in the nude.

Not that you have to do anything, I say, but you really get comfortable walking around with nothing on. It feels so nice. Really, there's nothing to it.

I don't know, he said. I don't know if I would like that.

His face is in profile, gorgeous mouth, a full lower lip, wide mouth like Gregory Peck, a mouth to be loved for sure, his sharp nose. All right, I think, that's fine with me. I'll love you up just the way you are, sit on your delicious lap, feel your delicious prick. Kiss your lovely mouth, brown eyes.

Instead I said: It's not so really very much, anyway, blushed and left the room.

Maybe he was just a happily married man—with remarkable resistance. Maybe he loved his wife in a way that my husband never loved me. I understand and respect him for that. I love him even more, in a sad way.

Because I was to be resisted. I am nice-looking. Long brown hair, green eyes, a sensuous mouth and a fresh look on my face—rather stunned innocence, but dynamite underneath. You know the type. Budding starlet, fucked every night—that's me.

And my figure? Long legs, good breasts. Wide-boned hips that sit out nicely when I walk.

This is only to suggest that I'm not a drag and could perhaps raise this boy's libido.

And it's not that Eugene was impervious to me. Not really at all.

Eugene and I were talking in the office about parties, and he said, Well, what about you? Why do you go to parties?

I don't really know. I wonder.

I know why I go, he says, if there is someone there I'm interested in.

Oh, yes?

We were at the same party. Eugene was standing off in the doorway, tall, handsome, dark, talking. Long fingers moving as he makes a point.

Later I am talking to his wife in the kitchen. She is very good-looking. Black hair, blue eyes, a real beauty. I even like her. She's smart, too. Biochemistry. But for some reason I find her much older. There is something cool about her. She reminds me of my mother.

Maybe she doesn't like me, I think. Maybe she knows.

I think back to hearing her give a lecture. She was intelligent, thorough. The same reserve, coldness. No, it can't be me.

In a way, I envy her. This distance, reserve. I am so unlike her. All excited, shy in public, inner passion, blushing face.

Again I think: There is a motherly quality to her.

Eugene and I talk about children.

Maybe that's what Tony needs, he says. It might make him feel more fulfilled.

I doubt that. What Tony needs is cunts. Cunts and cunts.

Wouldn't you like children?

I'm not ready for that.

I have dreams. Dreams. I would be screwed by children.

Maybe. Maybe not. He tells me about his little girl, his daughter. How she can draw and her mother is so pleased she puts her paintings on the wall. And he's proud of her too.

It is all very nice. But I am a little bored.

When I ask him, and gesture with my hands for emphasis, what he is living for? He says: My family, my child. To bring her up properly. Make a nice home for her.

I am—what can I say?—intrigued, dismayed. Children. What do I live for? I think in terms of meaningful existence, existential fulfillment, making the most of my life. In other words, selfish terms. Children. Well, to me that is disappointing. It's homely, but what? Where does it go?

Are you only to be another one of *Time*'s X million readers? I think.

Is that all you'll do? I say.

No, I'll have a job, which I'll do well, and I'll look after my family.

Well, that's nice.

But what about big things, I mean big things? Success, fame, etc.?

I'm not interested in that.

Well, no. I wouldn't think you are.

Sometimes I'm not too. I'm not interested in anything. But every time I come to, I think, and when I think I want and when I want there is no limit. It is for me a dream. I will stop at nothing. I will become the sun and the moon and the stars. Well, why not? Why not? It is all a fantasy held to reality.

With me what everything comes down to is that I get bored very easily. If I didn't get bored, crushingly bored so fast, perhaps life would be easier.

Sometimes I feel I am testing him. Leading him along a new path that he follows, but is afraid to understand.

Driving home from that party—they give us a lift, it is all chilly and frost in December and I am excited, sitting in the back seat of their car, fantasizing what I would like to do to him.

His wife chats eagerly. She is very sweet. At home I feel such a longing for him once he is gone.

I have a dream. What a strange dream! It is a lover's dream. Eugene is my lover and is gently caressing my shoulder, kissing my lips and I am filled with such an ache, tears, he is leaving me and I say, I love you, I love you so much and yes, he loves me too, he is so tender, so beautiful, so dark and he leaves and I am crying in the dream shedding tears sobbing. I wake up. I am depressed. It is as though I have lost my sweetheart. I feel foolish. My husband lies beside me asleep. I am depressed. I am sad beyond words.

I can't forget the dream. All morning and into the afternoon I am filled with the mood of the dream.

I do a foolish thing. A few days later, I mention the dream to him.

I say: I had a dream about you. I am fishing.

He is noncommittal.

You know, they say dreams are supposed to mean something.

That's what Freud says, isn't it? he says.

He tells me about a dream of his. In fact, he is confessing. I had a dream once, he says, about my brother. I wonder what that means? It could be homosexual. I've often worried about that dream. It's bothered me.

I didn't know he had a brother.

I am depressed.

We are in the lab drinking tea talking to someone else. Eugene looks down at my bare feet in sandals and my toenails painted sparkling silver. He reaches down and strokes my big toenail. I like that, he says.

Walking down the hall following me, he says, I knew it was you. I could smell your perfume on the elevator. It is Joy by Patou that I am wearing.

I see Eugene reaching up and plucking a large red mackintosh apple from an apple tree. He polishes the white dust off on the side of his pants and bites into it openmouthed with a crisp, crackling sound. His little girl sits high on his shoulders.

My husband is giving me no end of trouble. We have a lot of fights. I am very dissatisfied and sit and brood. I drink a lot. I drink when I get home from work and think of Eugene. While Eugene works at his books and goes down to the library and drinks cup after cup of coffee.

We play the radio in our apartment continuously. Somehow the evening passes.

My job gets me down. My heart is not in it. I am only doing it for the money. To support my husband through medical school.

Eugene is moved by beauty. He cries, yes, he actually sheds tears when he sees a lovely painting, his wife says, laughing.

I feel that way too.

I became convinced of something while I knew Eugene. Because of his perverseness, his obstinacy of character. And that was: Be what you are. No matter what you do or think or feel, you're never alone. There is always someone else like you.

Therefore, have courage.

I learned that from him.

Eugene had a friend. An unusual boy. Eccentric, long beard in the days when beards were exceptional. A flippant, taunting manner. Crusty. Very sexual.

This friend has flair. Walked with a knotty pine cane, quipped off insults, flirtations. Blushed deep within his bushy beard.

David was bisexual. Once he shouted after my husband and me while we were walking down the hall: Hey, Tony! Bend over! He jabbed his cane in the air in the direction of my husband's ass. My husband is a doll, and David would like to fuck his ass.

I told David, who was also a friend of mine, how my husband, being so well-built and sexy, attracted homosexuals.

I had the biggest laugh I said. We were coming into the foyer of our apartment when these two skinny French fags sitting on a couch whistled at my husband, you know, a cat whistle.

I was surprised and poor Tony crawled into his coat collar.

I can see why the boys go for him, David says. However Eugene says to me after in his office, You know, I can't figure David out. I don't know what he was getting at. I don't know what was bothering him.

David was in and out of his office several times a day. Dropping a few quips, leaving his books, stirring up the office.

Am I wrong? What is wrong with Eugene? David was gone on him. He appreciated a beautiful boy like that, I'm sure.

I don't think Eugene ever caught on. Or did he?

One Sunday in late February when it was snowing heavily, I decided to leave our apartment. My level of tension had built so high that I couldn't sit in a chair any longer and pretend to read. My husband was studying. I was fucked off. So I put on my snow boots, coat, mitts, and hat and left.

I'm going to the Art Gallery, I said.

Fucked off. Snow. Beautiful white. Plodding through the snow. Lifting my booted foot in the white deep drifts on the sidewalk, wet snow blowing in my face. Rejoicing, not knowing where I was going, so good to be out. Silent.

I had had two beers before.

I ended up at my place of work. Knowing perhaps, hoping Eugene would be there. Just curious to come upon. If he's there, I said, as I'm walking through the snow, I'll tell him how I feel, I don't care. I really don't care. Thinking of my husband and what a fucked-up mess there.

So I arrive. I unlock the big outside doors with my key, stamp off the snow from my boots and shake my hat and coat and walk up stairs.

Eugene comes down the hall.

I feel a panic. Torn between do I carry out my resolve, or do I think? Think, I say, think. I am panic-stricken. I am so far off, I know, in my fantasy, that it would be absurd to Eugene.

I have had another dream. This time an overtly sexual dream. Eugene and I are fucking.

I am so foolish, I say.

But my life is desperate.

Eugene comes by to my office and we have a cup of tea. We talk about politics and how things are going generally and Eugene sips his tea and looks over his steaming rim at me.

And I think, Fuck you. You are so damn dense.

Well, it is a big surprise to me when Eugene makes the first move. You can well imagine. I am coming home from my art class that I take four hours a week on Tuesday and Thursday evenings. Life drawing from the live model, which I enjoy very much. I like the tits on the girls. The boys unfortunately wear shorts. I am walking back from my art class carrying my roll of drawings in my hand. It is snowing as usual. Beside me going my way is a priest who also takes the classes. He leaves me in front of my place of work as I have forgotten a book that I must pick up.

Goodbye! Goodbye! I am walking up the stairs stamping my feet smelling of perfume and probably beer, which I had in quantity at supper. Deserted halls into my dark office picking up my book and down the hall.

Sure enough.

Eugene is at work. I see the crack of light under his door, and of course I knock on the door to his office.

I will show him my drawings, I think. My heart pounds in my chest.

He opens the door.

Surprised. Hello! he says. Dark, gorgeous, tall. He is really a beautiful boy. Briskly he says, What can I do for you?

I am awkward, blushing. Stupid. I wanted to show you my drawings. I hold out my roll of newsprint on which I have painfully drawn this evening's model. She was a middle-aged Negress. Teak brown. Big belly, lovely, long muscular legs and heavy breasts. Large tits. A wonderful model. She has a nineteen-year-old son. I couldn't believe it.

He smiles. No one is in the office. He holds out his hand and closes the door behind us.

My heart is still pounding. In situations like this, I am tongue-tied. Aching with desire, with love, I am helpless.

My cheeks feel hot.

But Eugene is assured, in control and takes my roll of drawings from me.

Let's see them, he says with genuine enthusiasm, as he pulls off the elastic and spreads out the sheets of newsprint on his desk. His desk is strewn with maps and pencils and erasers.

I feel like his little girl looking over his shoulder at my drawings.

They're good! He looks up at me.

I smile.

They're really good! He is impressed. My heart melts. Secretly I think they are good too, I have a talent for drawing, but I don't let on.

Thank you. I have no trouble blushing. His brown eyes are flecked with a little yellow. His nose is quite large. I find myself staring at his mouth, his lips. He notices too. I reach down for my drawings in confusion, ready to run in panic to escape my desire, my intense longing for him when he brushes my hand accidentally. A current goes through me. It must be accidental, I think, as I take my drawings, but he looks at me intently, he is trying to understand my face. Maybe I'm wrong, but I sense it, I feel it, this charge this tension between us and I am almost ready to touch him to risk everything to expose my sham of coming by to confess to him to pour out my lust for him, my craving, my obsession, my desire when he touches my fingers in mid-air and holds them.

I look at him. It is like a violent magnetic minute. Everything fierce hard passionate with aching. His long fingers tightly hold my hand and my heart is pounding too hard in my throat to speak or do anything but I look at him and the look in his eyes makes a jab of fire pass through my belly into my groin and I feel that I cannot resolve this moment that I shall collapse with the intensity of my desire and his that is facing me.

And then his arms are around me. I am swooning collapsing in his arms, suddenly sitting on his knee and kissing him in delirium. Blind passion, wild magnificent fear and joy, feeling and imagining, the two one, now real, caressing his lips his real lips touching mine feeling his hot body and warm wet breath, smelling him for the first time, feeling him for the first time.

I am ready to abandon everything.

Let the world, my world, crumble for this moment. I care nothing about anything, held in his arms.

He is too much. The smell of him, the taste of his mouth. I have my hands in his long black hair I am going wild with longing and fulfilled desire. I am the rainbow. I have reached the acme. No life before or after, I surrender. I am putty in his hands.

What surprises me is not my reaction. Not the intensity of my passion for him because I knew about this for a long time, but him, he is surprising me. What is this fierceness on his part? He squeezes me to death. He says, Angela. I wanted to do this for so long. You were driving me crazy. You're so beautiful. I wanted to touch you. I adore your long hair. You're so sexy. Oh Christ, why didn't you tell me I've been stuck on you for over a year, you silly bastard Oh Christ! I've been thinking of you nearly every waking minute and at night I dream of you and I'm just about going out of my mind.

He has his gorgeous hand on my breast. And I am trembling with desire and happiness.

Stroking my breast. Smoothing his hand over my swollen tits, cupping my firm round flesh, rubbing my nipple through my sweater with his thumb.

I lean down and bite his thumb. He leaves it in my mouth and I nibble on it and suck it while he outlines my mouth and lips and touches my tongue.

He is excited. His cock is standing up in his pants and I can feel it under me as I sit on him. And as I feel it under me I burn inside. Burning deep inside my cunt and belly, a sucking drawing desire, a mad blindness. My tits ache. Only one passion. Lie together naked. He on top of me, in me, feeling me, holding him inside. My cunt trembles, moist, ready to convulse, surrender.

He strokes my pussy. Then he does a beautiful thing he pushes his face into my lap and blows hot air on my cunt. I am still sitting on him.

He brings himself up and we look into each other's eyes.

I feel I have known him forever.

Forever. He is my archetype. My dream. My black prince, darling lover. I think nothing of my husband. My husband is a tiny scratch on my consciousness. I am thick in the foray. I would do anything for this man. I would risk everything for him.

I don't have to risk anything. No one need ever find out. I won't tell my husband.

I am rushing ahead of myself. I haven't risked anything yet, although Eugene has moved his hand from my lap along my thigh and placed his warm hand on my knee. He fingers my knee and I am begging him inside to touch my cunt, Oh, please, please, but I say nothing. I caress his beautiful face; it is so beautiful I even forget how much I want him to touch my bare wet cunt. I am lost in my dream of him I am lining his face with my fingertips as if he were a sculpture for he is truly that beautiful. Along his big nose to the dark nostrils, pointed tip of his nose, large soft lips, long chin with prickly black stubble. Teeth, touching them, first my fingertips then my lips, my tongue, squirming down on him holding him he holding me to him until I fear he will break me in two or his hard prick will crack me open. Somehow my legs open and I am spread wide across his knees and my open cunt fairly drips onto him. No drops, but I am soaking my pants and wide-open, sopping wet, and when he fingers my wet matted hair it is a relief like the coming of spring, such an ecstasy to feel him on me touching my hot lips rubbing my bare throbbing pussy, pressing with his rough fingers against my smooth, soft, puffy flesh.

Feel his fingers curling my hair opening my lips, stroking my smooth wet lips down to my gaping hole and slipping in quickly, squishy, making a soft sucking sound as he inserts his forefinger, poking with his long finger against the sides of my cunt deep into my hole, and then his middle finger, two fingers, splitting open my cunt hole stretching my opening playing cock in cunt, coming on his fingers.

He starts frigging me.

No! No! I say. My long wavy hair falls in my face. I am hot and damp.

No. I pull back his fingers. I don't want to come. There's a better way.

I sit back and unzip his pants. Free his hard bird, his white swallow, which pops up like a jack-in-the-box and stands out of his pants and sways back and forth.

I am awed. It is so big.

I do only what I know to do when confronted with such a big beautiful white prick swaying, trembling with eagerness. I go down on him.

He's not used to this because he immediately, almost panicky, asks me: What are you doing?

I look up and smile.

Don't you do this?

No. He likes it, I can tell.

I am holding his large erect prick in my hand and watching his fat bulbous end beat. The skin has dried because I haven't licked his prick with my tongue since I looked up at him. He fingers my nipple. This time under my sweater and bra which he has freed and I kiss him again on his tip, a wet kiss, a sucking kiss, and then I come up. He is holding my head in his hands and looking at me as though he can't stand it anymore, as grateful and amazed as if I had just sucked his ass instead of his cock.

I'll French him the next time, I think. The things you learn about people and never know. Oh you sexy repressed bastard what do you do with your black-haired wife? Fuck in the dark and never say fuck? You need to be unseamed licked open ready to come at all openings. I suppose you've never gone down on your wife then. Or fingered her asshole or fucked her asshole and sure enough later I ask him if he wants to fuck my asshole and he says no, and I say, do you not do that? and he says no. I changed all that. But right now he is drawing my head up and kissing my mouth and I am so glad to be kissing him drinking from his lips so joyous to be making love with my black-haired, white-skinned, fucking black prince that I don't need to be fancy and eat him or fuck his asshole I only need to hold his fingers and caress his cock and kiss his sweet soft open wet mouth. A tongue like I've never felt, a soft gentle tongue sucking my tongue my lips my nipple my belly button, for now my pink panties are down to my ankles and my skirt is pulled up to my waist and I am sitting on his lap my head thrown back and my belly and hairy cunt thrust in his face.

He kisses my pussy and blows hot breath on me. Then he parts my lips with his tongue and finds my clit, now hard as a red currant and standing up like a tiny cock in my fat swollen lips. And he licks me. The way he would lick an ice-cream cone and I can tell he hasn't had my experience, so I guide him and say, a little lower and he moves down and I say a little harder and he tongues me harder. There! I say, and he is right on. Right on.

He comes up and says, Do you like that? His big nose looking up at me and I think I could fuck that beautiful nose.

Yes! I say, yes. I like that.

Can you do it that way?

Jesus. This boy is naive. I am hanging on edge, hanging on the sharp-knifed joy his tongue was bringing. Aching for more.

Can you do it?

Yes. I smile. He is sweet and innocent and christly married for how many years.

How many years are you married? I say.

Six.

Six. Well, that should do plenty. And one child. I guess some people never get around to it.

Come on. I pull his head toward me. His big nose and mouth and fantastic large brown eyes. His thick black hair hangs in his face.

Come on, I say. Let's not get fancy. Come on. I am guiding his cock to the hard bristly hairs of my cunt, parting my lips, trying to insert his prick inside me. We are still sitting on the chair.

He squeezes me hard around my shoulders and kisses my free white fat floating breasts, sucks my pink nipples, nudges them with his nose, caresses my stomach, licks my belly button then my ear my nose my hair my lips.

Come on! Come on! I am delirious. He holds me and stands up looking around the room.

Where can we go? he says. Then he looks at his cluttered desk full of maps and compasses and rulers and says: Here.

He stands me on the floor and I watch him tenderly while he lifts off the maps, erasers, pencils, pens, desk blotter, books from the desk until there is a clear surface and then with his standing up prick jutting free out of his pants he walks to the door and takes his coat off the hook, checks the door that it is locked, then comes back over to me, spreads out his coat inside lining up, puts his arm around me and being so strong and tall, sweeps me off the floor, my long hair swaying and lays me out on the desk top on his coat. I put my hands on my belly and then on my knees and my legs automatically fall apart.

I look up and smile at him.

I stretch my legs out, still crooked, waiting for him.

Inside I am tingling, dancing, as if I had been sprinkled with hot pepper or invaded by an army of ants or hooked up to a Wimshurst machine and given bursts of static electricity.

There is nothing in this world but you and your prick. I delight in, I celebrate your glorious face and body and magnificent prick. The world begins and ends with your prick.

He puts it in. So simply.

I am like a bride consecrated. My lover, my husband slipping his white prince between my lips, breaking through the tightness of my hole, which resists at the edges, then gives and sliding it in feeling it rub all the way to the back and then tickling the back of my cunt as he draws back and inserts again and back and in hard to the limit and my legs are wide open like a pair of scissors and my bum flat on his desk my knees high and his white muscular ass and long thighs covered with thick curly black hair rising, contracting, pumping.

He has curly black hair in the small of his back, which I am fingering, then the thick hairy patch between his balls and asshole. He is moaning, I'm sure he's going to come. I grab his balls and gently squeeze them and he becomes so excited for he is drowning my mouth with his kisses, he is moaning and rocking in ecstasy, he is so excited that I become wild with his excitement and all I know is his hot balls in my sweaty hand and his hot throbbing prick in my cunt rammed to the back and bursting my walls filling my spaces with juicy cock and I come to a fever peak, a frenzy of excitement, a mountain of passion building, rolling in waves, over and over to the top.

I am shouting to him: Come on! Come on! He says: Come on, you fucker! Come on now! drawing out the now and suddenly arching and thrusting and bursting inside me against the back of my cunt as I clamp down on his hot hard prick in waves and waves of peak ecstasy, of electric desire, over rolling a fine sharp edge and coming down.

Inside I am all hot and coming and like a bees' nest still so excited.

He must know about this for he keeps thrusting his juicy prick squeezing out his spilled seed which is sopping my cunt, giving me quick sharp jabs with his prick like little punches, rubbing my clit with his pubic bone, punching me up to another climax—it is so easy and I am over the edge like a waterfall coming down dazzling I see flashes of light behind my closed eyes as I squeeze them so tight and a peak, a tight tingling coming, rings in my head, my cunt and it is even better than the first time more hurting, more coming, more aching, more fineness of feeling.

There we lie on top of his desk. Soaking wet between our bellies, breasts, thighs. His sperm leaking out of my cunt down onto the lining of his winter coat, his arms around me, his nose buried in my shoulder and hair.

He pushes himself back a little and smiles, such a sweet smile that I want him all over again.

Do you feel guilty? I ask.

Do you?

I shake my head.

Neither do I.

I want to tell him I want to say I love him. I want to tell him. It is so bad I feel my eyes filling with tears. But I hold back and touch his finger with my fingertip, caress it lightly, press against his finger in the air and say with a small smile, Do you like me?

Yes, Angela. He looks at me. He does. I like you.

Oh Christ! I know. I know he loves me. He loves his wife too. Yes, I love my husband. But we love each other. We love each other.

Come with me, I am saying inside to myself. You are so beautiful, it makes me ache. It makes me sick. Because you are so beautiful, I will do anything for you. I am helpless before you. I can't control myself.

And again I say: All my life I am looking for altars. Your beauty, your perfection, your newness, your prick, but only your prick because you are so beautiful and wild is my altar, I love you.

He is looking at me all the time, in my eyes, my green eyes as I say this inside to myself afraid to frighten him by telling him of the immensity of my passion.

But I think he would understand. He is just my type. A wild briar rose, but right now he is afraid. Of course, to me he is essentially innocent.

Innocent, sweet glorious, wild rose. My sweet. I would like to corrupt you to your bowels. Oh, my love. I would like to suck you into the quagmire of my lusts, couple you to my degradations.

I pull up my panties and straighten my skirt and blouse and he fixes himself up.

He is not trying to get rid of me.

I have to go, I say. I look at my watch. Ten-thirty. My husband expects me. Flushed cheeks, glitter in my eyes. He holds my hand and pulls me toward him and roughly kisses me.

You know, I can't believe it, I say. It's so unlike you. You were always so distant.

He smiles. I know.

I wait in silence.

Well. He finds it hard to express himself. His black hair covers his ears. I know I liked you. More than that. I thought about you in a way I shouldn't.

I shrug as if to say, Why not? And he says, Well, my wife—I love her. I nod, of course he does, but what has that to do with this?

And I feel guilty, he says, but then it became so bad and I couldn't help it anymore it ate out my brain everyday I couldn't get any work done I kept thinking about your breasts that you show so nicely in that sweater when you come to work and your round little ass in your skirt and legs, he is smiling, you're really a lovely girl, but he holds up his hand, it's not that completely, there's something funny about you—

Oh? I say.

Not laughable, but strange. Well, not strange, but different. Funny. You're not at all like the other girls. You must know that. You're not at all like my wife.

I look at him with a faint slow smile on my lips. Why should I be like his wife who housecleans every day after work and is very sweet, but doesn't go down on her husband or anyone else, who wants an everyday passion, a common existence?

I am greedy. I want fantasy, ecstasy. A rainbow. Eugene doesn't know it, but what it is in me that he can't name is greed. Passionate greed. I will eat up life, the jewels of this world, I will seek rainbow joys, mountain peaks of ecstasy.

I will float over wheat fields tickling my bare ass I will float over pine treetops tickling my cunt I will suck on the sun dream on the moon.

The world is a fantasy. A round oval coming back to a teardrop, a cunt, a shadow on the moon. A prick. A prick which is a blade of grass. A prick which is eternity.

Are you going to tell her? I ask.

No.

I smile and squeeze his hands. A look of complicity. You won't tell her?

No.

We have that secret then, I say. Eugene nods. I know he is mine. Mine for this moment.

Will you see me again?

He smiles and doesn't speak only looks at me. I know he'll see me again. He doesn't want to because he doesn't believe in it, he's not an adulterer, he loves his wife this is a mistake in his happy little life his world of maps and books and studies but he can't help himself he is torn by hate for himself and lust for me lust which will become love if he isn't careful because I am strange and I will get to him I am a disease which can destroy him ruin his peace his happy existence. I am dangerous because I am fearless. Wild. I will risk anything. He is frightened and fascinated. He is awakening to a new depth of living.

None of this is said. It needn't be. There is the passion and the fear. The fear and fascination. The passion and lust and longing and loving riding over it all.

A March day. Snowing heavily. On my way to work I see a couple kissing. They are obviously in love. I am stimulated and jealous.

In my office I sit mooning at my desk staring at the snowflakes piling on the ledge outside my window.

Of course I am thinking of Eugene. I haven't seen him for weeks. Only in the halls. He is terrified of me. I know I will see him again. It is simply a matter of time. I am patient. I can wait. For such a wonderful man I can wait.

As I said I am mooning at my desk writing a poem, which I call "The Kiss," thinking of the couple in the street, thinking of Eugene remembering how it was when we kissed that night.

I hear the swinging doors to the darkroom outside my office creak and the quick snap, snap of Eugene's fingers. The darkroom door slams and clicks shut as he snaps the lock.

I feel excited. A slight panic. Momentarily confused. What shall I do? It is as though my prize is trapped in that locked room. Oh the pain of this desire. Oh how it is driving me mad. I am not rational. There is no doubt about that. I long only to hold him make him mine. I realize that if I weren't married to my husband I would have married Eugene. If he had asked. Perhaps he would have. It would be a whole new world. Quite different from mine now but who can say less, even though I am happy, most of the time with my husband.

I am fascinated by other possibilities. The chance of new lives.

I can hear Eugene banging around in the darkroom. I sit rigidly at my desk listening, occasionally wetting my lips from tension.

The door snaps unlocked and the swinging door creaks. I wait. What is it I want? It is too much to hope for. Then Eugene's voice. He's walking over to me and standing behind me.

Done any more drawings lately?

Oh Christ! What does that mean? I blush crimson and look up at him.

For a girl who can fuck so well and uninhibitedly it is strange that I blush so often. Maybe it's the blushers who are the hottest.

I don't even answer him. Only look. Why pretend?

Then I say, What were you doing in the darkroom?

Developing some pictures for my project.

Oh.

I'm not finished. I'm timing the water rinse. He looks out of the window standing close to me.

A lot of snow, he says.

Oh why pretend, Eugene? I could cry. I am feeling so sorry for myself now, so paralyzed with wanting, a round ball wound up making my way through each minute like skeins of wool dodging desire, sick. Sick. Sad.

I can't even pretend to be sociable. Talk. I should. I want him so much I should try to impress him, be cheerful, vivacious, pretty. Entice him, win him. No.

My hopelessness must come across to him for he notices my silence and feels sorry for me.

I couldn't see you, he says.

I know. I stare at the radiator waiting. He pulls up a stool and sits in front of me. Then smiles.

Don't look so unhappy, Angela. He grips the side of the stool with his hands.

I shrug and smile.

No. I give a sigh. No. I smile.

It would ruin my marriage, he says.

I nod.

What about mine? No, it wouldn't ruin my marriage. I know that.

He keeps looking at me.

I don't care. I touch his hand. The black hairs on the back of his fingers.

I love you, I say. I say it simply. It is just a statement. A fact. I want nothing from him. I can smile now when I say it. There is nothing tragic about it. It is just nice. I love you.

His lips quiver. He is unnerved. You don't even know me.

Yes, I do.

This is wrong. Why are you doing this to me?

I'm not doing anything. Am I? What am I doing?

You're making me love you, he says.

Ah. Why can't we have an affair? A wonderful, beautiful, lovely affair? We don't have to leave our partners. Why can't we?

It would destroy us.

Why?

Because. He holds my hand and squeezes my fingernail. He looks at his knees jutting out on the stool, then at me, frightened. His black eyes black hair frightened. Because I love you too.

He wants to go. He's trying to leave he's pulling his hand away.

No, no! I try to hold him back. Don't go! Please, Eugene. I follow him to the darkroom through the swinging door. The door of the darkroom is ajar. He walks over to the sink full of running cold water and looks at his prints. I close the door behind me. His back is to me standing over the sink of water. I push the bolt in the door he doesn't move I walk over to him and place my arms around his waist my face against his back and hug him.

I can feel the tears coming down my cheeks.

We don't move. He has his hands on the rim of the sink his head bowed.

I squeeze him, so tight.

He starts to breathe harder. He is excited. I let my hands fall to his crotch and feel his prick big in his pants.

He turns with a sweet sigh toward me and hugs me to him. Lifts me off my feet, holds me high against his chest. Lowers me. Kisses my lips hot, hungry, wet, loving, sucking like a dying man a man drowning, raining kisses on my lips my nose and cheeks and eyes and then hugging me again against him so hard again and again.

I love you, he says. It's wrong, I know it's wrong, but I love you. I imagine my wife dead, my child gone. Just the two of us. It is terrible. Terrible. I can't see you again. Oh, but I love you. Just now. For now it's all right. It's all right. He is moaning in my long hair, murmuring. Touching my breast, it is coming all over again the joy of having him, loving him.

I caress his prick in his pants.

He fumbles with the zipper and lowers his pants until he is standing bare that same beautiful white prick that was in me before.

I gasp. What if someone comes? My God! Four in the afternoon. Everyone at work.

The door's locked, isn't it?

Yes. I am panting, throbbing. I am so excited. Confronted with his prick waiting for me.

I quickly take off my panties and stuff them into my brassiere. Then I hitch my skirt above my thighs and unhook my garter belt and pull down my nylons and we are standing together naked belly to belly and cock to cunt, but he is so tall his prick sticks into my belly too far from my hairy cunt so he puts his arms around me and draws me up on him while I open my legs and clasp my knees around his hairy white thighs. I am sitting on the tip of his prick and then suddenly he is in me going in hard violently to the back as I sink down on him and tighten my legs around his back.

He gasps and his eyes go hot and distant. I watch him I see his thrill, the excitement in his eyes, his delirium of his prick in my cunt me sitting up on him he leaning back thrusting his cock in me bumping, hugging me, groaning, crying, I want you, I want you I have to have you, Oh my beautiful fucker, he says, my lovely pet, do it to me again, fuck me again, come on my prick. Oh my Jesus, my fucking Jesus! Come on! Your prick in me so deep so hard I'm coming! I'm coming! and he thrusts like a wild bull still holding me up still plunging deep into my cunt me riding high and hard on the stallion of his prick coming coming and violently clasping my legs around him sinking down deep on his prick expiring: Ah! Ah! coming. Ah! A sigh. Such a sigh between us. Holding me. Kissing me, loving me. Nuzzling his big nose into my eye my neck my cheek.

Oh Eugene! I want to take you home with me. I want to love you. I want to live with you.

Yes, he says. Yes! I want that too. I want you too. I want you. He kisses my fat breast, me thinking my breasts are only for you to love, they are here for you. He lowering me, me coming off his softening prick sliding down. Standing now on my two stocking feet on the floor. The water still running in the sink. The room smelling of developer and fixer. The glow of the red lamp. My cunt dripping.

He plucks several Kleenex from a box on the counter and hands them to me and I stuff them between my legs into my dripping cunt.

The sound of the water gurgling in the sink. The red glow. His face. His limp prick hanging out of his pants with a drop on the tip.

A knock on the door.

Anyone there? A male voice.

Yes, Eugene says. I won't be long.

O.K., the voice says. Footsteps becoming quieter. Silence.

Sweetheart. Let me suck you, I say. He stands there smiling, his limp dripping prick that I take in my mouth. Soft like a sausage. A soft tube of rubber spongy, springy, small, filling my mouth. Taking his whole soft prick in my mouth soft and curled sucking on it, gently squishing it between my tongue and teeth, pulling on his limp prick with my lips. He grows in my mouth swells becomes longer pushes out of my mouth so I can no longer hold his prick in my soft cavern only half of it growing hard no longer his squishy little snail becoming so big so hard and stiff that only the tip now is between my lips and tongue and I hold on tightly to his stem with my hand and now I really suck him well licking, rubbing, caressing with lips and tongue and soft flesh and he pushes into my mouth and I softly touch his balls, caress them, then I go away from his fire hose for a minute and take one of his balls in my mouth suck it in, feel his curly hair against my lips and tongue I am holding his round egg in my mouth, gently stroking his hairy flesh between his cock and asshole, then I go back on his prick. Like a springy, spongy stick, a tuning fork, a magnificent rampant cock in my mouth and I suck and he loves it he loves it and fucks my mouth slowly easily gradually building until I am frigging his cord with my tongue at a fantastic rate and he's wound into his passion, his coming and I feel a spasm in his cock and balls which I am holding as he ejaculates once, twice, again, into my mouth, spurting gobs of white sperm, flooding my hot mouth, bumping, twitching again saying: Oh! Oh! grunting, gripping my hair, squeezing my face into his cock.

I swallow his sperm. A big swallow. Salty, going down in a lump. Egg white. His cock still in my mouth. Stroking my hair, sighing.

Then after: hugging me, holding me, my face on his shoulder. He says, You'll think this funny. I once went to a prostitute and she sucked me. I'd never had it done before.

I look up at him and as I do I lick his dripping cock and finger it in my slippery hand. I'll suck you every day, I say.

He has this angelic look on his beautiful face, his dark handsome face. This high-riding high-fucking hero of mine. He sighs.

Why doesn't your wife do this?

I don't know. I guess she thinks it's unnatural. She kisses it, but I once put it in her mouth, pushed it in while she was kissing it, and she choked. I never tried it again.

Don't you talk about these things? Don't you want it?

Yes, I do. We never talk about it.

You have such a beautiful prick, it should be loved every day. Every day I would kiss it. Cuddle it, suck it. You could come off in my mouth whenever you liked.

Eugene wavers against me.

You are my fucking orchid, I say, and caress his cock.

Knocking on the door.

Aghast! Did they hear? I whisper. Shhh!

Anyone there? Same voice.

Just five more minutes. Opening the refrigerator, banging shut a cupboard door.

O.K., the voice says. I have a meeting. I'll come back later.

We laugh together when he has gone. We squeeze each other we are happy. I feel like running down the hall and saying: Listen to this! You know what? I love Eugene. I am crazy about Eugene. I adore him. He has the most beautiful cock in the whole world. I just sucked his cock. Do you hear? I sucked Eugene's cock and I'll suck it again. I'll suck it again. I'll die sucking it again.

Eugene fingers my cunt. He rubs my clitoris and excites me, but it is me now who is anxious and saying, We have to go, lover. Eugene. We have to go. Eugene. Will you promise me something? I say.

Eugene smiles and places his hands on my breasts, slips his hands down to my bare hard nipples.

Yes, smiling, rubbing my nipples and bringing his mouth down to suck my tit.

Please. Listen to me. Will you think of me? Just to know you are thinking of me will make it bearable. Imagine streets, hallways all empty, evening skies, all my minutes, all my days without Eugene. Like a disease, living from minute to minute without him hour to hour.

Can I stand it? When it all comes together and I am in grief over my wanting him. Knowing this beautiful boy, so perfect, black, handsome, large funny nose, his face that haunts me. I see it everywhere I can't escape it. In my dreams. I dream of him. I want him by day. I want him at night. I am delirious.

Can I survive? We must all survive. One way or another.

107

But it makes me cry so much to see such a wonder, can you understand that he *is* beautiful, really beautiful? All my life I look for beautiful men and here he is. Yes. I am married to one. That is a fact. But there are troubles. Minor, maybe. We will survive, my husband and I, but for now, I have coming in me this longing, this spring, I am sprung from my husband because of his infidelity and I am looking, I suppose, for a new husband, knowing I will never leave my first, but here is this beautiful bastard—shit! he is good-looking. I am one of those girls who find it painful to see a gorgeous man because I want him so. It's not just good looks, no. There must be a quality and this boy has it. Dark, sexy, distant, detached. My men are not easy. They are so seldom.

Fuck. Here he is. One two three in a lifetime. And fuck that. Nothing more. Finished. Can't. Can't, he says. Oh, you doll, you sweet sweet dream.

Pretend we are in a Bergman film, you see, I say. See it now. Then we would have an affair. We would live out our desires to their completion. We would skewer ourselves on our destiny.

Life's not like that. You are so fucking romantic, he says. You make me cry too, like a painting.

Why don't we? Why don't we abandon everything? Wheee! like that. Cast it to the wind. Oh die together. Expire together. Be together.

His eyes are dark. Haunted. I temporarily sway him. He sees it too. Together. Running loving together.

We can be what we are. We can.

Ah! We must be realistic, my love. He touches my nose with his fingertip.

Realistic. He tips my lips. Bends to my eyelids. Lover.

I want to stamp my foot and shout: No! No!

What am I doing? Foolish again. One sweet child. Yes, he has a child. Ridiculous. This is nothing. I am only playing. It is only fucking. Nothing more. Such a power. Such a desire.

You obsess my life, Eugene.

We will never meet again, he says.

But why? Why can't we? I don't see why not. I am pleading. We could go on like this.

No, we can't.

Oh yes, please!

We can't. We can't. Oh, don't you see. Don't you see?

Please, I say, crying on his cheek, my tears on his eye. Say it please for me. Please say it now.

His mouth open on mine. His lips, wet with my tears.

Please.

Taking my hair in his hands drawing back my face and holding me.

Yes, I do. I'm sorry. I do.

Say it! Say it!

I love you. I can see the tears in his eyes. Oh, I'm sorry! I love you so much.

We hold each other tight as though we will break, numb, tingling with our tension, holding each other to last to the end of our lives.

Feel his long legs, his thighs against me feel his breath his hands, his belly his sweet belly pressed against mine. Feel him. Remember him. Oh please remember him.

We met once more. In a coffee shop. People coming and going. We accidentally met outside our building he coming, me going, but it was too much. There. In spite of everything. Feel it. Feel the tension. Feel the love. I could shout out in this fucking restaurant. Shout out. Oh, how I love this man! Look at him. Understand. Come with me, I say, across my cup of coffee. Come. I am nervous. My hand shakes and the cup trembles.

He is so beautiful. If only he were ugly. I imagine him ugly. It would be so easy then. Not that long body, that beautiful chest and shoulders and see him how he walks down the street with a friend, tight-hipped wide shoulders, a sweater, black hair afternoon sun. Remember how you wanted to run after him and hug him?

Sometimes it is too much. Feeling this. Yes, you understand. It is too much. The way you cry over a painting. It is the same thing, Eugene. Just the same.

BIG BLOW ON RAMROD KEY

SWINGING. CONDONED ADULTERY. My husband and I had swung once before. We weren't civilians, that's for sure. So we knew the score when we met the Ramsays down in Florida.

We were on our Christmas vacation. Same as they were. We met at a campsite on Ramrod Key. We had pitched our tent the night before; they arrived the next day in a VW bus.

I was standing on the beach, the wind blowing my hair, when suddenly I was approached by an extraordinarily good-looking man. Lean, excellent physique. Thin classic nose, mouth, blue eyes, brown hair. A dashing, flashing lad, one that could make me twinkle in an instant. However.

He said: Hi! extending his hand, white smile on his handsome face, I'm Neil. How are you?

I smile. Such a pleasure to be taken on by this good-looking boy out of nowhere.

How do you do? I smile. My hair blowing in the wind. Oh! Holding hands briefly. My name is Angela.

Are you staying long?

Before I can answer his wife appears at his elbow, a smiling round brown-haired dumpling. Nothing to look at. Short legs, plump face. No feature to hold on to.

Jesus. Without thinking I wonder how this guy can be married to her? And again without thinking, I am thinking: He's much better looking than my husband.

He reminds me of someone. I know he does.

Hi! his wife says, the friendliest girl around, broad smile, bubbling with enthusiasm. We're here on vacation. We're teachers. I'm collecting specimens. She has a jar of water in her hand and a tiny sandworm in it. She holds up the jar.

Oh, that's nice, I say. I appreciate sandworms because I took a course in invertebrate zoology in school.

We're science teachers.

Oh really?

Yes. Neil teaches grade ten science and I teach grade twelve biology. I'm trying to collect a few specimens for my class.

She has a beaming smile, small blue eyes and turned-up nose. Not ugly. But ordinary. Very friendly.

Her husband? What a catastrophe! He is unfortunately extremely good-looking. I am a little, but only a little amazed. She's a very nice person.

Her husband, bearing close at my shoulder, his bare feet pressing in the sand, says, What are you doing tonight?

I look back at our alpine orange tent for two and say: Nothing.

I see my husband bent emerging from our tent and coming toward us.

I introduce my husband to the new couple and Neil moves in quickly applying the same charm to my husband as he did to me.

Is he bi? I think. Christ! I'd like to see him in action. The Florida beach is beautiful on Ramrod Key. The waves crash in on the shore. The park ranger says there is a barracuda seventeen feet long off the beach between the island out there, which is perhaps five hundred feet away.

I am terrified when I go in the water. Staring down into the clear turquoise green water at the sand bottom. Watching each of my toes sink into the tan sand. Waiting to be attacked.

They have a VW bus.

We do this every year, his wife says around the campfire we have built that same night on the beach in front of our tent. This is our third year.

They're from Georgia. They have a southern accent, which I find enchanting. We are Canadians. From the north. You know, where they ski. Yes, that's us. No, we don't ski.

You talk funny, he says, the glow of the fire on his face. When you talk your voice rises in an inflection as if you are asking a question.

Oh? I laugh. I hadn't noticed, but then it becomes obvious. Well, I say, trying to find a reason, the French Canadians do that and yes, remembering an English girl I knew, the British too.

It's cute, he says. I like it. It's as though you are unsure of yourself.

I laugh a little. Yes, I am unsure of myself. I bite my nails. It is dark around the fire. No one can see my bitten nails.

We talk about my husband's work. He is a medical student. There are always a lot of anecdotes to tell when you are in medicine.

Yes, here's a good one. Talking about cutting up their corpse in anatomy. There were six of them on this body. An old woman.

Shriveled breasts, my husband says.

Yes! They laugh.

In medicine you get to see a lot of breasts. A lot of cunts.

You get used to it, my husband says.

We all giggle.

We're getting the inside story. What it's like to feel up a girl. Stick your fingers in her cunt and feel up her ovaries.

I don't know, Neil says. Imagine getting used to that!

They think this is great.

What's it like up in Canada? he says in his sweet Georgia accent. This drawl is getting to me. Fuck you.

Well. We aren't freaks you know, or Eskimos, we're just like you.

What's the morality like there? Ah, yes. Moving in. Do they screw around a lot in Canada? Drink a lot?

We are drinking some homemade grape wine they brought with them. It is very good. Strong, grapy, lightly sweet.

We search our minds.

What do we know about Canadian morality? We've fucked around ourselves, but do we represent Canada?

It's about the same, my husband says. Canadians drink a lot. They're great beer drinkers

We've had some parties, Neil says. He is eager, looking up over the fire, his eyes sparkling. Beth and I would go to a dance, you know one with three bands on three floors moving up from one level to the next drinking ourselves silly.

This is a grade ten science teacher from Georgia. A prize of a male specimen if I ever saw one. Oh, yes. A sweetheart. I bet he has hair on his chest, I think. Not a lot. But just enough that I could bite them with my teeth moving up to his throat. Then his lips.

Silence. Complete silence. The tide is out. We go down to look at the specimens laid bare on the tidal flat. There is a full moon. Salty air.

Look what I found here! his wife says.

Oh! It's a sea urchin.

She puts it into a jar. I'll have to save this. Walking barefoot in the sand on the coral stones, the moonlight pooled white on the sand. Gray shadows. Moon shadows.

His wife and I walk up to the can. The cement outhouse. Shadows so bright in the moonlight. The sea grapes by the cement house casting shadows on the sand.

You could read by this light, Beth says. The palm trees sharply etched across the path.

We are excited. On the way back we do a little dance on the path in the moonlight. She brushes against me and laughs.

115

We aren't ready for children yet, she says. We're having too much fun.

Neither are we! We've been married two years, screwing four.

Really? She laughs. Sometime before I'm thirty I'll have one. Not now! Ha! Ha! waving on the moon-shadowed sand path. Clear, bright. Such a glow. The whole camp asleep. Tents and trailers silent in the moonglow.

Sitting around the fire with the boys. Our voices are the only voices on the beach.

They must carry, I say, giggling. We're talking so loud. The wine is going down.

Neil says: We'd have this couple over to our trailer. They live in a trailer. They are building their own house on the weekends and every spare moment. I can see Neil's sharp nose, wide mouth, arms moving over his house.

Grade ten science teacher. Sex bomb builds his own house. Headlines.

Are they prejudiced? We are curious. This black problem is something we don't have in Canada. Because there are mainly no blacks.

It *is* a problem, she says in her southern drawl. We get along. Heavy on the drawl.

We recount how shocked we were about the signs in the gas stations: WHITES ONLY scrawled in black paint on the outside door of the can.

It's frightening down here, I say. Driving through those Georgia swamps at night with all that hanging moss, I was scared to death.

I've never seen so many black people before in my life, I think.

No, we aren't against them, Neil says. It's a problem. Georgia drawl. She's from Morgantown, West Virginia. Shit! We had breakfast in Morgantown on the way down.

Remember, honey? Virginia baked ham, southern fried potatoes, eggs sunny side up, toast, apple jelly and coffee. It had just snowed and they were scraping the snow off the sidewalks with shovels in front of the stores on the main street at the foot of the coal hills when we came through.

A one-horse town. I can see her coming out of one of those white wooden houses. Her drawl. The snow settling in. Not much beyond those triangular peaks, those limestone hills. Fuck. I took geology. I know all about those hills.

Where did she meet him? I wonder.

Yes, that couple. As I was saying we had this couple over to our trailer and did we ever let go. He laughs. I am staring at him over the fire. I can't take my eyes off him. He is so lovely. He reminds me of someone I used to know, as I said. I feel this longing.

His wife suddenly stands up and shows us how her knees are double-jointed. She can bend them out like this. Her leg bows out in an arc.

How can you do that? I say. I jump up and try it. I can't do it. She is wearing Bermuda shorts. I hate Bermuda shorts. I am wearing short shorts on top of which I

116

have my winter coat from Canada. There is a cool breeze coming in off the sea. We can see the lights on the bridges to the islands, strung like pearls on a chain, a lighthouse on the point, and far off on the horizon the shape of a tanker, a ship at sea.

What we used to do, Neil says, is lock the doors and forget the world outside for the weekend. Did we ever let go! You can imagine!

I am excited. The four of them. I don't care about the other three, only him. I see him letting go on the other woman.

I want to squeeze in there. Suddenly appear. Confront him.

The hard mahogany wood crackles and pops on the fire. The logs are wet.

Look at all those ants running around, Beth says.

Neil and Tony take a log on which there is an ant and dip it in the fire frying the ant. That's cruel, I say.

It's not. They're bastards, Neil says. They'll bite.

Peaceful star-filled night. The sky a mesh of stars. Full moon. Sitting in the moonlight on the beach in front of our alpine tent. The tide out. The moonlight washing the tidal beach.

Silent. The whole camp asleep. Our voices like silver spoons in the night tinkling on glass.

We are getting drunk on their homemade wine. Drinking out of the same paper cup and the top of their thermos jug. Passing the cup around. Now we are passing the bottle. It's almost gone.

I wish we had some more, Beth says, it's our last bottle.

She swings her foot above the sand. She is sitting in a deck chair and her legs are too short to reach the sand.

We would have brought more if we knew we were going to meet you all.

You all, I say. I love that! I love your accent!

Do you now? he says. Do you?

Look at his eyes across the fire. He's staring at me. Look how he is staring at me.

His wife and I go to the can again. She squats on the open toilet beside me. The moonlight shines through the open wood slats of the roof on to the cement walls and floor.

She unwraps a piece of paper and quickly slips something into her pussy.

She must have her period, I think.

Back on the beach sitting around our fire, which has burned to embers, we are drinking beer.

My husband has brought out the Budweiser that we bought earlier in the day and we're popping cans like eager fish.

Neil slops off the foam, takes a big gulp and says, Have you ever noticed how it's different when you've been married a few years?

My husband nods. Sure we have.

You get used to it, don't you? Neil laughs. At first we couldn't get enough of each other, always going at each other in a car, but it's different now.

How long have you been married? Tony asks.

Three years.

Four for us. Officially two. We all laugh.

We were walking along the beach today, Tony says, looking for shells. I was about five hundred feet ahead of Angela. You'd never know we were together.

I know, I say, it wouldn't have been like that a few years ago. I still feel badly. Any distance is a separation.

Collecting shells. We would have been hugging each other all along the beach, Tony says. I remember how we used to feel each other up in the library. Every time we walked past the circulation desk I had to put my hands in my pocket because I had a hard-on.

Ha! Ha!

Yes, that's the way it was, Tony says, snapping off another beer.

Better be quiet, Beth says. We'll wake up the camp. We are all laughing in the silent night. The tent next to us is about two yards away.

Oh no! Shhh! I bend over and kick my toe in the sand.

We're in the can again his wife and I.

Gee, this beer is flowing. Giggle. She wipes her crotch and looks at me.

Do you like Neil?

I'm quick. Yes, I do. Giggling. He's wonderful. Laughing.

Would you like to swap?

A sharp jab goes through my cunt. As I wipe myself I can feel my pussy swell and beat.

I'm no fool. I'm not going to blow this and I play cool.

Yes, I say.

She beams. Tremendous! I like your husband. He's a cute son of a gun.

Do you think so? Flushing the can.

Yes. He's real cute.

Well, a new perspective. An outsider's opinion.

So is yours.

Sure, but I'm used to Neil, she says.

We're washing our hands at the sink.

Just a minute, Beth says, and reaches for my hand. You're sure it's all right? She's patting my hand.

Yes, I'm sure.

Look how she's looking at me now.

118

Have you ever swung both ways? Her fingers are lingering on my hand. I'm just curious.

I look at her. Yes. Once before.

She has taken her hand away.

Did you like it?

Yes.

Would you swing with me?

Running the water and soap down the sink not looking at her.

Sure I'd swing with you, I say. I feel a thrill of excitement through my belly.

I'm glad, honey, she says. You're beautiful. Neil's going to love you. She pats me on the bum. I love the way you are.

We are both quite drunk. Pulling the paper toweling out of the dispenser, drying our hands.

Would you give me a kiss? she says.

She's much smaller than me, but that doesn't matter. I am thrilled by the taboo of this, kissing this ordinary looking girl who is going to fuck my husband who is saying I can fuck her husband who is a miracle of beauty to fuck, and the two of us now kissing it's thrilling. Coming together like this in the cement moonlit can off the beach, the Florida Strait, our husbands down on the sand in deck chairs sitting around the expiring fire talking while we do this, make things begin, the two of us girls ready to open it all up.

There they sit, the two men. We giggle at the end of the fire. We held hands on the way back, how exciting! Like two teenagers, but we are standing apart now and grinning at our husbands.

We have it all planned. She is going to ask my husband something. A medical question. Something private to get him away. Down the beach a little or just out on those tidal flats. I know what she'll do then, sitting beside him on some coral stone she'll go for his cock her hand in his pants before he knows what is happening. He won't protest. He'll be surprised (I can laugh just imagining) but he'll let her do it. Feel his cock. I can imagine her. She's probably an expert. An expert cocksucker. She'll have him off in no time flat. Before you can say, It's cold, or Here's another sea urchin.

He won't spurt out into the water. She'll catch him in her mouth. Will she spit his salty sperm into the sea or swallow it?

She'll swallow it I can tell. She's a marathoner. Look how she moved in on me.

And where does that leave me?

Back on the beach with her husband. Wow! I'm not complaining. He is one hunk of man. One beautiful lump of male. Shit. He is fuckingly good-looking. Give him a medal. Give the boy a medal. Grade ten science teacher from Georgia, building his own house wins award. Better looking than Paul Newman. Can you believe it? Paul Newman is some piece, but this boy is better.

I'm not exaggerating. Neil takes the cake. Beth is a nice girl and has a real good technique. But how the fuck she got this boy, I'll never know.

Sitting on the sand in our deck chairs. My husband fell for it. They are down on the tidal flat and I am here with Neil.

I am suddenly breathless. All gushy and goosey like a schoolgirl. I don't speak or move. I feel paralyzed.

Neil is smiling at me across the red and orange fire, white ash embers.

He hasn't caught on. But the way I am looking at him. He gets up and comes over to me.

Are you cold?

Yes. I still have this goddamn winter coat on from Canada, but I'm cold. Cold in Florida. Well it must be in the sixties, fifties.

He puts his arm around me to wrap my coat around my shoulders. He tugs on my coat. Just a minute. Stand up. I stand up and he sits down in my chair and pulls me down on his lap.

Well we both know what we are doing. I am sitting on the lap of what has to be the most adorable boy in this world and he is hot on me, he has been giving me hot eyes all night (his wife must have seen that) and it is at moments like this that I am glad that I am one hell of a sexy piece long hair, big tits wide hips a large hairy cunt long shapely legs a pretty face, come on. O.K. but look, I'll tell you this, Tony and I pulled into an orange grove in Winter Haven, Florida, for some orange juice and the woman selling the juice, a refined, tanned, blond, good-looking middle-aged woman put on the heat for me and said: Why don't you enter the Miss Universe Contest? (Why fuck me, is she kidding?) I'm a judge in the contest and you could qualify. Hair. Is it naturally curly? Eyes. I was stunned. Embarrassed. Impressed, let's face it. It was a thrill.

All this is to say that I'm glad I have something going for me as I sit on this fucker's lap.

He is looking at me and smiling so tenderly. I'm not used to such a sweet face.

Like the first couple we swung with. Nice-looking types, but not like Neil.

Please understand. I think guys like this should be put on a pedestal.

Seeing a face like Neil's, it's like, well, floating, or coming off in my head.

We share a beer. He takes a sip and I lick the foam from his lips. I take a mouthful and he places his lips on mine and takes the beer from my mouth. Our lips tingle the beer foams.

Metal taste. The taste of his tongue and lips and mouth in the bubbling beer.

He stretches back in his deck chair with me sitting on him and I can feel his bone in my ass. My legs hang over his knees like two limp rag dolls.

Neil nuzzles his face in my neck. He smells different. Nice. The smell of a new guy. I like that. His hair is brown and straight. Quite long. I am looking at his face up close. Fantastic. Seeing the bone in his nose, his large eyes. They remind me of the sea. I feel like the sea inside me. I am flowing inside, looking at this sweetheart.

Honey, he says.

Oh Jesus southern drawl! Let's go in there. He points to our tent.

Moonlight. I won't see him in there. I follow him holding his hand and we duck into our tent.

Kneeling on the tarpaulin floor. I take off my winter coat but when I get to my jersey top Neil places his hands on my breasts and fingers them, they're soft and full and my nipples stand out. I'm not wearing a bra. I never do. Men watch my boobs bounce under my blouses. I see their eyes looking for my nipples.

Neil's tongue and forefinger fondling my breast, his two hands cupped under my jersey, mouth parted, eyes on me kneeling in front of me.

You're a beautiful girl. He pulls up my jersey and his shirt and presses my bare boobs against his bare chest. I can feel his nipples, hair. Exciting. Like fine electric wires. He rubs my nipples against his hairy chest.

He squeezes me tight and says, Oh, honey.

Then he pulls back and unzips his pants, pushes them down to his knees, still kneeling.

I take off my jersey, unbutton my shorts. It is awkward undressing in the tent. He has to lean back, lie on his back to pull off his pants. There is moonlight coming in the tent through the front opening. The nylon mesh screen hangs limp across the entrance and the sand outside is white.

Once you are used to the light you can see a lot. I can even see the orange color of the tent canvas.

So I see his prick.

The moonlight licks one side of it like a long tongue. A stiff bone. Light on the top, his bulging end hanging over his tip. He has a lot of hair. Thick, curly, darker than on his head. A thick line of hair moves up toward his belly.

Lean hard ass as he turns. Good legs. Legs like a runner. When he sits up again I wait. This is too good to make the first move.

He places his hand between my legs. Rubs my inner thigh. I can tell already that he has polish. No hit-and-run.

He strokes my thigh close to my cunt, then takes a few cunt hairs and tugs on them while looking at me, his eyes are on me all the time.

I think he is taken with me. The same way I am with him.

I reach out and stroke his hairy arm, run up to his chest with my fingertips, then his nipple. His lips. Touching them with mine, surrendering myself to him on his lips. Drowning into him. Hearing the surf outside, the tide starting to move in.

Saliva, wet, salt tongue. His tongue is different. Hotter, harder, sharper tip. He licks the corners of my lips, under my tongue in front behind my teeth, where the spit pools, and the thin cord is like the cord on a cock. He tongues all my little mouth spaces while he holds my hair and strokes it.

I love long hair, he says. He sucks my hair between his teeth, breathes it. Twisting my long hair around his hands. I adore your hair. Pulling me down on him. You have such a beautiful face.

You have too. I rub his cheek rough with beard. His nose. What a nose! Sharp, fine. And his eyes. Smooth lips. I touch him lightly, gently as though he were a masterpiece.

You're really beautiful, Neil.

I don't have the nerve to say: How did your wife ever get you, sweetheart? That would break the mood.

But I feel like confessing. I feel I have to tell him how gorgeous he is. I don't care how many times he's heard it before; it does me good to say it again.

Neil. He's looking, listening. He goes for me. You're the sweetest thing I've ever seen.

He throws his arms around me and laughs and hugs me and pulls me down.

Wouldn't you like this to last forever? he says.

We tumble around on the double eiderdown sleeping bag.

Giggling. I can't stop laughing. Isn't this great? he says. Honey, I'd like to take you home to Georgia with me.

A threesome. I've thought of that since. The three of us fucking in their trailer, balling all around. But that leaves my husband out cold.

Shit! This guy is beautiful. I could kiss every part of him. I will. I will suck each of his ten toes, his ten fingers, his ears, his nose, his mouth, his prick, his ass.

A freshly washed ass, scrubbed well with soap. I'll tongue your ass, Neil.

Oh he is going wild on me panting, rubbing against me, hugging me so fiercely such kisses such love.

I am aching for it. I have to feel it between my legs or I will die. I will die. I must have it. Nothing will stop me. I will die having Neil's prick between my legs. He's pushing on top of my cunt grinding the wiry hairs of our two crotches together, poking his cock at my clitoris, holding it over my hole.

He's teasing me. He's making me delirious. He wants to hear me beg for it.

Oh I will beg for it, Neil. I will beg to have you in me.

Please. Oh Neil please! My mouth is wet and panting against his ear, his lips, open wanting. Put it in me, please! He nudges me thrusts against me.

I am tingling. Sharp hot chord. Fine wires of fire. Sucking. My cunt gasping. Oh Neil there is nothing more I want than you in me!

I put my hand on his prick and guide him through my jungle of wild hair, clear the way for his prick to my wet, waiting, open cunt. He touches my bare pussy and I throb. A pulse at the tip of his penis reflected through my cunt up to my belly everywhere, like lead sinking I am tipped on the edge begging crying, Oh I could cry, it is so strong so hard too much.

Neil slips it in. Glides like a sailboat through water, breaks through my flesh, in, going in in up to the back sinking his rod its full length. A length measured in the brain. A length like a steel pipe an oil rig, the sun flying high that high. A length that is every measure you have ever wanted ever taken coming to rest at the back his bulging hard cock against the small bone of my cervix nudged between thrusting out my flesh into my gut springing my insides stretching my cunt.

And then we begin the steady slow rhythmic gentle hard coming together. The building of a life together. The building of passion. Paddling on the sea, swimming in the sea, setting out on a journey, making round a whole completing a fantasy living a dream.

Beating, steady.

His hands caress my ass, he holds the cheeks of my ass in his hands squeezing them, bumping them, slapping them, hands wide open to hold their fullness, then suddenly his finger finds my asshole and he plays with my asshole around my tight opening pressing with his fingertip parting my opening pressing inside. Tight, sharp and then his finger is inside turning and rubbing and exciting my asshole coming on me like a big crap, feeling this excitement which makes his rod feel harder sharper to me more aware that he is in my cunt. Plugged in two ways to him, completing our circuit. I do the same to him. I feel out his asshole, buried in a mat of sweaty hair, hard to get his asshole clear of hair, finding his asshole and inserting my forefinger.

Neil groans and his balls draw up I have made him even more excited. Tripped his cock make him come begin to come, but he can hold back he wants me he wants me to fuck with him.

Honey, we're going to fuck together. I am going to make you. I'll make your ass I'll fuck your cunt I will drink your mouth suck your cunt we're going to come together, honey. His southern drawl against my hair, his finger in my asshole, his prick in my cunt.

Arching thrusting hugging sweating fingers in our assholes his cock in my cunt coming at the back of my cunt like a steam roller climaxing deep in my cunt clamping down on his bursting prick.

Now do it now baby!

Neil pumps. Hard fast jabs. Banging me open and closed.

Oh here I come! moaning, Here I come! I'm coming! crying out. Arching falling down on his prick grinding his belly into mine his legs between my wide-open cunt my legs wrapped high around his back glued together moving in a ball, in a vise his prick, his beautiful fat gorgeous prick in my cunt spilling over, finding me, reaching me, spilling his seed into me his beautiful seed all those lovely babies coming in me juicing me up while I love him and I love him my throbbing loves him my cunt loves him waves coming over him tight, sucking, pumping, hugging, lost to him flying to him floating away with him drifting together on a peak.

I bump on his prick. Squeeze his prick with my cunt. Sharp needle, pinpricks of sensation, a new climax.

Neil sighs and sleeps on my neck. I wiggle and kiss his wet hairy chest and the small hollow below his Adam's apple. We are soaking wet. His sperm spills out of my hole between our legs dribbling down onto the sleeping bag, staining the nylon. Proof of our love to be carried around forever.

I am hot inside. Burning. Hot pepper. I have to move. I am tingling, itching, still hot but I wait.

I kiss him. I taste the sweat on his sweet lips.

Neil. Ah!

Neil stirs. Opens his eyes. Curled long lashes looking. Smiles.

Hmmm, he says. His eyes gleam, his prick rises. Oh, he sighs. You're great. What a doll! I haven't had one like you for a long time.

I smile like an angel.

I can imagine all the cunts he's fucked all the breasts he's sucked. High school dances in the gym. He'd have them all. I'm glad to be one of his girls. One of his cunts.

But he's hard again and stretching my cunt. My cunt is a sopping, throbbing soft bed of hot flesh.

Let me fuck your asshole, he says.

OK.

We carry Vaseline with us just for this purpose. He smears his prick with Vaseline dabbing carefully his lips tight then a gob on my ass, around my swollen hole.

Inserting carefully, slowly. Sliding in better than my cunt, which is a gaping cavern, into my tight ass. Sucking my ass giving me a hot in my rump a hot jab up my rectum.

His cock feels longer in my asshole. Tight around my hole rubbing tingling like having my cunthole rubbed burning inside feeling I have to crap rubbing against my vagina. A swollen big prick up my bowels.

124

My legs are around his neck as he plunges into my ass. Rump fat cheeks pressing into his balls, legs high above his head. He draws back carefully methodically feeling out my rectum, tasting my shit with his prick. And he's all juice again, fucking my shit and I am coming like a storm in my cunt, my clit, my asshole. Inside I am waving roaring in ecstasy and he spurts his huge prick, gripped by my throbbing ass, bumping his juice inside me, spurting out his last drops of sperm expiring on my fat white ass, tasting my second hole.

Now it's sperm and shit and matted hair and we are sweating like pigs. My long hair is soaking at the back of my neck. Matted. My legs and arms throb from holding him so tight.

Neil is lying on me collapsed. Limp prick. Exhausted.

Oh, my doll! I nibble his ear. Suck his lips. Not to bother him. Taste him. Taste all his juices. Live in him.

We fall asleep. It must be late. Two, three o'clock when we awake. Our partners haven't returned. At first panicky, then not at all. They're all right.

Excited now to be still with him, sleeping with him even when all desire has been satiated, when all is past.

But I'm getting excited again being with him. We're hardly covered and it's cold, damp. His prick is hard. I can see it in the moonlight. It hits me like a knife in the night. He reaches for my hand and we clench fingers.

Oh throbbing again. Hot again. Doll face. Sleep tiredness gone. Still wet now cold and sticky where he fucked me before, still crazy for his ass his balls his lovely body.

Cold, stone hard sober in the middle of the night and as eager, as hot for him as before.

We decide to take a shower. This is crazy, Neil. We'll freeze our balls out there.

Come on. There's hot water.

What do we do, run naked?

We'll run naked, he says.

Oh for fuck's sake!

Running along the sandy path in the moonlight chasing me. Cool moon wet sand. Cool wind.

The cement can is creepy at night. But it's the same as when his wife and I were here. Still puddled in moonlight. The sea grapes overhanging the path.

No flashlight.

What if some creep is in there ready to murder us?

He's hugging me and laughing. We're giggling. Who the hell would be crazy enough to be in there now?

Some lady having a pee? I say.

We go into the Women's together. Snakes bugs. Nothing. None of my fantasies. Moonlight slanting through the roof. A strong sea breeze, cold blowing.

We huddle under the shower together and turn on the hot and cold.

We forgot the soap.

There's a bar on the sink that we use. Doesn't feel right soaping your cunt down with somebody else's soap so we half melt the bar under the hot and then feel right about using it.

Neil soaps me.

My tits, belly button. Crack in my ass. Asshole. I am bubbling sperm.

My guts gurgle.

I have gas, I say.

Come on fart on my finger, Neil says.

I can't.

Come on.

We're so excited. He reaches for my lips with his wet mouth under the stream of water and we kiss. His finger in my asshole, soap burning. I tongue his mouth ready to jump on his prick, which is standing up like a soldier ready to fire.

I fart on his finger.

His mouth is open, water running over his lips, his tongue. Kiss him. Kiss him kissing him under the shower. Honey. Oh my honey.

We'll drown, I say. Oh baby, we'll drown. And my long hair getting wet.

I'll die. I'll die of pneumonia. Oh Neil.

He holds my head back out of the shower, only the long hairs are wet, and the strands around my face. He holds my long hair in his hands and bends me over and puts his prick into my cunt. The shower flows down between us splashing off my belly as he holds me back, and floods between our thighs.

Neil turns down the water and turns me around and holds me from behind. My ass on his prick. He fingers my clitoris.

We are soaped all over. Clean in every hole. I washed his prick. Lathered hot his cock. Smoothed every crevice. Washed away all traces of my shit.

Neil keeps kissing me.

We'll freeze when we get out.

We forgot our towel.

Neil steps out and rips off yards of paper toweling from the dispenser on the wall.

I turn off the water.

He dries me. Patting me everywhere. Rubbing. Slapping my ass and thighs.

Jump up and down and you won't get cold, he says. I dry him bouncing on my feet rolling him around in paper toweling.

We run back. Towels streaming from us digging up sand with our toes.

Running by the palm trees through the sleeping tents and trailers.

Where are Tony and Beth?

Who cares, he says. Do you? Big smile when I look at him. We'll go in the VW where it's warmer.

When we open the back doors of their VW we see Tony and Beth lying together on a heap of pillows and blankets sound asleep.

The inside of their bus is hot and smells of blankets and leather seats.

They had it better than us here. We're shivering. Teeth chattering.

Watch out! Shhh! He puts his fingers to his lips. We don't want to wake them.

We crawl in the bus, around them. His wife stirs and sits up. Hello, honey. We were getting kind of cold on the beach.

She looks at me walking bare-assed, bare-boobed past her.

How're you doing, sweetheart? she says to me.

All right. I smile and look at her. Swing my boobs as I turn. Oh I don't want to sound too enthusiastic.

Us too.

Tony is sound asleep.

Looks like he's out, I say.

He is at that, Beth says. I think he's had enough for tonight.

Neil and I find a spare place and spread a blanket.

His wife sits watching us. Do you mind if I join you two? she says. I'm not quite sure what should happen now. Do I lie down with my husband? Trade places with her? Say goodbye to Neil?

I mean his wife here does kind of cool it, doesn't it?

But Neil has been through this before. He takes my hand and says, You're with me, remember?

I remember. Oh yes. But your wife, lover. Your wife.

Don't worry about her.

Her. His wife.

Don't worry about me, honey, she says.

Fuck. Neil smoothes the blanket and grabs two more over us. He's on me cuddling me blowing in my ear and saying, I'll warm you up. I'll keep you warm.

Fuck Neil. What about your wife?

She doesn't mind. She loves this. She'll go back to sleep.

Oh rolling around under those blankets, breathing hot air between us. Building up steam.

It's getting up, Neil. I gasp for air. Neil tickles me plays with my nipples and slides his face between my cunt.

127

Oh what are you doing?

He's eating cunt. Lapping me up. Eating my hole. His tongue sliding between my lips down to my cunthole, ringing it with his tongue, jabbing his tongue his tiny prick in and out and back up wet and quick to my clitoris. Flicking my head back and forth over my hard bone running along to my tip licking my hard bulbous edge, the seed of my joy.

My mouth opens I want him in my mouth, I have to have him in my mouth. I turn around. He keeps his mouth on my clitoris while I turn and then I am down on him feeling for his waving prick grabbing his monstrous organ in my mouth sucking and fondling and drawing his cock in.

Then his wife appears.

Honey, can I join you?

She is leaning over us. I take my mouth off Neil's prick and look at her.

I want to suck your pussy, she says.

When I don't understand she says, You go on sucking Neil, honey, and I'll suck you.

I don't mind as long as I get Neil. He sits up and moves closer to me. Lies across my face with his prick over my mouth. His wife moves in between my legs and fastens her lips on my cunt.

She does a good job. Better than Neil even though he was doing nicely, She's right on my tip, right on my needle-sharp sensation and I feel so grateful to her that I want to suck her pussy too, but I'm glad to have Neil's big prick in my mouth filling up my mouth. Something to grab on to and suck really well. I am panting and slobbering on Neil's prick and Beth is tonguing the clit off me. I raise my legs and suck harder on Neil slapping his ass telling him to come, Now! Now! She lets me go. Over the peak legs clit shuddering twitching coming off riding my peak Neil thrusting in my mouth jab jab hard now bursting beating pulsating together in rhythm together. Spilling into my mouth. Hot salty juicy sperm. Me throbbing squeezing out the last of my vagina clenching my legs together. Beth is breathing fast, she is hot and excited. I can hear her panting over my cunt. Neil is collapsed, sprawled to the side of my head his prick swollen and soft and wet in my mouth.

Her tongue flicks over my clit. Twitching me. Neil's prick draws out of my mouth, soft and limp. He's sleeping beside me.

I want to suck her. She made me come like that. I want to do the same to her. She puts two fingers in my cunt. I sit up and reach down to her.

Turn around, Beth, I whisper. I grab her ass as she turns and places her cunt in my mouth. Fastened together.

She's dripping wet. Sperm from my husband. Her clit is hard as rock. She's hot on me, starting, moaning and arching as soon as I begin to tongue her.

She'll wake the dead she's crying so much, no trouble coming. I am ready again and we beat our clits together, two fast eager tongues two hot mouths clamped on our girlish cunts.

She cries out when she comes and wraps her arms around my legs. Neil is fast asleep beside us. I fondle his prick and he murmurs and turns in his sleep.

Tony is awake. Beth's cries. He's kneeling over us looking at the two of us, his prick rigid. He brings his prick to my mouth next to Beth's cunt. He strokes my hair.

Now I want you to suck me, he says.

And I do. My mouth is aching. My jaws feel as if they'll drop off. But I do because he is excited and I can feel his excitement and I want to make him happy.

The next day they leave. They can't stay any longer. They're going to Miami for New Year's Eve, which is that night.

They want us to come for a party, but we can't. We have to go home.

Will you come back? Tony says.

Next year, Beth says.

We're going to Key West today to look at the big fish they bring in off the trawlers, Tony says.

When Beth leaves, he says to me: Well, what do you expect? It can't go on forever.

No, it can't.

I'm standing on the beach again by myself. My hair blowing in the wind, the same as the day before.

Neil comes up to me with a small blue book and pen.

I want your address, he says. He writes it down. Then his in my book, which I run to get.

Neil stands close to me on the beach handsome as ever smiling blue-eyed, the wind blowing his straight brown hair, standing on my feet in the sand rubbing my toes, and there before everyone he embraces me hard and kisses me.

The clear turquoise green water lies flat to the horizon and the tan sand shelled beach rises out of the sea in a bank of sand as we embrace and kiss forever.

CALL ME

WE MET BY chance at a college reunion. As it turned out we were both there for the champagne. Jack was something else. I have never met anyone like him. He had more imagination and daring than anyone I knew. Jack was wild. He was always surprising me, in fact, he was a way ahead of me. Jack was pure sex, pure adrenaline, pure rush. But it was dangerous; I never knew where it would take me. One thing that I knew for sure was that I couldn't resist him.

Jack and I met in our freshman year. I was seventeen and Jack a year older. His locker was two down from mine on the right. I had noticed him because he was tall with a big build and good-looking. Green eyes, thick curly dark brown hair and a sensuous mouth, always with a smile. Then one day he approached me and asked me to go to the frosh dance that Saturday. I said, No thank you, I've already been asked. In fact, I had been asked by seven other guys and had turned them all down because I was petrified that I might be chosen frosh queen and have to get up on the stage and say something. Conveniently, I came down with the flu that weekend, truly; none of my suitors needed to feel slighted.

A few months later, I found out that Jack had a crush on me. Jack's best friend, Bob, whom I was dating, said he had found someone else, and Jack who shared a locker with Bob, felt sorry for me and invited me to The Mirror Grill, a local restaurant, for coffee. We played music on the jukebox. I cried and Jack said, What can I say? Bob's a prick. After, we walked for hours in the snow sharing confidences, talking and laughing.

Ten years passed. I had married and separated and one Friday evening with nothing better to do decided to stop by a reunion at the college, drink some champagne and leave. I'm working on my second glass and don't know *anybody* when I turn and recognize a familiar face.

It's Jack!

What are *you* doing here? he says, amazed, and smiles.

Well, well, haven't seen you in ages! How are you? I bump against him, smile, and say, I'm here for the champagne.

Me too!

Hey, so what's been happening?

Well, I'm an engineer now—have my own business.

Good for you!

And you?

Working as an editor at the Geological Survey.

Hmm. Not bad. Married?

Was.

Oh, that's too bad. What happened?

Oh, didn't work out—different personalities, married young. You know, the usual story. So are you married?

Are you kidding?

What about girlfriends?

Dozens, Jack says, laughing.

Why am I not surprised? So who's the lucky girl now?

I'm in between girlfriends, but still looking.

The crowded room is emptying.

Looks like it's time for the President's speech, I say. Are you going?

Sure, why not?

We take our seats in the auditorium. Remember the Mirror Grill? Jack asks.

How could I forget?

That was cool, wasn't it?

Yes.

Did you know that I had a crush on you?

I suspected, I say.

You know, Jack says, when I saw you for the first time by the lockers—do you remember?

Yes.

I thought that you were the most beautiful woman I'd ever seen in my life.

Come on.

Yes, I did. I still do.

I'm blushing.

Look at me, his eyes are intense, you are.

I am feeling the two glasses of champagne and sitting so close to Jack—the object of my fantasy life for so many years.

Jack, I say, and smile, Do you *really* want to listen to the President's speech?

He looks at me, surprised and then laughs. No, I don't.

134

Do you want to leave and go somewhere we can talk?

Yes!

Do you know a place?

Sure, The Beagle. It's close by.

The pub is noisy and crowded and we sit close together on stools at the bar and order draft beer.

Can you believe this? Jack says. Talk about fate!

Yeah. Synchronicity . . . Tell me about yourself, I say, looking directly in his eyes, feeling giddy and my old desire for *good-looking* Jack.

You mean, he says, how I've fantasized about you for years?

I'd like to hear about that! I laugh.

I'd go home, he says, after university and lie in bed and wonder what it would be like to make love to you and I'd masturbate thinking about you.

You're kidding!

I'm not.

His confession leaves me breathless. We are sitting knees pressed together and I can smell him—we are close enough to kiss. I see his lips and his eyes and feel his leg pressed against mine and see the desire in his eyes and feel his longing for me in his voice as he talks and confesses his desire, his lust for me.

I didn't know that, I say, a breathless excitement overtaking me—moving up from my toes to my throat and capturing my breathing and smothering me in desire.

Look at that, he says, laughing.

What?

Our body language.

What do you mean?

Look how we are sitting, and he points to our posture—facing each other and legs wide open.

Hmm. You're right!

Interesting, he says.

I sigh. Well, I have to confess that I fantasized about you too. I thought that you were very sexy and good-looking.

Jack smiles.

I used to think of you when Tony and I were making love. In fact, we talked about you.

You did?

Yes.

What did you talk about?

Well.

What?

Ah . . . Tony talked about your sister. He knew her in high school.

Really?

Yeah, did you know that they once played spin the bottle at a party and kissed.

No! Jack chuckles.

Yes.

So anyway . . . we would fantasize that Tony would fuck your sister and I'd fuck you.

Hmm. You mean to say while I was jerking off over you, you were getting off on me?

Something like that.

When *you* do it, Jack asks, do you do it more than once?

I blush, flushed from the beer and excitement. Yes, I do. I mean, I usually do it three or four times, ah, at least two, one is never enough. Why stop, I say confidentially, leaning towards Jack, when you're all excited? It's getting there that takes the time, and once there—well, I can just roll it off, one after another—it's so easy.

Jack's eyes shine with admiration. Really? Most girls I know, only do it once.

I have *confessed* and feel suddenly liberated. Confessed to my desire. And one thing, I continue, emboldened, one thing I *never* do is fake it. Never. Never.

Never?

Never!

Jack laughs.

Tell me, I ask, What do you like to do?

I'm a voyeur. I like to watch. I watch films and masturbate. Fantasize and masturbate.

And dozens of girlfriends . . .

That's right. What do you say, Jack says, one more for the road?

Sure.

I'll be back—bathroom break.

Me too.

In the washroom, I feel acutely excited and reckless. I am ready to do anything with this wild man.

Drinking our last beers, Jack says, But what I want to know Angela, What about us? What about Angela and Jack?

Ah. I look at him intensely. That ache of desire. I gently touch his hand.

What about us? he repeats.

I don't know. Is there anywhere we can go?

Jack laughs. We could go to my car.

Where are you parked?

In the parking garage, second level. Do you want to go there?

I nod and smile. Yes, I do.

Jack pays the bill and we leave the bar.

We take the underground tunnel to the parking garage. Jack's car is a small red MG. Outside, the tail-end of Hurricane Hugo is raising hell, blowing rain and wind.

Get in, he says, and we roar off up the ramp to the top level and park in the rain in the deserted lot.

Isn't this wild! he says.

I love a storm! Wild wind rain.

Yeah, well, let's see . . . where were we?

Oh . . . Ah, you're between girlfriends.

Yep, that's right.

I have a boyfriend, I say.

Is it serious?

Yes, and no.

Are you living together?

No.

How long have you known each other?

Oh, about six months.

Look, he says, reaching over and placing his hand on mine, let's talk about us. You know, I was thinking about you several times in the last few weeks.

You were? What were you thinking?

Oh, what I would like to do to you if we were alone.

Like now.

Yes.

I sigh. Isn't this *amazing*?

Pure fantasy, he says.

Oh, god, I say and laugh—the wind, the rain and you!

Here, Jack says, Let's change sides. I'll go around and you shift over.

Jack opens the door and steps into the lashing rain and howling wind and runs around the car. He jumps in and slams the door.

God! You're wet, I say, laughing.

Not bad.

Here let me wipe you off. I take off my jacket and rub his curly brown hair vigorously. Jack laughs. I touch his wet face and he opens his mouth and bites my fingers.

Ah. I melt. My pussy aches. I lean over and touch his lips with mine and don't move.

Silent car, electric stillness and the raging wind and rain outside.

I touch his tongue with mine and run my tongue over his lips.

His breath quickens. I drop my left hand into his lap and he places his big fist over my hand and presses hard. I feel his erection under the soft material of his pants.

Jack is smiling at me—his face inches from mine, I can feel the heat of his skin.

Do you want to see something? he asks.

I smile.

Jack leans back in his seat and slowly, silently unzips his pants and takes out his hard cock. I have never seen Jack's cock before and I am amazed—it is huge—long, thick, maybe eight inches.

Oh, god. Lovely!

Touch it, he says.

I embrace his cock with my hand, wrapping my fingers tightly around his hard shaft and *squeeze*.

I look up at him. Do you like that?

I love it!

May I kiss it?

By all means.

I bend over and take his huge hard member into my mouth and slide my lips down as far as my mouth can go and then back up and lightly tongue his throbbing head.

Oh, god, he groans. All those years of wanting to fuck you and now you're doing this. Can I suck your tit, Angela?

I pull up my green knitted sweater and offer my voluptuous left breast to Jack who takes my hard nipple in his mouth and sucks. He sucks and tongue flicks and then bites my tit gently, yet firmly with his teeth and shakes his head. His fingers squeeze and rotate my other nipple and then he drops his hand to my white cotton skirt and slowly opens the ivory white buttons down the front until my belly is exposed and he caresses my soft skin to my panties and shaved sweet smelling pussy.

Oh, god. My pussy is so hot and engorged. Oh, Jack!

Sit on me, he says urgently, and I move over on top of him and slowly lower my body until the lips of my wet pussy make contact with his hard cock. I move a little, my lips sucking him up and I feel absolute agony, absolute bliss, and the wild breathless desire to plunge in deeper. Jack pulls me down hard—all this happens quickly, in seconds—and now he is in and how hard hard he is dragging on the side as he pushes deeply into me and I ride him.

I look in his eyes and see his thrill as he rocks me. My cunt is on fire, throbbing aching—ah!

Jack groans and suddenly pulls away from me and spurts hot gobs of cum on my belly. Oh, he moans. Oh. I'm sorry, baby. Too much.

No, no, I say, kissing his lips with quick little kisses. *Don't* be sorry.

Oh god, what a mess. I have some paper towel in the trunk—I'll get it.

Jack steps out into Hugo and I can't resist. I quickly pull off my remaining clothes and jump out of the car and walk around to Jack who is opening the trunk.

Ha! This is great! I say, as he hands me some paper towel.

The rain is coming sideways driven by the strong, steady howling wind.

Jack is soaked and laughing.

I wipe the rivulets of rain washed sperm dripping down my belly and thighs. The wind howls and blows the rain in slanting streams under the lamp standard.

I give Jack a hug. This is incredible!

Jack grins. Come on, he says, get in the car. You're soaking.

We put the heater on full and I dry off with my jacket and pull on my skirt and blouse.

That was exhilarating! I say.

You bet! Whenever we're together, he says, it is totally off the wall.

Blows my mind. I sigh. You know, I don't think we can see each other.

Bad timing?

Yes, unfortunately.

Ah, too bad. Just when I found you, you're gone.

Isn't that true, I say.

Are you sorry?

No, not at all! It was meant to be.

Life is amazing. You cross my path after ten years. Whenever we are alone together it *is* totally off the wall as you say. All night I dreamed about you. When I got up around eleven, the rain had stopped, but it was still cold and windy. You were going to run today and I thought, son of a bitch, he has balls. I couldn't get you out of my mind. After years of fantasy and forbidden desire, suddenly one night of truth. Will you call? I know you can't. *Such* a narrow line between fantasy and reality.

One month after Hugo the phone rings and it is Jack. I thought I'd call and see how you're doing, he says.

Oh, Jack! I didn't think you'd call.

Well, I have been thinking about four Fridays ago. It comes to me in a flash, he says, or just general circumstances.

Oh, me too. I was totally obsessed for two days—I mean night and day. It was mind-blowing fantasy, wasn't it?

Sure was. We sucked each other up, didn't we?

It took me two weeks to get over you. I wish we could have more.

Fantasy or reality?

Both.

Would you settle for fantasy? he asks. I insist on leading a healthy fantasy life. Living fantasy.

Well, I say, think of me as a blank sheet of paper on which you can write your fantasies.

I like that, he says. We'd need a rule.

What's that?

No touch.

For fantasy?

No, I mean if we were to see each other again.

Oh.

Well, you could watch me masturbate, and I could watch you, he says, that sort of thing.

Hmm.

Have you ever tried telephone sex?

No. Have you?

Yes. I did it with one of my girlfriends.

Did you like it?

Jack laughs. Sure. Telephone sex can be anything you want—no restrictions. Would you like to try it?

You'd have to start. I wouldn't know what to say.

All right, he says. Can I use the word 'fuck'?

Are you kidding? That's funny.

Let's go back to that stormy night. Do you remember when my hard cock pushed into your swollen wet pussy?

Jack's words are soft and flow easily from his mouth into the receiver and along the telephone lines to the receiver pressed to my ear and directly into my brain.

Yes, I say, breathless.

And how *good* it felt?

Yes.

Are you touching yourself? he asks.

Yes.

Do you want to know what I'm doing?

Yes.

I'm stroking my cock would you like to do that?

Yes.

I'm pulling down on my balls as I stroke my cock would you like my hard cock in your cunt—*words tumbling like soft fragrant petals*—do you remember how it felt, like it was amazing, wasn't it? all those years of fantasizing, and then suddenly come true would you like me to come inside? Yes, now yes—*the rush of my throbbing heart pounding in my ears*—Are you rubbing your clit? Yes. Squeezing your breast, what lovely breasts! I loved kissing your breast and taking your hard nipple in my mouth. Can you do it? Does it feel good? Do you want me to come? to shoot my load? Ah!—into your mouth . . . into your cunt . . . I'm coming! Oh, I am too, I am, oh my god! I sigh.

Breathless. Pussy throbbing, heart racing. That was *amazing* Jack! That was the most far out thing I've ever done, I can't believe it!

Did you like it?

Yes, yes!

Me too, he says. I'll talk to you again. Cheers.

Cheers.

Talking to Jack is a delight. What an aphrodisiac! Jack is a midnight fantasy—I love to hear him talk. He is so bad, so potent, so mind-obsessing!

I am in my kitchen looking out of the window at the pink crab trees and purple lilac in the backyard around the pool when the phone rings at three in the afternoon.

Hey, Jack says, I'm home early from work and, and I was just wondering if, if you have any fantasies for me.

Oh, boy! Just a minute—let me get settled.

A long pause.

OK, I'm back. I grabbed a beer in case I get thirsty.

So, do you have a fantasy?

Yeah, I do—you call from a downtown bar at midnight and suggest that we meet the next day in the parking lot outside a strip club, which is, if you can believe it, out in the country at a crossroads that has a gas station, a motel and a bar with strippers.

That's convenient, Jack says.

Sure is . . . well the next evening I am sitting in my car in the parking lot outside the strip club, waiting for your arrival. I'm a little early because I don't dare take the chance of missing you, since we have forgotten to say—wait at least half an hour. I am wearing my white straight skirt with the buttons down the front—the same one I had on the night of Hugo—but this time my blouse is a black embroidered blouse with open mesh that shows my hard pink nipples peaking through—

Oh, Jack groans, I *love* that!

Of course, I add, I am not wearing any panties.

Jack sighs.

Well, it's a little after seven and dark, and you approach my car and I only see you when you are at the door. You get into my car and say that you were already getting hard as you came up to my car. I murmur my appreciation and smile. You are wearing tan shorts—

I hate tan—

Is green OK?

Yes.

So you are wearing green shorts and you reach under the bottom of your left leg and pull out your cock and *show* it to me. *Well*! No matter how many cocks I've seen in my life, I'm always happy to see another. I lift up my skirt and show you my bare pussy. I part the lips and finger my clitoris. I say put your tongue here and point to my swollen clit. You do. I bend over and blow hot air on your cock. No touch, I say, teasingly. You say let's get in the back. We do. Fast forward to you saying, Where do you want me to come? In my cunt, I say. Or, I say, Between my breasts, in my mouth, and *here* pointing to my shaved pussy. As you can see, you have *a lot* of choices. All right—there are two versions—*first one*—you put it in hard and fast and pull out spurting all over my belly, or *version two*, we do the slow delicious cunt-cock teasing routine . . . your choice, Jack.

Two—

Ah, I'm *so* wet!

Are you rubbing yourself?

Yes. I've been lightly and slowly rubbing my clitoris the whole time. What about you?

I've been stroking my cock. I'm rock hard. I want to *fuck* you. Jack gasps. I *am* fucking you!

Fuck me! Come all over my face . . . your hot delicious sperm—

Ah! Jack groans. Ahh ahh—

I'm doing it *now*, Jack! Oh! Ohh!

What do you say we get together sometime, Jack says, recovering his breath.

I'd like that.

Mutual masturbation, he says.

No touch.

Exactly.

We're playing with fire, I say.

I like fire.

So do I. Do a dance, a little romance.

Jack chuckles. You betya!

Our encounters and talks are powerful, irresistible for me. I think he calls me on impulse. Jack thrills me.

I bought a nine-inch latex dildo for you, says Jack. Why don't you come over and we can play with it.

Only five days until we meet, I say. *That* will be an adventure.

There I am sitting on Jack's white couch, admiring this monstrous dildo, the realistic kind with all those veins, when Jack asks me if I want to *try* it.

Ha! That should be interesting.

Jack has an amused look on his face and a twinkle in his eye.

Well, it's not touching, he says.

Let's do it!

I watch Jack pull off his shirt and bend over to step out of his pants—very exciting.

My clothes are already on the floor and I lean back on the couch at one end and Jack takes the other end. He starts stroking his cock and I watch.

Does that look good?

A hard cock, yes.

He strokes some more and then I draw up my legs and face him, exposing my cunt.

Can you see?

Yes.

I finger rub my clitoris.

We are both excited. His cock is hard and swollen. Our calves touch slightly since there is not a lot of room on the couch. We look at each other and smile—the sexual tension is acute as Jack takes the big dildo firmly in his hand and touches my open pussy. Contact! He rubs the head of the dildo around my lips and teases the opening. Every movement I feel acutely because it is Jack's hand that is causing the motion and it is as if Jack is touching me. We watch each other and I see his excitement in his eyes and his cock, which is hard and standing straight up.

Total silence. Looking, rubbing, nudging—he works it in a little. Our legs are touching as he dildo plays my pussy. I take the dildo from him and spit on it and rub the tip on my nipple and then bring it to my mouth and suck on it . . . always looking at Jack in his eyes . . . *intensely exciting, breathlessly erotic.*

I love your breasts, he says.

Watching him, watching his face change with excitement, I twist the dildo in my mouth and then bring it to the tip of his cock and touch him. Big latex cock rubbing against the glistening tip of his hard smaller cock.

Now Jack takes the dildo and eases it into my cunt. I arch and squeeze my breasts and push my left breast to my mouth and suck on my hard tit as he rotates the huge cock in me, which is now in deeply, leaving only the rim for him to hold.

I watch Jack and rub my clit. I watch the excitement in his eyes. When he catches me looking, he smiles.

Can you do it?

I'm not sure. I feel choked. The rubber dick doesn't move when I contract on it.

Let's move over there, he says, indicating an easy chair.

I sit in the chair and he stands over me holding his hard cock and smiling. I watch his hand stroking his cock rapidly up and down, catching that point of intense arousal over the swollen head, over and over again, which I can see in his eyes as his eyes fix mine and his breath quickens, his lips part and I put my finger to my lips and lick it and then touch my nipple and put my nipple in my mouth. Then I wet my finger again and rub my clitoris and with my left hand squeeze my breast hard. Jack's head is bent down and his hand moving fast on his hard shaft—I watch him turn into the light and then away and then face me directly and I feel totally wanton and want him to fuck me and I go with his excitement as I rub myself over and over on that spot of exquisite feeling, my fingers slipping off, grabbing back on just as he grabs his cock hard and rapidly strokes his penis and says, breathless, where do you want it? In my mouth, and I open my mouth and see his beat, his going over the top, his coming in a moan, a spasm, a pulsating thrill and I come too seeing, seeing his cock spurting white cum into my mouth. The first shot hits the back of my throat and I have to swallow, and then a rogue shot hits me in my left eye. Hot and wild!

Oh, I say, laughing, ouch! That got me in the eye!

Oh no! All you all right?

Yes. I laugh, but holy shit that stings! Maybe I'll go blind—

No, no. It happens to everybody . . . every guy that is—go and rinse at the sink.

Ha! I shall.

Well, what do you think, he asks when I come back all rinsed, did you enjoy that?

It knocked me out Jack, no kidding. I *love* watching you.

Me too. You're gorgeous, he says.

You know, it's your game, Jack. I'd do *anything* for you. It's your fantasy.

I love the game, Jack says, don't you?

Yes, it's exciting!

And dangerous too, he says.

I wake up in the morning excited and very wet. Thinking of my evening with Jack takes my breath away. Strong images. What an addiction! And I think why don't I put on a porno and masturbate? At first I think, oh fuck, I should make coffee and get busy on all the shit I have to do. But no, look, if I don't give myself this time when will I ever get it? So I say, fuck, and go and get the Black Dick tape, the big latex dildo, wash myself, ditto dildo, come downstairs, put on the porno, sit in the chair and with drawn curtains watch the cocks and cunts on the screen. I have a great time playing with my tits and cunt and thinking of dear old Jack and his sexy cock. I do it six, seven, eight times. I don't count—I no longer count. What the fuck for?

But I get some good pulsating waves of intense excitement in my pussy thinking of that bad bad boy Jack. After that I feel relaxed, no more butterflies in my stomach and racing heart. So what's the difference? I think, partner or no partner? Ho! What a difference! Touching, silent communication, seeing that sexy look in his eyes. Knowing he's turned on—seeing that hard cock and coming off in front of a naked, erect, excited male.

Three weeks later the phone rings at one a.m. Hi! Jack says. I thought I'd give it a shot in the dark and call and see if you were still up or still receiving calls.

How come you're still up?

I was thinking what we could do.

Did you like our last get-together?

Absolutely!

Hmm—I had to indulge myself the next morning. Did you notice how we were silent most of the time?

Different modality.

On the phone we talk all the time.

Yeah.

God, you turn me on, Jack! It is so far out, so wickedly bad.

Well, we both love pornography, don't you think?

Yes.

Do you have any ideas?

How about meeting in a hotel sometime to watch?

I'd like that, he says.

Same rules?

Yes.

All right, but in fantasy, what would you like me to do to you?

Well, Jack says, I'm living in a downtown apartment, downtown New York, and you check into the . . .

The Waldorf Astoria.

Yes, the Waldorf Astoria on the top floor.

How do we know if there's apartment hotel across from the—

We don't—but I can see you across the courtyard between our buildings. You have told me when you will arrive and I watch your room with binoculars. I see you enter the room and turn on the light. I notice that you don't lock the door. You come to the window and push up the glass so that I have a better view of you. It so happens that I can conveniently see the single bed in your room to the right of the brown overstuffed chair. You sit on the edge of the bed facing me and look directly at me, looking through the binoculars at you, before you remove your dress.

What color?

Black, a black cocktail dress—you are returning from a dinner of exquisite French cuisine . . .

With friends?

No. You were alone—you are a woman of mystery, great secrets . . .

Yes.

As I was saying, you remove your black cocktail dress and then your black camisole, but leave on a lacy black bra, which gently cups your lovely white breasts, and now you are wearing only a black garter belt and black stockings. You are *not* wearing panties, although black panties would be nice, but I like it much better that I can see your bare white shaved pussy. You lie back on the bed still facing me and draw your legs up so that the soles of your feet are flat on the bed and your knees are in the air. You open your legs and take your right hand and rub your red nail polished fingers over your pussy.

I put down my binoculars, adjust my hard cock in my pants to conceal my erection and leave my room, locking the door behind me. I take the elevator to the basement and walk out a back door into a side street and go around to the front lobby and take the elevator to your floor, the ninth—

I thought I was on the top floor.

No, it's the ninth . . . and I come to the unlocked door of your room. I enter, unzip my pants, no underwear, while looking at you lying in disarray on the bed, and then I start to masturbate. You are sitting on the bed leaning against the propped-up pillows, your legs are bent in a V, knees up, feet on the bed and you have the sheet draped over you, but as soon as I enter the room, you pull the sheet away so that your cunt is exposed. You are wearing only a black bra, and black stockings fastened by a black garter belt. I say hello, you say hello, and then you say come here. I walk over to you with my erect cock. I walk right up to you and you open your mouth.

Do we fuck? I say, my heart taking a few extra beats.

Would you like us to?

Yes, let's fuck!

OK. How would you like to do it?

Why don't we try something different?

What do you have in mind?

Ass fucking!

Ha! You are getting bold!

Oh . . . if you want regular—

No, no no—personally, I would love to sink my hard cock deep into your ass!

Well, it just so happens that I've come prepared and sitting on the night table beside me is a small tube of KY jelly *and* a banana flavored safe.

Good thinking, Angela!

All right—I hand you the banana flavored safe, which you expertly roll on your swollen cock, which by the way, looks about twice it's normal size, and I say, Just a minute—let me suck you and taste that hard cock that you are going to dip into my ass. Well, you can hardly stand it and weave a little on your feet and I pass you the KY and say, I'm ready . . . and turn over on the bed and raise my ass in the air—

Which I slap, Jack says, I can't resist and I give your bum a few hard slaps—

And I say, Harder! Slap me harder! Jack, and you do and then gently massage my stinging flesh. I'm feeling tingly and hot on my ass and my pussy is wet and burning.

I take the KY, Jack continues, and generously lather on a gob over your asshole and the banana safe, and then on my knees and supporting my weight on my arms, I lower my body until my hard cock touches your pulsating asshole because by now your hot little ass is eager to receive my hard cock. Of course, you're a bit frightened because you've never done this before, but I reassure you and guide you—

No, no, that's not a comfortable position . . . I turn over and lie on my back and you kneel over me and raise my legs in the air and then you gently nudge my asshole with your cock and I relax until you can push in a little more and then more until you are in all the way and we both lie very still. I can feel you throbbing inside my ass, which is on fire, and I rub my clit as you slowly pull back and thrust in and now I can take it and you ram me hard *hard* bang! bang! Oh, God, I moan, I'm coming—whooo—

Me too! Ohhh, Jack groans.

Ah! I gasp. *That* was good.

Oh, yeah!

Until the next time, I say.

Goodnight, Jack says.

Good evening, says Jack.

Jack! It's been a while. I wondered if you'd made a New Year's resolution not to call me.

Jack chuckles. No, I haven't.

Well, good! Have you thought of any ways to be bad?

Heh! Heh! No, actually, I haven't had a chance. I've been so busy over the holidays, in fact, it was a relief to go back to work. What about you, any fantasies?

Well, I imagined us meeting at a shopping center—

You mean in the Christmas rush?

No, not at all—just meeting in a shopping center and then I go to your car and scrunch down in the back seat and you drive to your place . . .

Ha! that's risky—

Let me continue, uh, where was I? Oh, yes, uh, once you are in your garage, I get out and follow you into your family room and we sit down on a couch. You ask me what I want to drink and when you come back with my glass of wine I lift up my black skirt and show you my shaved white pussy. Then I part my outside lips and expose the pink flesh inside. I take a sip of my wine—*white*. You sit down beside me and I lean against you and undo your pants and free your cock, which by now is rock hard. Without saying a word, I take my two hands and guide your cock to my soaking wet pussy. Then I raise myself a little and place the lips of my cunt on your hard prick and push myself in.

Ah, he sighs, letting out a long breath. And then?

And then—well, I replay this over and over, you know, the part where you put it in, and all the while I am stroking my clit with a wet forefinger and two fingers of my left hand are deep inside my pussy, you know, pushing in and out, gush, gush, and while I am doing this, which by the way takes considerable finger power, I am thinking of you Jack, hotly stroking your cock and bringing that strong feeling forward in your cock, ready to release, and I do it once and then twice and, now lying still with a throbbing heart and quick breaths, I rub myself to another climax.

Whoo! That is hot! Hot!

What about you, Jack? Any wild ideas?

Hmm, I did think, a while back, before all this ho ho season, hum, I thought of meeting you in an underground parking garage—

Oh, creepy!

Not necessarily. We would follow each other in, of course, prearranging where to meet out in the street and then we'd drive down the ramp, I would be the front car, we'd take our tickets, drive into the garage, and then, since the garage is packed with cars from shoppers and workers—since this is a garage under a huge office shopping mega complex, we wouldn't be able to find a spot so we would keep going up and up until finally at the top level, where actually there are several spaces left, we pull in and park. I get out, and then you get out and I walk to the nearest EXIT and open the door and disappear.

That doesn't sound like much fun!

Just a minute . . . you are close behind and I hear you open the big metal door, which bangs shut and then your footsteps coming down the stairs.

Oh . . . there's no one around?

No one, and I am waiting for you at the next level in a corner casually leaning against the wall *and*, and I have my cock out, which by the way is hard, and my balls flopped out over the edge of my pants as *you* walk by.

God damn, Jack!

148

You linger and watch me shag my cock. I look you directly in the eyes as if to say . . . come and suck my cock.

Without a word, you come over, get down on your knees and start sucking, and oh, you do an excellent job of sucking my cock, wetly rimming my swollen head and then taking my full cock length into your mouth deep to the back of your throat.

Ahh . . .

Meanwhile, I start to unbutton your blouse when we both hear a heavy steel door slamming. You quickly stand up and I zip up and when two teenage kids, males, come bounding by, we are standing by the wall chatting.

As soon as they are gone, we resume our activities. Of course, we know we don't have much time to get off before someone else comes by.

What do we do? Do I go back to sucking you?

For a little bit—to get me hard—and then, you know what is coming, you know that I'm going to fuck you against the wall—ram it into your hot juicy cunt, and so you are ready . . .

I already have my skirt hiked up, don't I, Jack? And my bare pussy is exposed and I am so wet that when you take your cock in hand and push against my crack, you slide in, with a little resistance at first, and then you slide in like a dream. You've got me backed up against the cement wall and are lifting me with your hard cock and I have my legs around you and my back to the wall and you are pounding me over and over and I say now! Fuck me now! I'm coming! and you groan and pump gallons, gallons of hot fucking cum into my cunt.

Oh, Jack moans, oh fuck, Angela, I'm shooting!

Several days later Jack calls. The car episode, he says, in the garage stairwell where I have you backed up against the cement wall was excellent!

Don't you feel we've done it? I ask.

Almost. We need to go there. Make it real.

What about doing a video together? I say. No face or larger view shots.

Hmm. It's a possibility. I'll have to think about that.

We could use the no touch as an additional factor.

Yeah. You could bring a whole cornucopia of vegetables—like carrots, zucchini—um, *cucumbers*!

That would be good! What do we do—put a paper bag over our heads?

Ha! Ha! Noo, we'd just do close-ups of cucumbers and carrots. I could put a carrot in your ass—

Ha! ha! You're funny.

I'm serious.

Well, you know, I like to frame images in my mind—like snapshots or a deck of cards—but we'll need a few wild cards and jokers.

What do you suggest?

Well, how about fucking on the hood of my car on a country road in the sun? I mean—this is not being filmed, I'm just talking about wild cards.

We can explore that in the summer, Jack says.

Last night, I say, I was talking to Mike.

Who's Mike? Your boyfriend?

No, he's a guy I used to know.

Serious?

Uh uh. My ex and I knew him and his first wife in our swinging days.

Ah . . .

Anyway, we talked about you.

I see.

Yeah, well, Mike suggested that we could get together at his place and you could watch, respecting your *no hands* approach.

And I watch you two?

That's the idea. I mean . . . this is *Mike's* idea. And you could amuse yourself anyway you liked and if in the future you changed your mind we could try a threesome. Safe sex, of course.

Of course.

Mike wants me to go to a bar with him and flash.

Are you interested?

Well, I sigh, it's not something I would normally do. It's shocking and *that* appeals to me. Mike said it is *humiliation* that appeals to him, not knowing that he could fuck me. What about you Jack, are you a person of extremes?

You know I am. You are too. We know that, don't we?

Yes, I was teasing you. Stating the obvious.

I see it as a challenge . . . the flashing, I mean. A little *problem* to be solved. Mike has no guidelines; he's only seen it in a movie.

He also suggested picking up a guy and the three of us getting together. A *complete stranger*, can you imagine? I said, Are you kidding? and he said we would use safes. No, thanks, I said. I see what he is doing, using me for his own stimulation. It really doesn't have anything to do with me. However, when I said no, he dropped the whole idea.

Hmm . . . Angela . . . do you have a secret fantasy—something you've never told *anyone*?

Well, let's see, um, I've got something that's secret, but it's also real.

That sounds interesting!

Yeah, I mean, it's a secret fantasy, that, uh, almost played out.

Tell me.

Well, it's one of my lesbian fantasies where I go to a lesbian bar and chat up this pretty young lesbian in her early twenties—I don't like them *butch*—and she finishes the drink that I bought her, and invites me back to her place. Just as we're about to leave, her girlfriend, a real *ugly* shows up. Apparently, she's been watching us from across the room of the club, which by the way is called The Cave, and the music is loud techno with flashing strobe lights on the cement walls of the small crowded dance floor. Well, my pretty young lesbian can't leave.

Why not?

Her girlfriend won't let her.

Is she afraid of her girlfriend?

Probably. She sure was interested before her friend showed up.

Just a minute. This is a fantasy—you can do what you want.

I laugh, I know, but I am telling you a *real* story.

You mean, ah, you went to a lesbian bar and this girl—

Not exactly, yes, I did go, but I went with a guy who was going to do something unusual, he said, to please me, so he went up to the bar and chatted up this girl—he didn't buy her a drink, by the way, and the girl kept glancing back at me and then a woman came up to them and shortly after my friend came back to me . . . I was siting on a stool at the back of the dance floor . . . and said, she's interested, *definitely* interested, but her girlfriend won't let her.

Oh! I said, a little surprised at the whole undertaking, but he was doing it for me, since we had talked about my lesbian fantasies. God knows what would have happened if we had gone back to her place! I can imagine all kinds of things—like her ugly friend raging in and maybe, maybe shooting me—who knows?

Hmm . . . I like the hotel fantasy better, he says.

Oh, me too—you looking across the courtyard at the hotel windows and imagining me there.

Yes.

What will we do, Jack, when we run out of fantasy?

We won't. I'm fading, Jack, says.

Oh, my God, it almost three o'clock!

And I have to be up in four hours—

Poor baby . . . do you want to do it?

Let's save it for the next time.

Are you sure?

Sure—anyway, I've had a lot of cock rushes tonight.

Goodnight.

Wow! I'm obsessing about Jack. I just got a flash of him coming on the phone. He *really* wants to get into it! Too hot to leave—playing with fire, but that's part of the thrill. *The erotic as a means of self-discovery.* I just realized today, how much I miss Jack's calls and the *sound* of his voice. It is six weeks since he last called. I *love* the sound of his voice and I love how he takes me down a thrilling path. His words, each word, leads me further into excitement. When he describes how excited he is, I get excited, and when he describes what he would do to me, my heart speeds up, my breath becomes shallow, and my cunt beats. Six weeks is a long time. I had lost the thrill, but now I sit here with beating pussy, excited all over again, wanting Jack to *talk* to me. Talk to me and then we will *think* about fucking. Talk to me and we will plan to meet. I know how to do it now, to take action, to be bold. I could ask him to bring his finger or mouth close, but don't touch me. Or I could say would you like me to suck you? He'd say yes, and I'd say, but we can't, we have a rule. Let me show you how I *would* suck you, and then after showing him, I'd say, If you want me to suck you, you'll have to *beg* me, and of course, he does.

Jack calls and says, I'm dusting off some old fantasies. You probably thought I'd disappeared.

No, but I didn't think you'd call again.

Yeah, well, work has been crazy, and then there's all this social life, friends and relatives, so to speak.

Do you have any time? I ask.

To talk?

To see me.

In two weeks.

I'd like that, I say.

You know, Jack says, I was thinking today about you lying naked in your backyard on a sun bed.

Well, actually, today after my walk I lay naked in the hot sun on the cement patio by the pool. It was quite lovely—covered in pink petals from the crab trees. I was wet from the pool and I fantasized about you coming from behind and covering me with your cold, wet, naked body. I could almost feel the weight of your body on me.

Hmm, hmm, and then I'd slip my cock between the cheeks of your lovely ass.

Something like that, yes.

I had another idea and that was me with a camera coming upon you in your car in a garage and filming you.

Doing what?

Masturbating, naturally.

Ha! Of course, naturally, every time, no sometimes, when I'm alone in my car and my pussy is hot, I'll reach down—

I was going to film myself while talking to you on the phone, but after looking all over I couldn't find any blank tape. I'll get some and try to call you before we meet and get the tape to you, so you can watch what I'm doing while you're talking to me on the phone.

Ah! I sigh. It *never* ends, does it?

No. Speaking of such . . . when did you have your last orgasm?

Last night. I went to bed around one and I started thinking about you and I decided to try an experiment—using absolute minimal touch to keep myself on the edge of intense excitement. Ah, I wanted to observe my feelings. So I wet my finger and rubbed my clit very slowly, always staying on the spot and as I'm there, you know, *hovering*, my breathing almost stops, my heart gives a few extra beats—ba-dum, ba-dum, and my mind seems to drift, float on a stream of excitement. I did this for about ten minutes, *all the time thinking of you*. And when I was at peak arousal, holding there in a state of suspension, I talked to you in the most intense, arousing words.

Whoo! What did you say?

Well, I talked slowly and said, push-your-big-hard-cock-in-my-wet-throbbing-hole-cunt-aching-push-slowly-break-slide-ram-fuck-in-hard-swollen-tingle, and so forth. What fun! Well, that was fantastic and I came several times and then immediately a drugged sleep came over me, but I faded in and out, and I'd wake up still excited.

That *was* something! he says.

Well, Jack and I talk for over an hour and I do it at *least* eight times. I don't feel any deprivation about no contact, and I even wonder if he might go a little further the next time.

The phone rings a few minutes before midnight. Good evening, says Jack.

Good evening, I say. Three more days! I'm so excited!

He says, Speaking of a reality check, the conditions established in the beginning still stand—no contact?

Of course, I say, hiding my disappointment, I see quite clearly what you are saying about living pornography, this is just like watching a movie.

Exactly.

And no contact is the only way we can go.

I'm glad you understand.

Well, guess what? I went shopping for cucumbers today.

Wonderful!

Yeah, it was strange. My food selection was based on a different filter—this time I was not looking for the largest, but the right size. I felt strangely guilty as though people knew why I was selecting them. I felt as though I were being observed in an illicit act.

Ho! Ho!

I'm so distracted, Jack. I wish I could see you now. Maybe it's the six cups of coffee I've drunk today!

You'll rent the camera?

Yes. This is so bold! I've *never* done this before. Shit! I feel my heart beating harder.

Sitting in my car, parked under a bright light in a large outdoor parking lot, empty except for two parked trucks and two cars, I wait for Jack. The cool night air blows in through the open sunroof—jazz on the radio. Pale pretty face, orange lips, and green eyes and blond streaked auburn hair. Jack arrives and parks beside me. I motion for him to come and sit in my car. The purpose of our meeting is to transfer the camera and supplies, which Jack will take home with him, and then about ten minutes later, I'll come by his place.

I think they were suspicious at the video store, I say.

How come?

Well, the young Vietnamese boy kept clearing his throat as he filled out my order, and then he smiles and asks me if I had big plans for the camera.

He's just being friendly.

Yeah, except wrapped around the two tapes, there's a note—Don't give out blank tape when Mrs. X rents camera. She wants two tapes to purchase—exclamation mark!

Ah, I see what you mean.

Just when Jack is about to go, I say, Oh, I nearly forgot!

He looks surprised.

I want to show you something. I move my leg over the gearshift, open my legs, and pull up my skirt showing him my black stockings, garter belt, and bare pussy.

Very nice.

Do you like it?

Yes, very much. Here let me give you a preview, he says, unzipping his pants and pulling out his very erect cock.

Jack takes everything back to his place and I give him ten minutes and park a few blocks from his house and pick a moment when the street is empty to walk around the side of his house to the back and enter through the sliding patio doors.

Greetings again, and a look of complicity passes between us and then Jack gets drinks. The camera is already mounted on a tripod facing the couch.

This will be interesting, but Jack is full of imagination and patience—because it requires patience and care to frame the shots to exclude any identification—so really, what we're talking about is various vegetables in various orifices.

To begin with, we choose a cucumber to explore my cunt. Jack teases in about half an inch—the cucumber that I had carefully selected in the fresh produce store is too thick.

Probably an English cucumber would have been a better choice, I say.

Let's try the zucchini, Jack says, with enthusiasm.

Camera on, camera off. Jack is up and down with the camera since he has to screen the shot to keep only body parts in the frame.

This is a great shot! Jack exclaims, as he holds the green end of a greased-up thin carrot and carefully inserts it into my asshole. And then, with the carrot hanging out of my ass, Jack crouching over me, he slowly lowers his body until his ass is just touching mine and I can feel our legs lightly touching and the slightest warmth and pressure from his ass on mine.

Another great shot! Jack touching my nipples with the tip of his oozing cock, and then he *squeezes* my nipples with his fingers.

Oh, God!

I watch Jack's face, which the camera can not see, and I see the intensity in his face as he repeatedly brings himself to the brink of release.

And the end!

Where would you like it? he says.

There are *infinite* possibilities. I say. How about here? I point to my cunt and Jack immediately comes all over my bare pussy as I am rubbing my clitoris, now slick with his slippery cum, and I do it, and then *do* it again.

Our time together, I say, when we run out of tape, seemed like only five minutes. The next afternoon Jack calls around three to say that he could take some time to edit and transfer the tape. He calls back around five to say good news, bad news—the two-hour tape turned out very well, but in nearly all the shots, we are identifiable. So, I'm erasing it, he says.

At seven o'clock, he calls. I'm still erasing the tape. I'm scrapping the tape, he says. I'll throw it in a dumpster, and we can split the loss. I'll pay for half the camera.

Oh, no, you can, next time—

Get you a tabletop dancer.

Yes, all for myself, I say. Let's not have any money pass between us. So . . . the final sequence—

Didn't get erased. I ran out of time.

Can you imagine *that* in a dumpster downtown? I can't believe it!

Yeah, isn't that wild!

I wish I had seen the tape.

We'll do it again, Jack says. This time with my camera.

I had a dream about you last night, I say, it was this really weird dream—I was masturbating with *your* dildo against a Monet print.

You did that once before, didn't you?

155

Yeah. I took your dildo and placed it against the doorframe in the bathroom and watched myself in the mirror as I fucked the dildo.

I liked what I did with your nipple, Jack says.

Oh, me, too! And the end . . .

We were filming for hours.

Did you notice how silent we were? This erotic silence. No words.

I did, Jack says. Very powerful!

All we do on the phone is talk talk . . . I *love* the contrast.

Remember we talked about going to a strip club together?

Yes. I'd love that!

I'd get a table dance, he says, and then ask the girl to dance for you.

You know, Jack, this is interesting—under the catalyst of the camera, you did *touch* me.

Uh huh.

How do you feel about that?

I'm OK with it.

I feel as though we've crossed a line and gone deeper into the forbidden.

You mean partners in crime? *Taboo*, he suggests.

One of my *favorite* movies! Kay Parker, remember her?

Change in plans, Jack says, unavoidable.

I was disappointed.

Next configuration, he says. I wanted to call you, but couldn't. In the afternoon I went to the strip place myself and had a girl do many dances for me.

Did you have fun?

There was discrete touch, he says quietly, which made me excited.

What if we meet tomorrow night?

I'd like to kiss your nipple, he says, and then you kiss my nipple and we'd pass it back and forth.

Listening to Jack's hypnotic voice, there is *no* question about seeing him and being bad. A hidden, forbidden exploration of desire and perversity.

Well, it's after midnight and Jack hasn't called. I'm surprised. That seems strange to me. The next day he calls and says, I'm sorry about yesterday—unavoidable change in plans. Let's talk.

But you have to get up at seven.

I know.

You're a beast, I say.

Out of control, he says.

I wish you were.

Jack laughs. Scenario A, he pauses, is what we *can* do. Scenario B is what we'd *like* to do, but *can't*. Which do you prefer?

Definitely, B.

OK. You are bound by your wrists and ankles spread out to two trees, legs spread eagle with silk scarves about three feet above the ground, face down. You're suspended, sort of swinging free. I get down on my knees and part the lips of your cunt and have a close-up look and give it a few licks, and stick my tongue in your hole. I run my hands down your back and cheeks of your ass, inner thighs, and breasts. I see a glistening strand drop from your cunt.

I'm very wet, I say.

Yes, you are.

I mean *now*. I'm very wet and sticking two fingers into my wet squishy cunt. Can you hear that? I put the receiver down to my fingers squishing in and out making a sucking sound.

Yes, I can.

And, I say, speaking into the receiver, when I pull my fingers out there is a gob of clear slime that stretches two inches, three, no four between two fingers and then breaks.

There you go, he says, laughing. A glistening strand drops, he continues, from your cunt to the ground. I come up behind you and spread the cheeks of your ass. Are you still with me?

Yes, I say, breathy, but I don't know about being suspended that long—

Oh, it's a fantasy, he says, laughing, that doesn't matter.

Heh heh!

It's a fantasy. OK, so you're suspended and I'm approaching you . . . and I, he continues, wet your asshole and slowly push my cock into your ass. As he talks, I breathlessly rub my clitoris with saliva wet fingers although my whole pussy area is slippery with copious clear fluid.

I have opened up the Lowenbrau by this time and taken a few sips. Jack goes for a cold beer and when I ask, Did you get your beer, he says, yes, I'm going upstairs now—you're being carried up the stairs.

Ha! I'm portable.

Yes, you are. You know, Jack says, I'd like to pee on you when you're tied up.

Would you use your hands?

Oh, yes. I'd squeeze your breasts and part the lips of your cunt and the cheeks of your ass and stroke my hand over your back. You could pee on my cock and balls, he adds.

How about if we change my position of being suspended above the ground?

Wait a minute, he says, I haven't finished with you yet.

Oh . . .

157

There's a crabapple tree nearby he says, and I think, goody I like this, adding detail, and he says, I take two crabapples and place them in a condom with the crabapples at the head of the condom and I insert them into you and jiggle them around.

Oh, that's like the Chinese balls I have—

And I'd tug on them, he says, and push them around inside of you.

And you could put your cock in too.

Would that be in the safe or out?

Outside, I say.

All right.

My turn now, I say. I'm lying on the mossy ground, my arms are tied above my head around a tree and my feet are tied, legs apart, to two stakes in the ground . . . and while I'm peeing—

I'd put it in.

That would stop the flow, you'd have to rub my clitoris—

I would do that, he says.

And then it would start again.

While you're peeing, he says, I'd pee inside of you.

And I'd feel all your warm pee swelling up like a big cock, and then you would pull out, and your piss would flow into the soft green moss beneath me.

I take a sip of beer to wet my mouth.

You should see the *hard-on* I have! he says, you'd love it.

I *know* I would. God, I know I would.

You could do a lot of things with it.

I sure could. I'd put it everywhere. In my mouth in my cunt in my asshole. Oh boy!

Jack says, There. I'm back in bed. Broken thought.

Oh, where were you?

On the floor, he says, but I was getting cold so I got back under the covers.

I didn't notice, I say.

Good.

Is your house cold?

Yes, fairly.

And then he says, I'll have to go.

Don't you want to do it?

You mean rub myself and jerk off and come in big gobs.

Yes, I say, but I want you to tell me what you're doing.

Well, I'm holding my cock in my hand and stroking it and it's very hard.

Yes, I say.

Can you do it? he asks.

Yes, I can.

I am furiously rubbing my clitoris and the swollen lips of my pussy—charged, hot, eager to orgasm, and I hear him groan, oh, ah! ahh! and I rub and then the thrill is on and coming and I'm doing it too, and say oh! oh! my breath squeezed out of me as I come in a convulsion of muscle contractions, cunt squeezing, aching clitoris, tingling.

Hmmm. Very nice, I say.

Let's meet in the woods next Wednesday, he says. If I can't make it, I'll leave a message.

How often do you masturbate? I ask Jack the next time he calls.

At least once a day.

I thought so.

I'd like to lie naked beside you in your backyard, he says. Could that be managed?

Maybe, but too risky with neighbors around.

I like risk, he says, and you do too.

Yes, but it's not a risk for you, but it sure is for me.

I'm screening some videos, he says. Do you want to come over?

Hmm. I'd love to.

But it can't be a late night, is that OK?

When I arrive Jack is sitting in an easy chair dressed in a blue bathrobe. There is bottle of red wine on the fireplace beside him.

Hello, I say. Nice to see you.

What can I get you to drink?

Orange juice would be fine.

It's been a while, he says, coming back with orange juice and Perrier water.

Yes, but I've been busy. I climbed Mount Washington with my girlfriend.

That's impressive!

Thanks. And I'm taking another art class. Watercolor, this time.

While we are talking I sit on my knees on the floor beside his chair leaning over him, quite close to him, in a flirtatious way. He begins to rub my nipple through my black silk camisole.

I might as well take this off.

Please do.

Jack takes my breasts in his hands and gently rubs them.

That makes me excited, I say, when you stroke my breasts. I can feel it here, and I point to my pussy.

I'm glad, he says.

Here, let me undo this.

I untie his belt and open his robe.

If I could touch you, I say, this is what I would do. First, I would kiss you and rub my tongue against yours and then I'd move my finger down to your hairy chest and then here to your right nipple, left nipple, and then I'd go to your belly button and down here to your groin and I'd run my tongue over your balls and take them in my mouth and . . . moving my finger up and around . . . here, pointing to, but not touching, the bulging glans of his penis.

See where I've shaved, Jack says, showing me his shaved balls and inner thighs, and this gives me an opportunity to rub his legs. *A lot of touch* comes in feeling his shaved areas.

I take off my skirt—no panties—and he asks me, Do you still shave?

Yes.

Can I see it?

Yes.

I show him my bare pussy and then I show him the fine white line where the lips join that remains untanned.

Where the sun don't shine, he says.

Let's go somewhere where we can see, I say.

Here on the floor is all right, he says, and I lie back on the floor in front of his chair and put my legs up on the chair beside him. He looks at me and very soon moves off the chair and down beside me on the rug. I wet my fingers and rub myself and touch the tip of his cock and he rubs his cock against my cunt from clitoris to asshole and this goes on for the longest time until he stops to light a joint, first asking, Do you mind?

The air is filled with the sweet pleasant smell of grass.

Do you want some? he asks, choked.

No, thanks.

I watch him, watch his eyes, watch him watching the video behind me on the TV screen—occasionally I glance back—at one point as the man on the screen is shoving it in, I say, I'd kill for some of that!

I watch and wait. He sucks my nipple and I say, *Bite it*, but not hard, and he does.

I wet my fingers and rub them on the tip of his cock and he moves against my fingers, moves into my touch, so I facilitate his cock going a little into my cunt, and it feels *so good*.

Jack pauses and says, I have to take a pee.

Can I watch?

Sure. I'm going outside.

I say, pee on me.

We go outside on the patio and he says, Where?

Here let me sit down.

I sit on a small white plastic table and part the lips of my cunt.

Here, I say.

He pees and pees—a hard giant stream all over my cunt and I can hear it gurgling, the sound increasing as it hits against the opening of my pussy. As he is coming to the end, or just before, I put my mouth in the stream, and then my mouth fills with his urine, tastes chemical, maybe from the pot, and his hot piss runs out of my mouth and all over my breasts.

I have to go, I say, when he is finished. I try standing up in front of him, but can't get started, so I squat down and he walks away and I get it going. Here, put your hand under here.

He bends down and says, a good strong flow.

I make a big puddle on the patio.

I hope no one comes out here in the morning, I say.

Who would? There's no one here but me.

He turns on the water tap and brings the hose over.

Spray me here, I say, and he sprays my cunt and breast and mouth with the cold hose water. Are you going to wash yourself?

I don't need to.

No, of course not. You didn't get wet.

No, I'm going to wash off this puddle, he says, laughing, as he sprays the ground where I peed.

Jack brings me a towel to dry myself and we go back into the warm house. He sits in the chair and I on the floor in front of him and we talk again. Are you happy? I ask him.

Yes.

Anything you'd like to do that you haven't?

Maybe more travelling. I'm fortunate in having a good paying job that I like and I've learned to be happy in myself because if you're not, then when negative things happen, they affect you much more.

Let's talk dirty, I say.

Hard cocks and wet cunts, he says.

Yes, that's it.

He goes to get a beer.

Let me know when you want me to go.

One more beer, he says, and then we'll call it a night.

We return to our position on the floor and things go back to where they were before the pee break.

He says, do you want me to put it in, Angela?

Yes! I say.

He does and says, Ahh! He pushes hard a few times. I am rubbing my clitoris and am wildly excited. He groans and pulls out and says, I'm going to come! and comes on my open cunt and stomach. I rub my hard clitoris with his gooey slippery cum all over my open wet cunt and, as I am almost coming, I say *put it in* and he says, holding his hard cock in his hand and looking down, I can't. I continue rubbing until I come, and then I do some more and say I want you to fuck me in the ass, fuck me in the ass, and I come again.

That took me by surprise, he says, with a bemused look on his face.

Did you enjoy yourself? Did it feel good? I ask.

Yes. Did it feel good for you too?

Yes.

We both get dressed and say goodnight.

Can I hug you? I ask.

Sure.

I give him a big hug and he hugs me and I nuzzle my face and mouth in his neck and smell his cologne.

Call me when you can, I say.

He steps out for another pee.

And now three days later, I am obsessing about Jack all morning. I wash my hair, shave my legs, and pussy. Don't do my dishes, or bills, just pace around the kitchen talking to myself. Up so high, so wired. Words like hard cocks and cunts and, Do you want to put it in? come to mind.

I wonder what he meant about being caught off guard. I decide that he was surprised how quickly he came, not that he crossed the line and put it in—it blew him away. I knew we would touch and I know in time we will end up fucking. It seems the more I talk about the limits as a *hard fact* and unbendable rule—the more he slips through them—it's his love of the forbidden and risk.

Do you know that thinking of the illicitness and *absolute* wrongfulness of all this gives me a charge? Do you know that being bad excites me, being wicked, evil pleases me? *Corrupt.*

I have a dream—we are in bed talking about our planned rendezvous when suddenly I *realize* in the dream that we are in bed and I say to Jack feel me—feel how wet I am from our talk. He does and *it is like an explosion*! I can feel him touching me, then grabbing me, and I reach for his swollen cock and the excitement is intense—unfortunately, I wake up.

Jack doesn't call. Light swish of rain outside my open window. The night is warm and humid. I like it. *Jack is a hot mental fuck*! I love the forbidden.

Oh God, you call!

Two months! I say, surprised.

I know. I've been really busy. What have you been up to?

Nothing much.

Do you have some time?

What have you in mind?

I'd like to fondle your tits. Maybe we could drive down the highway and I'd feel your tits.

Oh, I sigh.

Would you like that?

Yes.

How are we going to do this?

Meet me in the Home Depot parking lot in twenty minutes.

I should have brought some beer, Jack says, when he walks over to my car.

We can go and get some.

Good idea. I'll get in the back seat. I want to fondle your tits while you're driving. Jack takes off the headrest, and I take off my coat. I am wearing my black silk camisole with no bra and a black woolen jacket, the same as I wore the last time we met.

You're looking good, he says, taking in my wild curly hair, green eye shadow, and red lipstick. Driving down the main street, Jack is sitting forward in the back seat with his arms around my seat and his hands on my breasts and his fingers gently, yet firmly, rubbing and rolling my tits.

Christ! This is exciting!

It is hard to concentrate on driving, I say, excited. We stop at the liquor store and I wait in the car. Jack strides back tall and handsome to my car, brown bag in hand, and I think how good he looks! And then we drive back to our spot on a lonely access road by a storage warehouse and sit in the backseat—Jack with his Jack Daniel's.

Lusty Lady, he says.

I like that, I say, smiling.

Do you mind if I smoke?

No, go ahead.

Jack steps outside and lights up—a few deep inhalations. Do you want any? he asks in a smothered voice, holding the cigarette out to me.

Oh, no. Thanks.

A car and then a truck pass by on the road about 500 feet away. The lights beam on us and pass.

Let's get back in, he says, pinching out the burning tip of the cigarette.

Jack is concerned about the steamed up car.

I say, If anyone is close enough to notice, it would be too late.

Jack kisses my nipples and squeezes my breasts.

Oh, I like that . . . will you lick me Jack?

He looks up at me and smiles and then runs his tongue down to my clitoris and rapidly tongues me. Slow circular strokes and rapid flicks.

Ah, oh, I moan.

I am leaning back in the corner of the back seat and Jack is on his knees. He reaches down to his cock and brings his warm hard cock up to my wet pussy and pushes against the lips of my cunt. I rub my clitoris as he nudges the head of his cock into my swollen wet flesh. Ah! Ahh! Jack groans as he pushes in slowly and deeply just as I am about to come.

Look at me Jack!

He looks at me as I come—holding still and then pulling out.

That was amazing control, I say.

Ha!

Jack opens the back car door beside him and I feel a breeze of cold air on my cunt.

I have to take a pee, he says.

Do you want to do it in me?

I'll have a smoke first, he says.

We step outside into the cool late November air. Cool enough that at one point when we were in the car, it started to snow lightly, and the snow melted in fine raindrops and ran down the front windshield

Let me try it, I say, when Jack lights up again.

I inhale and cough.

Jack takes a long drag. I try again and hold the smoke as long as I can. My head feels dreamy, floating.

Here, have another—this is the good stuff at the end.

Jack holds the hot burning tip to my lips and I suck in deeply.

Thanks, my voice suffocated, and now, Jack's face seems to blur and is less defined, almost fluid as though his face is shrinking a little. Ha! ha! I feel *zonked*, Jack!

We take off our remaining clothes—me in my black stockings and garter belt and my jacket still on.

How do we do this? I say. Ha ha!

I lean against the car door and part the lips of my bare pussy, tilting my palms slightly forward. I can lie on the hood, I offer.

No turn around, he says. Bend over.

I bend over with my breasts hanging down and my arms by my side while Jack inserts his hard cock into my cunt. We hold still. Silence. Then I feel pressure, a feeling of expansion. Jack pulls out and a gush of hot urine flows out of my pussy, and it is as if I am peeing now. A huge flood. He finishes off his pee in an arcing stream in the snow.

Jack! I gasp, laughing. I'm standing in your piss!

Let's get back in the car.

We run the motor and turn the heat on high for a few minutes. Jack sits back in his seat and looks at his soft cock and says, Doesn't it get to squirt?

Sure. I giggle. I didn't know if you wanted to.

How are we going to do it? he asks.

Anything you want . . . anything . . . do anything that gets you excited, I say, stroking his cock and taking it in my mouth and sucking on it.

Does that feel good even when it's soft?

Yes. He sighs and shifts in his seat and moves above me. I guide his cock to my cunt, his cock that is becoming hard, and put it in, sinking it deep into my cunt, pulling back and thrusting to the side of my cunt, feeling the length of his hard cock. I move with him tingling to his stroke. A few more thrusts and he pulls out and comes all over his belly and leg and my cunt.

We lie wet together, blissful, happy in my dark car on a dark deserted road with snow lightly falling outside in the cold November night. After we wipe up and put on our clothes. I don't bother with my stockings and garter belt.

I drive Jack back to his car. He waves, smiling, and drives off quickly. My head feels bright and spacey from the pot.

Home alone, he says. Would you like to join me?

Hmm.

Freshly shaved balls—watching some videos.

I'll be right over!

Did you like me feeling your tits while you drove?

I loved it! And the peeing—

That was good!

Jack, you're the only person I know that likes porno and fantasy as much as I do.

Well, I remember what you said.

What's that?

Consider me a blank sheet and write your own fantasies.

Ah, yes, I did say that. I mean it too. I think everyone should have a secret life.

I agree.

We both like the forbidden, don't we?

Yes.

And we are both bad, I say.

I'll leave the patio door open for you, he says.

When I arrive, Jack is sitting in his chair in his open blue bathrobe, feet stretched out, pulling on his erect cock and watching a video.

Hi, he says, looking up and smiling.

Hi.

Can I get you a soda?

I'll have a beer this time.

While Jack is getting our drinks I watch a pregnant woman being fucked on the TV screen.

This is different, I say, when he comes back.

He chuckles. Well, I like variety.

I brought the Polaroids. A few cocksucking shots from my past.

Hmm. Thank you.

I hand them over and reach out to touch his cock. Cold hands. I bend down and take his cock in my mouth. Jack takes a drag on his joint and offers me some. I take a long inhalation and feel a head swoon. Like a sexual swoon and then I do some *intensive cocksucking* on Jack's hard cock.

I'm surprised I haven't forgotten how to do this, I say. I'm just making a pig of myself.

Go ahead and be a pig!

This is what feels good on my tit, I say, offering my breast to him. Hold it between your teeth and suck it.

Jack gently takes my nipple between his teeth and sucks.

Ahh! nice, I say, and then suck his hard cock in deep strokes.

Another drag each. As I feel the swoon, I say, breathlessly, I want to sit on your cock.

Jack smiles. We'll have to save that for another time.

Just one more, I say, bending my mouth to his cock and sweeping my hair up and away from my face. Here's the famous shot.

Mm-hmm.

You'll love the pictures, I say. Lots of cocksucking.

Good.

Jack calls. I have to return the pictures, he explains, there is no safe place to hide them.

We meet at the Playmate Club in the afternoon. The place is crowded. Jack squeezes my tit and slips his hand up my skirt and touches my cunt, which is partially available to him when I cross my right leg over my left and lean on my left arm. We order beer and a beautiful dancer for me.

A COUNTRY GIRL

She asks, Is this your husband?

No, a friend.

I danced for a woman for a year and a half, she says. She came in with a friend.

How about another beer? Jack asks. And another dance?

Jack is really enjoying himself. The second dancer says to me, He's a real sweetie—so polite and quiet.

In the washroom, a woman is saying to a stripper. I really enjoyed your show.

I ask Jack when I'm back at our table, Did you notice that there are more women here than men? What's with that?

Maybe they're getting their needs fulfilled, he says.

Another stripper, who is sitting at the next table, starts talking to me and introduces us to her fiancé.

We're getting married in September, she says. I'm 26 and have four kids. She has a beautiful body.

When we finish our beer, Jack asks me, Do you want to fool around?

Sure.

Do you want me to give you all I've got, he says with a smile and a twinkle in his eye.

Yes, and more!

We go to Jack's car, which is parked in a lot by a bus stop, partially screened by some bushes.

I loved the Polaroids, Jack says, and as a thank you, I made one for you.

Oh, thank you! It is a composite shot of all my cocksucking pictures fanned around the erect fat head of his cock.

I love it!

Do you want to smoke?

Sure. You really come prepared. I take a deep drag and feel the melt in my head and body, a real erotic trance of intense desire. Jack watches for people outside, such as the taxicab parked beside us, while I do an expert suck on his cock.

What do you like? I ask, when I sit up again.

Oh, a variety of things. It is a linear progression . . . and I like to keep it going.

How can I sit on you?

I turn away from him and position myself over the gear box and lower my body so that his cock goes in a little, just the head really, since I can't get past the gears, but oh, how exquisite it feels, how my pussy burns with aching desire, and how I want to plunge his cock in deep and hard.

You know, I say, frustrated with the limitations on penetration, they *should* have planking platforms in the city where you can go and do it, just like they have washrooms.

Where can we go? he says.

I could just bend over a garbage can and you fuck me, I say. *Oh, it feels good to be this excited*!

I suck him again.

I have to leave, he says. I'm late.

I am very wet and wipe myself with my finger and wet his cock. I wet my finger again with my cunt juice and put my finger in his mouth. He sucks on my finger and his breath quickens. His cock is rock hard.

What a scene! Daylight—taxis beside us, people on the other side of the hedge waiting for the bus and walking by on the sidewalk.

I wet my fingers and stroke the head of his cock as he plays with himself.

Do you want me to suck you? I ask.

Yes. Should I do it?

Yes.

I encircle his fat swollen prick below the head and slowly move my hand and there is a spurt and Jack says, Whoops! and white cum spurts into my hand.

I say, next time, I'll catch it in my mouth.

Four or five tissues later, and Jack is cleaned up.

What a huge amount! Have you not done it recently?

Yes, I have, that's just me.

You'll have a lot of kids, I say, and he laughs.

Jack has to meet some friends and he's late so we part.

When I leave, walking past the taxi stand with no drivers, I give a small wave of my hand and Jack winks. I don't look back, but I wonder how I look as I walk away.

Oh my, oh my. This side of heaven Jack is! He called from a pay phone. I'm out having a few celebrating and thought I'd take a chance and call. How about if I go home, he says, and we talk on the phone.

I don't know about that, I say, I have a catchy throat and would cough, so that wouldn't work.

Well, he says, why don't you come by and I'll suck your tit. Bring a movie.

I do and we are sitting side by side on the couch sharing Jack's cognac in a glass and a joint. Pass the pot, Jack says. And wow! it zonks my head—a swoon of desire.

I thought of you last night, I say, playing with Jack's cock, which is wrapped in a white elastic that goes under his balls, and I thought of you rubbing your cock across my cunt and you coming in the car. Would you rub your cock across my cunt if I lie down?

Yes.

I lie down and Jack says, Play with your cunt, and I slip two fingers into my cunt and all around the lips of my pussy.

We both take turns taking a drag and a drink.

Jack watches the porno peripherally and watches me while he jerks his hard swollen cock and rubs it across my cunt and then he pushes it in, oh sweet dream in my cunt, so hot and burning while I finger my clitoris. Many times he pushes it in and takes it out and then back again sinking down on me and I say to him, you hooked me in the car in the storm.

Can I hold your ass? he asks as he fucks me and yes do, and he presses deep and says I want to fuck you and oh, there . . . ah . . . there, moaning and holy fuck, I am burning with his hot cock, burning with his sweet delicious hard deep cock.

Ow! I say when he presses in deeply.

Are you all right?

Yes, I love it! I love it! I love your cock and I love doing this!

Where do you want me to come?

In my cunt.

You want me to come in your cunt?

Yes . . . what is your policy?

I should probably come outside between your breasts in your mouth where do you want it?

In my cunt.

You want it in your cunt?

Yes.

How about if I come in your mouth?

Yes, come in my mouth, I say, as I rub my clitoris and frig myself with two fingers in my pussy—look at me, look at me while I come, and he is excited, so excited, milking his cock and he says, Are you ready, are you ready? Yes. Open your mouth and I open my mouth and big hot gobs spurt in my mouth and flow out and I rub my nose over his wet gobby head all slime dripping down my cheeks and into my hair.

Ah terrific! I spit his cum outside in the garden. He smiles. Still holding it in your mouth?

I can still feel my cunt hot and burning with your cock inside.

Sweet dreams, I say when I leave.

You too.

The phone rings and it is Jack.

I was just thinking of you, I say.

Jack laughs. You made me do it. Next week, he says, I'll have some time. How about coming over and I'll suck your tits.

I'll go upstairs and call you back, I say. Think of something bad. Upstairs, clothes off and dildo on the bed, I call.

I *love* to hear you talk Jack.

I'm lying on my back naked, he says, cock standing up, holding it in my hand. I loved it the last time when I was sucking your tit . . .

And you were leaning down to me and put your cock in and pushed it hard to the back and moved it around.

Uh hmm. I love holding your ass and drawing you to me and grinding our pelvic bones together. I want to pee in your ass. I want to fuck you in the ass.

I loved last Monday in the car, I say, it felt *so* great when you put it in.

I know. I should have been wearing shorts, he says, in the club so you could reach in and feel my hard cock.

Hmm, I'd like that.

I love you sucking my cock I wish you could do that now.

Did you like it? I say.

It feels like it *belongs* there.

It does.

I want you to pee while I fuck you, he says.

Ah, I know a remote road close to my place where we could go. You could go to the neighborhood strip club, have a few pints, watch the girls, then call me up and I'll meet you.

I'll keep that in mind.

Tell me something exciting Jack.

Here's something for you, he says. In the morning when I wake up I get excited. Just yesterday I wondered whether to call you or not, but thought not. Ah, hum, you might not be alone—

You could always take a chance.

Well, I thought about things we had talked about and decided to put a well-greased finger up my ass. I stuck my left forefinger in a jar of Vaseline and with my cock hard, balls shaved, and an elastic band around my cock, I . . . ah, worked my finger into my ass and massaged my prostate.

How did *that* feel?

Felt *good*, a very good feeling.

Like how?

Like the smell of crunchy leaves in the fall.

Wow!

And I thought of how you would like to do that.

Uh, huh.

I want to put my cock in your ass Jack says, and a dildo in your cunt. I'd start with a soft pliable vegetable . . .

Like what?

Well, what would be soft, I can't think of any . . . uh—a banana pepper—

Too hot!

Well, how about a carrot . . . I'd insert a carrot into your cunt, and then my cock and—

I want you to fuck me in every orifice—

I'd slide it in all wet and hard and . . .

Oh, I'm coming, I moan—

And, huh, Jack groans, I'm all slimy up your, ah, ass, and whew, ah, your cunt—

Ah, I'm coming again! Ah, another! Jeez! Jack, I did it four times!

Beer break! he says. I'll be right back.

How good it feels, Jack continues when he is back, to go into your cunt and press deep and it feels so *good* and I want to push it deep into your cunt and ah! I'm going to come huh! ah! A big mess here.

Kisses everywhere, and until the next time you call.

No pining, Jack says.

No, of course not, only fantasies. So until the phone rings, I say.

And you come out of some black hole.

Yes, that's it.

That was an hour ago when Jack called and my pussy is still swollen.

I say, I went to a reggae concert the other afternoon with my girlfriend. I wondered if you were there, but then I figured you were probably sitting in someone's back yard.

Jack laughs.

What time is it?

Eleven-forty.

Before I tell you something . . . I want to ask if you are ready for bed, or, ah, can you go out?

Sure, I can.

Same place?

You know how to get there?

Yes. I'll be there in about 20 minutes, I say.

Before I leave I grab a musty old sleeping bag from the basement, just in case.

Driving through downtown, a half August moon hanging in my front window, a truck ahead, no traffic and the warm moist air blowing through my open windows. Speeding in the dark night to see him, my anticipation so great, awakening my pussy—I become aware of a part I didn't know I had until it is in turmoil . . . like flopping butterflies.

Several turns later on the other side of town and then right on a road going into the dark nowhere and a little down that road, a few more turns and then I see some lights off to the side on a little run-in road. I pull in and stop. The interior light of the car ahead flicks. I get out of my car.

Friend or foe? I ask as Jack steps out of his car.

Jack has brought along a large bottle of leftover wine to which he added vodka and mix.

Tastes like wine, I say. We are sitting on the front bumper of my car. Stars gorgeous, big, popping out of the sky and the half moon, fat, pale, brassy yellow, hanging low in the sky.

I fondle him through his shorts. Jack looks good in brief shorts and tank top.

He says, I'm surprised it is cold.

Feel how cold my hands are, I say. All that wild air blowing against my skin as I raced out here.

Jack smiles and pulls down his shorts and I cuddle his soft cock in my hand. His cock and balls are warm and gave off a moist warm heat. Jack brings out a reefer, lights up and takes a long deep drag. Ah . . . he slowly exhales and smiles.

Here have some.

No thanks.

I lean over his cock, watching him as he takes his cock in hand, and the smell of the sweet grass gives me a vicarious rush, a feeling in my cunt of excitement and my breath quickens and I am in that suspended state again of head dizziness, cunt rush, and I say to Jack, surprised, I can feel that.

It's called a contact high, he says.

Really?

Yeah.

So here we are on my bumper, I say, and squat down in front of him, open my blouse, and take his cock in my mouth.

Just a minute. He pinches his cigarette and pulls his shorts down his legs and steps out of them. My skirt is hiked up baring my legs. As I work over his cock with my mouth, he leans forward and grabs my breasts, squeezing them, pushing them forward and up against my chest. I slowly suck his shaved balls into my mouth and pull on them with my lips, gently tugging with suction. His cock swells. When my legs start to hurt from squatting, I stand up for a rest.

Are you all right? he asks.

We share a drink from the large bottle. I lift my skirt and he says, Do you want me to put it in?

Yes . . .

Here, turn around, he says.

I turn around and lean over the hood on the musty sleeping bag.

I say, Rub it across me, and he rubs his hard cock over my pussy. I wet my fingers and slime up my pussy and he pushes his cock in. Oh, sliding in hard to the back as I bend over the hood, he pushes and pokes and the fucking rush is delightful—rush in my head, rush in my cunt, oh, bent over, his cock deep in my cunt and my wet fingers rubbing my taut clitoris, sharp tip excitement, an ache inside, an ache wanting to squeeze my muscles my cunt swollen, beating on his hard cock as he moves in and out to the back, side hard—bang bang across my bum, rubbing the cheek of my ass with his hand and then a light slap, then another and me saying *harder* slap me *harder* and he slapping me harder and my whole cunt ass hot with excitement. Slap my other cheek, I say. Slap! Slap! My knees are up on the bumper, and now with hard thrusting they are starting to hurt.

I have to move, I say, and slide the sleeping bag down onto the bumper. Now I am standing in wet mud and soil and when Jack enters me again, the toes on my right foot dig into the dirt, and I love that. *I love the whole fucking thing.* Christ! it's exciting, rubbing my clit with a brilliant sharp thrill and a deep aching, throbbing inside as his hard thrusting cock rams into my wet fleshy soft cunt and he groaning, Ahh! Ahh! and my whole body swooning, swirling into my center, my precious source of life and pleasure.

We stop for a rest. I have to go pee and move over to the side in the dark, squat down and wait, wait for the pee to come. I am completely naked except for my wedge-heeled sandals. I hang my head down to concentrate and finally a little comes and then a stream so that we can hear the gurgle as my urine hits the dirt. Watching me from the bumper, leaning back holding his cock, but not clear in the dark, although the moonlight and starlight provide some light, he asks, Do you want me to put it in your mouth, do you want to suck my cock while you go?

Oh, yes! So he comes over and I reach up and take his cock in my mouth as he leans forward and then I am able to start my pee again, but only a little left now so no gurgle only wetness dripping down my pussy on to the ground. I stand up feeling dizzy and then we walk over to the car.

Ah, I say, I loved you asking from the dark, Do you want me to put it in your mouth, and then coming over and doing that.

We sit on the bumper again. I go down on him and suck his balls into my mouth. Does that feel good?

Yes.

The hood is warm, and especially hot on the bumper and the smell of oil as I bend down, take his cock in my mouth and look up at the brilliant plentiful stars in the black night. Crickets singing shrilly, air smelling of moist hay. A delight, and the moon, a fat lush gob over my right shoulder sinking below the horizon. Setting moon. I suck on his cock and then pull his balls into my mouth all stretchy until again my knees hurt and I stand up. A drink for both, another smoke. I lean back on the hood, a swirl in my head, look up at the stars and say, *Van Gogh* stars! and so they are because my head is swirling and so are the stars.

We sit on my front bumper and chat so long that Jack goes soft. I'd like to pass your sperm from my mouth to yours, I say.

We could try that.

What about my cornfield fantasy?

You mean where we fuck between the rows of corn?

Uh huh.

Where I would find you down a cornrow sitting back, legs parted, waiting for me to appear, holding my hard cock in my hand, and then I would kneel down and stroke your wet pussy with my glistening cock and—

I sigh. Yes!

Or, or we could take a cob, carefully select it, and I could fuck you, you know, but I wouldn't rape you with the cob . . . I'd, uh, just tease you . . .

And push it in—

We could take a picture of that . . . a variety of corncob penetrations—but I'd use a condom. You never know, fungus, or whatever.

I never thought of that. Jeez—a condom on a corncob!

Well, you have to be careful.

How about a black condom?

You wouldn't see the corn in the photograph.

Oh, of course not. Then clear—it has to be clear.

We could try a whole variety. Ribbed, variegated.

I like the idea. Adds another dimension.

You're weird, he says.

Now don't *you* tell me I'm weird, I say, laughing.

What else would you like?

Two cocks—sucking two cocks.

How about fucking two cocks?

You mean a sandwich?

No, I mean two in your cunt.

God! I don't think I could get two in.

What about *you* getting a black boyfriend? he asks.

Girlfriend too.

And we'd have a threesome with a *big black cock*.

Absolutely!

Jack is pulling on his soft cock, working it like an expert, watching it grow. I watch too, touching my mouth to his back and arm, which smell of soap—watching him, breathing, silent and then saying, It's exciting watching you do that.

I'm glad, he says.

I like to watch you and imagine you at home in the morning pulling on your cock, rubbing it, making it hard, thinking of what we did.

Jack's cock is growing, he is getting excited listening to me talk about him getting excited. His cock gets bigger and bigger as he pulls it and adroitly twists it.

Do you want to do it? I ask.

Do you want me to do it?

Yes.

Do you want me to put it in first?

One more time, I say.

He looks at me, stroking, rubbing his cock and says, between breaths, if I do that I'll blow my load.

That's OK, I say. You can do that.

He groans. Can I shoot in your mouth?

Yes.

Oh, he is starting to come. I place my mouth over his cock and catch the spurts.

Ahh, he groans.

When he is finished, I say, Do you want it in your mouth?

No, thank you. The moment has passed.

I smile.

Do you want to spit it out?

I guess so. His cum is all frothy in my mouth. I move to the side and bend over letting his frothy sperm drip from my mouth and watch the foam land in the dirt.

Next time, I'll swallow it, I say, moving back to the car. So you changed your mind I see.

He smiles.

When it's finished, it's over.

It's not like that with me. It keeps on going. Next time, ha! I'll have to get you before you do it!

Jack laughs.

We put on our clothes and say goodbye. It is my turn to back out into the dark with a fogged window. I look out my window to see where I'm going. I'm getting used to this—don't need to open my door to back out—just take a quick look to see that monstrous puddle and drive back to the side of it. I notice that he goes clump and revves right through the puddle.

A final wave and I'm off down the dark road and turn left until I find my exit to the highway. Drive home on a deserted, gray fogged road playing K.D. Laing's 'Moon Drives Me Crazy,' the moist wind blowing through my sunroof and open windows. *I am in fucking heaven.*

Did you think about last time? I ask Jack.

Yes. A couple of times I'd wake up in the morning and think about different things and then masturbate.

I guess you were alone.

Yes. He gives a little laugh. It was interesting he says, when we were sitting on the bumper and how we went off on a different tangent.

You mean when we were talking?

Yes. I liked that.

You sitting there soft, I say, no chance of anything, talking.

Yeah.

You know Jack . . . you really are a drug. Yesterday when I was running back home by a cornfield, I imagined that I ran into you going the other way and we, ah, decided to meet in the cornfield on the east side of the road.

Hmm.

I wanted to slip into the cornfield—the light was *perfect*—it was, ah, around five-thirty, but I didn't—there was a car parked on the shoulder down the road and I thought if I disappeared into the corn, the people in the car might come after me.

Oh, my God!

No, listen, my plan was to do something *bold* to tell you about. I was going to take a pee and probably give my clitoris a little rub while I peed just to get a little excitement going—I knew this would excite you. And it would be a little scary because I knew that I would feel vulnerable with my pants down in a cornfield taking a pee.

Well, when I ran by the car there was a young woman looking unhappy at the wheel and two anxious children in the back seat. It was as though they were all waiting for something . . . maybe the mother was upset and couldn't drive . . . maybe they had car trouble. I thought of asking if they were OK, but I didn't want to interfere.

Jack says, Why don't you shove your tit in my mouth?

What do you mean?

Well. What time is it? he asks.

You mean . . . I am flabbergasted.

Sure why don't you?

All right, I'll be there by a quarter to eleven.

Don't bother getting ready, he says, Just bring your tits and your cunt.

Ha!

Go to the same bar, he says. We'll each have a beer and I'll watch you to see if I can get a glimpse of your pussy.

When I arrive he isn't there. I order a beer. Then I see him sitting at the bar so I move with my beer to the bar.

The bartender says, Oh, you've moved to the bar.

I place my cowboy booted right foot up on the rung of the next stool and pull up my skirt over my knee and angle my body towards Jack, showing him my black stockings. There is no way that I can expose my bare pussy and black garter belt. It is enough that I sit here alone with my black silk lace teddy showing and my skirt up above my knee.

The bartender says, What brings you here so late?

Taking a break from work.

What do you do?

I'm an editor.

Oh, that sounds interesting, he says.

Strange, sitting here on the barstool, running my hand along my stocking—so aware of Jack, but not acknowledging him.

An ugly burly friendly man comes to the bar between us and in no time introduces himself to Jack and they shake hands. And then after talking to Jack, he turns to me and introduces himself.

It's my second time here, he says. I just met Jack.

Do you know him? I ask.

No, I don't.

I am enjoying myself enormously.

Jack leaves first and when I go outside he is sitting in his car parked beside mine looking like the cat's pajamas. Smiling. He winks at me.

Follow me, he says.

I follow his car and we end up parked somewhere, I don't know where, under huge hydro towers in a deserted industrial park. *Surreal.* Like out of a movie. We are parked side by side facing in opposite directions.

I slide my seat forward and Jack comes into my car. We sit in the back because of the bucket seats in front. Heat turned up high and the windows steam up quickly—it is November.

Well, well, well. I say, Jack, you're the greatest. *Numero Uno.*

You're bad, Angela.

Thank you. Coming from you, that's a real compliment.

We do a toke and I say, Go down on me.

Lift your leg, Jack says, I want to suck your cunt.

He takes his finger and strokes around my clitoris slowly and it is excruciatingly exciting.

Ah! Take it in your teeth, I say.

Jack moves up to my breasts and sucks on each breast, filling his mouth, and then he takes one, my left, in both hands, holds it, shakes it, and draws it out and points it at his mouth and says, Come on squirt me with your milk.

Oh, I would *love* to squirt you with my milk, I say, breathless—fill your mouth be all over you at once—my open wet *cunt* my breasts my mouth all over your cock your ass your mouth.

Jack sucks my tit, my tit without milk.

I *love* stroking your cock, Jack. I rub his cock, wetting my fingers and hand and encircle his hard swollen head and caress him.

Jack groans. Oh!

I'm so wet, I say, feel me. I want to sit on your cock.

Then I sit on him and shove my tits in his face.

My tits are shooting milk, I say.

They're *real* tits! he says. Squirt your milk in my mouth, Angela. Come in my mouth, sweet milk.

I wish I could. You could get me pregnant and when my breasts fill with milk for our baby, I'd give you some.

Feed me, he says, suckle me with your sweet milk.

And, I say, when my belly is swollen and hard with your baby, you could fuck me slowly and feel my belly quiver and contract and play with my stretched uterus and tightly pulled clitoris and feel my orgasm spread all over my swollen belly as I come.

Jack's eyes are hot intense, his prick enormous, hard as I squeeze him and touch my lips to his lips and run my tongue over his lips, touch his tongue, rub my nose against his cheek, head and breathe hot breaths into his ear while he pushes his hard big cock deep inside me, and it feels delicious, hard, warm, beating, and his mouth on my nipples and breasts.

And Jack, I groan . . . I am lying in the hot sun in my backyard by the pool thinking about you. The sun is hot on my pussy, hot on my inner lips and clitoris and I imagine you coming along and slowly putting your cock in. And then I turn over, and now, now, I am on my knees and arms, bum in the air and you push in, ah, push in deeply, you are very hard and, ah, ah, and now we are in the pool fucking, fucking in the pool . . .

Jack is pushing hard inside me and pulls out, holds back in excitement, he is close. I see the look on his face and in his eyes and oh, does he love that! I can feel a tingle in my cunt as I rub my clit and clench my cunt together and rub in a beat until I come *on the look* in Jack's eyes.

We step outside of the now chilled car into the cold November air to take a pee. Silent crisp night, sound of the car door shutting, cool air on my crotch as I stand, lips parted, trying to pee, but can't, waiting for him to shoot, seeing him leaning back against my white car, tall long legs, milking his cock, such a sexy image. *Oh, God*!

Imagine who called? Jack.

I've been very busy over the holidays, he says.

Have you done any thinking? I ask.

Yes. Things we've done. The last time in the car.

I'd like to take your cock in my mouth, I say.

Yes, push it against your cheek.

It feels *so* good when you push your cock against the back of my cunt beside my cervix. I can hear his breath quicken.

I'm lying back on the bed, he says, my cock is very hard, standing up. I have an elastic band pushing my balls up—the veins are standing out on my hard, purplish head.

Describe how it feels when you are coming.

I feel it coming in my balls and ah! he groans and I rub myself furiously and come too.

Breathy, I say . . . call me next time . . . you have a chance and, ah, I'll hop in my car.

Just like that?

Yes, *just* like that. I would race across town in the middle of the night to meet you!

We say goodbye.

I'm lucky to know Jack, I think. He's someone I can talk to—he's smart, creative, adventurous, *explorative*—the quintessential observer. He is the *only* person I know like that.

A man like Jack, I think, who uses his cock well—hard, swollen, curious, gentle, a cock with a *personality*, will always have me longing for more.

The phone rings at nine-fifteen in the morning. You're awake Jack says, surprised.

Of course! You just caught me—a couple of more minutes and I would have been in my car on the way to the bank.

Well, I'm at home and have a little time before going downtown and I'm puttering around in the kitchen and walking around with a hard-on.

What were you thinking of? I ask.

Different things, things we've done and imagined.

Why don't we meet during one of these morning hours that you have off?

How about that country road when the weather is better?

What would you do? I ask.

Lean against your car and pull my cock out of my shorts and rub myself. And you could do whatever you wanted.

Well, I say, that's *everything!*

Jack says, Where was the last place you had an orgasm?

Two nights ago in bed with the big latex dick . . . It all started when I was getting into bed, I decided to caress my legs and arms and breasts and touch my face with the palm of my hand just to see what it felt like, Then I lay down on my bed and squeezed my bare fat pussy—that feels so good—all soft and squishy and I pulled on my pussy and *that* pulls my clitoris and then I put a finger in my hole and clamped and squeezed my muscles tight to feel what that feels like. Then I tried doing Kegels—

Kegels?

Oh, they're these vaginal contractions, you know, you contract your muscles—imagine if you cut off your pee, those muscles—so I was doing 25 fast 25 slow, but that got me really worked up so I stopped and went and got Jack and that's how I did it—doing Kegels on big rubber dick Jack. Oh, you'll like this—earlier in the evening when I was blow drying my hair, don't you love that word? I turned the hot dryer on my pussy. I was standing naked in front of the bathroom mirror, and I decided to blow hot air on my pussy, just to see what that felt like, and if you can believe it, my pussy lips involuntarily contracted.

Imagine that! says Jack, and laughs. Well, Do you want to know some of the places where I've had an orgasm recently?

Of course, I do!

In the morning when I get up and I'm going to have a shower, sometimes I'll do it. I'll rest my balls on the cool porcelain of the sink and jerk into the sink in front of the mirror.

A while ago, I say, I took the latex cock and did it in front of the mirror to see it going in. In fact, it was the day you called the last time. I like to stand in front of the mirror and open up the lips of my pussy and look at the inner lips and clitoris or I'll turn sideways, part the lips and see the inner lips hanging. Very *cunty*, I say.

Ah! Jack murmurs approval.

I also like to, he says, ah, kneel down in front of the toilet and place my balls on the cold rim of the toilet seat and, ah, jerk off into the toilet. The cold enamel feels good.

I am so excited and slippery wet rubbing my clit that I do it when he says that he shot into the toilet bowl. Fuck!

I'm going to do it, he says and groans. I'm doing it, it's coming!

I rub myself some more, hard, and do it again.

Breathless, we say goodnight. I am wet all day after that.

What were you going to tell me the day before? Jack asks.

About standing naked at my bedroom window and staring at the full moon and masturbating. I imagined that I was fucking the moon—that the moon was my lover. I didn't break my gaze, just looking and rubbing and coming three times.

So you fucked the moon?

I did.

Good for you!

What can we do? I ask. I want to do something bad.

What's bad?

Something risky, I say. What about the downtown washroom scene? Is it possible?

Yes, he says.

When could we do it?

How about tomorrow? Do you know the Forest Pub?

Yes.

Let's rendezvous there at one-thirty. We won't indicate that we know each other and then after a draft, you follow me to a particular washroom and I'll go in first to see if anyone is there, and I'll let you know, and you can come in and go to one of the cubicles. I'll stand at a urinal in front of the cubicle and pull out my cock to piss. You are watching me through the crack in the door. I'll walk over to you and you can tongue me and I'll push it in your mouth—if there's a noise at the door, I'll go back to the urinal.

Do you mind if I finger myself?

No, go ahead, Jack says in his liquid, seductive voice . . . so you're watching me through the crack in the door, while I'm masturbating furiously at the urinal, and then when no one is around, I'll come up to you and shove my hard cock in your mouth and—

Oh, god! Jack! I can . . . hardly stand it, ah! ah! I'm so *excited*—

Would you like to do that?

Yes, I gasp on the edge of orgasm. I'd *love* to!

So you'd give it a try?

Yes! Ah . . .

Why don't you pull Jack out? he suggests.

Don't go away, I say. I'll be right back. I have to go pee.

I'm back to the phone before he is, and I sip my beer and run my hand over my pussy.

Hi, he says.

Hi, I've got Jack.

Good.

Do you want to hear what I did in front of my bathroom mirror?

Go ahead.

Well, on the way to the bathroom, the other evening, I paused in front of the mirror and looked at my naked body—wild hair, fat white breasts, shaved smooth pussy and the large flesh colored bulbous-headed, vein-marked dildo that I am now holding in my right hand, and thought what would it be like to stand in front of the mirror in all my white nakedness and fleshy bare cunt and slip the hard latex cock between the pouting lips of my pussy?

Hmmm . . .

The dildo goes in with ease, but at least three inches stick out—rather like the flat snout of a fat pig, ha!—but very convenient to butt up against the edge of the counter to push against and fuck, ah, fuck, like a real man cock.

Now that my right hand is free, I part the nude lips of my pussy and expose the soft pink flap of inner lips that droop like a large engorged clitoris. The sight of myself in the mirror with this indecent fake cock . . . thick and hard . . . jutting out of my cunt excites me and . . . I start to play with my clitoris. I rub hard—

Hang on, Jack says, I have a beep.

A long pause, and then Jack returns.

Sorry about that. We'll have to pick this up another time—I've got company.

Oh . . . Anything I should know about?

No, it's not important.

Well, I think, when we hang up, *no point* in wasting the moment, so I squeeze my left breast and pinch my nipple and draw it out and with my right hand I rub the dildo on my pussy. Then I switch to my fingers and rub my clitoris and swollen lips thinking of Jack's hard cock stroking slowly, and then slapping my excited wet, swollen, slippery pussy flesh—think of the intensity in his eyes as he does this—and how good it feels to be cock whipped and I trip, roll over into an exquisite climax, savoring the throb and then still rubbing trip again, now thinking of Jack's hard thrusting cock pounding inside me and I come again. *Delightful!*

The washroom scene doesn't work out. Jack shows up at the pub about five minutes after I sit down, looks at me, but shows no sign of recognition. I do the same. He orders a beer at the bar and then about 10 minutes later, I see him standing at the entrance. He looks at me, serious face, and gives the slightest shake of his head and then is gone.

The next day Jack calls. Just calling, he says, to let you know that I'm alive and well. The washroom was locked, and there was no way I could let you know.

Maybe they only unlock the door when there is a conference going on.

That's probably true.

How was your company? I ask.

Oh, you mean the other night? Hmm, let's see, it was a big-breasted blond from an escort service—

Jack!

My neighbor stopped by—he has this real good pot that he's been growing—

OK, OK—

I have a few ideas kicking around, he says. Do you have any?

What are yours?

How about meeting at the Moulin Rouge for a drink. It's a strip club, but just so you don't build up any expectations, I want to be home by 11 and *in bed*.

Jesus. You're worse than Cinderella. At least she had until midnight.

I'd never been to the Moulin Rouge and when I enter through the pool hall entrance downstairs, I ask a young Chinese pool player where the club is. He looks at me and asks, Are you dancing?

Dancing? No.

It's upstairs.

Do you have an escort? the girl at the entrance asks.

No. Just then I see Jack rising from the ranks of the room to come forth as my escort.

There's a girl at my table, he says in a hushed voice. I said that I was expecting a friend.

The girl at Jack's table is young, about 18. Short blond hair and exceptionally thin. She is sloshed. She takes to me right away.

What should I do, she asks, pointing to her pussy, about a rash I get from shaving down here?

I shave too, I say. Powder helps, and with time you don't get a rash.

It's so nice to talk to you! she says. You are *real* cool.

Another girl, Veronica, with huge lovely breasts dances for Jack while I watch intently. When Jack suggests she dance for me, she is shy and flustered and says, I'll have to ask my manager.

She comes back and says, It's OK with my manager, but I don't feel comfortable.

Oh, I completely understand, I say.

Are you a lesbian? she asks.

I laugh. That's the first time anyone has asked me that! No, I'm not. But I have done things with women.

Oh, I've been with women too.

When Veronica leaves, Jack says, wouldn't it be neat to do a hit while looking at those big tits.

Why not? I say.

I've never done it in these circumstances, he says.

The thin friendly girl comes up and sits down beside me.

I'll dance for you, she says. Your friend said that you like to watch and are interested in erotica.

That's true.

I'm interested in erotica, she says, smiling at me. You're well-educated too.

How can you tell?

Oh, by the way you talk, I can tell. Are you his wife?

No, Jack says. A couple, occasionally.

That's *neat!*

What's your name? I ask.

June.

I'm Angela.

Jack watches the bouncers and manager and patrons and then leaves for the washroom. June leaves to dance.

When Jack comes back, I say, Pass the pot and on the way to the washroom, pass a psycho balding man who keeps staring at me and says something that sounds like German, but it turns out that he is gesticulating and talking to someone else. What a fucking feeling leaning up against the washroom cubicle taking a couple of deep drags feeling a spin coming over me and all I want to do is suck Jack's cock!

Back to the table and I tell Jack about the psycho—next thing you know he'll go into the washroom and come out spraying bullets. Now I'm emboldened and kiss Jack's neck when luscious breasted, pretty-faced Veronica comes over smiling to chat. So there's lovely V in front of us and she does another table for Jack and I have my hand under Jack's bum and apply pressure at particular moments. I lean against him and whisper in his ear, I want to suck your cock. Another stripper dances for Jack. She is flat-titted, not good-looking, but flirtatious—leans against him, the-play-with-her-clit kind of girl.

She made me hard, Jack says, after she finished dancing for him.

Did big-breasted Veronica make you hard?

No, he says, there has to be some intimacy established.

June, the thin young blond returns and says, I *hate* that bitch, referring to the plain stripper who just left.

Why?

She stole my clothes and threatened to kill my cat.

You're kidding!

184

No. I could kill her. Do you have any lip gloss or lipstick that I could put on my lips before I go on?

I reach into my purse and turn up my pink lipstick, which she applies and then I turn it back and put it in my purse. I won't use it again.

We stay drinking more beer, running out of money and taking hits in the washroom. Several times we try to do our washroom fantasy scene, but finally give up.

Jack sends the young blond into the washroom to get me—she didn't know why I was there.

When I'm back, he says, The managers are watching from the bar. They really keep tabs on things, no doubt to keep down prostitution and fast money.

After fond goodbyes from Veronica and June to me, we make a final attempt to do the washroom fantasy downstairs in the pool hall, but no luck. Too many watchful staff.

The moon is full, hanging high in the sky across the street when Jack and I walk out of the Moulin Rouge. We have *both* decided that I will suck Jack's cock.

I go to my car and he follows, but soon he is no longer behind me and I'm in the dark street alone and I wonder what happened, but I continue on to my car, get in and sit there. Wait in the dark under a street lamp. Then a car pulls in behind me and parks with lights on and I get worried and lock the doors only to have Jack rapping at my window. It is his car. I let him in. He unbuttons his jeans and I lovingly give him a long suck. Jack lights up and we share half a joint.

I ask Jack to pull down his pants a little to free his cock and balls and as we are doing that, a thin shifty-eyed man suddenly appears in the doorway of a bar which is beside the closed and barred porno shop that we have both separately frequented in the past.

Oh, oh, Jack says. We better move.

Then almost simultaneously a car with lights pulls up in the parking spot behind as Jack says urgently, Pull out and as I do, I look back and see the lights on the roof.

Holy fuck! It's a cop car—probably the prick in the bar called the cops thinking it's a prostitute with a John, who knows?

We drive straight ahead and after indecision about which way to turn, I turn left and go down a side street. I do a U and think of parking in front of a building when Jack says, Go ahead, turn in here.

The parking garage?

Yes.

So down we go, take a ticket and I turn down to the back and a darkened corner.

We've talked about this on the phone—the underground parking garage and here we are sucking tits outside the car on the hood. I am lying back on the hood of my car,

185

black skirt up, black stockings, garter belt—bare shaved pussy, but not freshly, so a little stubble—just like the stubble on his balls as this was all impromptu, my green cowboy boots flat on the hood for grip as he puts his cock in. Due to the angle—he's standing and I'm draped over the hood, we can't get deep penetration, but he pulls me down to the edge. We play this over and over—passing dubie, me rubbing my clit, sticking my finger in my cunt, *teasing*. And we get that lovely poking to the side, the pot spinning our minds, and our cunt and cock playing with each other—it is mind-blowing!

Occasionally there is an alert—footsteps, a squeal of tires and I get down off the hood, pink-cheeked, and back up again. Then Jack takes a piss against the garage wall. I go over and put my mouth on his cock. He stops the stream. I tap his cock to indicate that he should pee, which he does and my mouth blows up like a balloon and then I spit it out. We do that again. His urine is very dilute and tastes like hot tea and I comment on how mild it is and that I'm thirsty, mouth bone dry, and I should have swallowed some.

You're crazy, he says.

He loves to watch this, do this, but double standard, he says, I couldn't do it myself.

There is more on the hood and then I say I have to put my legs down. I'm surprised how I can lie on that hard hood for so long with my legs and heavy boobs in the air, so I put my legs down and he turns me on my side and now I'm lying on my side on the front of the hood, right leg hiked up to expose my cunt and ass and I ask him if he'd like to fuck me in the ass and he says, Yes. So he plays around with his cock to my cunt but the lateness is getting to us and he's not as hard, although it's more the fucking awkwardness of trying to get your cock into a cunt, which is elevated on the hood of a car.

We hear a noise and I get off the hood and we check the time.

Disastrous! Three-fifteen in the morning.

Time to go!

I get in my car and he stands framed in the open window on the driver's side where I am sitting. He strokes his cock and then stops and buttons and belts up.

Oh, no! I say. It's like a movie and this is the end.

We need more time and not so late, he says.

We discover that there is a barricade across the exit to the garage. The attendant comes up walking from somewhere. Two dollars, but we have no money. Jack finds a quarter. I find a dollar. As we are about to drive away the attendant asks, Do you need a cab?

No, of course not, I say.

I am insulted.

Do we seem drunk, I ask Jack, or is it because we have no money and are driving out of the parking lot? Do you think they have us on surveillance cameras?

I wouldn't worry about it, he says, relaxed, smiling.

I drop Jack off in the street and he disappears in the dark walking to his car and I drive home. On the bridge I pick up a car of young black men at a light as I'm blasting my Cajun music. They look over and smile. For a while they're behind me, and I wonder if they are following me, but then they pass and turn off to the right. There are no other cars on the road. Warm moist air is blowing in my open windows and I am joyous.

A month goes by before Jack calls again. I have just taken a shower, washed my hair, shaved my legs and pussy when the phone rings.

Well, hello, I say. How are you?

Can you come over? he asks. And why don't you pick up a few items?

Before I leave, I go over my supplies in a bag—four cold Smithwicks, a mickey of Smirnoff, a bottle of tonic, one lime, and just in case, anal beads in plastic, never opened, and KY jelly.

When I walk in through the open patio door, Jack is sitting on a sofa watching a porno and stroking a huge erection.

After greetings and drinks, I am sitting on his hard cock, my back to him and his hands on my breasts. I take a deep drag, two, and feel orgiastic throughout my body. Hot. Exciting.

Then we are sitting side by side, both masturbating while watching a video of black erotic moments . . . when he gets up to make a drink, he has such a great erection that I say, We shouldn't let this go to waste. He stops and I lie down on the white couch and pull up my loose silk skirt, and spread my legs. Jack pushes his big swollen cock into my cunt.

We fool around for a long time. I suck his balls, put both in my mouth. He sucks my breasts. I suck my nipples. We do tit rubbing—my tits against his. Then he says, Do you want me to slap your cock with mine?

Yes.

He slaps and rubs and I rub my clitoris and the feeling is *exquisite. The head of his cock on my parted lips.*

So tantalizing—he wants to thrust in, me too, but doesn't. Just hanging there in an erotic trance. We continue to watch the images on the screen.

On the floor—hard and pumping. And then, on my side, he jabs so hard that it hurts, but hurts good, and I rub my clit until I am close to orgasm.

Then he goes for a pee. When he comes back, he says, I want to watch you masturbate.

I put my right foot on the arm of the chair, legs parted, and open my cunt with my fingers, put two fingers, three in, and rub my clitoris.

You, he says, all hot watching, you have a lovely hole and this cock wants to go in there.

As I am close to doing it, I say, I want you to put it in, and I rub my cunt . . . here, indicating my wet swollen pussy lips. I want you to . . . put it, ah, in my wet cunt—

Jack is watching me intently.

Do you want me to put it in?

Yes.

I'll watch, he says.

So I play with my clit to the point of fine delicacy and then he puts his finger deep inside.

Do you like that?

Ah! I do it once, twice, as he plays with his hard swollen cock, choked by the thick white elastic under his balls.

Would you suck it? he asks.

I take his cock in my mouth.

Ah! ah! he pulls out and comes in huge deep spurts and convulsive thrusts over my breasts. I watch him come, closing his eyes and groaning. Hot. My breasts are bathed in cum—shiny like glycerin from tits to belly. I run my hand over his sperm and smooth it all around. My little pussy is tingling, beating and warm.

How was your trip? he asks.

Sailing was great.

He is very chatty. Guess what I did earlier?

What?

I stuck the narrow neck of a wine bottle up my rectum and imagined that you were doing that to me. Do you want to hear what I did this week?

What did you do?

I woke up in the morning with a hard-on and went into the bathroom and masturbated in front of the mirror thinking of you lying on the hood of the car in the parking lot. I came all over the mirror.

Huh! I am rubbing myself as Jack talks. I hear him take a deep breath.

The smell of grass, I say, makes me think of when we were in the garage and you were profiled, framed in the open driver's window jerking your cock—you were a headless man. I could see only your upper thighs, cock in hand and chest in the window, except when you lowered your head to smile at me.

Yeah, that was good! How about the bus stop? Behind the hedge.

That was amazing! You *really* do something to me, Jack.

I want you to piss on my shaved balls, he says.

This is a change for him, so I carry it further and say, I'd like to piss on your asshole and it would drip down to your balls and onto your cock and I'd grab your cock all wet and slimy with my urine and put it in my cunt.

Yes! he says . . . and you could piss on my cock, pee on my balls . . . Do you want to hear what I did today driving down the thruway?

Tell me.

I was driving down the thruway and I slipped my cock out of my shorts and stroked it to let it lie on my right thigh. As I'm driving by the cars I look at them and when the driver is a woman, I think, how would you like to have this cock in your mouth? How's this, he says, we are driving the thruway in separate cars, I'm stroking my hard cock laid out on my thigh, my shaved balls also outside the leg of my shorts and you are in your car playing with your pussy, stroking your clitoris, all wet and excited. Or . . . we could both be in the same car, and you are watching me, I am looking down to my hard cock laid out on my leg and then over to you frigging your pussy, and then you are coming—No, he says, we're in separate cars and pulling off the road . . . thank god, I think, let's go for a big fuck . . . and then we park and both get out of our respective cars and you lean back against your car and play with yourself and I do the same and I watch you come and then I shoot out into the air white cum, falling on green grass, green leaves, gobs of white on green and we smile at each other, total strangers, gather ourselves up and get into our separate cars and drive away.

The ultimate highway fuck fantasy! I say. God, I just did it seven times! I can't believe it!

Magic seven, he says, and we sign off.

The next time he calls, I say, do you want to hear this?

What?

It's called 'Ode to a Wet Cunt'.

Sure.

I'm out running, I say, doing my three miles. It is hot and humid and my legs are burning. I am thinking of you. Thinking of longing and fantasy and reality and that's why I'm out running because I am excited like a restless mare in a stall and if I don't move I'll explode or go crazy, so I put on my beat-up Nikes and take to the suburban streets. Familiar, comforting—houses and trees pass by. An old man raises his thumb in salute and says, That's the way to do it, as I pass him sweating, smiling and think yes, I'll do it, I'll run three fucking miles without stopping. I've never done it before, but I'll do it now because I'm high, I'm excited. Thinking of our knee to knee contact in the pub that started it all, thinking of our exciting talk, our fantasies, ideas, encounters—scenes before my eyes like a movie—virtual reality in the flesh. This gets me through the three miles. My legs go from burning to numb to aching and it is all part of the sweet cunt ache that comes when I see your cock or your cock touches my hand, my mouth, the lips of my cunt or the wet aching walls of my pussy.

Waiting for Jack's call when I think he might have some time, and then he doesn't call. Waiting. Not being in control of my state of mind. Resolving never to anticipate his call again. Sitting on pins and needles, all excited in my pussy, wondering if the ringing phone will break the silence—Jack feeds into my elemental self.

At 11:35 p.m. the phone rings. I had gone to bed at 10 because I was sleepy and bored and when the phone rings, I'm in a quasi-sleep. Jack!

I have been surrounded by *friends* all evening, he says, but finally they've left!

We rendezvous at the usual place. Last call, the bartender says, so I order a draft. I don't see Jack at first, but then I see him, looking the other way, and partially obscured behind a pillar. I finish my beer and leave. I wait in my car, which is parked in the parking lot in front. About five minutes later Jack comes out.

I follow his car here and there, everywhere, over dark roads. Sometimes I put out my lights and just follow his car ahead. We stop at one point and discuss suitable locations.

Do you want to try a construction site? he asks.

Immediately, I have a fantasy of lying on bare wooden planks in an open structure, and I think good thing I have shoes on so I won't step on any nails, but when we get there we discover that everything is lit and houses and cars are on either side of the street.

No, not here, I say. You know how suburban people are—they're at their windows twenty-four hours of the day and they'd call the police in a minute thinking that we are going to vandalize the place.

You're right, he says, I know a better place. What's that about the lights? he asks. Is there something with the lights?

No. I was just trying not to be obvious.

We are off again. The other place he has in mind is down a deserted dirt road with woods on either side that looks promising until we come to a dead end and a turnabout by an old house with a bright yard light. Must be the original farmhouse, I think.

Jack stops, rolls down his window and says, Bright yard light.

No kidding! It would be like being on stage—a private performance for the occupants of this solitary house, off in the woods.

Back down the road and then he turns off the road and we stop on a dirt gradient with a huge bulldozer with a forklift silhouetted against hazy lights on the horizon.

Deserted. We get out and stand by the trunk of his car—night air moist, quiet, crickets, bright stars above.

Jack has a pop bottle with a gin and tonic mix and we take a drink. I pull up my skirt and say, Feel how wet I am. Jack moves his fingers over the lips of my cunt and twists them inside a little.

Hmm, he says.

I give him a sideways hug and kiss his cheek, run my hand over his hard cock in his shorts, reach my hand up the leg of his shorts and grab his cock and ask, Are these the shorts you were wearing when you took your cock out driving down the thruway?

They are, he says.

He takes out a joint, lights it, and inhales deeply, many times, and passes it to me. I take a couple of light ones, and it goes to my head in a swoon.

Dark night. Crickets ringing. Smell of moist fresh air and this exploding head and tingling cunt.

Jack leans back against his trunk and I say, Do you think it will dent?

Probably.

Let's sit on my hood. It's already dented.

I climb up on the hood, which snaps as the metal bends, move back to the windshield to give him room. He has his pants off, and sandals on his feet. We both part our legs and watch each other masturbate. I part the lips of my cunt and expose myself. Can you see? I ask. There is a surprising amount of light.

Yes, he says, as I rub and he strokes.

Then he brings his hard cock up to my cunt and pushes in, but the angle isn't good so I sit on him and he leans back with his head hanging over the hood of the car, his throat all exposed, and me sitting on his hard cock and putting my hands under the back of his neck to support his head. We do that for a little bit and then I suggest that he sit back against the windshield and I sit on him that way and reach my finger around to his ass and with his help push my forefinger a little into his asshole.

I have to take a pee, he says.

Wait a minute, don't let it go to waste.

I jump down and take his cock in my mouth and he pees into my mouth.

Tell me when to stop, he says.

I let my cheeks fill out and then tap his cock and pull my mouth away and let his urine run out. I put my mouth back on his cock and he recommences, my cheeks filling out again and then he says, That's it, before I had to stop.

I let it run out and put my finger into the urine flowing out of my mouth.

There, just rinsing my bummy finger.

You're funny, he says.

Now I have to pee. Let me pee on you. Not in your mouth, but on your balls.

All right . . .

Let's go back to the hood. He takes up his position again with his back against the windshield. I've removed all my clothes and placed my skirt behind his head as a pillow. He is naked except for his sandals.

Do you want these to get wet? I ask.

Oh, no, the least evidence the better.

I remove his sandals and drop them on the ground. Then I squat down. He masturbates while I rub myself and try to coax the urine out of me. I'm all engorged. I stand above him and look up at the stars above and my head swirls. Well, I try and try, but can't pee, so squat down, and say, It's hard to pee when all swollen.

Jack strokes his cock rapidly and says, Piss on my balls, piss on my shaved balls.

I feel his smooth balls, stroke my cunt and concentrate. I don't look at him and put my mind to this task of peeing on his balls and cock. I think of squatting in the New Hampshire woods and peeing on the leafy, ferny floor. This does it. I feel the warm urine coming out slowly. Then I can't believe it—it stops. I get it back and more urine flows out, warm. I feel it running off his leg onto the hood where my feet are. There's more, I say, and then when no more comes, I rub his cock all over my wet cunt and push it against my hole.

Now we feel the cool wetness and become aware of the cool moist night air. You're cold, I say.

We get up.

Have you a towel? Jack asks.

Yes.

Jack dries himself and then puts on his clothes and so do I. We sit on my front bumper and lean against the hood and talk.

One thing I regret, I say, is that we didn't come together sooner. I'm not being mushy, but we have a lot of resonance.

To be buddies, he says.

Yes. I like talking to you—we hardly ever talk.

Jack looks perplexed.

I mean we talk, but about other things.

Such as ice cocks?

Ice cocks? You mean melting down with all that heat into nothing?

Like now, he says, looking down at his soft cock. We both laugh.

What time is it? I ask.

He looks at his watch.

Around three?

Very close, he says, five to.

Oh, God! We've done it again.

192

The night is very foggy and my back window is opaque. To back down the slope and turn left into the road, I have to open my window to see. I follow his car and he stops at an intersection.

I go this way? I ask, pointing to the left.

He nods, smiles and we wave and go our separate ways in opposite directions.

When I get home, I am too tired to masturbate, but then I start a little and then decide to do it, thinking of Jack fucking me. I do it so hard and so many times that my arm and wrist and hand are aching, crippled, painful, but I keep rubbing through the pain, stopping a couple of times, and it feels *really* good.

Jack calls and I tell him all about my recent trip to Paris. He talks about our last encounter.

Did you like that when I peed on your balls on the hood of the car?

Yes. A blast! he says, being on the hood of your car—I fantasized about us standing in front of your car—me with an erection, and we're talking.

What are we talking about?

Oh many things—such as the machinery around digging up the ground! Or . . . both of us in front of the mirror . . . Or I'll wake up and think about the two of us, and rub my cock until I come, and then go back to sleep.

Jack gets a beep as we are talking and the phone goes dead shortly after. I run upstairs and dress to go out—black stockings with a seam, garter belt, no panties, my black lacy camisole.

The phone doesn't ring so I call back. After many rings he answers, breathlessly. Family calls, he says. He's waiting for another.

I dressed to go out, just in case.

He says, I'm sorry to disappoint you, but it won't happen tonight.

How about tomorrow afternoon?

That would be better. We can meet downtown.

Will you call back tonight? I ask.

I don't know.

Well, let's save it for tomorrow, I say. If you're not going to call back tonight, I think I'll go out for a beer. I'm all worked up.

Oh, poor thing, he says, and laughs. I'll think of you.

You know, Jack, I've become used to our phone calls. Not that they aren't exciting—they are, but in the beginning, they totally blew my mind. Now I want *more, more.* Do you know what I'm saying?

Yes, I do.

Up the juice, I say. Change the environment, circumstance, and then what do we do?

There's a lot of territory to explore there, he says.

Time. If only we had time, but we don't.

No, we don't.

I sigh. Well let's talk about what we *do* have.

Woods, he says, fucking you in the woods.

How about the cornfield? Just a minute . . . do you want to hear my two biggest fantasies?

Let me guess. Well, the cornfield—

Yes.

And, let's see, uh, let's see . . . tied to a tree in the woods?

Ho! No, you're not going to guess this one—I want to be fucked over my gravesite!

What? I don't like cemeteries, he says.

Oh, I love them! I feel the closest I can get to *infinity*, and timelessness in a graveyard. Anyway, listen, what I want to do is celebrate *life*, and say *fuck you death* . . . so with the right person, which could be you, we would go to my plot—the one I bought a few years ago in a gesture of romantic fatalism—it's in a country graveyard overlooking rolling green hills, and we'd bring along a picnic basket . . . you know, green grapes, cheese, crackers, fruit, bread that kind of stuff, ah, and of course wine, maybe even a bottle of champagne. It would be the harvest moon, a full moon, and you would fuck me on the ground above where one day I will lie below dead. I just think of it as a celebration of life.

Consecrate the ground with a stream of sperm, Jack says.

That's it! You got it! I just want to live above ground before I'm down below dead.

The next time we are together, I say, rubbing the sensitive tip of my clitoris with a wet finger and feeling an exquisite sharp burning thrill, I want you to suck my clitoris. I want you to rub your tongue over my hard shaft and circle the tip with your tongue and take it between your teeth and suck on it. I want to fuck you with my little cock that would grow into a big cock and I'd slowly insert it into your tight asshole . . . you'd have to relax . . . push past the tight rim, and deeply in and I'd reach forward and grab your hard cock—

And you are a woman with fat breasts and big hard tits and a wet succulent fleshy cunt and you are turning your desire into a throbbing cock so you can bum fuck me—

Ahh! Yes . . .

And I'd take my hard swollen cock and shove it up your cunt and, ah, oh . . . we'd be two cocks, ah, fucking each other. Jack moans, and I do it several times with two fingers thrusting wildly inside while I rub my clit with my other hand.

Hmmm! I sigh. Most delightful!

After, I sit for a long time on the toilet waiting for my swollen pussy to go down so I can pee.

What are you doing? I ask Jack when he calls.

Oh, at loose ends. What about you?

Me too.

I'm watching a foreign movie that I rented and I'm getting hard.

So what would you like to do? I ask.

I'd like to feel your tits. Why don't we take a drive along the highway—remember when we did that before?

Yes.

Did you enjoy it?

Mm-hmm.

Do you want to try it again?

Yeah.

Let's meet at our usual bar, he says.

I'll leave my car unlocked and go in and have a beer.

I rush around in a flurry—first a shower, a little makeup, find the right clothes. Try on a loose silky black teddy that dips down in front showing my ample breasts. Black garter belt, stockings with seam, skirt, jacket, black suede high-heeled Italian sandals, and finally my long silk mauve raincoat. A splash of Joy perfume. I leave looking, I think, dramatic, pretty, and sexy.

The thruway is very busy. I arrive at the pub just as he arrives and parks beside me. Jack goes into the pub first. Seeing him again *inflames* me! I sit at a table looking at a silent TV screen showing sports statistics and hockey players whizzing around on the ice. He sits at the bar.

As I anticipated, when I am two-thirds through my large draft, he goes to the washroom. I watch the clock, which moves slowly from 11 to 11:20, remembering his words on the phone about expectation and time frames so that I wouldn't be disappointed and that he had to be back between 12 and one.

All the while as I sit with my back to the bar, my cunt tingles and warms with a glow. I am excited and I feel like I am in Paris again. I observe the strong white light on the bare branches of a tree outside the bar window and the illumination is specific, a frozen image, as if in a painting. Jack comes out of the washroom and turns to the room behind, dallying at the video machine. I drink my remaining beer and go to the washroom. In the washroom while I pee, I look through the crack in the door and imagine him masturbating at the sink, but knowing that he can not enter the women's washroom, which is like a well-lit stall for female piglets. When I leave the washroom Jack is standing at the crowded bar and I have to slightly twist my body to move past him, not looking, and out the door.

We drive down the highway in my car and Jack, who is sitting behind me in the middle of the back seat with his head visible in my rear view mirror, reaches forward and strokes, squeezes and fondles my breasts and nipples through my silk chemise and under the silk on my bare skin.

Feel how soft they are, I say.

Ooo . . . like silk, Jack says, caressing my breasts.

I take a sip of beer that he has popped open and passed to me and I hear him rustling around for his spliff. The whole car smells of grass. I reach back and fondle his cock. Red lights down the highway . . . so we turn off into the city streets.

Why don't you get in the front seat so you can fondle my pussy too? I say.

We stop on a side street and Jack gets in the front seat. As we drive, he pops open another beer and we share it back and forth. I follow Jack's directions and turn off to the right and we are now driving through dark country with pyramidal, ghostly cedars, fences and painted wheels at the end of driveways. How do you know these roads? I ask.

I cycle here.

Later when we are on a potholed road, I ask, Do you cycle here?

No, I run here.

Ah! I'm impressed. I can see him cycling, running, stretching, leaning into the wind, a solitary hero with a mission, a conviction. How I admire that drive.

All the while I'm driving he's dragging on his joint and stroking his cock and we're passing the beer between us. I drive with one hand on his cock. The road after several turns becomes narrow and after we pass a house with a light, I ask if there is anywhere we can pull over.

Here, he says, so I pull over, first on the shoulder by a deep ditch.

You'd better go back on the road.

I stop further down the road where there is more shoulder and we step out into the balmy night for a pee. I'm squatting trying to pee, the wind blowing on my cunt, which feels good, refreshing, and he hands me the reefer.

Do you want some?

I take a toke and holy fuck after about 10 seconds my head swims and there is no way I can pee so I pass the joint back to him and squatting, focus on peeing. I center my whole mind on peeing and become one with peeing and then I start—a few drops, a little burst and then a steady stream bubbling in the soil, making a hard gushing sound and as soon as he hears this he starts to pee in a hard noisy steady stream. When I have finished and he is still going I turn to him and put my tongue in the stream—

Stop! I say, and take his cock in my mouth, tap his cock for him to continue and receive his urine in my mouth until my cheeks fill, balloon and I turn away, spit out and go back to his cock and he fills my mouth yet again, and again I spit, and then only a few dribbles.

Amazing amount of urine! Eight mouthfuls! How long since you've gone?

In the restaurant, he says.

Since we are getting cold in the wind and shivering, we go back into the car and turn the heater on full.

I want to play with your tits, he says.

We get into the back seat. Jack sucks my tits, and I suck his cock, and we both get into a *fucking* sexual trance. Christ!

Jack says, when he is really hard and big, Turn your back to me.

He has trouble getting in—first he's too far back and we're fumbling for the right hole when he says, A car stopped behind.

Of course, I can't see anything because I have my face in the leather seat and my ass in the air. We quickly disengage and sit up, groping for our clothes. Jack steps out pulling on his pants and buttoning up. I look behind through the foggy back window and see some lights. It's getting late, about one a.m. and he has to go. So I do a U-turn and we're gone.

Maybe the people in the house called someone, he says, you never know.

I can't believe that, I say. Surely the cops have better things to do.

Maybe they saw the lights and thought it was suspicious.

Well, I drive. He unzips. Do you mind if I smoke? he asks.

No, not at all. Do you want some?

No, not while I'm driving. Before me is a two-lane road lost in the blackness of the dark countryside with only my high beams illuminating the road ahead.

Do you want me to drive?

Oh no, that's all right.

I'll take the wheel, he says, when again he offers me the smoke.

I take a drag, blows my mind, all the while with easy pressure on the gas while he steers. Fuck! This is the closest to levitation I've come, I say. *Mesmerizing.*

We continue like that—sometimes he steers while I drag or I steer while he does, stroking his cock, squeezing my breasts and me squeezing his cock. Such an incredible experience!—the road going on forever—through dark woods, such a surreal experience, pure magic—sexual desire stretched out, run out on a ribbon of road. Time seems forever.

Pull over here, he says, when the city lights are on the distant horizon. Only half an hour has passed.

Jack strokes his hard cock and I lean over and wetly, fondly suck his cock, all the while the motor is running, the interior light on. I tell him to come all over my dashboard and he tips the head of his hard cock towards him, considers it, and then pumps hard and spurts on the windshield, splat! a lovely long arc of cum dripping down the window.

Wow! white rain, I say, as I catch the spray with Kleenix before it drips into the heating vents. Lovely.

Did you like that?

I smile and sigh. Yes.

We return to the parking lot and Jack gets out.

Thanks, Angela, it was a very exciting time!

Jack, it was incredible!

Then he gets in his car and drives away.

Jack calls at eleven-twenty, two nights later.

I loved driving along the highway, I say, and you in the back seat feeling my tits—

Feeling how big and hard your tits get . . . feeling your warm, wet mouth on my cock . . . and then, when we were in the back seat.

Huh! and peeing, ah, my cheeks filling with your pee—oh, I would like you sometime to pee all over me . . . from the top to the bottom.

Even your hair?

Yes, in my hair too. My hair, my face, my mouth, my tits, and my cunt. I'd have my lips parted, I add.

What about a pee enema? he asks.

That's an idea. You could pee in my ass and then come in my ass.

Hmm . . .

Are you rubbing your cock?

Yes.

I'm rubbing my clit.

Feels good, doesn't it?

Yes.

Jack, I want to watch you masturbate all over the dashboard of my car and my mouth . . . I'd catch your shooting sperm, ah, Jack, I'm close—

Just a minute, he says.

A long pause.

He says, I have to go. I *love* that idea. Let's meet next Tuesday and you can catch me on my run.

I'll check out a spot tomorrow, I say.

I found a gravel parking lot off the road where Jack runs. Completely deserted. No one will come along and wonder why we're there and besides, we'll be siting side by side, and it will look like we're talking.

When Tuesday arrives, I select what to wear—lacy, see through black corset—no stays or elastic, just lace and hooks down the front to close, white breasts and pink nipples showing through and the bottom closing just above the sweet curves of my bare pussy and smiling dark slit. Black nylons with a seam down the back and then over this a full black skirt and my black jacket with low neck. A silk blue scarf draped in the neckline to cover and then finished off by Italian suede sandals. And two cold Lowenbrau beer, in case he wants anything. I arrive at the site at eleven in the morning. He doesn't come by.

He says, Do you want an excuse?

Well, I thought something came up.

Yes, I had a meeting with a client that I had completely forgotten about and I didn't get away until later and had very little time.

That's OK.

What happened the other night?

Well, I've gone out a couple of times with a girl from work and she had some late night crisis.

Ah, girlfriend trouble . . .

Something like that, but she's not my girlfriend.

I see.

Look, he says, I went into the washroom yesterday near the parking lot and it was completely deserted and I thought maybe you were nearby and I fondled myself and became erect.

Did you do anymore?

No. This morning, he says, when I woke up . . .

Were you alone?

Yes. I was aroused and I stood in front of the bathroom mirror looking at myself with a hard cock and I had some fantasies.

What fantasies?

They have to do with bondage.

Oh, I say.

We are in the woods completely naked and I tie your hands above your head to a tree and your ankles are tied too. You are kneeling, he says. Your head is tied back also. I come along—I'm naked—and, oh, yes, you're blindfolded too and I rub my cock, the head of my cock, over your lips. You open your mouth and I put my cock in your mouth and move it around. You can't move your head or body, all you can do is open and close your mouth and move your tongue.

What else?

How kinky do you want to get?

What do you have in mind?

Well, I'd clip your nipples and all the folds of flesh around your cunt—

And twist them—

And put a clip on your clitoris and move it with my tongue, and then, ah, take it off and lick you and then gently place it back on—

Then, now, I'm all tied up with clips on my nipples and clitoris and I uh, ask you to, ah, pee on my face!

No, not on your face, he says, in your mouth and you would swallow it. I would have drunk a lot of beer and you too and after some time has passed, you would pee in my mouth . . . and then, I would pee in your mouth and, ah, eventually we would be recycling our own pee.

Wow! What a neat idea! I say. You know, I read about hash smokers in Morocco drinking each other's piss to get the drug.

Really?

Jack . . . I think if we were together for a few days, huh, something would really evolve, change . . . we would create something new—am I right?

Yes, he says.

I've *never* had that opportunity with anyone. I've never been able to go the distance, take it to the limit. Never! You know, I think you would be a good person to do that with.

Silence.

What do you think?

Uh huh. I'm taking it all in. I'm enjoying listening to you talk.

Blank sheet, I say. Complete freedom, no consequences.

Jack takes a deep breath. Keep talking—I'm on the way to the washroom.

Oh, I laugh, here we go again.

Heh, heh.

Have I ever told you about my detachable cock dreams?

No.

Well, I think it would be fantastic to be able to take home the cock of, ah, a guy that I'm crazy about, you know, sort of put it in my pocket—it would be like a *delicious* hand warmer—and when I got home I could shove his cock into my cunt and keep on *being* with this fantastic guy! Of course, his detachable cock would live, on its own, stay warm, and be naturally hard, and I would return it to him the next time I saw him. I would only be borrowing his cock, *you see*, and he wouldn't need it until we were together again—oh, I never considered how would he go pee—Well, that doesn't matter, does it? This is a fantasy—my detachable cock fantasy. You know, I've thought about this so much that I've actually dreamed this. I laugh. *Pretty fucking weird*, don't you think?

Ha ha! Not if you love cocks, he says.

On Jack's next trip to the bathroom his phone goes dead. I call back. You cut us off.

Nope.

Call back.

It's not that, he says. Dead phone.

Call back.

It's the battery.

You're kidding! Don't you have another phone?

No.

Call back.

He's laughing. I'm afraid it's goodnight.

Fuck! Goodnight, I say.

Jack's laughing. Goodnight, he says. Thanks.

Well indeed! We ran out of battery power.

I see him running by. He doesn't look, so I honk. He stops and runs over. His face is beaded with sweat. He has to get back to work.

I'll come back tomorrow—as long as you have something to read.

Oh, yes, here. I reach for the little book *Cold Mountain* on the dashboard and show it to him.

Are you watching that?

No, no. It's Chinese poetry.

Oh good, as long as you can amuse yourself because I never know what will happen . . . and then the weather.

Did you see the parking lot? I ask.

Yes, I ran by there.

Perfect, isn't it?

The next day I wait on the shoulder of the road beside a row of elm trees, bare branches and dark trunks that screen wide open fields and distant farm houses. I read for over an hour Jeanne de Berg's *Erotic Imaginations*, which I quite like, particularly the S&M scene in New York—but Jack, regretfully, does not come by. Today, I am dressed in black nylons with seams, and a low cut blueberry sweater—I am reading pornography, ready for my fantasy, living my fantasy, even if he doesn't come by.

Five days later, the phone rings. Holy surprise! It's Jack! Turns out I have some time, he says.

What *do* you do Jack, when you're not talking to me?

Do you really want to know?

Yeah, I'm curious.

Well, there's work, colleagues, friends, relatives, sports, reading, and yes, the occasional date.

What do *you* do?

Right now, I'm watching Fawlty Towers.

And the rest of the time?

Same as you.

Are you still seeing your boyfriend?

Which one?

Ho ho!

The serious, not serious one.

Sometimes.

Do you want to go back to Fawlty?

Oh, no! I'd rather talk to you.

I'm sorry about the dead phone. Jack chuckles, but it happens all the time.

Well, do you want to know what I did after the phone went dead?

Tell me.

I had a fantasy about my brother, but I won't go into it in case it turns you off.

Oh, no, no. I'd like to hear it.

OK . . . so I'm left lying on the bed with a small amount of vodka and tonic in a glass on the bedside table, and thinking, well, let's just continue. So I go to the cupboard and take out the monster nine-inch latex dildo, you know—*Jack*, and I go into the bathroom and stand in front of the mirror, insert Jack and rub my clitoris. This is not particularly working so I move up to the counter, press the end of the dildo against the rounded edge of the counter, which leaves about one inch visible. This is much better because now I can *pretend* that I'm being fucked. I rub some more, but my outer lip is getting sore from the short hairs due to shaving—ouch!—so I figure I need some intensity, after all, we're looking for *effect*, so I bring in BROTHER. Brother is now outside the bathroom door . . . I am stepping out of the bathtub where I have been soaking for about twenty minutes, and by the way, playing with myself, but not to orgasm, and I wrap a soft white bath towel around my slim luscious seventeen year old body—

Uh, what is brother doing?

He's standing in front of the open linen closet in the hall and I—

What is his name?

Ah, ah . . . his name is *Charlie*!

Is that his real name?

Of course not, Jack—I don't have a brother! But if I *did* have a brother, this would be my brother fantasy—

All right, so Charlie, your brother, your, ah, fantasy brother—

My *real* brother, Jack.

OK, so your *real* brother, Charlie, is in front of the linen closet, and—

And, I walk right up to him and pretend to look for a new towel . . . my towel is wet, you see—

Yes, of course.

And I *notice* that my brother, Charlie, has a huge erection bulging in his pants. Well, what do I do? I turn to him and press against him. Naturally, he is surprised, but that doesn't stop him from parting my towel and teasing me with his hard cock.

Do you want your brother to put his cock inside you? he boldly asks.

I gasp. I am very excited, and when I recover from my shock, I whisper, *Yes*!

Well, Charlie slips it in—my brother slips his hard cock inside me, and then he says, Do you want your brother to fuck you? Well! by now, standing in front of the mirror going through this fantasy of me and my brother, I am just about to faint with excitement, and all the while I'm looking at myself in the mirror and pushing against a rubber cock, which is deep into my cunt. Ha! I'm rubbing my clitoris, and squeezing my left nipple hard enough to make me come and then my cunt beats and beats on the dildo so that it feels like the dildo is beating and then *Jack*, I go back to *you* because I only used my brother to kick me up, but it is *you*, Jack, that I want to fuck and I do it again and again—my cunt beating on the rubber cock and the rubber cock beating back.

Man, it was a great fuck! No kidding! And then finally, at three a.m. I go to sleep.

I love it! he says. Do you have any more? It makes me very excited!

Oh . . . maybe.

What did *you* do?

Well, I played a little with my erection, which then waned, and I decided to pack it in.

Let's see, I say . . .

Suddenly Jack says, Good*night* with a rising inflection on 'night'.

Whoops! Looks like Jack has company. This time I don't go into any fantasies, but instead go back to watching Fawlty Towers.

Next time I'm watching a Bruce Lee movie when Jack calls.

Am I interrupting anything?

No. Just watching a movie.

I replayed your brother fantasy, he says, and I found it very exciting. I really appreciate you telling me these personal things.

You know, Jack, I think I'm imprinted to like the forbidden.

What about tomorrow? Jack asks.

Can't—a birthday dinner for a girlfriend. How about the next night?

That would work, he says.

Well, call me and let me know. You know, I say, this is so much like Alice in Wonderland. I'm always saying to you—tell me what you want to do—anything!

What I would like, he says, is a woman that we could play with. Remember we talked about this after the friendly stripper episode?

Yes, I do. I still have her number. You know what I'd love to do?

No! I can't guess. Tell me!

I'd like to sit on you, I say, while you're watching a girl who is right in front of your nose.

You know, you can watch two girls doing it, private, he says. I've seen it advertised in *The Sun*.

I'd do that, I say. We could watch and masturbate and play with each other and even, you could rub your cock against her ass, *if* this is allowed, and squeeze her breasts.

Uh huh! Yeah!

Have you ever considered getting together with another couple?

Uh huh.

Would you?

Ha ha! What do you think?

Well, Tony and I had some good times . . . do you want to play a game?

Always.

Well, let's imagine one of your old girlfriends—do you have a favorite?

Ah, actually, yes.

So what does she look like?

Blond, very fit, fabulous boobs—

Why the hell did you break up?

She wanted to get married and I, ah, just . . . wasn't ready.

OK.

We have this gorgeous girl, and naturally she's bi, right?

Right!

So, she would be very happy to have me in the picture—well, Ok, this is the scene . . . you and I and—

Barbara.

Barbara. Well, Barbara and I are sitting out in my backyard on the patio by the pool while you, you are naked except for a chef's apron, you are at the barbecue turning over the Bratwurst!

Do I have a hard-on?

Of course you do, because while you are tending to the sausages, you glance over at Barbara and me—we are also naked—to see us kissing and fondling each other's breasts.

A knowing smile comes on your face as we both get up and move towards you, smiling.

Ah, yes!

Slow motion as we approach you and silently kneel down and together, our lips touching, give you the best blow job you've *ever* had in your life!

Oh, God! I'm close to coming!

No, no! Not yet. There's more. This reminds me, I say, of the time I was invited over to a friend's house to meet his new wife, his second. Turns out they are swingers and he suggests that his wife and I get acquainted, so we sit down on the couch together—

Just a minute—

A long pause.

I heard a noise, he says, when he comes back.

Oh? What do you think it was?

Don't know . . . things have gone fairly flat here.

Well, I say with quickening breath, well, while you were gone I was rubbing myself and had to stop so that I wouldn't do it.

Good for you, he says.

We'll just have to kick you up again, Jack. I'd take that soft cock of yours and make it all wet and suck it into my mouth and take it in as far as I can, pushing it into my soft wet cheek. Then I'd take your mouth-wet-cock, which is now hard as a rock and grown to an enormous length, and slide it between my fat breasts—you are fucking my breasts, Jack, that are like a big fat cunt. You're fucking a big fat whore, Jack, a whore with a huge fat juicy cunt.

Jack groans, and says breathlessly, I'm going to do it, is that OK?

Yes, do it! I am frigging my clit furiously. Do it! You're fucking a whore's fat cunt.

Jack sucks in air and says, I'm doing it! and I am almost there and keep rubbing through his silence and come too and say gasping, Well! *Call me*, and I'm going to keep doing it after we hang up.

I am still rubbing and twitching on my come, when he says, Goodnight, and I breathe a little quick breath as he hangs up and think, *neat*, what a way to end a conversation in the middle of an orgasm, and I keep on rubbing and do it again.

Jack is returning some videos that I lent him. We are sitting at separate tables in a cozy British pub on a sunny Saturday afternoon in January. Jack can't stay, but we talked about meeting in the upstairs washroom on the second floor at the end of a deserted dining room.

When I told him on the phone earlier that I had a shower, shaved my pussy and washed my hair, he said, Oh, then you're all ready for a lapping. That stopped me right there.

Picture this, I said, I am leaning against the wall outside the ladies, or it could be inside, and you come along and get down on your knees and start licking my clitoris.

Yes, I'd like that, he said.

In the pub, I glance over at Jack who seems to have finished reading the newspaper and is tapping his thumbs and fingers together, listening to the music. He seems ready and restless so I'll watch what he does. Will he call me on the telephone here or not? Will he call the pay phone in the entrance of the pub as we had arranged? Jack continues to tap his fingers and then gets up from the table and walks upstairs. After a discrete interlude, I follow. There is a solitary male at a table in the large upstairs room—he is drinking with his back to the washrooms. I go into the ladies and have a pee, then open the door wide. I see Jack in the single men's cubicle and motion him over. He shakes his head, moves toward me and says that people could come upstairs. I step back into the doorway, lift up my full black skirt and show him my bare pussy and the bottom of my black lace teddy. Then I unbutton my tailored black jacket and while he watches I lift up my black silk blouse and show him my luscious breasts beneath the black lace teddy with my pink round hard nipples peeking through the holes. The teddy, which is embroidered with little pink roses is hooked down the middle to my nude pussy. Jack's eyebrows go up and his eyes widen. He looks pleased. He then pulls on his erect cock in profile, just as we had talked about on the phone, and looks at me. Fuck! I am ready to rape him on the spot. I imagine him walking over to me and putting it in. Nothing would stop him; he is saving his cock for me. He will always fuck me, but no, can not do, so fuss around in the bathroom and when we emerge I ask him if he has the tapes and he says, No, they're in his car.

Are you going to call me? I ask.

Yes.

We walk downstairs separately and I return to my table and have a coffee. I watch Jack sitting across the room, purposely not catching his eye. He is writing in a notebook, looking around, tapping, sometimes not too pleased, and then at other times as if he is enjoying himself.

The phone rings. I am deep into my book when the old bartender comes over and asks if my name is Angela?

Yes, I say.

The phone's for you. I take it behind the bar.

Jack says, I'm calling from the phone in the vestibule, which I turn to see. I'm sorry but we can't go anywhere, I'm meeting some friends.

I turn away and say OK. I'm parked near you, he says. So go out to your car and I'll give the tapes to you. After he hangs up, I keep on chatting. I walk back to my table, finish my coffee, pay and leave. I go to my car in the back parking lot, run the motor to warm up, and after about five minutes Jack comes out. I can see him peripherally, I don't look, but as he passes I glance his way and he smiles. I have already popped my trunk for him to put the tapes in. I fantasize that he does this and then gets into the car. Instead, he starts up his car and pulls out of the parking lane, giving me a signal to follow. He turns right. This is better than I thought, I think, he's going *somewhere*. He goes down the first side street and then turns left into a parking lot.

Terrific! I was thinking of suggesting just drive down the road and park on any side street and then you can jerk off.

However, here we are even closer and I pull alongside of him. He looks at me and points ahead. I nod—I don't know what he means—he pulls ahead, turns his car around and drives back beside me, his nose at my ass.

Oh, I say, rolling down my window. Just like cop cars.

Yeah, he says, unmarked, undercover cars.

We laugh. Then we have a playful chat and I invite him into the passenger seat.

But I'm already late for a skiing date with colleagues.

Is skiing a priority? I ask, smiling.

He smiles, acknowledging my thrust, my attempt.

What's 10 minutes more? I say. I could watch you masturbate. Think how you would feel.

Yes, he says, smiling, a little wet spot. Rather than coming off quickly and that's it, a quick spurt, I'd like to come off over a long time, slow motion, savor it. Let's save it for another time.

OK. Very frustrating, I add.

But it was fun, he says. The little things we did.

Yes, it was fun. I wanted to fuck him, but that was unrealistic to think this could happen in the upstairs washroom of the pub. And we did do our fantasy—he holding his cock and seeing me in all my voluptuous loveliness.

Jack calls. I have something new we could try. It is cyberspace, he explains, really neat. What I did, he says, is call the talk live connection listed in the newspaper and by charging $10 to your telephone bill you can talk live for 30 minutes. You leave a message on the line and then people who are on line can choose to respond—you can choose to connect live or leave a message or go on to the next caller.

I choose as my message a woman who is looking with her boyfriend for another guy for a threesome. I get replies and talk to one guy, Rob, who asks me to call him at work—he is taking inventory.

We talk about what we like to do. No Greek for him, oral is all right. He is divorced after two years of marriage, 230 pounds, six foot three, blond hair, blue eyes, about 10% interested in guys, mainly women. When I ask him what he would do—he's done this before, but never two women, he says he'd like it one guy at the top, one at the bottom giving a fingertip and tongue massage. He described all the parts and crevices where the tongue could wander. Man on pussy would taste pussy and then let the woman taste herself. She couldn't do anything until a prearranged time and then what would *you* do? Rob asks.

Well, I'd like to suck, can we use language here?

Most certainly . . .

Two cocks at once.

Oh that's easy—the two guys would kneel with cocks tip to tip.

Oh, no, I say, I don't mean that, I've already done that—I mean take the two cocks in my hand and put my mouth over the top of them and run my tongue around.

Oh, yes, he says.

Or double penetration, I say.

Oh, you like it in the ass?

Sure. And I'd like to have both shoot in my face.

I bet you love to swallow!

Well, sometimes, if I'm trying to impress my partner.

He laughs and says, Where have you been all my life?

I've heard that one before.

I want to meet you, he says. Do you do *one on one*?

Depends, I say, on the one.

Of course, he says.

What do you look like?

Well, long curly blond hair. People think that I'm attractive and I would agree with that.

I bet you have gorgeous legs.

Well, not bad.

How much do you weigh?

I'm five four and 120 pounds. What I *really* like, I say, are my breasts—nice and full.

Thirty-seven, he adds.

No, more like 36. A mouthful—you couldn't get it all in your mouth.

Depends how you try, he says, laughing.

No, he has not seen *The Crying Game*, and he has never tried coke, but he's done some weed.

What about safe sex? I ask.

I get tested every few months with my job because I travel a lot in the Caribbean and I wouldn't get in without the tests.

You know about the three-month window?

No.

I say, my boyfriend and I are interested in watching a live sex show—two women getting together.

You can do it, but it will cost you $150.

That's a lot.

I know some people, he says. I could get it for you for free.

You know, I'd like a black guy, but that's hard to arrange.

Oh, I know some guys. I could introduce you to them.

That's pretty dangerous, isn't it?

Oh, well, you can insist on safe sex.

He gives me his beeper number and to leave a number where he can reach me and he'll call back in twenty minutes, if he can, if not, he'll destroy the number.

At the time I think I might call back *the next day*, and I tell Jack this when I connect with him on line.

Then Jack and I go off line and Jack says, I replied to a woman saying that she was calling to see what was out there. I connected with her, but she couldn't leave her number and neither could I. She said that she was forty and that was probably too old, and I laughed, and said that I liked older women.

Ha ha!

Jack says, you know the washroom in the pub?

Yeah.

Well, I come over to your side and step into the ladies and you're leaning up against the wall and I touch your open pussy with the tip of my cock.

And, I want you to shove it in.

I put my hard cock deep into your mouth, your mouth closes on it in an O and you can't move your lips or tongue and I come in the back of your throat, my cum trickling down the back of your throat . . . would you like that?

Yes! I sigh, rubbing my clit furiously and come once, twice. Did you do it? I ask.

Not yet, he says. Are you tired or would you like to continue?

Oh, continue, I say.

Have you anymore stories about your brother, he asks, something that would make me come quick?

I tell him about the dining room scene—I am doing my homework and my brother comes up behind me and puts his arms around me and places his hands on my breasts and says he loves me. Or . . . you might like this one, Jack, I am standing on a ladder in my bedroom washing my walls—I am very fastidious, heh, heh, and my brother, ah, my brother—

Charlie—

Yes, Charlie is standing at the bottom of the ladder looking up at my bare legs in short shorts. He smiles and says, How's it going?

I notice that he has a huge erection in his pants . . . and, ah, I say, the fantasy, ah, always ends with penetration. That's about it . . . Ah, Jack, what would *you* do, if you were my brother?

Well, it so happens that one time after your bath you come out of the bathroom with a towel wrapped around you and as you are going to the hall cupboard to get a fresh towel you happen to glance towards your brother's bedroom across the hall. His door is drawn closed, but not completely, so that you see him lying naked on his bed stroking his *huge* cock. You have never seen an adult cock before and you feel a sudden rush of confusing emotions—excitement, shame, and fascination. You quickly turn away with your new towel and go back to the bathroom.

You are now a prisoner in the bathroom because you don't dare leave with your naked brother across the hall masturbating. As it is, about five minutes later, there's a knock on the bathroom door and it's your brother—

Charlie . . .

Yes, and Charlie is knocking on the door and wants to know when he can use the bathroom. You are quite flustered, but manage to calmly say that you are finished. *Well* . . . you can't get the image of your brother masturbating out of your mind.

What happens when I come out of the bathroom?

Oh, nothing. *Not* yet.

Oh.

So anyway this is the situation—your parents have gone out to a Sunday matinee movie and your brother has gone out with his friends. That means you are *home alone*. And what do you do, as a virginal teenager at home alone?

I masturbate!

Of course! Now, you are already excited, just knowing that you are going to do this incredibly exciting thing to yourself, but this time you choose to go into

210

your brother's bedroom and lie on his bed and in the very same spot that you saw him playing with his cock, you play with your pussy. The room is warm—sunlight is streaming through the window and you become lost in the wet juices of your virginal pussy and when you make yourself come, you leave a small damp spot that smells of virginal pussy, on Charlie's bed. You open your eyes and look up to see Charlie's reflection in the bathroom mirror and realize with shock and delight that he has been watching you—*all this time*—masturbate. A sharp thrill shoots through your belly down to your pussy and your heart races. And now he knows that you know and emboldened, you get off the bed and move towards the bathroom. Charlie turns away from the mirror and you look at each other and hold eye contact while Charlie jerks off his huge hard cock and his sperm spills to the cold tiled bathroom floor. And now, you, ah, ah, GET DOWN ON YOUR HANDS AND KNEES AND LICK IT UP!

I am breathless. I am so carried away by the continuous stimulation that I do it again, twice, and I am sure that he has too . . .

Would you like to do that? he calmly asks.

Yes! Yes! I'd lick up your sperm, ah, Charlie's sperm . . . off the bathroom floor, which I know is clean. Ohh, I groan and do it again.

Well, Jack *continues*, intensely absorbed in his narration, another day has passed and, he hesitates—what do I do next?

I say, I want you in the bed . . .

Charlie comes to your bed, he says, with renewed vigor, and you are lying there with your legs wide apart, quivering, wanting to feel the tip of his hard cock—well, I am so fucking swollen and raw it's amazing and also *exhausting*, but still I continue defying all laws of nature as to arm and hand power and energy—and now, Jack says, you *know* that Charlie is going to shoot his sperm inside you.

Oh, God!

You say to Charlie, Jack says, Pretend you're Daddy and I'm Mummie and we are making us . . .

Oh, God, Jack! I'm going to do it! and Jack's voice and my mind become one and I feel my cunt all swollen and engorged, like free floating flesh and I say to him fuck me *brother*, fuck me I want you to come inside me and I hear him coming, groaning and *wow*! I am totally, mentally and physically fucked out as I tumble over the waterfall.

We say goodbye.

In the bathroom, out of curiosity, I look at my smarting cunt and see two vastly swollen areas—one the size of a pea pod around my clitoris, which has completely disappeared in a mass of red swollen flesh, and then on the other side, there is a huge swollen water bubble of flesh. I touch it and feel the liquid underneath and it's like touching a water blister the size of a quarter. After all this I ache, I hurt, I am so stimulated so raw and ragged and I think of Jack getting up early in the morning and know that he will have a hard day.

I had just returned from a two-week sailing holiday when the phone rings. How was your sailing? Jack asks. Did you touch yourself on your trip?

No. I laugh. Although lying on the deck one night, I touched my bare pussy and my clitoris, but didn't do anything.

Were you naked?

No. I could hardly walk around naked, and it was cold too. I haven't done anything for *three weeks*! Oh, Jack, I want to feel you all over me. I want you to touch me everywhere. What would you do to me?

I'd like to outline your face with my cock. I'd trace my cock along your cheek, neck, chin, ear, eye, nose, nipples, navel. I'd squeeze your breasts, cup them from behind, as I have done before, and press them together until your nipples are touching. Then I'd turn you over and take my cock and slap your lovely large ass with it and I'd rub my cock between your cheeks and over your asshole and lightly nudge it in. I'd suck your clit as hard as I can and I'd lap you several times, let the saliva flow in my mouth and spit on your clitoris and run the spit to your cunt. I'd take my cock and play it all over your clitoris and the swollen flesh and run it to the edge of where your cunt opens. I can feel where this is and would press against the hot wet slippery swollen hole and then push my cock in and feel all that wet swollen flesh around my hard cock.

All the time Jack is talking, I'm rubbing, excited, and breathing hard. My face is flushed and my heart races and my body burns.

I'd lift my bum up off the bed, I say, and push myself into you and move on your cock, squeeze your hard cock with my cunt and feel you inside.

I'm really hard, he says. And so our breath flows, talking, breathy words, pauses and groans. I let myself become one with my excited clitoris and pussy and breathing and see him in my mind, hear his voice touching me and licking me and sucking me and fucking me. I become so excited that a hot orgasm *floods*, waves over my cunt without me moving, an ache, sweet and exquisite.

Where would you want me to spurt? he says.

What do you want?

He sighs. I want to come all over your side window as you sit in your car with the window rolled up—your face pressed to the glass, eyes wide open and I would shoot and my sperm would splash all over the glass and then the image would decay. The sperm would run down the glass.

I would rather have it directly in my face, so that I could feel your hot sperm and taste it.

212

I'm ready to shoot, he says, urgently. I'm going to do it.

I have been rubbing all this time and when I hear him grunt and breathe into the phone, I come again. We do it together.

Goodnight, I say. It was *so* nice to talk to you.

Down your rabbit hole, Alice.

Ha ha!

Goodnight.

I ran by the parking lot on Friday, he says, to see if you were there.

Too much work, I say.

Let's call the talk line, he suggests, and get off.

I go on line and leave a message saying my boyfriend and I are here getting it on and he has a big cock and we are wondering what it would be like to have another guy here. Give me a call and then I listen to Jack's message.

He says, I'm sitting here in the kitchen seven and a half cut, uh, rock hard, looking for some action, uh, horny, anyone out there wants to work with it? His voice is breathy—I find it terribly exciting.

I listen to a couple of messages—one a guy with leather jacket, boots, eight-inch hard cock looking for someone, *you*, he says, come through the door and see what we can do. You could *start* by sucking my balls.

I answer, Wow! sounds really interesting! What would you do with my boyfriend and what would you do with me?

Well, he calls back—*jeez* once I dropped my message every time I press the number to return to the line, there is *you have another caller who wants to talk to you*. After a while—I am continuously listening to messages callers have left for me and decide it's time to check out the line again to see what is new. I hear the same messages—one guy sounds like he is jerking off on the phone and then there is a black guy desperate for someone's number. He lost it and gives his number so I respond to this and ask if he would be interested in a woman or was he only into guys? I don't have time to wait for a reply since it's been over half an hour and Jack hasn't come on line so I figure he is on the phone to an outside caller. I get off line and call him. The phone rings a couple of times and his answering machine comes on.

I return to the line. In fact, I am really enjoying myself. One guy responds to me by saying, This is a dream come true—my favorite fantasy. He sounds sweet and what is *he*? Slim, brown-eyed, seven-inch cut. Well, don't we talk the lingo. I want to call him back, but I am getting a continuous stream of *another caller wants to talk to you*—talk about drawing them out of the woodwork! The leather jacket guy responds by saying in a rough, husky, biker voice, well, what I'd like to do—your boyfriend

213

walks in the door and comes over and starts sucking my *cock* and *balls* and I'd take his hard cock in my hand and suck on it. I give *great* head and then I'd sit back and I'd jerk myself off. OK, this guy is gay, but flexible, right?

I never get an answer from the black guy desperate for the lost phone number. And after Jack's answering machine picks up again, I don't feel like going back to the line so I think of Jack and masturbate and bring myself off in a wave of ecstasy.

The next day I decide to drive by the parking lot and see if Jack runs by. So I'm cutting across a farm field on the way to the lot when I see a runner and as I get closer I see that it is *indeed* Jack. I slow down and stop. Greetings! He is returning from the parking lot and has to get back and be in the showers in the next five minutes. His face is covered with beads of sweat, but not flushed. I get out of my car and give him a hug. I embrace him and feel how he's wet and pat his back. He doesn't quickly pull away, so we hug.

Get back in the car, he says, and suck your tits.

I get back in the car while he stands by my car and watches me pull up my blouse and expose my alabaster tits.

You want me to suck on them?

He smiles and nods.

I pull my smooth plump breast up to my lips and lick the pink nipple, fondle my breasts, and then show him my white shaved pussy below the lace—no panties of course.

Very nice, he says. Look at the effect, and he points to his cock swelling in his blue running shorts.

I'm getting excited too, I say, I want to put your cock in my mouth.

Jack smiles, reluctant to go.

He says, I was in the process of leaving you a message on the line last night when you called. I had to pack it in—too late. I hope you weren't disappointed.

A little, but I went back on line and listened to a few more messages. Then I thought of you.

Did you do it?

Uh huh.

What were you thinking?

You standing by my car, your cock swelling in your running shorts.

Like now?

Yes.

I was by last week, he says.

Tomorrow, I'll be here.

He smiles.

214

This is what we can do. You sit over there, I say, indicating the passenger seat, and I'll turn to you and expose my pussy, open my legs wide so you can look and stroke yourself.

That would do it, he says. I don't know how much sperm production I'll have with the running.

I just smile at him.

He looks around, lingers. We are parked by a flat field, totally visible from a great distance.

Well, not here, he says.

You'd better go, I say, tapping his hand. Call me. I have so much to talk to you about. I want you to come by my place.

Jack looks at me as if I'm crazy.

Sure, I say, all I have to do is turn out the light at the first sound of noise and you'll disappear like a ghost in the night.

Jack wants to stay. At this rate, I won't even have time for a shower, he says.

Off he goes. I'm left behind with a tingling cunt. I'm *always* surprised at the effect he has on me.

I did go by, he says, but too many people, so I turned away. I thought afterwards about the other day. I could have pulled down my pants a bit so you could see my cock. I'd give it a few pulls and then if someone was coming by, I'd put it back.

Jack's words excite me, the image.

I am captivated, I say. But we were out in the open on flat ground—silhouetted.

I know, he says.

After, I went to the pub where we met upstairs, and had a pint and thought about you. I was excited, and surprised . . . I mean, we haven't seen each other in a long time, and I was hoping, hoping that when you took your shower . . . you would masturbate—but I thought it's probably all out in the open.

No, he says, his voice low, sexy, catching, no *actually*, there are closed shower stalls, and in fact, I did play with my cock. It was nice and hard and, ah, with the warm water flowing over me, I imagined it was your warm piss, and I thought that maybe our encounter would make you excited.

Well, then I was thinking the same thing at the same time.

There is a pause.

Did you do anything?

No, I thought, well time to get on with it, because I had to get back to work.

Ah.

What do you say we call the line?

Don't you have to go to work tomorrow?

Jack laughs. Yes. But we could talk and then get off.

The line isn't too exciting. I recognize Rob, the big guy with his own business. We have our regulars. In my message I add that my boyfriend is a cross-dresser and that draws out a guy who is interested, but never had the courage to try and didn't have the clothes, but he'd like to meet us. Then Jack sends me a message marked 'boyfriend' that really turns me on. He talks about masturbating, spreading the lips of my cunt far apart all glistening and poking his fingers in and then his voice trails off.

When we reconnect off line, I ask him what was he saying and he says he was talking about all the things that I could put in my cunt. Do you have an automatic or a stick shift? he asks.

Automatic.

Well, you could sit on the stick shift.

We'll just have to use your car, I say.

I'd sit facing you, he says—

Wait a minute—Do we use a safe or would it be clean?

Ah . . .

Clean, I decide.

OK, clean, and you lower yourself until the stick shift *disappears*.

And the sparkling white wine I brought—

I wouldn't drink it, he says, but you could bring it along and we'd peel off the foil and you could put *that* in your cunt.

And it has a bulbous top too, like a cock. Just a minute, I say, a bathroom break.

When I get back he says, I have to wrap it up—it's five to one now.

While I was on the toilet, I say, I rubbed my clitoris, which is all swollen and I peed on my fingers. I hear him taking a long inhalation. You know what?

What?

You are standing beside my car and you are going to shoot through the open window all over my face.

I'm ready to do it, he says.

Do it, I say, rubbing my clitoris, all excited, and hear him groan as he shoots at the other end of the phone, maybe five miles away, and I continue, you're coming through the window and all over me, and I do it. When I know that Jack is finished, I say, I'll let you go, but I'm going to continue . . .

Good for you, he says.

Until the next time, I say.

Until the next time. We hang up and I proceed to rub and poke, and *not* counting, do it at least another 10 times.

216

On my way to bed with a glass of red wine, the phone rings. I went by our new spot, Jack says.

I thought you would. I was thinking of you at the time, I say, as I was pulling into my garage. I couldn't go by because I had an appointment.

Well, for your information, he says, when I went back and took a shower—no one there and I thought of what we could do in the car. I'm wearing shorts and I'd slip it out the side—it was a hot day—and I ran the cool water over me and noticed that things were getting engorged and I started stroking myself and getting hard standing straight up and I thought that I could go ahead and do it, and said why not? So I did it.

Where did it go?

Down the drain. He chuckles.

I see his sperm circling down the drain at the bottom of the shower stall.

And then I was all set to go back to work, he says, and laughs.

This morning, I say, I was driving by where the corn is usually planted and saw nothing and thought *Oh no*, No corn this year—

It would be the size of grass now, you couldn't see it.

Oh.

Several times, he says, I've come off thinking about the corn fantasy. I'd come across you down one of the cornrows and you are lying back . . . he gets a beep. I gotta go, he says. Sorry.

Should I call you back?

Yes.

I hang up and find the super-sized dildo that Jack gave me. I run it under the tap in the bathroom until Jack's all drops of water on his non-absorbent latex surface, and then in front of the large mirror, I suck Jack, poke him in the lips of my cunt, and do a little display waiting for the phone to ring. No ring. I call back. Jack's recorded voice comes on. I try four more times. Same thing. Well, who knows what goes on at the other end of the telephone line?

Jack calls to explain what happened the night before. I got a late night call—I heard your beeps. How fast can you get here? he asks.

You must be joking!

No, not at all.

What would you do to me?

You're lying here, he says, legs apart, and it is obvious that I can have my way with you, and I do, thrusting deeply, hard, pulling back and out and then teasing you and slapping your pussy with my big hard rod and you are aching to have me inside again, waiting, and then I slowly push in long hard strokes until you are moaning, *Please don't stop*—and I do it twice listening to Jack.

217

I drive out to a prearranged road in the green wooded country and Jack comes along running—I'm reading *The Hero Within*, waiting for him and look up and see him in my rear view mirror.

Hello! he says.

Hey, nice to see you. He is pouring beads of sweat.

You too. He smiles. *God, he looks good.*

I hand him a water bottle filled with tap water and two ice cubes and he squirts the water over his face and in his mouth.

Thanks.

What do you think? I say, looking around at the green woods and narrow road.

I think you should move down the road—better visibility in both directions. That way we won't be surprised by a runner or a car.

Good idea.

Down the road, Jack comes up to my open window and squirts water in his mouth, drinks some, and then pulls out his cock, which is not small or totally flaccid, but already of some size although hanging softly and pallid, blanched in color. He strokes himself.

It's getting hard, he says, and what a sight, his heavy, hanging, swollen head and cock growing hard.

I take in the view of his pale pink cock in his hand hanging out of his red nylon shorts and the green bushes and trees behind and the absolute silence of the road. No birds, although earlier I heard the chirp of birds. This is all new to me. I don't know what will unfold.

I notice you're not wearing too much, he says, looking at my dress.

I am wearing a low-necked sleeveless cotton vest. I had covered up with a mauve tank top while driving here, but when I pulled off the road to take a pee in the weeds with the fluff of a grey dandelion ball tickling my pussy, I took off my top.

Do you like it? I ask as I take my two full white soft, luscious voluminous breasts and pop them out of my black top, presenting them like two, yes, white doves.

Lovely sight, he says.

Yes. Lovely sight, you too, I say.

He strokes his cock and I look at it—one eye.

It's like looking at a snake. I can't see Jack's face, only his one-eyed cock in his hand and his body up to his neck.

I should have a convertible, you know, because the roof gets in the way.

Jack is dripping sweat on the black leather paneling and down on me.

I'm dripping all over your car.

That's OK.

I take his cock in my mouth and see this sexy image in my side mirror, my cheeks drawing in as I suck him, emphasized by my high cheekbones.

What a fantastic image! I say, and he, an artist and pornographer asks me to adjust my mirror to accommodate him. I do and then he sees what I see.

He strokes himself and I lean forward and just add to his stroke by putting my lips on the head of his cock and taking his rhythm with my tongue and lips open and soft to rub against his stroking cock. Without seeing him, I know he is excited.

Do you want me to shoot?

Yes!

Now I know, *this is the come by and watch me shoot in the car* scenario that we talked about!

Where do you want it? On your face in your mouth?

Both.

Open your mouth.

I open my mouth and close my eyes and he begins to spurt, a big warm burst of liquid in my mouth on my face dripping off my chin into the car and it is sweet, wet, warm and I swallow it.

He groans as he comes.

It's a time freeze frame—the perception—all happening at once and only for a few moments—the anticipation, sensation of imminent coming—the warm hot shot in my mouth and dripping down my mouth and chin and the awareness of his pleasure—protracted, held and then as I swallow his cum. It is sweet—the reflection, I would call it, later, of a cum. Ah, yes, the mirror, his cock, my breasts, and the green green bushes.

We arrange to meet in a cornfield in the lunch hour. I drive to our meeting place and wait in my car. I sip on a fruit juice drink and look around at the cornfields, which are precisely as he has described them. I pull down the mirror to look at myself—I am enjoying the fall corn, cool late September day, looking like rain, when I turn to my right and to my surprise see Jack standing against the wire fence, a little breathless.

Hello! he says.

What a surprise! I smile and roll down my passenger window. I thought you weren't coming.

What do you think? he asks, looking around. It's a little wet.

That's the season, I say. Do you have time?

He nods.

Where would we go?

He points out the clump of corn in the field to our right.

OK. How do I get there?

Just walk in by the gate and straight along, he says.

Well, you go first.

He leaves running and then stops, points down the road and then back to the cornfield and I think, he's going that way and then coming back. I nod and he runs away. After a couple of minutes, I get out of my car, lock up and walk out to the intersecting road. I don't turn into the path to the field—of course not—too obvious for all those unseen observers, I turn right into the intersecting road, and walk briskly as if I am going somewhere. After about 30 feet, I stop, and turn to see Jack running in the other direction and then as I watch he stops too and turns while I walk back to make a left turn into the road where my car is parked and then turn into the cornfield. I walk forward for about 50 feet, and make a right into a row of corn and suddenly I am swallowed up, protected. I wait. *This is fun!* A few minutes later I see Jack coming along looking for me. I am invisible. As he gets closer, I say, *I'm here*! You can't see me, and he turns my way.

We spend the next few minutes searching up and down the cornrow for the right sized cob. I laugh because they all seem so inappropriately BIG.

Isn't this funny, I say, maybe we have to bring our own cob from the supermarket.

We peel back a few. They are all black moldy-tipped. I brought along a safe as Jack suggested to cover the cob. I break off the black end of one and now have half a cob—too thick.

Jack is peering down the row and comes up with one that has a nicely rounded tip, but black, so I go back to one a few stalks down that I had unpeeled with no black tip.

How about this one?

Whatever you like, he says, smiling, it's your choice.

Ha! ha!

Now that we have selected the cob I pull up my skirt and sit down in the cornrow on the ground, which is a little muddy from the recent rain. Jack pulls the safe that I have given him over the corn—clear as he suggested, but we don't have a camera, and squats beside me and teases my bare pussy with the tip. I have opened his pants and finger his swollen cock. I rub my clitoris and Jack gently inserts the cob of corn into my cunt and fucks me. Cold wet mud on my warm ass, hot hard cock in my hand and a cob of corn fucking my cunt.

Can you do it? he asks.

Yes.

Go ahead, he says, and I come, rubbing my clit, on the cob of corn.

I fondle his cock and say, Here, let me suck you.

I'd love that, he says, but I'm afraid I'm out of time. Let's save it for another time. He smiles. You'll take care of that? indicating the safe on the corncob.

Sure, I say, laughing because it is all so bizarre. Don't worry, I won't throw it away.

He stands up, tall above me, and steps out of the cornrow and disappears.

I stand up and become aware that my bum is cold with wet mud. I unsheathe the cob and put the safe in my pocket and walk out of the cornrow, thinking, that was fucking *amazing*!

I am in the kitchen wrapping Christmas presents when Jack calls. I am surprised since I haven't heard from him in months. Merry Christmas! he says.

Same to you, Jack.

I'm sitting in the family room with a bottle of cognac and a cigar, he says, watching some porn, and stroking my cock. I wanted to wish you a Merry Christmas.

Ho ho Santa, I think.

Well, I say, I thought you had vanished.

No . . .

So you called to wish me Merry Christmas, or did you want to talk?

A little of both.

Well, what would you like to talk about?

Let's call the line and leave messages to each other.

OK. Why not? I think.

I play it to the hilt—I have many callers. One guy is a Scout leader. He leaves a message saying he wants to be tied up and would do anything except anal sex. I reply how much that appeals to me—being tied up. Jack leaves messages asking if I am stroking my pussy, am I wet? I send back messages about what I said to the Scout leader and how I'd like Jack to come all over me from mouth to tits, belly, cunt, and back again to my mouth. He answers that he really likes this. Then he says, Maybe we can get together sometime later in the week.

Sure. But I don't expect him to call—I figure he's got a girlfriend.

Nine days later I receive an unexpected call.

I'm calling from a pay phone in a strip mall, he says.

Friends and relatives over, I say, I'll call you back.

I am late calling Jack and when I call he says, When you took so long to call back, I imagined that you had come out to my place and were calling from a pay phone on the chance of seeing me.

Well, the idea crossed my mind, but I take my cues from you. I don't want to fuck myself with you, Jack.

You wouldn't, he says.

What do you want to talk about?

Something bold!

Well, I say, how about I outline your nipples in a bright red lipstick—

And I coat the head of my penis—

Fabulous!

Why don't you come out here?

Let's talk.

Remember the time on the floor, he reminisces, when without even knowing, I pushed it in?

Oh God! How could I ever forget! And what about the first time you broke your rules of no touching, and, oh, I sigh, that was the *last time* of no touching.

Why don't you come out here?

It's late, like ten to one. I'm tired and anyway, I love listening to you, and in fact, I am ready to do it.

Why don't you?

Look, I say. Do you *really* want me to come out there?

Yes, he says. Just throw on some clothes—no fussing and come out here. But I should say that we'll watch each other masturbate. Just so you won't be disappointed. Is that all right with you?

Sure.

Now I'm off in my car driving through the deserted streets. His house is the only one with a light on when I arrive.

There he is sitting on the couch, T-shirt, bare feet with a flask of wine on the end table and a porno on the video.

Well, do we have a good time! He *permits* me to suck his cock and when I offer him a nipple he takes it. He calls the personals and talks and gives the phone to me at times. I take out my lipstick and draw a bright red line around his nipples and then say, Put some here—indicating my clitoris, and he circles my clit in bright red. Do my nipples too, I say.

Crazy wild desire! The time melts. I am sitting with my pussy lips open, head back, masturbating, fingering myself while facing him. He is lying back on pillows rubbing his cock. I can see only his face and not his cock. After a while, he says, I'll have to call it a night.

God! It's *six* a.m.

Go ahead and do it, he says.

Do you mind?

Not at all.

I continue to rub my lipstick-coated clitoris and do it once, twice, and then look up at him stroking his cock.

Did you watch?

Oh, yes! Uh uh! he groans and milks white cum over his belly.

Three weeks later we are talking on the phone. How good it felt to see my cock disappear into your mouth into nothingness, he says.

No sleep, that was tough.

But it was worth it, he says. I can't believe the abandonment.

What do you mean—me, or you?

Me, he says.

I love . . . Jack . . . what I would call *desperate desire*—you know, that euphoric feeling that you get smoking a joint and you just want to be fucked, no matter what.

You want me to come inside, don't you?

Yes.

I love putting my cock in your fleshy wet cunt.

So you really like fucking me?

Yes! And I like you watching me come all over your face.

Oh, I remember when we were in the car for the first time, and it was incredible!

I know—all those fantasies and finally doing it.

I couldn't believe it! I was excited for two days after.

And me, he says, pushing deep into your cunt.

Did you like the lipstick?

Yes. I love having a bleeding red cock.

And now, after I have done it four, five, or more times, Jack is in his bathroom and about to jerk off in front of the mirror.

I say: Jack . . . you get up at night to go to the bathroom and I am sitting on the cold ceramic edge of the bathtub . . . or, as you are peeing into the toilet and looking down, you see that you are peeing into my *mouth* as I am now on my knees by the toilet.

Powerful, isn't it? he says.

Sure is. Next time you take a piss in the middle of the night, you'll think of me.

A pause.

He says, I'm back on my bed—I'm lying naked on the bed, ah, and . . . you come along and sit astride me, legs parted, and, ah, pull up your skirt and show me your bald cunt. I put my cock, he says breathlessly, to your wet cunt and slowly penetrate in as far as it will go . . .

And then, I pull back slowly—

Ah yes! he says.

223

And my cunt is a huge wet mouth sucking on your cock.

Like a straw loaded with cum—my cock swollen and full of cum in your cunt. Oh, Jack!

I am rubbing my swollen, all-ready-come-off-five-six-times clitoris, rubbing frantically over the hard cord, clenching my ass together, tightening my cunt walls and—

I'm ready to do it! I say.

Let it go, Jack groans, and uh! uh! I'm squeezing my ass together, my, oh, virgin ass, and I'm coming!

I am too! And I do it again.

I'll let you go, I say, between short breaths, and clean up.

Did it feel good?

Yes! Yes!

Until the next time, he says.

I am aglow when we hang up.

A month has passed and I am again at Jack's sitting on his cock on the couch. There is a warm log fire burning and we are drinking homemade wine. His cock is deep and hard inside me. I am your brother, he says, and you are sucking your brother's cock, your brother's cock is between your voluptuous breasts, and I look into his eyes and see his excitement, and mine too—his cock deep inside, exquisite, achy, a cunty thrill. I go down on my hands and knees before the fire, spread my cheeks and say boldly, Put it in, Jack.

Jack puts his cock in my cunt and there is *such* delicious ramming.

We go back to the couch and he squeezes my breasts making two full hands and shakes them hard.

Oh, that feels good.

Did you notice that my balls are cool?

Yes, I did.

How about some ice cubes? I suggest.

Uh huh. Sure.

I go out to the kitchen and fill a glass with ice cubes from the freezer. One I rub over his balls and cock and a second ice cube I put in my mouth and suck on it. Then I suck his cock with the ice cube melting in my mouth.

A little later when I'm taking a bathroom break, I say, I want you to do something when I come back.

What's that?

I want you to slap my bum.

Hand or whip?

Do you have one?

Yes.

What do you use it for?

Can't say.

Hand, I say.

When I come back, I get down on my knees and bend over the couch, face on the cushion and after what seems like a long pause he gives my left cheek a hard stinging slap. I am surprised as that is much harder than his previous slaps on other occasions.

Ouch!

Then he slowly rubs the slapped area, massages it and gives me another slap. He varies his slaps from quick light to hard stinging.

Ouch! Ouch! That hurts, I protest, but then the stinging starts to feel warm and now what I really want him to do is to fuck me so I move my legs far apart and he strokes my ass lower down, but then stops after another good slap and sits back on the couch.

Was that more than you had anticipated?

Yes, I'm surprised.

It's getting late, he says, around four.

Oh, I sigh. I should go.

Jack is stroking his hard cock.

But before I go, I say, licking and sucking his nipple, Why don't you do it?

Where do you want it?

You know . . . but how about my mouth?

So I put my mouth over his cock and he comes off in my mouth with me sucking his cock and I let his cum ooze out of my mouth into my glass of ice cubes. What a night!

And then I'm driving through the empty streets and arrive home at four-thirty. The next day all I want to do is think of Jack—all that fucking and slapping. It seems we are going even deeper.

How did you like the last time? Jack asks three weeks later.

I loved it!

Didn't you like it going in, sitting on it?

It was overwhelming! Just thinking about it makes me excited.

I masturbated several times thinking about it, he says. I liked the slapping.

Me too.

So you want to talk?

Sure. Just a minute . . . I'm all dressed. I'll pull off my clothes . . . There.

Have you done anything exciting recently? he asks.

Well, a few days ago, I was fingering myself on the toilet and I could see my reflection in the open mirrored bathroom cupboard. I thought of you coming in the sink, and so I went to the sink and watched myself in the big mirror as I rubbed my clit, squeezed my breasts and, ah, my body so white, ah, I imagined a *big black cock* pushing into the fat shaved lips of my pussy—ah, what it would be like going in.

Did you have anyone in mind?

No, no one—just the cock, ah, that's all I wanted and well, I rubbed myself *furiously and frantically*, and did it watching myself climax, flushing, abstracted look in my eyes and then, I did it again!

I'm close, he says. I can do it anytime, I'm just holding off, I'd, ah, like to shoot in your mouth and watch it spurt in.

I'd suck it all up, I say.

I'm going to do it! It's coming, and he groans.

I'm rubbing myself, I say.

Ah! ah! That feels good. I hope you enjoyed that.

Yes, I did.

Talk to you later, he says.

Your brother, he says, taking a toke, followed by a brief pause while he regains his ability to speak, is upstairs and has just come out of the shower and you go innocently into the bathroom.

Jack's talk is breathy back and forth, a little weed, a little pause—all the time I am wetting my finger and rubbing my clit, on the edge, and have to stop or I'll do it, so pacing, and then we get to the climax. I lean up against the sink, bend over and brother puts his huge hard cock between my virginal pussy lips. And in it *goes*, says my delightful raconteur, pushing into your sweet girl cunt and you feel it all the way in and as I listen to him, I am palpitating, throbbing with this daring outrageous violation, and rubbing my clit, I come off.

I can do it anytime, he says.

It excites me immensely when I hear him groan repeatedly as he does it, and I do it again.

We should make a video, he suggests, next time we're on the phone.

That night I dream our talk and wake up throbbing and excited. All day my pussy is warm and throbbing. What a thrill—Jack, playing my brother. Jack is *exciting* and forbidden.

I turn down the road where Jack runs past green fields, and I see him, standing tall with his hands on his hips as he looks out over the fields—brown curly hair, green shorts, no top, his back to me as I slowly roll up alongside him and say, Don't I know you?

He turns, surprised and smiles, but almost not that surprised. Was he looking for me across the fields? He is dripping wet.

We chat. The road is busy with cyclists and cars.

Maybe we should go somewhere else, I say.

Jack points out a distant curve in the road.

How about there?

Jack runs ahead and I turn the car around and drive slowly after him. While I'm driving, I unbutton my outside blouse and flop out my breasts over the top of my camisole . . . now I look like the bare-breasted ladies of the French court. I pass him running and pull over on the curve ahead and wait for him to arrive.

How do you like this? I ask, when he is on the driver's side.

Very nice . . . I called you yesterday morning around ten, but you had already left. I was going to suggest that you hop in your car and show me your tits.

Jack looks around for approaching runners, walkers, cyclists, motorists.

Can you take it out? I ask.

He smiles and takes out his cock and touches his erect cream colored budding cock against the black rubber molding at the bottom of my open window.

Can I touch it?

He looks around and nods. I touch his cock.

I'd love to suck it.

Give it a try, he says, and I eagerly put my mouth on his cock and suck, briefly. The sweat is dripping off the tip of his nose, his chin in profile, as he looks ahead.

I'd love to rub your sweaty face all over my tits, I say.

Yes, isn't it great? I *love* to watch you suck your tits.

So I oblige him and leave a pink moon fragment of lipstick on my nipple. My breasts are full and white and luscious. Do you like them? I ask.

Mmm. Uh huh, he replies.

Well, cutie, I say.

What?

Cutie, I repeat.

He smiles.

You look nice.

Well, thanks.

Every time someone passes I cover my naked breasts.

Why don't you drive me down the road, he suggests, and I can fiddle with you?

He steps back from my car and laughing, says, you'll have to wash your car.

Why?

Salt from my sweat.

Oh, that's all right.

He opens the passenger side, steps in, sits down on the black leather seat, and pulls out his pink cock and reaches over to rub my nipple.

How does that feel? he asks.

Terrific!

He shags his cock in his hand. How does this look? he asks.

Even better.

When no one is coming and he on the lookout, I duck down and take his hard cock in my mouth and greedily suck it. Down and up, on and off, depending on the traffic. Cars turning, people walking. I show him my bare pussy—no panties. I'm all wet. Feel this, I say and take his hand.

He touches and fingers my wet pussy, and goes back to his cock.

Do it, I say, sucking him.

Just drive slowly down the road.

Why don't you do it?

We see a walker in the distance.

I'm close, he says.

Have to watch out for the leather.

That's the problem.

Here, I'll take this off, I offer, and quickly whip off my long-sleeved blouse, leaving me with a scanty pink camisole, and arrange it in his lap around his cock while he is stroking.

I don't think I'll have much for you.

Meanwhile the walker is getting closer. Why don't *you* do it? he asks.

I don't think I can do it in such a short time.

No, I mean jerk me off.

Oh. I take his cock and stroke it, shag it a few times and he comes huge white gobs on my navy blue silk blouse all bunched up, fluffed up under his cock.

I am excited. We reach the main road—the walker has long passed and I turn left and then at the next light he gets out of the car and wishes me a good trip. I am flying to Paris tomorrow with my girlfriend.

How exciting and amazing our chance meeting! That he should be there, standing, dripping sweat, like a luscious ripe fruit to be plucked, as I drive by late, our chance of meeting remote, but he was hoping to meet me and I came by like a dream.

When I'm back from ten days in Paris, I get a seven p.m. call from Jack.

I'm downtown, he says. I'm going home. Call me in twenty minutes.

I have a shower and frantically look in my closet for something to wear. When I call he is preparing a sandwich.

How was Paris?

Fantastic! I went to a live sex show in Pigalle.

With your girlfriend?

No, she had already gone home. I went with a small tour group.

I'm impressed, he says. I've never been to Paris.

It's my favorite city. You would have loved the show, Jack. I sat up front by the rotating stage. Actually, I was the only one there on my own. No, there was a German, old guy, white beard who had a wife back in a hotel. Am I boring you?

No, not at all.

There was a rotating glass stage, which was illuminated from underneath. Four of the five acts were two women making out, kissing, using a double dildo with condoms. And then there was the stud-fucking scene—I liked that one and believe it or not the naked fucking couple left the stage and went to the back row of the tiered theatre, which had only our small group of six, except for a young guy and two women in the back row. I couldn't believe it, the woman stretched out across the laps of these three and they caressed her with the studly, short, hairy man looking on. Maybe they knew each other. Our group had already left since we had to meet our bus, but the German was still there. I didn't want to go and wanted to see the first act that we had missed, so I stayed and look, this is the best part. The women do a strip tease first and this one, a pretty petite woman, say about 25, comes over to me where I am sitting in the front row and bends down and offers her bra for me to unhook. S'll vous plait, Madame? she asks. So I unhook her bra. What a thrill, Jack! I was in stripper heaven!

I bet!

Can I call you back? I say. I have to go pee.

After I pee, I look for the latex dildo, but can't find it so take the nine-inch hard plastic one that I don't like.

What? he says, laughing, when I call back, you've lost Jack?

While we talk I rub my clitoris and get flashbacks of past events—on my knees on the floor at his place, feeling him in me, his cock going into my cunt.

I like taking roles, he says.

Like what?

Brother.

You know I like that, I say, how excited it makes me.

What do you like about it?

Well, I think it's the excitement of the forbidden—it's like that with us. But that's not the only reason. I *always* was interested in you . . . but the forbidden draws me even more. What about you? What do you like about the role-playing?

Playing in left field, he says, something out of the ordinary, not the usual.

229

Yeah. That's me too. Listen to this, I say. I place the telephone receiver down to my two fingers that I am moving in and out of my wet cunt. Do you hear that, Jack?

We both listen to the wet sucking sound of penetration and withdrawal.

I want to shove my hard cock in your wet fleshy hole and push in deep to the back and make you feel deliciously full and sharply aching.

Ahh! I groan, I'm doing it!

Jack says, I feel like coming over there right now and putting my cock in your warm, wet, swollen cunt.

Hmm. Ah . . .

I want to lie on the cement deck by your pool in the sunshine and play with you as you lie naked and get you *very aroused*, he says. You would turn over on your back and let the sun shine on your bare pussy.

I know. My pussy in the sunshine glows with heat . . . almost like a small animal.

We could masturbate.

I don't know if there's enough tree cover.

It's all in the angle, he says.

Yes, true.

I would suck your clitoris, suck your clitoris into a little cock. Are you inflamed?

God, yes! I'm so hot, *so* pussywet!

My cock is all veiny and hard, he says, and I'd love to shove it in you.

I want a double dildo inside me, I say, and the other end rubbing your cock. Cock meets cock . . .

Ah ah! Jack groans, and I do it again.

Jack comes by running, suddenly emerging between the clumps of dry yellowing corn and he looks surprised, but takes it all in stride, and comes to stand by my open car window dripping sweat and catching his breath. What a lovely sight! It's like watching him in the throws of orgasm, seeing him breathless and sweating.

What are you reading? he asks.

I show him *Henry and June*.

Hmm. Did you see the movie?

Yes, I did.

Like it?

Very much. So, Jack, anything new sexually?

No, most of the time my cock is this limp thing between my legs.

Ha! That sure isn't my experience.

What did you like about our last talk?

Ah . . . all that evolving, changing stuff. We had a clitoris changing into a penis, all mouths, organs, and hands busy.

Yeah, I was really turned on, he says.

Jack runs on down the road and I drive by him and wait at our stopping spot. Warm breeze blowing through the open windows. Finally he comes by sweating, dripping sweat.

Do you want to see if I can get a hard cock? he says, and smiles.

Get in, I say, and he slides in on the black leather seat beside me.

Well, it's fun isn't it? he says, and winks.

Uh huh. I give him a big smile as he pulls out his soft pink cock and shaved loose balls and my hand goes to him and I play with him and watch his cock swell and the head grow plump. Seeing him sitting there—blue shorts, bare legs, his pink hard cock in his hand . . . ahh! Too much! Tell me when you see a car, I say, looking around to a clear road and then wrapping my wet mouth around his hard standing up cock.

So I'm down on his cock, which is pulled out of the side of his pants, and I am gently wetly sucking, tasting feeling him rock hard . . . his silence is tribute to his pleasure. I come up, still no one around.

How do you like that? he asks.

I love it. How do *you* like it?

Feels wonderful.

A few, three or four lovely, long sucks, a little tongue around the tip and he says, there's someone coming.

I look up to see a car in the distance.

I don't have a low-necked top, I say, but I can pull it up.

I like that, he says, and smiles. Wouldn't it be nice to come all over those lovely tits?

All over everywhere!

Let me rub my cock on your nipple.

I bend over holding my breast out and take my tit in between my thumb and forefinger and rub it against his cock—a familiar image.

Ah! my cock is fucking your tit, he says.

This is all *very* exciting. Now there is a dog runner in the distance so I cover up. We have sociable conversation while runner and dog pass.

Well, how do you like to have a hard cock in your car?

Oh, *don't* ask. More tit and cock rubbing, but two runners are approaching so we drive back to the bend in the road where we were parked before.

I get out, bare feet and take a package of tissues out of the trunk, which Jack tucks into his shorts for use—since we both want to see his lovely member shoot. But now a single runner approaches.

Better be prudent than sorry, I say.

I agree, he says.

I turn the car around. As we're driving I hold and squeeze his hard cock and grit my teeth. I *love* the feel in my hand. Like clay in my hands, I say.

We should make a clay cock for you.

I laugh. Oh, yes, but then I'd complain, wouldn't I? Cold, not warm and then it would break.

Ho ho!

Time is running out. The last possibility is a road to the left, but there is a man on a grass mower going by so that's out and what is left is to drop him off at a red light. Jack removes the tissues from his shorts and says, I better get rid of these.

Stroke yourself in the shower, I say, and think of me.

Waiting at the red light he leans in the passenger window, casually, like a runner stopping to chat to a friend at a light.

Call me, I say, even if you don't have a lot of time.

And so we say goodbye.

Jack is at home with a cold and thinks that I might like to know that he has been in bed for two to three hours masturbating, cock up and down, drifting, and now I have a big hard-on, he says.

Have you done it?

No, but I'm about to and then I have to leave. Are you *ready*? he asks.

Yes. I'm rubbing my clit lightly as I sit on the edge of the bed. There is no way I'm going to do it, but that's not why he called—he called for me to eavesdrop on his orgasm.

I love to hear him come—he lets out soft moans like a quiet erotic song, whispered, breath exhaled, squeezed out in ecstasy. Love it! Little waves of excitement going from my pussy to my belly. *Sex with an edge is what I like.*

I drive by our country spot, but Jack is half an hour late so we can't do what we had planned. He was going to sit in my car and I'd watch him masturbate. I am wearing a purple chemise with falling down straps and a black G-string to pull apart to show my freshly shaved pussy. Pull up black stockings and full black skirt to conceal and reveal all. We chat. I expose my plump white breasts, and then I part the G-string.

Will you do it in the shower?

That's an idea, he says. I shave my balls, freshen up.

You can think of me there, I say, sucking your cock, the water streaming down my face.

232

Well, you can think of me tonight getting licked and sucked, poked and squeezed. He looks off in the wind across the empty farm fields and says, musing, it's amazing how many verbs describe pleasure.

I can see that he is quite happily thinking about all those verbs of squeezing, sucking, licking and enjoying each one as the cool wind blows across his long bare legs, skimpy thin shorts, light shirt—a cool, very cool spring day with a pale weak sun, no warmth, all the surrounding fields bare and exposed, only a green haze on the branches, no hiding places for adulterers.

I get a beep on the phone when I am talking to an old boyfriend who is in town.

Hey. It is Jack who says he is naked, rented a couple of videos, about to have a snack—just the sound of his voice recharges me and makes me excited.

Jack calls back and suggests that I come over *now* and watch videos.

I can't come, I say, but let's talk about what we would do if I did.

Well, I'd leave the patio door slightly open—this detail I find exciting—and I would wait for you while keeping myself hard and when I hear you come through the sliding door, I'd stand up naked, my hard cock directed toward you to show you my interest. I'd walk over to the glass door, lean against it, spread my legs and stroke my cock. Then we'd go over to the couch, and I'd ask you to go up to the video image on the TV and get down on your hands and knees—you're wearing a skirt and no underwear—and I'd come from behind and expose your pussy and put my cock between the cheeks of your ass and lightly spank you. I would be *intensely* excited, just knowing that your pussy is exposed, and I could fuck you if I wanted to.

Ohh! I *like* that, Jack.

What are you doing now? he asks.

I'm rubbing my clitoris.

Are you wet?

I slip two fingers into my pussy and I'm all slimy. Yes. Just a minute. Listen. I put the phone down to my two fingers going in and out of my wet pussy with a gush *gush* sound. Do you hear that?

Yes, he says breathlessly.

I am *smelling* my fingers, Jack, which have a light tangy, musky, brook water smell—very pleasant.

Ah! Hmm . . . Do you want to go on line and look for someone who wants to talk?

Sure.

The response is overwhelming. So many men want to do it. Two give me their home numbers. One man, Tom, says ask for a live connection and call your friend and I'll pay for the call.

We get a three-way going. Tom says he likes sex toys. He picked one up that had a bulb that fits over the tip of the penis and there is a little hose and a ball that you squeeze and this thing moves all along the penis. Oh feels really good, he says.

How do you do it? I ask.

A little baby oil.

I like to talk to someone on the phone rather than alone, he says.

How often do you do it?

Once a day. Or every couple of days. I can hold him back that long.

I had a threesome, he says, me and another guy and girl. We both fucked her. Then ten minutes later we jerked each other off with the girl watching. That's the only thing I've done with another guy. I would like to watch two girls doing it.

I've done that.

Did you like it?

Immensely.

I can do it, Tom says, by squeezing the tip of my cock hard and with a little motion or rubbing come off.

No, Jack says, I've never done it that way.

Tom says, I like to stick my finger in my ass when I'm coming.

I did that with a boyfriend of mine, I say. Drove him *crazy*.

You never told me that, Jack says.

Yeah. You know what I like, I say. I like a good slap on my bum, all tingly and hot and wanting it.

You're a wild one, Tom says.

Yes, I sure am!

Jack says, I like to have her down on all fours and slap her ass. I like to slap her ass and shove my cock in from behind.

Oh, I'm going to come, Tom says. Ah! ah!

Are you spurting? Jack asks.

Uhmm, yes, *yes*!

Big gobs of cum, Tom?

Jack and I meet near his place—it is Easter Sunday and there are eight inches of snow on the ground. Wow! So fantastic sitting in his car and he is *such* a bad boy. We have returned to the no contact rule, but in spite of this, he says, Kiss it, and I do. Another time he says, Put your mouth on it.

I am confused.

Open your mouth wide, he says, and put your mouth over it.

I do.

He says, *Control.*

I breathe in and out on his cock with my mouth an O around it, not touching.

A second time he says, kiss it. I do. His cock is wet with pre cum.

I masturbate and have three orgasms while he watches and then I stroke him off. *It is all so exciting.* It is slow and lingering like a dream. At one point, he opens up the sunroof and chunks of wet snow fall on the gearshift and us.

When we leave, he first, I am left behind scraping my car—his tracks are solitary in the snow. I follow them back to his house where they turn into his lane and then I continue home, driving carefully in the snow.

I like face-to-face, I say, next time we are talking on the phone.

I agree, he says, except phone or voice contact allows the inner self to come out, don't you think, without the visual prejudices, say someone is fat or old.

You're right.

Jack is in his kitchen with his cock out, working on it, drinking some wine and keeping his eye on a pizza, which he takes out when it is done. While we talk, I do it at least four or five times.

How about if I go out for some beer and we meet, he suggests. I want to show you my cock.

I'd love to, but I have to prepare for a meeting tomorrow.

I understand, he says.

If you are doing it later, I say, call me.

A little after eleven he calls. I've picked up three pornos, he says, teenage sex, transsexuals and group grope.

More hot talk. Hot, hot. Lusty naked teenagers kissing and sucking cock and oh, ah, and I do it again and again and *again.*

I love it when you're a sex pig! he says.

Me too.

I'm having *another* cock rush, he says, breathless. Ah! I can feel it in my balls and ah . . . it's coming up my cock and ah, here it comes—gobs and gobs. What a mess! I'd better clean up. Until the next time, he says. Goodnight.

Jack suggests that I meet him tomorrow at a park near his place, if it's not raining, and I can watch him masturbate.

I could give you a present, he says for your next birthday. And maybe tomorrow morning we could . . .

But the *rules*, Jack—

Well, you can masturbate me.

Sure . . .

235

He says, I like to think of all the different places, occasions that we have gotten together.

The next morning it is raining, but he calls as prearranged and says, It looks like it's off. So I relax into having some breakfast, reading, not bothering to wash. Half an hour later the phone rings and he says the rain has stopped at his place—it's like an Irish mist.

It's still raining here, I say.

Would you like to come out?

Yes.

I wash, fluff my hair, and leave in rain, which becomes heavy as I am driving and then diminishes to nothing. An Irish mist, as he said, where he lives. I wait in the parking area of the park. There is another car parked with a man at the wheel. Jack comes along running, sweating. As he approaches the car I am surprised how tall and *big* he is. He looks good for a man running in a light drizzle, dripping, catching his breath. And, green eyes.

Jack gets in my car and we chat.

Do you want to see my cock? he asks.

Yes. It is all so playful.

He releases his cock from his running shorts. Soft, he says, flopping it on his leg. He begins pulling back the skin sliding it up and down until it is a little turgid. Heavier, he says.

I feel it, lift it. Yes, definitely. Spongy.

Soon he has his cock hard.

I'll pull down my pants a little, he says, as he slides them down to his knees. He inclines the seat and leans back with his cock straight up in the air. So you want to do this? he asks.

Yes.

I spill my ample white breasts out of my low cut dress.

Very nice.

Jack plays with my right nipple. You can have the other one, he says.

I take him in hand, stroke him easy, hard.

Take your other hand, he says, and grab my sack and pull my balls away from my body. Pull down. Yes, that's it.

We do this for a few timeless minutes. The rain is tapping hard on the car, and all the windows are fogged.

Isn't this *great*? he asks. Sitting here in the car in the rain and masturbating?

I smile and nod.

Yes, it *is* great! I am enjoying this very much.

Do you want me to do it now or should we continue a little until the rain stops?

Let's continue.

Timeless time. I watch him intensely, all the time stroking, sliding his hard upright cock, occasionally pausing to dab the clear oozing fluid from the small hole at the tip of his penis and rubbing the fluid over the head of his cock.

When I come, he says, let go of my balls and stroke lightly, not hard.

And that is precisely what I do. He comes in gallons, moaning in ecstasy, shooting hot spurts of cum like a geyser flowing all down my clenched hand. The first shot splashes on my other forearm. I've never seen so much wet slimy, white cum before! It is thrilling. What a turn-on! He reaches for a tissue from the back seat and I mop up.

This image of his erect spurting cock shooting pornographic volumes of cum is in my mind forever.

Jack calls at nine in the morning and leaves a message: Hello, sleepy head.

Jack has called nearly everyday . . . sometimes twice a day.

Jack defines the erotic for me. I'll probably never meet anyone like him.

More messages from Jack—

Hey Angela, how are you doing? Thought I would say a quick hi. I'm sure you figured out what happened yesterday, just sounded like my friend, ah, was all of a sudden around the corner as it turned out not to be the case, but I didn't even get a chance to say a proper, oh sorry, gotta go, sort of routine. Anyhow, I'm not sure what type of day you had yesterday and after you got things done if you felt horny started fantasizing about sex cock cum masturbation and all that stuff, *oooh*, who knows? Neat doing it, isn't it? I've seen you masturbate I've seen you suck on your tit seen you finger yourself spread your pussy for me and I've slapped your pussy remember those days? Those occasions . . . those times . . . when I wasn't supposed to put my cock inside you? We were so high so, uh, horny and high on sex . . . we were so high and horny on sex that we let it go in a bit—forbidden! Forbidden sex is fun, isn't it? I've got my cock rock hard right now talking to you. My girlfriend is still upstairs we had great sex yesterday, sucked and licked each other, fucked each other, exchanged bodily fluids. I'd like to have you masturbate and watch, ah, maybe, ah, lick her pussy, when my cock's inside her, ah, talk to you later.

Hey! How are you doing sleepy head? Just checking to see if you might be up at this hour. It's a quarter after nine Saturday morning. Anyhow, just checking in to see if I can catch you with your panties down.

Message marked urgent!

Hi! Good morning Angela. How are you doing? Just checking in on the off chance that you might be leaving your phone on. It's early Saturday morning—it's seven o'clock, just lying here sliding my foreskin up and down on the top of my shaft over my head and I can feel my balls moving bouncing on my asshole nice and hard thinking about sex. How are you doing? Enjoyed coming with you before. I assume that nobody else is listening to these messages ah, your messages, hence this type of message.

Hey—how are you doing? Just was thinking about you listening to my message. I know you're busy, things like that, but I know that you are going to listen to the message. Anyway, the whole process has kinda aroused me and maybe I'll just try to catch you and leave a message for you to listen to, anyway, going for a run, all my clothes off. I started playing with my nipples and my balls decided to sit down and put my feet up on the coffee table and get myself, get myself, ah, completely hard, which I am, guess what's going to come out of my cock in a second—hmm um, yep, you got it, ah! Take care. Hmm.

Jack says, I have good news and bad news. What do you want to hear first?
The bad news.
All right. My girlfriend left me.
You're kidding!
Nope. Seems she likes the guy at work more than me.
How do you know this?
She told me.
Oh, Jack, I'm sorry.
Don't be. I could see it coming.
How do you feel about it?
Surprisingly, OK.
Well, that's good.
Do you want to hear the good news?
Oh, yes.
I have a present for you. A birthday present.
But it's not my birthday.
It's an early birthday present.
Oh. Can you tell me what it is?
No. It's a surprise.

Jack says, Take one, as he clacks the small chalkboard.
A and J, take one, Jack says, showing the chalkboard to the camera, and clacks again.

Ha ha!

I am sitting demurely on his white couch wearing a loose blue cotton dress patterned with quarter moons and stars. Jack has placed small yellow lights on the back of the couch to be festive. I smile and run my fingers through my curly hair.

Oh, boy! I say, reaching for my glass of champagne, I'm signing up for filming—give me a contract.

I look up and smile at Jack as he sits down beside me and reaches for his champagne glass. He leans towards me and puts his arm on the back of the couch.

Jack smiles and turns to me, You're looking good, he says.

Well, thank you. So are you.

Cheers, he says.

Cheers.

We click our glasses of Veuve Clicquot Ponsardin.

Here's to erotica, says Jack.

Here's to rampant sex—

Yeah—

And unbridled passion, I say, as I rub his cock.

Jack looks at me intently and then smiles and puts his glass down on the coffee table and leans forward.

Hmm . . . oh, my goodness. I say, laughing and put down my glass.

We tongue kiss, our tongues touching, poking, caressing, and I give a slight bite to his tongue.

Ha! Jack laughs and kisses the side of my mouth and around to my neck as I lean into him and he brings his hand to my cheek and kisses my neck, throat, shoulder and rubs his thick curly hair against my head.

Ah ah! I sigh.

Jack tilts his head back and I kiss his throat and we embrace and kiss and then he sweeps my hair up and back off my face. I rub his cock as he leans back and smiles, and then I hold his face in my hands and smooth his forehead and eyebrows and caress his face as he looks at me and kisses me.

Yeah, he says, smiles, and gets up to turn off the camera.

Oh boy, Jack . . . that's some red hot kissing!

Uh huh. You betya! Let's try some close-ups.

I pull off my dress to reveal black stockings, garter belt, and a low cut black chemise. I am wearing black leather wedge-heeled sandals.

Jack is holding the camera.

Hey, should I hold the camera?

No.

All right.

I am standing in my Italian sandals, black stockings, garter belt, black teddy and leaning into the camera. Jack, who is holding the camera, is filming my breasts and my hand, which is holding my champagne glass.

Give it a little dip, Jack says.

Give it a dip, OK.

Make sure it's nice and hard.

I stroke his cock and kiss his mouth.

Yeah, ah, . . .

We kiss again and again as I continue to caress his cock.

OK, all right, I say, laughing, *this* is how I like to drink my wine and I take his hard cock and bend it down to my glass. Can you dip it in?

Ho!

And I dip the tip of his cock into my champagne.

Ahh! sighs Jack.

I take a sip of my champagne and put my tongue in the glass and then I bring the glass back to his hard cock.

Hmmm . . .

Instead of an olive—ha ha—I like a little *cock* with my wine!

I bring the glass to my fat breast, only the nipple goes in, and push my breast up to my mouth and suck on my champagne tit.

Nice.

I smile at Jack.

Jack changes the camera position—sets it on a chair across the room for a whole body shot.

We return to the couch and he leans back on the sofa and I straddle him with my white ass in the air. I kiss him and nuzzle his neck and he slaps my bum.

Smack! Smack!

Harder, Jack!

A stinging slap. I kiss his lips, his eyelids, his nose and cheeks, and behind his ear, all the while caressing, drawing out his long, thick, curly brown hair.

Oh! Jack!

He leans back on the couch as I run my tongue down his hairy chest to his left nipple and take it lightly between my teeth and suck.

Oh, he groans, and his cock surges as I move down to his belly button and make it wet with my spit and then run my tongue down to his *rock hard* cock and take it *deeply* into my mouth.

Oh, god! Ah, that's *good*!

Ah, I say, maybe we should change the camera position for a close-up. What do you think?

Jack smiles and gets up with his huge hard-on and walks over to the camera and turns it off.

What are you doing?

He comes back and smiles and takes my hand.

Never mind the camera, he says, let's go into the bedroom.

Ah!

But what about filming?

Jack shakes his head.

It's time for your birthday present, Angela. And I'm going to give it to you.

Hmm . . . Ah, you mean—

Yes, gobs and gobs—

A geyser of—

White cum exploding—

Oh, Jack!

I've *always* wanted to . . . do this, Angela, and, and now, *finally* . . . after all these years . . . I am going to *really* fuck you.

EPILOGUE

LIGHT. A PREOCCUPATION with light.

Color. Little cones of fire. Orchid, red, pink, blue. Her brain soaked in color.

She had ideas of color. Sometimes she was green. Sometimes orange, often pink. Her world was contaminated by color.

Silence. Silence is like light. There is no point comparing the two. They are the same.

She got off the bed.

There is a quality to your love-making that I particularly like, she said, stretching back on the white pillow. It is suffused with light.

I liked the part best where the hero fucks the girl in the ass. So true to life.

She's reading and he's bum-fucking.

Please pick a rose for me. I like pink best. Did you see the drops of dew on that pink one, the pale pink one, the one you just picked for me?

What are we going to do?

She went back to sleep.

There's a small stuffed duck in the window of Bergdorf Goodman that I want you to get for me. I pointed it out to you.

Do it to me.

I'll turn over and you can do it to me.

Do it to me now.